Nathaniel Hawthorne (1804–64) was born in Salem, Massachusetts, the son and grandson of proud New England seafarers. In 1825, he graduated from Bowdoin College and returned to Salem, determined to be a writer of short stories. For the next twelve years, he was plagued by unhappiness and self-doubt as he struggled to master his craft. He finally secured some small measure of success with the publication of *Twice-Told Tales* (1837). *The Scarlet Letter* (1850) brought him tremendous success, and was followed by the even more popular *The House of the Seven Gables* (1851).

Katherine Howe is the author of the *New York Times* bestselling novel *The Physick Book of Deliverance Dane*. She is completing her PhD in American and New England Studies at Boston University, where she taught an undergraduate seminar on witchcraft in North America, and she holds an undergraduate degree in art history and philosophy from Columbia University.

Brenda Wineapple is the author of acclaimed biographies including *Hawthorne: A Life*, winner of the Ambassador Award of the English-Speaking Union for Best Biography of 2004. Formerly the Washington Irving Professor of Modern Literary and Historical Studies at Union College, she now teaches in the MFA programs at Columbia University and the New School.

Nathaniel Hawthorne

THE HOUSE
OF THE
SEVEN GABLES

A Romance

With a New Introduction by
Katherine Howe

and an Afterword by
Brenda Wineapple

SIGNET CLASSICS

SIGNET CLASSICS
Published by New American Library, a division of
Penguin Group (USA) Inc., 375 Hudson Street,
New York, New York 10014, USA
Penguin Group (Canada), 90 Eglinton Avenue East, Suite 700, Toronto,
Ontario M4P 2Y3, Canada (a division of Pearson Penguin Canada Inc.)
Penguin Books Ltd., 80 Strand, London WC2R 0RL, England
Penguin Ireland, 25 St. Stephen's Green, Dublin 2,
Ireland (a division of Penguin Books Ltd.)
Penguin Group (Australia), 250 Camberwell Road, Camberwell, Victoria 3124,
Australia (a division of Pearson Australia Group Pty. Ltd.)
Penguin Books India Pvt. Ltd., 11 Community Centre, Panchsheel Park,
New Delhi - 110 017, India
Penguin Group (NZ), 67 Apollo Drive, Rosedale, North Shore 0632,
New Zealand (a division of Pearson New Zealand Ltd.)
Penguin Books (South Africa) (Pty.) Ltd., 24 Sturdee Avenue,
Rosebank, Johannesburg 2196, South Africa

Penguin Books Ltd., Registered Offices:
80 Strand, London WC2R 0RL, England

Published by Signet Classics, an imprint of New American Library,
a division of Penguin Group (USA) Inc.

First Signet Classics Printing, June 1961
First Signet Classics Printing (Howe Introduction), October 2010
10 9 8 7 6 5 4 3 2 1

CONTENTS

INTRODUCTION

The House of the Seven Gables does not exist. Nathaniel Hawthorne himself is careful to insist on this point almost before any other, when he suggests in his preface that the ensuing story of one cursed nineteenth-century Salem family be called a "romance" rather than a "novel." Analysis of the difference between the novel and the romance forms the basis of most classical criticism of *The House of the Seven Gables*, for in drawing this distinction, Hawthorne positions his text within a long heritage of fictional works more concerned with imaginative, rather than historical, truth. "Truth of the human heart," as Hawthorne calls it in his preface, which can be constructed from pure writerly imagination.

Of course, it's hard to take Hawthorne at his word. For the story of the Pyncheon family—proud spinster Hepzibah; her misunderstood brother, Clifford; fresh and wondrous cousin Phoebe; upstanding yet wicked cousin Jaffrey; and Holgrave, the mesmeric artist lodger—unfolds in a Salem so familiar to his readers that after publication Hawthorne and his wife would feel compelled to stay away from Salem permanently to spare themselves their neighbors' rage. The Pyncheon family name is borrowed from a real Salem family, and the lingering taint from their involvement in the Salem witch trials belongs to Hawthorne's own family. Even Holgrave, the daguerreotypist who rents one of the unused gables, voices attitudes about the Pyncheons' relentless obsession with their past that are difficult not to ascribe directly to our author. "To plant a family! This idea is at the bottom of most of the wrong and mischief which men do. The truth is," Holgrave remarks, "that, once in every half century, at longest, a family should be merged into the great, obscure mass of humanity, and forget all about its ancestors." Hawthorne's omniscient narrator, who often addresses the reader directly, actively ushers us through the description or action as it unfolds, rather than melting invisibly into the background, thus intensifying the sensation of this being Hawthorne's story, as if he is whispering it in our ear.

The romance tells the tale of the few remaining members of the Pyncheon family, last vestiges of a proud New England dynasty who live within the oppressive walls of the house of the story's title. The mansion was erected by their dour ancestor: a judge at the Salem witch trials, who contrived to condemn one Matthew Maule as a wizard in order to help himself to Maule's land. Maule curses Colonel Pyncheon from the scaffold, saddling him and his descendants with the leaden weight of guilt, together with a mysterious tendency to choke to death on their own blood. From this one historic wrong stem generations of downward spiral, as the Pyncheons slip from Puritan aristocracy to such destitution that the action begins with Hepzibah opening a little cent shop in the ground floor of the house. The Pyncheons nurture dreams of a lost key to wealth, a hidden deed to great swaths of land, which if only it could be found would restore them to their imagined greatness. This mythical lost land also finds its shadow in Hawthorne's own family past.

The house, like other Gothic houses in American literature, serves multiple functions, of which Colonel Pyncheon's oft-quoted goal of "planting a family" is only one. Like all houses, it shields its occupants from the incursions of the outside world—incursions so acutely painful to long-isolated Hepzibah that whenever the new shop bell rings to announce a customer for her cent shop, the sound shatters her sense of security and well-being as thoroughly as if a cannon had blown a hole in the wall. At the same time, if the house's walls keep the rest of the world at bay, Hawthorne is careful to remind us that houses can also keep their occupants trapped inside. When Hepzibah's fragile, elderly brother Clifford rejoins the household, finally freed from prison with the few remaining shreds of his sanity, he cries out against their continued residency in the family house, itself a sort of prison. "Why should we live in this dismal house at all?" he wails, wondering why they don't instead light out for Paris, Naples, Venice, Rome. His tirade is interrupted by the tinkling of the hated shop bell.

Indeed, the house itself acts as much more than a mere setting for the interactions of the characters: Hepzibah and her young cousin Phoebe in the shop, Phoebe and Holgrave in the garden, Hepzibah and Clifford in the parlor, Phoebe and Clifford in the summerhouse. The house instead serves as a character itself, and Hawthorne lavishes such attention on its details of furnishing and decay that we feel that we know its rotted roof, with a flower shrub sprouting from the shingles (posies, planted by the celebrated Alice Pyncheon of one hundred years' remove), and its arched front window, where Clifford likes to perch and blow soap bubbles into the street. We smell the mackerel that Hepzibah makes for Clifford's first breakfast at home, just as we smell the moist earth of the overgrown garden around the possibly enchanted well. Most of all, we come to know intimately the portrait of Colonel Pyncheon, the patriarch and spirit overhanging the entire narrative, mounted on the wall in the very room where the man himself was found sitting in a great armchair by a band of waiting guests, lifeless, having choked to death on his own blood. The house has such an immediacy and vibrancy both within the story and within Hawthorne's own life that from the moment of the book's publication theories swirled about which Salem house was the "real" House of the Seven Gables. From the outset, the borders between the purely fictional and the historical have been hazy, intersecting in the physical corpus of this most mysterious of houses.

And so, on a cold and drizzly February afternoon, I toured the House of the Seven Gables in modern-day Salem, Massachusetts. I *ooh*ed and *aah*ed over its tiny cent shop, just like the one Hepzibah is driven to open by the onward crush of her poverty, which is tucked behind the "Colonial" kitchen. I mounted its staircase hidden behind the dining room hearth. The central contradiction of my actual visit to a fictional house approaches some of the themes that await us in *The House of the Seven Gables*: history, heritage, selfhood, and the multifarious ways, both conscious and not, that we look to the past to tell us who we are and remake it to echo what we want to hear.

The House of the Seven Gables (1851) was Hawthorne's first novel to appear after he had finally, at long last, tasted literary success with *The Scarlet Letter* (1850). Both texts are impossible to read without being overshadowed, to some extent, by Hawthorne's own embattled relationship with his New England roots. Indeed much of his writing, whether romances, sketches, or short stories, pays either visit or homage to the dour Puritans who were a scant few generations removed from Hawthorne himself. It is difficult to consider this Romantic writer, a member of the short-lived Fourierist collective Brook Farm in 1841, and a luminary among what literary critic Susan Cheever has called the "American Bloomsbury" of Ralph Waldo Emerson and his Transcendentalist circle in mid-nineteenth-century Concord, as so close, in generational terms, to the Puritans, who formed the basis of his fiction. But it wasn't until Hawthorne's own generation that his name finally settled on its current spelling, rather than the more malleable and archaic "Hathorne" of his Salem judge ancestor. *The House of the Seven Gables* in many respects serves as Hawthorne's expiation, his purging of the shame and sorrow that he felt for descending from a man who, until his dying day, never regretted the part that he played in hanging nineteen people as witches in 1692.

Nathaniel Hawthorne was born in Salem, Massachusetts, in a little Georgian house then located on Union Street, in 1804. He lived in Salem for much of his adult life, attended college at Bowdoin, married Sophia Peabody in 1842 (after a long and public flirtation with her sister, Elizabeth), and eventually gained a position in the Salem customs house in 1846. He had attained some local interest for his story collections *Twice-Told Tales* (1837) and *Mosses from an Old Manse* (1846), written during the three years that he and Sophia lived in the Old Manse in Concord, Massachusetts. However, real literary success had eluded him, and as he labored away at his dull political appointment in Salem, he expressed intense frustration at his inability to write. He lost his position with the changing of the political climate in 1848, and left Salem amid a storm of vituperation, made worse by the scathing 1850 introduction to *The Scarlet Letter,* called "The Custom-House," which did not hesitate to vent his professional and personal frustrations with his native city. *The Scarlet Letter* went on to become a bestseller, and finally brought Hawthorne the recognition that he craved, though echoes of his years of aggravation appear in his infamous complaint, in a letter to his publisher from 1855, that "America is now wholly given over to a d—d mob of scribbling women, and I should have no chance of success while the public taste is occupied with their trash—and should be ashamed of myself if I did succeed." Hawthorne would spend the rest of his life moving between the Berkshires, Concord, and Europe, but his mind never fully left Salem behind.

And so we scour Salem for traces of Hawthorne, looking for clues to unlock his literary achievement, and in so doing happen upon a possible House of the Seven Gables. The Turner-Ingersoll mansion on present-day Derby Street, now widely considered to have served as the inspiration for Hawthorne's romance, was first built for a ship captain in 1668 as a simple two-room, two-and-a-half-story affair facing south over Salem's harbor. It underwent several generations of remodeling and change for the Turner family in 1680, 1692, and

1725, spiraling forward in time through different periods and styles before passing into the hands of the Ingersoll family, relatives of the Hawthornes. When Hawthorne visited the house as a young man in Salem, it had three gables, but his cousin Susannah Ingersoll reportedly showed him the places under the eaves of the house where other gables had once stood.

In 1908 the house came up for sale, with three gables and a reputation as the inspiration for Hawthorne's dark tale of history and oppression intact, and was acquired by one Caroline O. Emmerton. By that time the neighborhood in Salem where the building stood was almost entirely populated by Polish workers, part of the leather and manufacturing industries that had arisen in Salem as the harbor silted in, causing the city to lose its grip on shipping and trade. Emmerton, a wealthy philanthropist active in numerous historical and progressive causes, concocted the novel idea of establishing the House of the Seven Gables as a historic museum, proceeds from which could be used to support a settlement house for the education and Americanization of the surrounding immigrant community.

The question of "Americanization" looms large at this point in the house's story. The late nineteenth century had seen an explosion both of European immigration to America and of xenophobic nativism in response. Some progressives responded to increased immigration not with paranoid protectionism, but with aggressive assimilationism. Many philanthropists, like Emmerton, worried about how the new immigrants could possibly be incorporated into American society when barriers of language and culture stood between them and the "real"—that is, native-born—Americans. Settlement houses attempted to resolve this problem by not only providing the poor with charity and practical job training, but also by introducing them to the reigning ideologies of American politics, religion, and culture. Benevolent societies arose during this period for the preservation of American history and culture not only for its own sake, but as a way of laying claim to a truer American heritage, to resist the change implied by growing diversity and immigration. Emmerton, like many other settlement house proponents, believed that physical contact with historic American architecture could itself provide a beneficial influence as part of the Americanization process, as though the ideals of democracy could somehow be leached straight out of the post-and-beam structure itself.

Of course, there was one problem: The Turner-Ingersoll house didn't much resemble the untouched seventeenth-century dwelling of Hawthorne's narrative. It had grown and changed over the generations, and by 1908 was a hodgepodge of styles ranging from Federal to Victorian, with a bit of everything in between. Emmerton enlisted the aid of architect Joseph Everett Chandler, an expert in the Colonial revival, to return the mansion to its idealized *proper* form.

The Colonial revival was itself a nostalgic enterprise, born in part of the Progressive-era fetish for the supposed simplicity and healthfulness of past modes of domestic architecture. It was also the architectural and cultural expression of the same ethnic anxiety that undergirded much of the drive for Americanization. Chandler, also known for his work on the Paul Revere house in Boston, set to refashioning the Turner-Ingersoll mansion not to a complete version of its earlier self, but to an imagined ideal of what a Colonial-era mansion should be, with a healthy consciousness of the expectations that readers of Hawthorne's novel might bring to the building when visiting. Today the kitchen persists as an example of the Colonial-revival aesthetic: a rebuilt open hearth, with simplicity of form trumping actual usefulness, and with muskets hanging over the fireplace, where they would have been sure to explode in a real Colonial kitchen. Chandler also supplied a simulacrum of Hepzibah's cent shop, which had never existed as such in the house's actual historical life, but which was designed to heighten the experience of walking into a page from Hawthorne's romance. Chandler even created a secret winding staircase behind the rebuilt hearth, once thought to have been part of the original structure of the house, but which in recent years has been revealed as yet another example of the fictional nature of historical memory.

When Hawthorne's birthplace was in danger of being torn down for a parking lot in 1958, it was sold to the settlement house foundation for one dollar and moved to its current location, perpendicular to the House of the Seven Gables. These two buildings, together with the Hooper-Hathaway house, which was restored half to seventeenth-century parameters and half to eighteenth-century, for use as a bed-and-breakfast where visitors could choose the historical period they wished to sleep in, now form a bustling and important museum of historical preservation. The museum complex still supports the efforts of the settlement house, though its project now is less one of "Americanization" per se and more one of community building and social services. In effect, a visitor to the modern incarnation of the House of the Seven Gables discovers that Hawthorne's project still rings true: History becomes a story that we tell ourselves about the past, from which we endeavor to learn who we are in the present. Today, of the seven extant gables that can be seen, four date from the twentieth-century restoration.

Of course, Hawthorne's text itself has a complicated relationship with history. Though the usual critical approach to *The House of the Seven Gables* concerns its relationship to the tenets of the romance, and so to the difference between what is probable and what is possible in fiction, Hawthorne himself undermines such a straightforward distinction by peppering his narrative with identifiable places, names of actual people, and even details taken from the historical record. He notoriously placed the actual curse that accused witch Sarah Good hurled from the scaffold to Revered Nicholas Noyes, "I am no more a witch than you are a wizard, and if you take away my life, God will give you blood to drink," and put it instead in the mouth of Matthew Maule. (That Hawthorne's righteous accused witch is a man neglects a central fact important to recent historiography, which is that most witches at Salem, and in New England more generally, were women.) Just the idea that some extant houses in Salem at the end of the nineteenth century could credibly lay claim to being Hawthorne's inspiration would seem to contradict Hawthorne's own insistence on the House of the Seven Gables as a place of pure fantasy. History weighs too heavily on Hawthorne, as it does on his troubled Pyncheon family, and yet Hawthorne, the Pyncheons, and even Caroline Emmerton rely on Puritan history to tell themselves who they really are. But they draw different conclusions. Emmerton felt that the Puritan past embodied salutary influence: indoctrination into a true sense of the American. Hawthorne found in that past an inspiration, but for the Pyncheon family, it sets a deadly trap.

The strange nature of a real visit to a fictional house speaks to our desire to have a memento mori when encountering history. Today, a visit to the House of the Seven Gables is less an act of literary tourism—many people who pass through the rooms have never read the book, and some have never heard of Hawthorne—than it is a desire to stand in the actual presence of history. For an episode like the Salem witch crisis, which looms so large in the American consciousness and yet which has left almost no tangible reminders behind, the appeal of a house that can be entered, touched, and explored, that itself bore witness to those terrible events, exerts a powerful magnetism. Most of us encounter history through the comforting lens of fiction, which can supply tidy narratives, accessible reasons, defined characters, and, most important of all, a coherent ending. History gives us none of these things, and for an event as anomalous and discomfiting as the Salem witch crisis, in which nineteen people were put to death by the state for what, to the modern mind anyway, amounts to senselessness bordering on madness, the inability of history to force that period to make sense is at the least unsatisfying and at the most unacceptable. Hawthorne's narrative supplies a rational explanation for this madness. Greed, we learn, lay at the heart of the Salem witch crisis. Greed and the desire "to plant a family."

In effect, *The House of the Seven Gables* is about the possibility of redemption. Hawthorne's story implies a moral decrepitude that infects a family following the choices made by its founding member, establishing an entire dynasty on a foundation of scheming and blood-thirsty selfishness. And yet the idea of intrinsic debility is inseparable from the idea of nativist worth; if we are what our forbears doom us to be, for better or for worse, then the most optimistic ideals of the American experiment, in which we are a nation of opportunity and reinvention, seem impossible to reach. Does Hawthorne believe we can be free of our past or not? I'm not sure I know. For that matter, I'm not sure he knows. The abrupt, tidy, and relentlessly cheerful conclusion to Hawthorne's narrative—in which past wrongs are righted, the evil are punished, the good are redeemed, and everyone lives happily ever after (there's even a kiss)—occasionally strikes readers as too anomalous to be believed. Emmerton surely believed in redemption; it lay at the heart of the settlement-house project. Literature, and architecture, and history, a nexus of American culture, all brought together for the betterment of those who would free themselves from a less privileged past.

In the end, the many onion layers involved in paying a real visit to a real house redone so it better resembles a fictional house that is itself inspired—supposedly—by a real house, and done to supply funds for the "real"-ization of would-be (i.e., fictional) Americans who are now real is itself a story about the contested relationship we have with history. Throughout the narrative, Hawthorne, coy to the last, conjures images of generations of long-dead Pyncheons all trapped within the House of the Seven Gables, gathering at midnight in the room where the colonel died in his great chair, worrying over their legacy. Worrying, that is, until the final freeing moment of escape. "The past," Hawthorne gives Clifford to remark while riding in flight on his very first train, "is but a coarse and sensual prophecy of the present and the future."

—Katherine Howe

THE HOUSE
OF THE
SEVEN GABLES

Preface by the Author

WHEN a writer calls his work a Romance, it need hardly be observed that he wishes to claim a certain latitude, both as to its fashion and material, which he would not have felt himself entitled to assume had he professed to be writing a Novel. The latter form of composition is presumed to aim at a very minute fidelity, not merely to the possible, but to the probable and ordinary course of man's experience. The former—while, as a work of art, it must rigidly subject itself to laws, and while it sins unpardonably so far as it may swerve aside from the truth of the human heart—has fairly a right to present that truth under circumstances, to a great extent, of the writer's own choosing or creation. If he think fit, also, he may so manage his atmospherical medium as to bring out or mellow the lights and deepen and enrich the shadows of the picture. He will be wise, no doubt, to make a very moderate use of the privileges here stated, and, especially, to mingle the Marvelous rather as a slight, delicate, and evanescent flavor than as any portion of the actual substance of the dish offered to the public. He can hardly be said, however, to commit a literary crime even if he disregard this caution.

In the present work, the author has proposed to himself—but with what success, fortunately, it is not for him to judge—to keep undeviatingly within his immunities. The point of view in which this tale comes under the Romantic definition lies in the attempt to connect a bygone

1

time with the very present that is flitting away from us. It is a legend prolonging itself, from an epoch now gray in the distance, down into our own broad daylight, and bringing along with it some of its legendary mist, which the reader, according to his pleasure, may either disregard, or allow it to float almost imperceptibly about the characters and events for the sake of a picturesque effect. The narrative, it may be, is woven of so humble a texture as to require this advantage, and, at the same time, to render it the more difficult of attainment.

Many writers lay very great stress upon some definite moral purpose, at which they profess to aim their works. Not to be deficient in this particular, the author has provided himself with a moral—the truth, namely, that the wrongdoing of one generation lives into the successive ones, and, divesting itself of every temporary advantage, becomes a pure and uncontrollable mischief; and he would feel it a singular gratification if this romance might effectually convince mankind—or, indeed, any one man—of the folly of tumbling down an avalanche of ill-gotten gold, or real estate, on the heads of an unfortunate posterity, thereby to maim and crush them, until the accumulated mass shall be scattered abroad in its original atoms. In good faith, however, he is not sufficiently imaginative to flatter himself with the slightest hope of this kind. When romances do really teach anything, or produce any effective operation, it is usually through a far more subtle process than the ostensible one. The author has considered it hardly worth his while, therefore, relentlessly to impale the story with its moral as with an iron rod—or, rather, as by sticking a pin through a butterfly—thus at once depriving it of life, and causing it to stiffen in an ungainly and unnatural attitude. A high truth, indeed, fairly, finely, and skillfully wrought out, brightening at every step, and crowning the final development of a work of fiction, may add an artistic glory, but is never any truer, and seldom any more evident, at the last page than at the first.

The reader may perhaps choose to assign an actual locality to the imaginary events of this narrative. If permitted by the historical connection—which, though slight, was essential to his plan—the author would very willingly have avoided anything of this nature. Not to speak of other objections, it exposes the romance to an inflexible and exceedingly dangerous species of criticism, by bringing his fancy pictures almost into positive contact with the realities of the moment. It has been no part of his object, however, to describe local manners, nor in any way to meddle with the characteristics of a community for whom he cherishes a proper respect and a natural regard. He trusts not to be considered as unpardonably offending by laying out a street that infringes upon nobody's private rights, and appropriating a lot of land which had no visible owner, and building a house of materials long in use for constructing castles in the air. The personages of the tale—though they give themselves out to be of ancient stability and considerable prominence—are really of the author's own making, or, at all events, of his own mixing; their virtues can shed no luster, nor their defects redound, in the remotest degree, to the discredit of the venerable town of which they profess to be inhabitants. He would be glad, therefore, if—especially in the quarter to which he alludes—the book may be read strictly as a Romance, having a great deal more to do with the clouds overhead than with any portion of the actual soil of the County of Essex.

LENOX, January 27, 1851

❦ 1 ❧

The Old Pyncheon Family

HALFWAY down a bystreet of one of our New England towns stands a rusty wooden house, with seven acutely peaked gables, facing towards various points of the compass, and a huge, clustered chimney in the midst. The street is Pyncheon Street; the house is the old Pyncheon House; and an elm tree, of wide circumference, rooted before the door, is familiar to every town-born child by the title of the Pyncheon Elm. On my occasional visits to the town aforesaid, I seldom failed to turn down Pyncheon Street, for the sake of passing through the shadow of these two antiquities—the great elm tree and the weather-beaten edifice.

The aspect of the venerable mansion has always affected me like a human countenance, bearing the traces not merely of outward storm and sunshine, but expressive, also, of the long lapse of mortal life, and accompanying vicissitudes that have passed within. Were these to be worthily recounted, they would form a narrative of no small interest and instruction, and possessing, moreover, a certain remarkable unity, which might almost seem the result of artistic arrangement. But the story would include a chain of events extending over the better part of two centuries, and, written out with reasonable amplitude, would fill a bigger folio volume, or a longer series of duodecimos, than could prudently be appropriated to the annals of all New England during a similar period. It consequently becomes imperative to make short work with most of the traditionary

5

lore of which the old Pyncheon House, otherwise known as the House of the Seven Gables, has been the theme. With a brief sketch, therefore, of the circumstances amid which the foundation of the house was laid, and a rapid glimpse at its quaint exterior, as it grew black in the prevalent east wind—pointing, too, here and there, at some spot of more verdant mossiness on its roof and walls—we shall commence the real action of our tale at an epoch not very remote from the present day. Still, there will be a connection with the long past—a reference to forgotten events and personages, and to manners, feelings, and opinions, almost or wholly obsolete—which, if adequately translated to the reader, would serve to illustrate how much of old material goes to make up the freshest novelty of human life. Hence, too, might be drawn a weighty lesson from the little-regarded truth that the act of the passing generation is the germ which may and must produce good or evil fruit in a far-distant time; that together with the seed of the merely temporary crop, which mortals term expediency, they inevitably sow the acorns of a more enduring growth, which may darkly overshadow their posterity.

The House of the Seven Gables, antique as it now looks, was not the first habitation erected by civilized man on precisely the same spot of ground. Pyncheon Street formerly bore the humbler appellation of Maule's Lane, from the name of the original occupant of the soil, before whose cottage door it was a cowpath. A natural spring of soft and pleasant water—a rare treasure on the sea-girt peninsula, where the Puritan settlement was made—had early induced Matthew Maule to build a hut, shaggy with thatch, at this point, although somewhat too remote from what was then the center of the village. In the growth of the town, however, after some thirty or forty years, the site covered by this rude hovel had become exceedingly desirable in the eyes of a prominent and powerful personage, who asserted plausible claims to the proprietorship of this, and a large adjacent tract of land, on the strength of a grant from the legislature. Colonel Pyncheon, the claimant, as we gather from whatever traits of him are preserved, was characterized by an iron energy of purpose. Matthew Maule, on the other hand, though an obscure man, was stubborn in the defense of what he considered his right; and, for several years, he succeeded in protecting the acre or two of earth which, with his own toil, he had hewn out of the primeval forest, to be his garden ground and homestead. No written record of this dispute is known to be in existence. Our acquaintance with the whole subject is derived chiefly from tradition. It would be bold, therefore, and possibly unjust, to venture a decisive opinion as to its merits; although it appears to have been at least a matter of doubt whether Colonel Pyncheon's claim were not unduly stretched, in order to make it cover the small metes and bounds of Matthew Maule. What greatly strengthens such a suspicion is the fact that this controversy between two ill-matched antagonists—at a period, moreover, laud it as we may, when personal influence had far more weight than now—remained for years undecided, and came to a close only with the death of the party occupying the disputed soil. The mode of his death, too, affects the mind differently, in our day, from what it did a century and a half ago. It was a death that blasted with strange horror the humble name of the dweller in the cottage, and made it seem almost a religious act to drive the plow over the little area of his habitation, and obliterate his place and memory from among men.

Old Matthew Maule, in a word, was executed for the crime of witchcraft. He was one of the martyrs to that terrible delusion, which should teach us, among its other morals, that the influential classes, and those who take upon themselves to be leaders of the people, are fully liable to all the passionate error that has ever characterized the maddest mob. Clergymen, judges, statesmen—the wisest, calmest, holiest persons of their day—stood in the inner circle round about the gallows, loudest to applaud the work of blood, latest to confess themselves miserably deceived. If any one part of their proceedings can be said to deserve less blame than another, it was the singular indiscrimination with which they persecuted not merely the poor and aged, as in former judicial massacres, but people of all ranks; their own equals, brethren, and wives. Amid the disorder of such various ruin, it is not strange that a man of inconsiderable note, like Maule, should have trodden the martyr's path to the hill of execution almost unremarked in the throng of his fellow sufferers. But, in after days, when the frenzy of that hideous epoch had subsided, it was remembered how loudly Colonel Pyncheon had joined in the general cry, to purge the land from witchcraft; nor did it fail to be whispered that there was an invidious acrimony in the zeal with which he had sought the condemnation of Matthew Maule. It was well known that the victim had recognized the bitterness of personal enmity in his prosecutor's conduct towards him, and that he declared himself hunted to death for his spoil. At the moment of execution—with the halter about his neck, and while Colonel Pyncheon sat on horseback, grimly gazing at the scene—Maule had addressed him from the scaffold, and uttered a prophecy, of which history, as well as fireside tradition, has preserved the very words. "God," said the dying man, pointing his finger, with a ghastly look, at the undismayed countenance of his enemy, "God will give him blood to drink!"

After the reputed wizard's death, his humble homestead had fallen an easy spoil into Colonel Pyncheon's grasp. When it was understood, however, that the Colonel intended to erect a family mansion—spacious, ponderously framed of oaken timber, and calculated to endure for many generations of his posterity—over the spot first covered by the log-built hut of Matthew Maule, there was much shaking of the head among the village gossips. Without absolutely expressing a doubt whether the stalwart Puritan had acted as a man of conscience and integrity throughout the proceedings which have been sketched, they, nevertheless, hinted that he was about to build his house over an unquiet grave. His home would include the home of the dead and buried wizard, and would thus afford the ghost of the latter a kind of privilege to haunt its new apartments, and the chambers into which future bridegrooms were to lead their brides, and where children of the Pyncheon blood were to be born. The terror and ugliness of Maule's crime, and the wretchedness of his punishment, would darken the freshly plastered walls, and infect them early with the scent of an old and melancholy house. Why, then—while so much of the soil around him was bestrewn with the virgin forest leaves—why should Colonel Pyncheon prefer a site that had already been accursed?

But the Puritan soldier and magistrate was not a man to be turned aside from his well-considered scheme, either by dread of the wizard's ghost or by flimsy sentimentalities of any kind, however specious. Had he been told of a bad air, it might have moved him somewhat; but he was ready to encounter an evil spirit on his own ground. Endowed with common sense, as massive and hard as blocks of granite, fastened together by stern rigidity of purpose, as with iron clamps, he followed out his original design, probably without so much as imagining an objection to it. On the score of delicacy, or any scrupulousness which a finer sensibility might have taught him, the Colonel, like most of his breed and generation, was impenetrable. He, therefore, dug his cellar, and laid the deep foundations of his mansion, on the square of earth whence Matthew Maule, forty years before, had first swept away the fallen leaves. It was a curious and, as some people thought, an ominous fact that, very soon after the workmen began their operations, the spring of water, above mentioned, entirely lost the deliciousness of its pristine quality. Whether its sources were disturbed by the depth of the new cellar, or whatever subtler cause might lurk at the bottom, it is certain that the water of Maule's Well, as it continued to be called, grew hard and brackish. Even such we find it now; and any old woman of the neighborhood will certify that it is productive of intestinal mischief to those who quench their thirst there.

The reader may deem it singular that the head carpenter of the new edifice was no other than the son of the very man from whose dead gripe the property of the soil had been wrested. Not improbably he was the best workman of his time; or, perhaps, the Colonel thought it expedient, or was impelled by some better feeling, thus openly to cast aside all animosity against the race of his fallen antagonist. Nor was it out of keeping with the general coarseness and matter-of-fact character of the age that the son should be willing to earn an honest penny, or, rather, a weighty amount of sterling pounds, from the purse of his father's deadly enemy. At all events, Thomas Maule became the architect of the House of the Seven Gables, and performed his duty so faithfully that the timber framework fastened by his hands still holds together.

Thus the great house was built. Familiar as it stands in the writer's recollection—for it has been an object of curiosity with him from boyhood, both as a specimen of the best and stateliest architecture of a long-past epoch, and as the scene of events more full of human interest, perhaps, than those of a gray feudal castle—familiar as it stands, in its rusty old age, it is therefore only the more difficult to imagine the bright novelty with which it first caught the sunshine. The impression of its actual state, at this distance of a hundred and sixty years, darkens inevitably through the picture which we would fain give of its appearance on the morning when the Puritan magnate bade all the town to be his guests. A ceremony of consecration, festive as well as religious, was now to be performed. A prayer and discourse from the Rev. Mr. Higginson, and the outpouring of a psalm from the general throat of the community, was to be made acceptable to the grosser sense by ale, cider, wine, and brandy, in copious effusion, and, as some authorities aver, by an ox, roasted whole, or, at least, by the weight and substance of an ox, in more manageable joints and sirloins. The carcass of a deer, shot within twenty miles, had supplied material for the vast circumference of a pasty. A codfish of sixty pounds, caught in the bay, had been dissolved into the rich liquid of a chowder. The chimney of the new house, in short, belching forth its kitchen smoke, impregnated the whole air with the scent of meats, fowls, and fishes, spicily concocted with odoriferous herbs, and onions in abundance. The mere smell of such festivity, making its way to everybody's nostrils, was at once an invitation and an appetite.

Maule's Lane, or Pyncheon Street, as it were now more decorous to call it, was thronged, at the appointed hour, as with a congregation on its way to church. All, as they approached, looked upward at the imposing edifice, which was henceforth to assume its rank among the habitations of mankind. There it rose, a little withdrawn from the line of the street, but in pride, not modesty. Its whole visible exterior was ornamented with quaint figures, conceived in the grotesqueness of a Gothic fancy, and drawn or stamped in the glittering plaster, composed of lime, pebbles, and bits of glass, with which the woodwork of the walls was over-spread. On every side the seven gables pointed sharply towards the sky, and presented the aspect of a whole sisterhood of edifices, breathing through the spiracles of one great chimney. The many lattices, with their small, diamond-shaped panes, admitted the sunlight into hall and chamber, while, nevertheless, the second story, projecting far over the base, and itself retiring beneath the third, threw a shadowy and thoughtful gloom into the lower rooms. Carved globes of wood were affixed under the jutting stories. Little spiral rods of iron beautified each of the seven peaks. On the triangular portion of the gable that fronted next the street was a dial, put up that very morning, and on which the sun was still marking the passage of the first bright hour in a history that was not destined to be all so bright. All around were scattered shavings, chips, shingles, and broken halves of bricks; these, together with the lately turned earth, on which the grass had not begun to grow, contributed to the impression of strangeness and novelty proper to a house that had yet its place to make among men's daily interests.

The principal entrance, which had almost the breadth of a church door, was in the angle between the two front gables, and was covered by an open porch, with benches beneath its shelter. Under this arched doorway, scraping their feet on the unworn threshold, now trod the clergymen, the elders, the magistrates, the deacons, and whatever of aristocracy there was in town or county. Thither, too, thronged the plebeian classes as freely as their betters, and in larger number. Just within the entrance, however, stood two serv-ingmen, pointing some of the guests to the neighborhood of the kitchen, and ushering others into the statelier rooms—hospitable alike to all, but still with a scrutinizing regard to the high or low degree of each. Velvet garments, somber but rich, stiffly plaited ruffs and bands, embroidered gloves, venerable beards, the mien and countenance of authority, made it easy to distinguish the gentleman of worship, at that period, from the tradesman, with his plodding air, or the laborer, in his leathern jerkin, stealing awe-stricken into the house which he had perhaps helped to build.

One inauspicious circumstance there was, which awakened a hardly concealed displeasure in the breasts of a few of the more punctilious visitors. The founder of this stately mansion—a gentleman noted for the square and ponderous courtesy of his demeanor—ought surely to have stood in his own hall, and to have offered the first welcome to so many eminent personages as here presented themselves in honor of his solemn festival. He was as yet invisible; the most favored of the guests had not beheld him. This sluggishness on Colonel Pyncheon's part became still more unaccountable when the second dignitary of the province made his appearance, and found no more ceremonious a reception. The lieutenant governor, although his visit was one of the anticipated glories of the day, had alighted from his horse, and assisted his lady from her sidesaddle, and crossed the Colonel's threshold, without other greeting than that of the principal domestic.

This person—a grayheaded man, of quiet and most respectful deportment—found it necessary to explain that his master still remained in his study, or private apartment; on entering which, an hour before, he had expressed a wish on no account to be disturbed.

"Do not you see, fellow," said the high sheriff of the county, taking the servant aside, "that this is no less a man than the lieutenant governor? Summon Colonel Pyncheon at once! I know that he received letters from England this morning; and, in the perusal and consideration of them, an hour may have passed away without his noticing it. But he will be ill pleased, I judge, if you suffer him to neglect the courtesy due to one of our chief rulers, and who may be said to represent King William, in the absence of the governor himself. Call your master instantly!"

"Nay, please your worship," answered the man, in much perplexity, but with a backwardness that strikingly indicated the hard and severe character of Colonel Pyncheon's domestic rule. "My master's orders were exceeding strict; and, as your worship knows, he permits of no discretion in the obedience of those who owe him service. Let who list open yonder door; I dare not, though the governor's own voice should bid me do it!"

"Pooh, pooh, master high sheriff!" cried the lieutenant governor, who had overheard the foregoing discussion, and felt himself high enough in station to play a little with his dignity. "I will take the matter into my own hands. It is time that the good Colonel came forth to greet his friends; else we shall be apt to suspect that he has taken a sip too much of his Canary wine, in his extreme deliberation which cask it were best to broach in honor of the day! But since he is so much behindhand, I will give him a remembrancer myself!"

Accordingly, with such a tramp of his ponderous riding boots as might of itself have been audible in the remotest of the seven gables, he advanced to the door, which the servant pointed out, and made its new panels re-echo with a loud, free knock. Then, looking round, with a smile, to the spectators, he awaited a response. As none came, however, he knocked again, but with the same unsatisfactory result as at first. And now, being a trifle choleric in his temperament, the lieutenant governor uplifted the heavy hilt of his sword, wherewith he so beat and banged upon the door that, as some of the bystanders whispered, the racket might have disturbed the dead. Be that as it might, it seemed to produce no awakening effect on Colonel Pyncheon. When the sound subsided, the silence through the house was deep, dreary, and oppressive, notwithstanding that the tongues of many of the guests had already been loosened by a surreptitious cup or two of wine or spirits.

"Strange, forsooth—very strange!" cried the lieutenant governor, whose smile was changed to a frown. "But seeing that our host sets us the good example of forgetting ceremony, I shall likewise throw it aside, and make free to intrude on his privacy!"

He tried the door, which yielded to his hand, and was flung wide open by a sudden gust of wind that passed, as with a loud sigh, from the outermost portal through all the passages and apartments of the new house. It rustled the silken garments of the ladies, and waved the long curls of the gentlemen's wigs, and shook the window hangings and the curtains of the bedchambers; causing everywhere a singular stir, which yet was more like a hush. A shadow of awe and half-fearful anticipation—nobody knew wherefore, nor of what—had all at once fallen over the company.

They thronged, however, to the now open door, pressing the lieutenant governor, in the eagerness of their curiosity, into the room in advance of them. At the first glimpse they beheld nothing extraordinary: a handsomely furnished room, of moderate size, somewhat darkened by curtains; books arranged on shelves; a large map on the wall, and likewise a portrait of Colonel Pyncheon, beneath which sat the original Colonel himself, in an oaken elbowchair, with a pen in his hand. Letters, parchments, and blank sheets of paper were on the table before him. He appeared to gaze at the curious crowd, in front of which stood the lieutenant governor; and there was a frown on his dark and massive countenance, as if sternly resentful of the boldness that had impelled them into his private retirement.

A little boy—the Colonel's grandchild, and the only human being that ever dared to be familiar with him—now made his way among the guests, and ran towards the seated figure; then pausing halfway, he began to shriek with terror. The company, tremulous as the leaves of a tree, when all are shaking together, drew nearer, and perceived that there was an unnatural distortion in the fixedness of Colonel Pyncheon's stare; that there was blood on his ruff, and that his hoary beard was saturated with it. It was too late to give assistance. The ironhearted Puritan, the relentless persecutor, the grasping and strong-willed man, was dead! Dead, in his new house! There is a tradition, only worth alluding to as lending a tinge of superstitious awe to a scene perhaps gloomy enough without it, that a voice spoke loudly among the guests, the tones of which were like those of old Matthew Maule, the executed wizard—"God hath given him blood to drink!"

Thus early had that one guest—the only guest who is certain, at one time or another, to find his way into every human dwelling—thus early had Death stepped across the threshold of the House of the Seven Gables!

Colonel Pyncheon's sudden and mysterious end made a vast deal of noise in its day. There were many rumors, some of which have vaguely drifted down to the present time, how that appearances indicated violence; that there were the marks of fingers on his throat, and the print of a bloody hand on his plaited ruff; and that his peaked beard was disheveled, as if it had been fiercely clutched and pulled. It was averred, likewise, that the lattice window, near the Colonel's chair, was open; and that, only a few minutes before the fatal occurrence, the figure of a man had been seen clambering over the garden fence, in the rear of the house. But it were folly to lay any stress on stories of this kind, which are sure to spring up around such an event as that now related, and which, as in the present case, sometimes prolong themselves for ages afterwards, like the toadstools that indicate where the fallen and buried trunk of a tree has long since moldered into the earth. For our own part, we allow them just as little credence as to that other fable of the skeleton hand which the lieutenant governor was said to have seen at the Colonel's throat, but which vanished away as he advanced farther into the room. Certain it is, however, that there was a great consultation and dispute of doctors over the dead body. One—John Swinnerton by name—who appears to have been a man of eminence, upheld it, if we have rightly understood his terms of art, to be a case of apoplexy. His professional brethren, each for himself, adopted various hypotheses, more or less plausible, but all dressed out in a perplexing mystery of phrase, which, if it do not show a bewilderment of mind in these erudite physicians, certainly causes it in the unlearned peruser of their opinions. The coroner's jury sat upon the corpse, and, like sensible men, returned an unassailable verdict of "Sudden Death!"

It is indeed difficult to imagine that there could have been a serious suspicion of murder, or the slightest grounds for implicating any particular individual as the perpetrator. The rank, wealth, and eminent character of the deceased must have insured the strictest scrutiny into every ambiguous circumstance. As none such is on record, it is safe to assume that none existed. Tradition—which sometimes brings down

truth that history has let slip, but is oftener the wild babble
of the time, such as was formerly spoken at the fireside
and now congeals in newspapers—tradition is responsible
for all contrary averments. In Colonel Pyncheon's funeral
sermon, which was printed, and is still extant, the Rev. Mr.
Higginson enumerates, among the many felicities of his distinguished parishioner's earthly career, the happy season-
ableness of his death. His duties all performed, the highest
prosperity attained, his race and future generations fixed
on a stable basis, and with a stately roof to shelter them,
for centuries to come—what other upward step remained
for this good man to take, save the final step from earth
to the golden gate of heaven! The pious clergyman surely
would not have uttered words like these had he in the least
suspected that the Colonel had been thrust into the other
world with the clutch of violence upon his throat.

The family of Colonel Pyncheon, at the epoch of his
death, seemed destined to as fortunate a permanence as
can anywise consist with the inherent instability of human
affairs. It might fairly be anticipated that the progress of
time would rather increase and ripen their prosperity than
wear away and destroy it. For, not only had his son and
heir come into immediate enjoyment of a rich estate, but
there was a claim through an Indian deed, confirmed by
a subsequent grant of the General Court, to a vast and as
yet unexplored and unmeasured tract of Eastern lands.
These possessions—for as such they might almost certainly
be reckoned—comprised the greater part of what is now
known as Waldo County, in the State of Maine, and were
more extensive than many a dukedom, or even a reigning prince's territory, on European soil. When the pathless
forest that still covered this wild principality should give
place—as it inevitably must, though perhaps not till ages
hence—to the golden fertility of human culture, it would
be the source of incalculable wealth to the Pyncheon
blood. Had the Colonel survived only a few weeks longer,
it is probable that his great political influence, and powerful connections at home and abroad, would have consummated all that was necessary to render the claim available.
But, in spite of good Mr. Higginson's congratulatory elo-

quence, this appeared to be the one thing which Colonel Pyncheon, provident and sagacious as he was, had allowed to go at loose ends. So far as the prospective territory was concerned, he unquestionably died too soon. His son lacked not merely the father's eminent position, but the talent and force of character to achieve it: he could, therefore, effect nothing by dint of political interest; and the bare justice or legality of the claim was not so apparent, after the Colonel's decease, as it had been pronounced in his lifetime. Some connecting link had slipped out of the evidence, and could not anywhere be found.

Efforts, it is true, were made by the Pyncheons, not only then, but at various periods for nearly a hundred years afterwards, to obtain what they stubbornly persisted in deeming their right. But, in course of time, the territory was partly regranted to more favored individuals, and partly cleared and occupied by actual settlers. These last, if they ever heard of the Pyncheon title, would have laughed at the idea of any man's asserting a right—on the strength of moldy parchments, signed with the faded autographs of governors and legislators long dead and forgotten—to the lands which they or their fathers had wrested from the wild hand of nature by their own sturdy toil. This impalpable claim, therefore, resulted in nothing more solid than to cherish, from generation to generation, an absurd delusion of family importance, which all along characterized the Pyncheons. It caused the poorest member of the race to feel as if he inherited a kind of nobility, and might yet come into the possession of princely wealth to support it. In the better specimens of the breed, this peculiarity threw an ideal grace over the hard material of human life, without stealing away any truly valuable quality. In the baser sort, its effect was to increase the liability to sluggishness and dependence, and induce the victim of a shadowy hope to remit all self-effort, while awaiting the realization of his dreams. Years and years after their claim had passed out of the public memory, the Pyncheons were accustomed to consult the Colonel's ancient map, which had been projected while Waldo County was still an unbroken wilderness. Where the old land-surveyor had put down woods, lakes, and rivers, they marked out the cleared spaces, and dotted the villages and towns, and calculated the progressively increasing value of the territory, as if there were yet a prospect of its ultimately forming a princedom for themselves.

In almost every generation, nevertheless, there happened to be some one descendant of the family gifted with a portion of the hard, keen sense, and practical energy, that had so remarkably distinguished the original founder. His character, indeed, might be traced all the way down, as distinctly as if the Colonel himself, a little diluted, had been gifted with a sort of intermittent immortality on earth. At two or three epochs, when the fortunes of the family were low, this representative of hereditary qualities had made his appearance, and caused the traditionary gossips of the town to whisper among themselves, "Here is the old Pyncheon come again! Now the Seven Gables will be new-shingled!" From father to son, they clung to the ancestral house with singular tenacity of home attachment. For various reasons, however, and from impressions often too vaguely founded to be put on paper, the writer cherishes the belief that many, if not most, of the successive proprietors of this estate were troubled with doubts as to their moral right to hold it. Of their legal tenure there could be no question; but old Matthew Maule, it is to be feared, trode downward from his own age to a far later one, planting a heavy footstep, all the way, on the conscience of a Pyncheon. If so, we are left to dispose of the awful query, whether each inheritor of the property—conscious of wrong, and failing to rectify it—did not commit anew the great guilt of his ancestor, and incur all its original responsibilities. And supposing such to be the case, would it not be a far truer mode of expression to say of the Pyncheon family that they inherited a great misfortune, than the reverse?

We have already hinted that it is not our purpose to trace down the history of the Pyncheon family, in its unbroken connection with the House of the Seven Gables; nor to show, as in a magic picture, how the rustiness and infirmity of age gathered over the venerable house itself. As regards its interior life, a large, dim looking glass used to hang in one of the rooms, and was fabled to contain within its depths all the shapes that had ever been reflected there—the old Colonel himself, and his many descendants, some in the garb of antique babyhood, and others in the bloom of feminine beauty or manly prime, or saddened with the wrinkles of frosty age. Had we the secret of that mirror, we would gladly sit down before it, and transfer its revelations to our page. But there was a story, for which it is difficult to conceive any foundation, that the posterity of Matthew Maule had some connection with the mystery of the looking glass, and that, by what appears to have been a sort of mesmeric process, they could make its inner region all alive with the departed Pyncheons; not as they had shown themselves to the world nor in their better and happier hours, but as doing over again some deed of sin, or in the crisis of life's bitterest sorrow. The popular imagination, indeed, long kept itself busy with the affair of the old Puritan Pyncheon and the wizard Maule; the curse, which the latter flung from his scaffold, was remembered, with the very important addition that it had become a part of the Pyncheon inheritance. If one of the family did but gurgle in his throat, a bystander would be likely enough to whisper, between jest and earnest, "He has Maule's blood to drink!" The sudden death of a Pyncheon, about a hundred years ago, with circumstances very similar to what have been related of the Colonel's exit, was held as giving additional probability to the received opinion on this topic. It was considered, moreover, an ugly and ominous circumstance that Colonel Pyncheon's picture—in obedience, it was said, to a provision of his will—remained affixed to the wall of the room in which he died. Those stern, immitigable features seemed to symbolize an evil influence, and so darkly to mingle the shadow of their presence with the sunshine of the passing hour that no good thoughts or purposes could ever spring up and blossom there. To the thoughtful mind there will be no tinge of superstition in what we figuratively express, by affirming that the ghost of a dead progenitor—perhaps as a portion of his own punishment—is often doomed to become the Evil Genius of his family.

The Pyncheons, in brief, lived along, for the better part

of two centuries, with perhaps less of outward vicissitude than has attended most other New England families during the same period of time. Possessing very distinctive traits of their own, they nevertheless took the general characteristics of the little community in which they dwelt; a town noted for its frugal, discreet, well-ordered, and home-loving inhabitants, as well as for the somewhat confined scope of its sympathies; but in which, be it said, there are odder individuals, and, now and then, stranger occurrences, than one meets with almost anywhere else. During the Revolution, the Pyncheon of that epoch, adopting the royal side, became a refugee; but repented, and made his reappearance, just at the point of time to preserve the House of the Seven Gables from confiscation. For the last seventy years, the most noted event in the Pyncheon annals had been likewise the heaviest calamity that ever befell the race; no less than the violent death—for so it was adjudged—of one member of the family by the criminal act of another. Certain circumstances attending this fatal occurrence had brought the deed irresistibly home to a nephew of the deceased Pyncheon. The young man was tried and convicted of the crime; but either the circumstantial nature of the evidence, and possibly some lurking doubt in the breast of the executive, or, lastly—an argument of greater weight in a republic than it could have been under a monarchy—the high respectability and political influence of the criminal's connections, had availed to mitigate his doom from death to perpetual imprisonment. This sad affair had chanced about thirty years before the action of our story commences. Latterly, there were rumors (which few believed, and only one or two felt greatly interested in) that this long-buried man was likely, for some reason or other, to be summoned forth from his living tomb.

It is essential to say a few words respecting the victim of this now almost forgotten murder. He was an old bachelor, and possessed of great wealth, in addition to the house and real estate which constituted what remained of the ancient Pyncheon property. Being of an eccentric and melancholy turn of mind, and greatly given to rummaging old records and hearkening to old traditions, he had brought himself, it is averred, to the conclusion that Matthew Maule, the wizard, had been foully wronged out of his homestead, if not out of his life. Such being the case, and he, the old bachelor, in possession of the ill-gotten spoil—with the black stain of blood sunken deep into it, and still to be scented by conscientious nostrils—the question occurred whether it were not imperative upon him, even at this late hour, to make restitution to Maule's posterity. To a man living so much in the past, and so little in the present, as the secluded and antiquarian old bachelor, a century and a half seemed not so vast a period as to obviate the propriety of substituting right for wrong. It was the belief of those who knew him best that he would positively have taken the very singular step of giving up the House of the Seven Gables to the representative of Matthew Maule, but for the unspeakable tumult which a suspicion of the old gentleman's project awakened among his Pyncheon relatives. Their exertions had the effect of suspending his purpose; but it was feared that he would perform, after death, by the operation of his last will, what he had so hardly been prevented from doing in his proper lifetime. But there is no one thing which men so rarely do, whatever the provocation or inducement, as to bequeath patrimonial property away from their own blood. They may love other individuals far better than their relatives—they may even cherish dislike, or positive hatred, to the latter—but yet, in view of death, the strong prejudice of propinquity revives, and impels the testator to send down his estate in the line marked out by custom so immemorial that it looks like nature. In all the Pyncheons, this feeling had the energy of disease. It was too powerful for the conscientious scruples of the old bachelor; at whose death, accordingly, the mansion house, together with most of his other riches, passed into the possession of his next legal representative.

This was a nephew, the cousin of the miserable young man who had been convicted of the uncle's murder. The new heir, up to the period of his accession, was reckoned rather a dissipated youth, but had at once reformed, and made himself an exceedingly respectable member of society. In fact, he showed more of the Pyncheon quality, and had won higher eminence in the world, than any of his race since the time of the original Puritan. Applying himself in earlier manhood to the study of the law, and having a natural tendency towards office, he had attained, many years ago, to a judicial situation in some inferior court, which gave him for life the very desirable and imposing title of judge. Later, he had engaged in politics, and served a part of two terms in Congress, besides making a considerable figure in both branches of the State legislature. Judge Pyncheon was unquestionably an honor to his race. He had built himself a country seat within a few miles of his native town, and there spent such portions of his time as could be spared from public service in the display of every grace and virtue—as a newspaper phrased it, on the eve of an election—befitting the Christian, the good citizen, the horticulturist, and the gentleman.

There were few of the Pyncheons left to sun themselves in the glow of the Judge's prosperity. In respect to natural increase, the breed had not thriven; it appeared rather to be dying out. The only members of the family known to be extant were, first, the Judge himself, and a single surviving son, who was now traveling in Europe; next, the thirty years' prisoner, already alluded to, and a sister of the latter, who occupied, in an extremely retired manner, the House of the Seven Gables, in which she had a life estate by the will of the old bachelor. She was understood to be wretchedly poor, and seemed to make it her choice to remain so, inasmuch as her affluent cousin, the Judge, had repeatedly offered her all the comforts of life, either in the old mansion or his own modern residence. The last and youngest Pyncheon was a little country girl of seventeen, the daughter of another of the Judge's cousins, who had married a young woman of no family or property, and died early and in poor circumstances. His widow had recently taken another husband.

As for Matthew Maule's posterity, it was supposed now to be extinct. For a very long period after the witchcraft delusion, however, the Maules had continued to inhabit the town where their progenitor had suffered so unjust a death. To all appearance, they were a quiet, honest, well-meaning race of people, cherishing no malice against individuals or the public for the wrong which had been done them; or if, at their own fireside, they transmitted, from father to child, any hostile recollection of the wizard's fate and their lost patrimony, it was never acted upon, nor openly expressed. Nor would it have been singular had they ceased to remember that the House of the Seven Gables was resting its heavy framework on a foundation that was rightfully their own. There is something so massive, stable, and almost irresistibly imposing in the exterior presentment of established rank and great possessions that their very existence seems to give them a right to exist; at least, so excellent a counterfeit of right, that few poor and humble men have moral force enough to question it, even in their secret minds. Such is the case now, after so many ancient prejudices have been overthrown; and it was far more so in ante-Revolutionary days, when the aristocracy could venture to be proud, and the low were content to be abased. Thus the Maules, at all events, kept their resentments within their own breasts. They were generally poverty-stricken; always plebeian and obscure; working with unsuccessful diligence at handicrafts; laboring on the wharves, or following the sea, as sailors before the mast; living here and there about the town, in hired tenements, and coming finally to the almshouse as the natural home of their old age. At last, after creeping, as it were, for such a length of time, along the utmost verge of the opaque puddle of obscurity, they had taken that downright plunge which, sooner or later, is the destiny of all families, whether princely or plebeian. For thirty years past, neither town record, nor gravestone, nor the directory, nor the knowledge or memory of man, bore any trace of Matthew Maule's descendants. His blood might possibly exist elsewhere; here, where its lowly current could be traced so far back, it had ceased to keep an onward course.

So long as any of the race were to be found, they had been marked out from other men—not strikingly, nor as with a sharp line, but with an effect that was felt rather than spoken of—by an hereditary character of reserve. Their companions, or those who endeavored to become such, grew conscious of a circle round about the Maules, within the sanctity or the spell of which, in spite of an exterior of sufficient frankness and good-fellowship, it was impossible for any man to step. It was this indefinable peculiarity, perhaps, that, by insulating them from human aid, kept them always so unfortunate in life. It certainly operated to prolong in their case, and to confirm to them as their only inheritance, those feelings of repugnance and superstitious terror with which the people of the town, even after awakening from their frenzy, continued to regard the memory of the reputed witches. The mantle, or rather the ragged cloak, of old Matthew Maule had fallen upon his children. They were half believed to inherit mysterious attributes; the family eye was said to possess strange power. Among other good-for-nothing properties and privileges, one was especially assigned them—that of exercising an influence over people's dreams. The Pyncheons, if all stories were true, haughtily as they bore themselves in the noonday streets of their native town, were no better than bond servants to these plebeian Maules, on entering the topsy-turvy commonwealth of sleep. Modern psychology, it may be, will endeavor to reduce these alleged necromancies within a system, instead of rejecting them as altogether fabulous.

A descriptive paragraph or two, treating of the seven-gabled mansion in its more recent aspect, will bring this preliminary chapter to a close. The street in which it upreared its venerable peaks has long ceased to be a fashionable quarter of the town; so that, though the old edifice was surrounded by habitations of modern date, they were mostly small, built entirely of wood, and typical of the most plodding uniformity of common life. Doubtless, however, the whole story of human existence may be latent in each of them, but with no picturesqueness, externally, that can attract the imagination or sympathy to seek it there. But as for the old structure of our story, its white-oak frame, and its boards, shingles, and crumbling plaster, and even the huge, clustered chimney in the midst, seemed to constitute only the least and meanest part of its reality. So much of mankind's varied experience had passed there—so much had been suffered, and something, too, enjoyed—that the very timbers were oozy, as with the moisture of a heart. It was itself like a great human heart, with a life of its own, and full of rich and somber reminiscences.

The deep projection of the second story gave the house such a meditative look that you could not pass it without the idea that it had secrets to keep, and an eventful history to moralize upon. In front, just on the edge of the unpaved sidewalk, grew the Pyncheon Elm, which, in reference to such trees as one usually meets with, might well be termed gigantic. It had been planted by a great-grandson of the first Pyncheon, and, though now fourscore years of age, or perhaps nearer a hundred, was still in its strong and broad maturity, throwing its shadow from side to side of the street, overtopping the seven gables, and sweeping the whole black roof with its pendent foliage. It gave beauty to the old edifice, and seemed to make it a part of nature. The street having been widened about forty years ago, the front gable was now precisely on a line with it. On either side extended a ruinous wooden fence of open latticework, through which could be seen a grassy yard, and, especially in the angles of the building, an enormous fertility of burdocks, with leaves, it is hardly an exaggeration to say, two or three feet long. Behind the house there appeared to be a garden, which undoubtedly had once been extensive, but was now infringed upon by other enclosures, or shut in by habitations and outbuildings that stood on another street. It would be an omission, trifling, indeed, but unpardonable, were we to forget the green moss that had long since gathered over the projections of the windows, and on the slopes of the roof; nor must we fail to direct the reader's eye to a crop, not of weeds, but flower shrubs, which were growing aloft in the air, not a great way from the chimney, in the nook between two of the gables. They were called Alice's Posies. The tradition was that a certain Alice Pyncheon had flung up the seeds, in sport, and that the dust of the street and the decay of the roof gradually formed a kind of soil for them, out of which they grew, when Alice had long been in her grave. However the flowers might have come there, it was both sad and sweet to observe how Nature adopted to herself this desolate, decaying, gusty, rusty old house of the Pyncheon family; and how the ever-returning summer did her best to gladden it with tender beauty, and grew melancholy in the effort.

There is one other feature, very essential to be noticed, but which, we greatly fear, may damage any picturesque and romantic impression which we have been willing to throw over our sketch of this respectable edifice. In the front gable, under the impending brow of the second story, and contiguous to the street, was a shop door, divided horizontally in the midst, and with a window for its upper segment, such as is often seen in dwellings of a somewhat ancient date. This same shop door had been a subject of no slight mortification to the present occupant of the august Pyncheon House, as well as to some of her predecessors. The matter is disagreeably delicate to handle; but, since the reader must needs be let into the secret, he will please to understand that, about a century ago, the head of the Pyncheons found himself involved in serious financial difficulties. The fellow (gentleman, as he styled himself) can hardly have been other than a spurious interloper; for, instead of seeking office from the king or the royal governor, or urging his hereditary claim to Eastern lands, he bethought himself of no better avenue to wealth than by cutting a shop door through the side of his ancestral residence. It was the custom of the time, indeed, for merchants to store their goods and transact business in their own dwellings. But there was something pitifully small in this old Pyncheon's mode of setting about his commercial operations; it was whispered that, with his own hands, all beruffled as they were, he used to give change for a shilling, and would turn a halfpenny twice over, to make sure that it was a good one. Beyond all question, he had the blood of a petty huckster in his veins, through whatever channel it may have found its way there.

Immediately on his death, the shop door had been locked, bolted, and barred, and, down to the period of our story, had probably never once been opened. The old counter, shelves, and other fixtures of the little shop remained just as he had left them. It used to be affirmed that the dead shopkeeper, in a white wig, a faded velvet coat, an apron at his waist, and his ruffles carefully turned back from his wrists, might be seen through the chinks of the shutters, any night of the year, ransacking his till, or poring over the dingy pages of his daybook. From the look of unutterable woe upon his face, it appeared to be his doom to spend eternity in a vain effort to make his accounts balance.

And now—in a very humble way, as will be seen—we proceed to open our narrative.

❧2❧

The Little Shopwindow

It still lacked half an hour of sunrise, when Miss Hepzibah Pyncheon—we will not say awoke, it being doubtful whether the poor lady had so much as closed her eyes during the brief night of midsummer—but, at all events, arose from her solitary pillow, and began what it would be mockery to term the adornment of her person. Far from us be the indecorum of assisting, even in imagination, at a maiden lady's toilet! Our story must therefore await Miss Hepzibah at the threshold of her chamber; only presuming, meanwhile, to note some of the heavy sighs that labored from her bosom, with little restraint as to their lugubrious depth and volume of sound, inasmuch as they could be audible to nobody save a disembodied listener like ourself. The Old Maid was alone in the old house. Alone, except for a certain respectable and orderly young man, an artist in the daguerreotype line, who, for about three months back, had been a lodger in a remote gable—quite a house by itself, indeed—with locks, bolts, and oaken bars on all the intervening doors. Inaudible, consequently, were poor Miss Hepzibah's gusty sighs. Inaudible the creaking joints of her stiffened knees, as she knelt down by the bedside. And inaudible, too, by mortal ear, but heard with all-comprehending love and pity in the farthest heaven, that almost agony of prayer—now whispered, now a groan, now a struggling silence—wherewith she besought the Divine assistance through the day! Evidently, this is to be a day of more than ordinary trial to Miss Hepzibah, who, for above a quarter of a century gone by, has dwelt in strict seclusion, taking no part in the business of life, and just as little in its intercourse and pleasures. Not with such fervor prays the torpid recluse, looking forward to the cold, sunless, stagnant calm of a day that is to be like innumerable yesterdays!

The maiden lady's devotions are concluded. Will she now issue forth over the threshold of our story? Not yet, by many moments. First, every drawer in the tall, old-fashioned bureau is to be opened, with difficulty, and with a succession of spasmodic jerks; then, all must close again, with the same fidgety reluctance. There is a rustling of stiff silks; a tread of backward and forward footsteps to and fro across the chamber. We suspect Miss Hepzibah, moreover, of taking a step upward into a chair, in order to give heedful regard to her appearance on all sides, and at full length, in the oval, dingy-framed toilet glass that hangs above her table. Truly! well, indeed! who would have thought it! Is all this precious time to be lavished on the matutinal repair and beautifying of an elderly person, who never goes abroad, whom nobody ever visits, and from whom, when she shall have done her utmost, it were the best charity to turn one's eyes another way?

Now she is almost ready. Let us pardon her one other pause; for it is given to the sole sentiment, or, we might better say—heightened and rendered intense, as it has been, by sorrow and seclusion—to the strong passion of her life. We heard the turning of a key in a small lock; she has opened a secret drawer of an escritoire, and is probably looking at a certain miniature, done in Malbone's most perfect style, and representing a face worthy of no less delicate a pencil. It was once our good fortune to see this picture. It is a likeness of a young man, in a silken dressing gown of an old fashion, the soft richness of which is well adapted to the countenance of reverie, with its full, tender lips, and beautiful eyes, that seem to indicate not so much capacity of thought as gentle and voluptuous emotion. Of the possessor of such features we shall have a right to ask nothing, except that he would take the rude world easily, and make himself happy in it. Can it have been an early lover of Miss Hepzibah? No; she never had a lover—poor thing, how could she?—nor ever knew, by her own experience, what love technically means. And yet, her undying faith and trust, her fresh remembrance, and continual devotedness towards the original of that miniature, have been the only substance for her heart to feed upon.

She seems to have put aside the miniature, and is standing again before the toilet glass. There are tears to be wiped off. A few more footsteps to and fro; and here, at last—with another pitiful sigh, like a gust of chill, damp wind out of a long-closed vault, the door of which has accidentally been set ajar—here comes Miss Hepzibah Pyncheon! Forth she steps into the dusky, time-darkened passage; a tall figure, clad in black silk, with a long and shrunken waist, feeling her way towards the stairs like a nearsighted person, as in truth she is.

The sun, meanwhile, if not already above the horizon, was ascending nearer and nearer to its verge. A few clouds, floating high upward, caught some of the earliest light, and threw down its golden gleam on the windows of all the houses in the street, not forgetting the House of the Seven Gables, which—many such sunrises as it had witnessed—looked cheerfully at the present one. The reflected radiance served to show, pretty distinctly, the aspect and arrangement of the room which Hepzibah entered, after descending the stair. It was a low-studded room, with a beam across the ceiling, paneled with dark wood, and having a large chimney piece, set round with pictured tiles, but now closed by an iron fireboard, through which ran the funnel of a modern stove. There was a carpet on the floor, originally of rich texture, but so worn and faded in these latter years that its once brilliant figure had quite vanished into one indistinguishable hue. In the way of furniture, there were two tables: one, constructed with perplexing intricacy and exhibiting as many feet as a centipede; the other, most delicately wrought, with four long and slender legs, so apparently frail that it was almost incredible what a length of time the ancient tea table had stood upon them. Half a dozen chairs stood about the room, straight and stiff, and so ingeniously contrived for the discomfort of the human person that they were irksome even to sight, and conveyed the ugliest possible idea of the state of society to which they could have been adapted. One exception there was, however, in a very antique elbowchair, with a high back, carved elaborately in oak, and a roomy depth within its arms, that made up, by its spacious comprehensiveness, for the lack of any of those artistic curves which abound in a modern chair.

As for ornamental articles of furniture, we recollect but two, if such they may be called. One was a map of the Pyncheon territory at the eastward, not engraved, but the handiwork of some skillful old draftsman, and grotesquely illuminated with pictures of Indians and wild beasts, among which was seen a lion; the natural history of the region being as little known as its geography, which was put down most fantastically awry. The other adornment was the portrait of old Colonel Pyncheon, at two-thirds length, representing the stern features of a Puritanic-looking personage, in a skullcap, with a laced band and a grizzly beard; holding a Bible with one hand, and in the other uplifting an iron sword hilt. The latter object, being more successfully depicted by the artist, stood out in far greater prominence than the sacred volume. Face to face with this picture, on entering the apartment, Miss Hepzibah Pyncheon came to a pause; regarding it with a singular scowl, a strange contortion of the brow which, by people who did not know her, would probably have been interpreted as an expression of bitter anger and ill will. But it was no such thing. She, in fact, felt a reverence for the pictured visage, of which only a far-descended and time-stricken virgin could be susceptible; and this forbidding scowl was the innocent result of her nearsightedness, and an effort so to concentrate her powers of vision as to substitute a firm outline of the object instead of a vague one.

We must linger a moment on this unfortunate expression of poor Hepzibah's brow. Her scowl—as the world, or such part of it as sometimes caught a transitory glimpse of her at the window, wickedly persisted in calling it—her scowl had done Miss Hepzibah a very ill office, in establishing her character as an ill-tempered old maid; nor does it appear improbable that, by often gazing at herself in a dim looking glass, and perpetually encountering her own frown within its ghostly sphere, she had been led to interpret the expression almost as unjustly as the world did. "How miserably cross I look!" she must often have whispered to herself; and ultimately have fancied herself so, by a sense of inevitable doom. But her heart never frowned. It was naturally tender, sensitive, and full of little tremors and palpitations; all of which weaknesses it retained, while her visage was growing so perversely stern, and even fierce. Nor had Hepzibah ever any hardihood, except what came from the very warmest nook in her affections.

All this time, however, we are loitering faintheartedly on the threshold of our story. In very truth, we have an invincible reluctance to disclose what Miss Hepzibah Pyncheon was about to do.

It has already been observed that, in the basement story of the gable fronting on the street, an unworthy ancestor, nearly a century ago, had fitted up a shop. Ever since the old gentleman retired from trade, and fell asleep under his coffin lid, not only the shop door, but the inner arrangements, had been suffered to remain unchanged; while the dust of ages gathered inch-deep over the shelves and counter, and partly filled an old pair of scales, as if it were of value enough to be weighed. It treasured itself up, too, in the half-open till, where there still lingered a base sixpence, worth neither more nor less than the hereditary pride which had here been put to shame. Such had been the state and condition of the little shop in old Hepzibah's childhood, when she and her brother used to play at hide-and-seek in its forsaken precincts. So it had remained, until within a few days past.

But now, though the shopwindow was still closely curtained from the public gaze, a remarkable change had taken place in its interior. The rich and heavy festoons of cobweb, which it had cost a long ancestral succession of spiders their life's labor to spin and weave, had been carefully brushed away from the ceiling. The counter, shelves, floor had all been scoured, and the latter was overstrewn with fresh blue sand. The brown scales, too, had evidently undergone rigid discipline, in an unavailing effort to rub off the rust, which, alas! had eaten through and through their substance. Neither was the little old shop any longer empty of merchantable goods. A curious eye, privileged to take an account of stock, and investigate behind the counter, would have discovered a barrel—yea, two or three barrels and half ditto—one containing flour, another apples, and a third, perhaps, Indian meal. There was likewise a square box of pinewood, full of soap in bars; also, another of the same size, in which were tallow candles, ten to the pound. A small stock of brown sugar, some white beans and split peas, and a few other commodities of low price, and such as are constantly in demand, made up the bulkier portion of the merchandise. It might have been taken for a ghostly or phantasmagoric reflection of the old shopkeeper Pyncheon's shabbily provided shelves, save that some of the articles were of a description and outward form which could hardly have been known in his day. For instance, there was a glass pickle jar, filled with fragments of Gibraltar rock; not, indeed, splinters of the veritable stone foundation of the famous fortress, but bits of delectable candy, neatly done up in white paper. Jim Crow, moreover, was seen executing his world-renowned dance, in gingerbread. A party of leaden dragoons were galloping along one of the shelves, in equipments and uniform of modern cut; and there were some sugar figures, with no strong resemblance to the humanity of any epoch, but less unsatisfactorily representing our own fashions than those of a hundred years ago. Another phenomenon, still more strikingly modern, was a package of lucifer matches, which, in old times, would have been thought actually to borrow their instantaneous flame from the nether fires of Tophet.

In short, to bring the matter at once to a point, it was incontrovertibly evident that somebody had taken the shop and fixtures of the long-retired and forgotten Mr. Pyncheon, and was about to renew the enterprise of that departed worthy, with a different set of customers. Who could this bold adventurer be? And, of all places in the world, why had he chosen the House of the Seven Gables as the scene of his commercial speculations?

We return to the elderly maiden. She at length withdrew her eyes from the dark countenance of the Colonel's portrait, heaved a sigh—indeed, her breast was a very cave of Aeolus that morning—and stepped across the room on tiptoe, as is the customary gait of elderly women. Passing through an intervening passage, she opened a door that communicated with the shop, just now so elaborately described. Owing to the projection of the upper story—and still more to the thick shadow of the Pyncheon Elm, which stood almost directly in front of the gable—the twilight, here, was still as much akin to night as morning. Another heavy sigh from Miss Hepzibah! After a moment's pause on the threshold, peering towards the window with her nearsighted scowl, as if frowning down some bitter enemy, she suddenly projected herself into the shop. The haste, and, as it were, the galvanic impulse of the movement, were really quite startling.

Nervously—in a sort of frenzy, we might almost say— she began to busy herself in arranging some children's playthings, and other little wares, on the shelves and at the shopwindow. In the aspect of this dark-arrayed, pale-faced, ladylike old figure there was a deeply tragic character that contrasted irreconcilably with the ludicrous pettiness of her employment. It seemed a queer anomaly that so gaunt and dismal a personage should take a toy in hand; a miracle that the toy did not vanish in her grasp; a miserably absurd idea that she should go on perplexing her stiff and somber intellect with the question how to tempt little boys into her premises! Yet such is undoubtedly her object. Now she places a gingerbread elephant against the window, but with so tremulous a touch that it tumbles upon the floor, with the dismemberment of three legs and its trunk; it has ceased to be an elephant, and has become a few bits of musty gingerbread. There, again, she has upset a tumbler of marbles, all of which roll different ways, and each individual marble, devil-directed, into the most difficult obscurity that it can find. Heaven help our poor old Hepzibah, and forgive us for taking a ludicrous view of her position! As her rigid and rusty frame goes down upon its hands and knees, in quest of the absconding marbles, we positively feel so much the more inclined to shed tears of sympathy, from the very fact that we must needs turn aside and laugh at her. For here—and if we fail to impress it suitably upon the reader, it is our own fault, not that of the theme—here is one of the truest points of melancholy interest that occur in ordinary life. It was the final throe of what called itself old gentility. A lady—who had fed herself from childhood with the shadowy food of aristocratic reminiscences, and whose religion it was that a lady's hand soils itself irremediably by doing aught for bread—this born lady, after sixty years of narrowing means, is fain to step down from her pedestal of imaginary rank. Poverty, treading closely at her heels for a lifetime, has come up with her at last. She must earn her own food, or starve! And we have stolen upon Miss Hepzibah Pyncheon, too irreverently, at the instant of time when the patrician lady is to be transformed into the plebeian woman.

In this republican country, amid the fluctuating waves of our social life, somebody is always at the drowning point. The tragedy is enacted with as continual a repetition as that of a popular drama on a holiday; and, nevertheless, is felt as deeply, perhaps, as when an hereditary noble sinks below his order. More deeply; since, with us, rank is the grosser substance of wealth and a splendid establishment, and has no spiritual existence after the death of these, but dies hopelessly along with them. And, therefore, since we have been unfortunate enough to introduce our heroine at so inauspicious a juncture, we would entreat for a mood of due solemnity in the spectators of her fate. Let us behold, in poor Hepzibah, the immemorial lady—two hundred years old, on this side of the water, and thrice as many on the other—with her antique portraits, pedigrees, coats of arms, records and traditions, and her claim, as joint heiress, to that princely territory at the eastward, no longer a wilderness, but a populous fertility—born, too, in Pyncheon Street, under the Pyncheon Elm, and in the Pyncheon House, where she has spent all her days—reduced now, in that very house, to be the hucksteress of a cent shop.

This business of setting up a petty shop is almost the only resource of women in circumstances at all similar to

those of our unfortunate recluse. With her nearsightedness, and those tremulous fingers of hers, at once inflexible
and delicate, she could not be a seamstress; although her
sampler, of fifty years gone by, exhibited some of the most
recondite specimens of ornamental needlework. A school
for little children had been often in her thoughts; and, at
one time, she had begun a review of her early studies in the
New England Primer, with a view to prepare herself for the
office of instructress. But the love of children had never
been quickened in Hepzibah's heart, and was now torpid,
if not extinct; she watched the little people of the neighborhood from her chamber window, and doubted whether
she could tolerate a more intimate acquaintance with them.
Besides, in our day, the very A B C has become a science
greatly too abstruse to be any longer taught by pointing a
pin from letter to letter. A modern child could teach old
Hepzibah more than old Hepzibah could teach the child.
So—with many a cold, deep heartquake at the idea of at
last coming into sordid contact with the world, from which
she had so long kept aloof, while every added day of seclusion had rolled another stone against the cavern door of
her hermitage—the poor thing bethought herself of the ancient shopwindow, the rusty scales, and dusty till. She might
have held back a little longer; but another circumstance,
not yet hinted at, had somewhat hastened her decision.
Her humble preparations, therefore, were duly made, and
the enterprise was now to be commenced. Nor was she entitled to complain of any remarkable singularity in her fate;
for, in the town of her nativity, we might point to several
little shops of a similar description, some of them in houses
as ancient as that of the Seven Gables; and one or two, it
may be, where a decayed gentlewoman stands behind the
counter, as grim an image of family pride as Miss Hepzibah
Pyncheon herself.

    It was overpoweringly ridiculous—we must honestly
confess it—the deportment of the maiden lady while setting her shop in order for the public eye. She stole on tiptoe to the window, as cautiously as if she conceived some
bloody-minded villain to be watching behind the elm tree,
with intent to take her life. Stretching out her long, lank

arm, she put a paper of pearl buttons, a jew's-harp, or whatever the small article might be, in its destined place, and straightway vanished back into the dusk, as if the world need never hope for another glimpse of her. It might have been fancied, indeed, that she expected to minister to the wants of the community unseen, like a disembodied divinity or enchantress, holding forth her bargains to the reverential and awe-stricken purchaser in an invisible hand. But Hepzibah had no such flattering dream. She was well aware that she must ultimately come forward, and stand revealed in her proper individuality; but, like other sensitive persons, she could not bear to be observed in the gradual process, and chose rather to flash forth on the world's astonished gaze at once.

The inevitable moment was not much longer to be delayed. The sunshine might now be seen stealing down the front of the opposite house, from the windows of which came a reflected gleam, struggling through the boughs of the elm tree, and enlightening the interior of the shop more distinctly than heretofore. The town appeared to be waking up. A baker's cart had already rattled through the street, chasing away the latest vestige of night's sanctity with the jingle-jangle of its dissonant bells. A milkman was distributing the contents of his cans from door to door; and the harsh peal of a fisherman's conch shell was heard far off, around the corner. None of these tokens escaped Hepzibah's notice. The moment had arrived. To delay longer would be only to lengthen out her misery. Nothing remained, except to take down the bar from the shop door, leaving the entrance free—more than free: welcome, as if all were household friends—to every passer-by, whose eyes might be attracted by the commodities at the window. This last act Hepzibah now performed, letting the bar fall with what smote upon her excited nerves as a most astounding clatter. Then—as if the only barrier betwixt herself and the world had been thrown down, and a flood of evil consequences would come tumbling through the gap—she fled into the inner parlor, threw herself into the ancestral elbowchair, and wept.

Our miserable old Hepzibah! It is a heavy annoyance

to a writer, who endeavors to represent nature, its various attitudes and circumstances, in a reasonably correct outline and true coloring, that so much of the mean and ludicrous should be hopelessly mixed up with the purest pathos which life anywhere supplies to him. What tragic dignity, for example, can be wrought into a scene like this! How can we elevate our history of retribution for the sin of long ago, when, as one of our most prominent figures, we are compelled to introduce—not a young and lovely woman, nor even the stately remains of beauty, storm-shattered by affliction—but a gaunt, sallow, rusty-jointed maiden, in a long-waisted silk gown, and with the strange horror of a turban on her head! Her visage is not even ugly. It is redeemed from insignificance only by the contraction of her eyebrows into a nearsighted scowl. And, finally, her great life trial seems to be that, after sixty years of idleness, she finds it convenient to earn comfortable bread by setting up a shop in a small way. Nevertheless, if we look through all the heroic fortunes of mankind, we shall find this same entanglement of something mean and trivial with whatever is noblest in joy or sorrow. Life is made up of marble and mud. And, without all the deeper trust in a comprehensive sympathy above us, we might hence be led to suspect the insult of a sneer, as well as an immitigable frown, on the iron countenance of fate. What is called poetic insight is the gift of discerning, in this sphere of strangely mingled elements, the beauty and the majesty which are compelled to assume a garb so sordid.

❧ 3 ❧

The First Customer

MISS HEPZIBAH PYNCHEON sat in the oaken elbowchair, with her hands over her face, giving way to that heavy down-sinking of the heart which most persons have experienced, when the image of hope itself seems ponderously molded of lead, on the eve of an enterprise at once doubtful and momentous. She was suddenly startled by the tinkling alarum—high, sharp, and irregular—of a little bell. The maiden lady arose upon her feet, as pale as a ghost at cock-crow; for she was an enslaved spirit, and this the talisman to which she owed obedience. This little bell—to speak in plainer terms—being fastened over the shop door, was so contrived as to vibrate by means of a steel spring, and thus convey notice to the inner regions of the house when any customer should cross the threshold. Its ugly and spiteful little din (heard now for the first time, perhaps, since Hep-zibah's periwigged predecessor had retired from trade) at once set every nerve of her body in responsive and tumul-tuous vibration. The crisis was upon her! Her first customer was at the door!

Without giving herself time for a second thought, she rushed into the shop, pale, wild, desperate in gesture and expression, scowling portentously, and looking far better qualified to do fierce battle with a housebreaker than to stand smiling behind the counter, bartering small wares for a copper recompense. Any ordinary customer, indeed, would have turned his back and fled. And yet there was nothing fierce in Hepzibah's poor old heart; nor had she, at the moment, a single bitter thought against the world at large, or one individual man or woman. She wished them all well, but wished, too, that she herself were done with them, and in her quiet grave.

The applicant, by this time, stood within the doorway. Coming freshly, as he did, out of the morning light, he appeared to have brought some of its cheery influences into the shop along with him. It was a slender young man, not more than one or two and twenty years old, with rather a grave and thoughtful expression for his years, but likewise a springy alacrity and vigor. These qualities were not only perceptible, physically, in his make and motions, but made themselves felt almost immediately in his character. A brown beard, not too silken in its texture, fringed his chin, but as yet without completely hiding it; he wore a short mustache, too, and his dark, high-featured countenance looked all the better for these natural ornaments. As for his dress, it was of the simplest kind: a summer sack of cheap and ordinary material, thin, checkered pantaloons, and a straw hat, by no means of the finest braid. Oak Hall might have supplied his entire equipment. He was chiefly marked as a gentleman—if such, indeed, he made any claim to be— by the rather remarkable whiteness and nicety of his clean linen.

He met the scowl of old Hepzibah without apparent alarm, as having heretofore encountered it and found it harmless.

"So, my dear Miss Pyncheon," said the daguerreotypist— for it was that sole other occupant of the seven-gabled mansion, "I am glad to see that you have not shrunk from your good purpose. I merely look in to offer my best wishes, and to ask if I can assist you any further in your preparations."

People in difficulty and distress, or in any manner at odds with the world, can endure a vast amount of harsh treatment, and perhaps be only the stronger for it; whereas they give way at once before the simplest expression of what they perceive to be genuine sympathy. So it proved with poor Hepzibah; for, when she saw the young man's smile— looking so much the brighter on a thoughtful face—and heard his kindly tone, she broke first into an hysteric giggle and then began to sob.

"Ah, Mr. Holgrave," cried she, as soon as she could speak, "I never can go through with it! Never, never, never! I wish I were dead, and in the old family tomb, with all my forefathers! With my father, and my mother, and my sister! Yes, and with my brother, who had far better find me there than here! The world is too chill and hard—and I am too old, and too feeble, and too hopeless!"

"Oh, believe me, Miss Hepzibah," said the young man, quietly, "these feelings will not trouble you any longer, after you are once fairly in the midst of your enterprise. They are unavoidable at this moment, standing, as you do, on the outer verge of your long seclusion, and peopling the world with ugly shapes, which you will soon find to be as unreal as the giants and ogres of a child's storybook. I find nothing so singular in life as that everything appears to lose its substance the instant one actually grapples with it. So it will be with what you think so terrible."

"But I am a woman!" said Hepzibah, piteously. "I was going to say a lady, but I consider that as past."

"Well, no matter if it be past!" answered the artist, a strange gleam of half-hidden sarcasm flashing through the kindliness of his manner. "Let it go! You are the better without it. I speak frankly, my dear Miss Pyncheon, for are we not friends? I look upon this as one of the fortunate days of your life. It ends an epoch and begins one. Hitherto, the lifeblood has been gradually chilling in your veins as you sat aloof, within your circle of gentility, while the rest of the world was fighting out its battle with one kind of necessity or another. Henceforth, you will at least have the sense of healthy and natural effort for a purpose, and of lending your strength—be it great or small—to the united struggle of mankind. This is success—all the success that anybody meets with!"

"It is natural enough, Mr. Holgrave, that you should have ideas like these," rejoined Hepzibah, drawing up her gaunt figure, with slightly offended dignity. "You are a man, a young man, and brought up, I suppose, as almost everybody is nowadays, with a view to seeking your fortune. But

I was born a lady, and have always lived one; no matter in what narrowness of means, always a lady!"

"But I was not born a gentleman; neither have I lived like one," said Holgrave, slightly smiling. "So, my dear madam, you will hardly expect me to sympathize with sensibilities of this kind; though, unless I deceive myself, I have some imperfect comprehension of them. These names of gentleman and lady had a meaning, in the past history of the world, and conferred privileges, desirable or otherwise, on those entitled to bear them. In the present—and still more in the future condition of society—they imply not privilege, but restriction!"

"These are new notions," said the old gentlewoman, shaking her head. "I shall never understand them; neither do I wish it."

"We will cease to speak of them, then," replied the artist, with a friendlier smile than his last one, "and I will leave you to feel whether it is not better to be a true woman than a lady. Do you really think, Miss Hepzibah, that any lady of your family has ever done a more heroic thing, since this house was built, than you are performing in it today? Never; and if the Pyncheons had always acted so nobly, I doubt whether an old wizard Maule's anathema, of which you told me once, would have had much weight with Providence against them."

"Ah! No, no!" said Hepzibah, not displeased at this allusion to the somber dignity of an inherited curse. "If old Maule's ghost, or a descendant of his, could see me behind the counter today, he would call it the fulfillment of his worst wishes. But I thank you for your kindness, Mr. Holgrave, and will do my utmost to be a good shopkeeper."

"Pray do," said Holgrave, "and let me have the pleasure of being your first customer. I am about taking a walk to the seashore, before going to my rooms, where I misuse heaven's blessed sunshine by tracing out human features through its agency. A few of those biscuits, dipped in sea water, will be just what I need for breakfast. What is the price of half a dozen?"

"Let me be a lady a moment longer," replied Hepzibah, with a manner of antique stateliness to which a melancholy smile lent a kind of grace. She put the biscuits into his hand, but rejected the compensation. "A Pyncheon must not, at all events under her forefathers' roof, receive money for a morsel of bread from her only friend!"

Holgrave took his departure, leaving her, for the moment, with spirits not quite so much depressed. Soon, however, they had subsided nearly to their former dead level. With a beating heart, she listened to the footsteps of early passengers, which now began to be frequent along the street. Once or twice they seemed to linger; these strangers, or neighbors, as the case might be, were looking at the display of toys and petty commodities in Hepzibah's shopwindow. She was doubly tortured; in part, with a sense of overwhelming shame that strange and unloving eyes should have the privilege of gazing, and partly because the idea occurred to her, with ridiculous importunity, that the window was not arranged so skillfully, nor nearly to so much advantage, as it might have been. It seemed as if the whole fortune or failure of her shop might depend on the display of a different set of articles, or substituting a fairer apple for one which appeared to be specked. So she made the change, and straightway fancied that everything was spoiled by it; not recognizing that it was the nervousness of the juncture, and her own native squeamishness as an old maid, that wrought all the seeming mischief.

Anon, there was an encounter, just at the doorstep, betwixt two laboring men, as their rough voices denoted them to be. After some slight talk about their own affairs, one of them chanced to notice the shopwindow, and directed the other's attention to it.

"See here!" cried he. "What do you think of this? Trade seems to be looking up in Pyncheon Street!"

"Well, well, this is a sight, to be sure!" exclaimed the other. "In the old Pyncheon House, and underneath the Pyncheon Elm! Who would have thought it? Old Maid Pyncheon is setting up a cent shop!"

"Will she make it go, think you, Dixey?" said his friend. "I don't call it a very good stand. There's another shop just round the corner."

"Make it go!" cried Dixey, with a most contemptuous

expression, as if the very idea were impossible to be conceived. "Not a bit of it! Why, her face—I've seen it, for I dug her garden for her one year—her face is enough to frighten the Old Nick himself, if he had ever so great a mind to trade with her. People can't stand it, I tell you! She scowls dreadfully, reason or none, out of pure ugliness of temper!"

"Well, that's not so much matter," remarked the other man. "These sour-tempered folks are mostly handy at business, and know pretty well what they are about. But, as you say, I don't think she'll do much. This business of keeping cent shops is overdone, like all other kinds of trade, handicraft, and bodily labor. I know it, to my cost! My wife kept a cent shop three months, and lost five dollars on her outlay!"

"Poor business!" responded Dixey, in a tone as if he were shaking his head. "Poor business!"

For some reason or other, not very easy to analyze, there had hardly been so bitter a pang in all her previous misery about the matter as what thrilled Hepzibah's heart on overhearing the above conversation. The testimony in regard to her scowl was frightfully important; it seemed to hold up her image wholly relieved from the false light of her self-partialities, and so hideous that she dared not look at it. She was absurdly hurt, moreover, by the slight and idle effect that her setting up shop—an event of such breathless interest to herself—appeared to have upon the public, of which these two men were the nearest representatives. A glance; a passing word or two; a coarse laugh; and she was doubtless forgotten before they turned the corner! They cared nothing for her dignity, and just as little for her degradation. Then, also, the augury of ill success, uttered from the sure wisdom of experience, fell upon her half-dead hope like a clod into a grave. The man's wife had already tried the same experiment, and failed! How could the born lady—the recluse of half a lifetime, utterly unpracticed in the world, at sixty years of age—how could she ever dream of succeeding, when the hard, vulgar, keen, busy, hackneyed New England woman had lost five dollars on her little outlay! Success presented itself as an impossibility, and the hope of it as a wild hallucination.

Some malevolent spirit, doing his utmost to drive Hepzibah mad, unrolled before her imagination a kind of panorama, representing the great thoroughfare of a city all astir with customers. So many and so magnificent shops as there were! Groceries, toyshops, dry goods stores, with their immense panes of plate glass, their gorgeous fixtures, their vast and complete assortments of merchandise, in which fortunes had been invested; and those noble mirrors at the farther end of each establishment, doubling all this wealth by a brightly burnished vista of unrealities! On one side of the street this splendid bazaar, with a multitude of perfumed and glossy salesmen, smirking, smiling, bowing, and measuring out the goods. On the other, the dusky old House of the Seven Gables, with the antiquated shopwindow under its projecting story, and Hepzibah herself, in a gown of rusty black silk, behind the counter, scowling at the world as it went by! This mighty contrast thrust itself forward as a fair expression of the odds against which she was to begin her struggle for a subsistence. Success? Preposterous! She would never think of it again! The house might just as well be buried in an eternal fog while all other houses had the sunshine on them; for not a foot would ever cross the threshold, nor a hand so much as try the door!

But, at this instant, the shop bell, right over her head, tinkled as if it were bewitched. The old gentlewoman's heart seemed to be attached to the same steel spring, for it went through a series of sharp jerks, in unison with the sound. The door was thrust open, although no human form was perceptible on the other side of the half window. Hepzibah, nevertheless, stood at a gaze, with her hands clasped, looking very much as if she had summoned up an evil spirit, and were afraid, yet resolved, to hazard the encounter.

"Heaven help me!" she groaned, mentally. "Now is my hour of need!"

The door, which moved with difficulty on its creaking and rusty hinges, being forced quite open, a square and sturdy little urchin became apparent, with cheeks as red as an apple. He was clad rather shabbily (but, as it seemed, more owing to his mother's carelessness than his father's poverty), in a blue apron, very wide and short trousers, shoes somewhat out at the toes, and a chip hat, with the frizzles of his curly hair sticking through its crevices. A book and a small slate, under his arm, indicated that he was on his way to school. He stared at Hepzibah a moment, as an elder customer than himself would have been likely enough to do, not knowing what to make of the tragic attitude and queer scowl wherewith she regarded him.

"Well, child," said she, taking heart at sight of a personage so little formidable, "well, my child, what did you wish for?"

"That Jim Crow there in the window," answered the urchin, holding out a cent, and pointing to the gingerbread figure that had attracted his notice, as he loitered along to school. "The one that has not a broken foot."

So Hepzibah put forth her lank arm, and, taking the effigy from the shopwindow, delivered it to her first customer.

"No matter for the money," said she, giving him a little push towards the door; for her old gentility was contumaciously squeamish at sight of the copper coin, and, besides, it seemed such pitiful meanness to take the child's pocket money in exchange for a bit of stale gingerbread. "No matter for the cent. You are welcome to Jim Crow."

The child, staring with round eyes at this instance of liberality, wholly unprecedented in his large experience of cent shops, took the man of gingerbread, and quitted the premises. No sooner had he reached the sidewalk (little cannibal that he was!) than Jim Crow's head was in his mouth. As he had not been careful to shut the door, Hepzibah was at the pains of closing it after him, with a pettish ejaculation or two about the troublesomeness of young people, and particularly of small boys. She had just placed another representative of the renowned Jim Crow at the window, when again the shop bell tinkled clamorously, and again the door being thrust open, with its characteristic jerk and jar, disclosed the same sturdy little urchin who, precisely two minutes ago, had made his exit. The crumbs and discoloration of the cannibal feast, as yet hardly consummated, were exceedingly visible about his mouth.

"What is it now, child?" asked the maiden lady rather impatiently. "Did you come back to shut the door?"

"No," answered the urchin, pointing to the figure that had just been put up. "I want that other Jim Crow."

"Well, here it is for you," said Hepzibah, reaching it down; but recognizing that this pertinacious customer would not quit her on any other terms, so long as she had a gingerbread figure in her shop, she partly drew back her extended hand. "Where is the cent?"

The little boy had the cent ready, but, like a trueborn Yankee, would have preferred the better bargain to the worse. Looking somewhat chagrined, he put the coin into Hepzibah's hand, and departed, sending the second Jim Crow in quest of the former one. The new shopkeeper dropped the first solid result of her commercial enterprise into the till. It was done! The sordid stain of that copper coin could never be washed away from her palm. The little schoolboy, aided by the impish figure of the Negro dancer, had wrought an irreparable ruin. The structure of ancient aristocracy had been demolished by him, even as if his childish gripe had torn down the seven-gabled mansion. Now let Hepzibah turn the old Pyncheon portraits with their faces to the wall, and take the map of her Eastern territory to kindle the kitchen fire, and blow up the flame with the empty breath of her ancestral traditions! What had she to do with ancestry? Nothing; no more than with posterity! No lady, now, but simply Hepzibah Pyncheon, a forlorn old maid, and keeper of a cent shop!

Nevertheless, even while she paraded these ideas somewhat ostentatiously through her mind, it is altogether surprising what a calmness had come over her. The anxiety and misgivings which had tormented her, whether asleep or in melancholy daydreams, ever since her project began to take an aspect of solidity, had now vanished quite away. She felt the novelty of her position, indeed, but no longer with disturbance or affright. Now and then, there came a thrill of almost youthful enjoyment. It was the invigorating breath of a fresh outward atmosphere, after the long torpor and monotonous seclusion of her life. So wholesome is effort! So miraculous the strength that we do not know of! The healthiest glow that Hepzibah had known for years had come now in the dreaded crisis, when, for the first time, she had put forth her hand to help herself. The little circlet of the schoolboy's copper coin—dim and lusterless though it was, with the small services which it had been doing here and there about the world—had proved a talisman, fragrant with good, and deserving to be set in gold and worn next her heart. It was as potent, and perhaps endowed with the same kind of efficacy, as a galvanic ring! Hepzibah, at all events, was indebted to its subtile operation both in body and spirit; so much the more, as it inspired her with energy to get some breakfast, at which, still the better to keep up her courage, she allowed herself an extra spoonful in her infusion of black tea.

Her introductory day of shopkeeping did not run on, however, without many and serious interruptions of this mood of cheerful vigor. As a general rule, Providence seldom vouchsafes to mortals any more than just that degree of encouragement which suffices to keep them at a reasonably full exertion of their powers. In the case of our old gentlewoman, after the excitement of new effort had subsided, the despondency of her whole life threatened, ever and anon, to return. It was like the heavy mass of clouds which we may often see obscuring the sky, and making a gray twilight everywhere, until, towards nightfall, it yields temporarily to a glimpse of sunshine. But, always, the envious cloud strives to gather again across the streak of celestial azure.

Customers came in, as the forenoon advanced, but rather slowly; in some cases, too, it must be owned, with little satisfaction either to themselves or Miss Hepzibah; nor, on the whole, with an aggregate of very rich emolument to the till. A little girl, sent by her mother to match a skein of cotton thread, of a peculiar hue, took one that the nearsighted old lady pronounced extremely like, but soon came running back, with a blunt and cross message that it would not do, and, besides, was very rotten! Then there was a pale, care-wrinkled woman, not old but haggard, and already with streaks of gray among her hair, like silver ribbons; one of those women, naturally delicate, whom you at once recognize as worn to death by a brute—probably a drunken brute—of a husband, and at least nine children.

She wanted a few pounds of flour, and offered the money, which the decayed gentlewoman silently rejected, and gave the poor soul better measure than if she had taken it. Shortly afterwards, a man in a blue cotton frock, much soiled, came in and bought a pipe, filling the whole shop, meanwhile, with the hot odor of strong drink, not only exhaled in the torrid atmosphere of his breath, but oozing out of his entire system, like an inflammable gas. It was impressed on Hepzibah's mind that this was the husband of the care-wrinkled woman. He asked for a paper of tobacco; and as she had neglected to provide herself with the article, her brutal customer dashed down his newly bought pipe and left the shop, muttering some unintelligible words, which had the tone and bitterness of a curse. Hereupon Hepzibah threw up her eyes, unintentionally scowling in the face of Providence!

No less than five persons, during the forenoon, inquired for ginger beer, or root beer, or any drink of a similar brewage, and, obtaining nothing of the kind, went off in an exceedingly bad humor. Three of them left the door open, and the other two pulled it so spitefully in going out that the little bell played the very deuce with Hepzibah's nerves. A round, bustling, fire-ruddy housewife of the neighborhood burst breathless into the shop, fiercely demanding yeast; and when the poor gentlewoman, with her cold shyness of manner, gave her hot customer to understand that she did not keep the article, this very capable housewife took upon herself to administer a regular rebuke.

"A cent shop, and no yeast!" quoth she. "That will never do! Who ever heard of such a thing? Your loaf will never rise, no more than mine will today. You had better shut up shop at once."

"Well," said Hepzibah, heaving a deep sigh, "perhaps I had!"

Several times, moreover, besides the above instance, her ladylike sensibilities were seriously infringed upon by the familiar, if not rude, tone with which people addressed her. They evidently considered themselves not merely her equals, but her patrons and superiors. Now, Hepzibah had unconsciously flattered herself with the idea that there

would be a gleam or halo, of some kind or other, about her
person, which would insure an obeisance to her sterling
gentility, or, at least, a tacit recognition of it. On the other
hand, nothing tortured her more intolerably than when
this recognition was too prominently expressed. To one or
two rather officious offers of sympathy, her responses were
little short of acrimonious; and, we regret to say, Hepzibah
was thrown into a positively unchristian state of mind by
the suspicion that one of her customers was drawn to the
shop not by any real need of the article which she pretended to seek, but by a wicked wish to stare at her. The
vulgar creature was determined to see for herself what
sort of a figure a mildewed piece of aristocracy, after wast-
ing all the bloom and much of the decline of her life apart
from the world, would cut behind a counter. In this particular case, however mechanical and innocuous it might
be at other times, Hepzibah's contortion of brow served
her in good stead.

"I never was so frightened in my life!" said the curious
customer, in describing the incident to one of her acquaintances. "She's a real old vixen, take my word of it! She says
little, to be sure; but if you could only see the mischief in
her eye!"

On the whole, therefore, her new experience led our
decayed gentlewoman to very disagreeable conclusions as
to the temper and manners of what she termed the lower
classes, whom heretofore she had looked down upon with
a gentle and pitying complaisance, as herself occupying a
sphere of unquestionable superiority. But, unfortunately,
she had likewise to struggle against a bitter emotion of a
directly opposite kind: a sentiment of virulence, we mean,
towards the idle aristocracy to which it had so recently been
her pride to belong. When a lady, in a delicate and costly
summer garb, with a floating veil and gracefully swaying
gown, and, altogether, an ethereal lightness that made you
look at her beautifully slippered feet, to see whether she
trod on the dust or floated in the air—when such a vision
happened to pass through this retired street, leaving it tenderly and delusively fragrant with her passage, as if a bou-
quet of tea roses had been borne along—then again, it is to

be feared, old Hepzibah's scowl could no longer vindicate itself entirely on the plea of nearsightedness.

"For what end," thought she, giving vent to that feeling of hostility which is the only real abasement of the poor in the presence of the rich, "for what good end, in the wisdom of Providence, does that woman live? Must the whole world toil, that the palms of her hands may be kept white and delicate?"

Then, ashamed and penitent, she hid her face.

"May God forgive me!" said she.

Doubtless, God did forgive her. But, taking the inward and outward history of the first half day into consideration, Hepzibah began to fear that the shop would prove her ruin in a moral and religious point of view, without contributing very essentially towards even her temporal welfare.

❧ 4 ❧

A Day Behind the Counter

TOWARDS noon, Hepzibah saw an elderly gentleman, large and portly, and of remarkably dignified demeanor, passing slowly along on the opposite side of the white and dusty street. On coming within the shadow of the Pyncheon Elm, he stopped, and (taking off his hat, meanwhile, to wipe the perspiration from his brow) seemed to scrutinize, with especial interest, the dilapidated and rusty-visaged House of the Seven Gables. He himself, in a very different style, was as well worth looking at as the house. No better model need be sought, nor could have been found, of a very high order of respectability, which, by some indescribable magic, not merely expressed itself in his looks and gestures, but even governed the fashion of his garments, and rendered them all proper and essential to the man. Without appearing to differ, in any tangible way, from other people's clothes, there was yet a wide and rich gravity about them that must have been a characteristic of the wearer, since it could not be defined as pertaining either to the cut or material. His gold-headed cane, too—a serviceable staff, of dark polished wood—had similar traits, and, had it chosen to take a walk by itself, would have been recognized anywhere as a tolerably adequate representative of its master. This character—which showed itself so strikingly in everything about him, and the effect of which we seek to convey to the reader—went no deeper than his station, habits of life, and external circumstances. One perceived him to be

52

a personage of marked influence and authority; and, especially, you could feel just as certain that he was opulent as if he had exhibited his bank account, or as if you had seen him touching the twigs of the Pyncheon Elm, and Midaslike, transmuting them to gold.

In his youth, he had probably been considered a handsome man; at his present age, his brow was too heavy, his temples too bare, his remaining hair too gray, his eye too cold, his lips too closely compressed, to bear any relation to mere personal beauty. He would have made a good and massive portrait; better now, perhaps, than at any previous period of his life, although his look might grow positively harsh in the process of being fixed upon the canvas. The artist would have found it desirable to study his face, and prove its capacity for varied expression; to darken it with a frown, to kindle it up with a smile.

While the elderly gentleman stood looking at the Pyncheon House, both the frown and the smile passed successively over his countenance. His eye rested on the shopwindow, and putting up a pair of gold-bowed spectacles, which he held in his hand, he minutely surveyed Hepzibah's little arrangement of toys and commodities. At first it seemed not to please him—nay, to cause him exceeding displeasure—and yet, the very next moment, he smiled. While the latter expression was yet on his lips, he caught a glimpse of Hepzibah, who had involuntarily bent forward to the window; and then the smile changed from acrid and disagreeable to the sunniest complacency and benevolence. He bowed, with a happy mixture of dignity and courteous kindliness, and pursued his way.

"There he is!" said Hepzibah to herself, gulping down a very bitter emotion, and, since she could not rid herself of it, trying to drive it back into her heart. "What does he think of it, I wonder? Does it please him? Ah! He is looking back!"

The gentleman had paused in the street, and turned himself half about, still with his eyes fixed on the shopwindow. In fact, he wheeled wholly round, and commenced a step or two, as if designing to enter the shop; but, as it chanced, his purpose was anticipated by Hepzibah's first customer, the little cannibal of Jim Crow, who, staring up at the window, was irresistibly attracted by an elephant of gingerbread. What a grand appetite had this small urchin! Two Jim Crows immediately after breakfast—and now an elephant, as a preliminary whet before dinner! By the time this latter purchase was completed, the elderly gentleman had resumed his way, and turned the street corner.

"Take it as you like, Cousin Jaffrey!" muttered the maiden lady, as she drew back, after cautiously thrusting out her head, and looking up and down the street. "Take it as you like! You have seen my little shopwindow! Well! What have you to say? Is not the Pyncheon House my own, while I'm alive?"

After this incident, Hepzibah retreated to the back parlor, where she at first caught up a half-finished stocking, and began knitting at it with nervous and irregular jerks; but quickly finding herself at odds with the stitches, she threw it aside, and walked hurriedly about the room. At length, she paused before the portrait of the stern old Puritan, her ancestor, and the founder of the house. In one sense, this picture had almost faded into the canvas, and hidden itself behind the duskiness of age; in another, she could not but fancy that it had been growing more prominent, and strikingly expressive, ever since her earliest familiarity with it as a child. For, while the physical outline and substance were darkening away from the beholder's eye, the bold, hard, and, at the same time, indirect character of the man seemed to be brought out in a kind of spiritual relief. Such an effect may occasionally be observed in pictures of antique date. They acquire a look which an artist (if he have anything like the complacency of artists nowadays) would never dream of presenting to a patron as his own characteristic expression, but which, nevertheless, we at once recognize as reflecting the unlovely truth of a human soul. In such cases, the painter's deep conception of his subject's inward traits has wrought itself into the essence of the picture, and is seen after the superficial coloring has been rubbed off by time.

While gazing at the portrait, Hepzibah trembled under its eye. Her hereditary reverence made her afraid to judge the character of the original so harshly as a perception of the truth compelled her to do. But still she gazed, because the face of the picture enabled her—at least, she fancied so—to read more accurately, and to a greater depth, the face which she had just seen in the street.

"This is the very man!" murmured she to herself. "Let Jaffrey Pyncheon smile as he will, there is that look beneath! Put on him a skullcap, and a band, and a black coat, and a Bible in one hand and a sword in the other—then let Jaffrey smile as he might; nobody would doubt that it was the old Pyncheon come again! He has proved himself the very man to build up a new house! Perhaps, too, to draw down a new curse!"

Thus did Hepzibah bewilder herself with these fantasies of the old time. She had dwelt too much alone—too long in the Pyncheon House—until her very brain was impregnated with the dry rot of its timbers. She needed a walk along the noonday street to keep her sane.

By the spell of contrast, another portrait rose up before her, painted with more daring flattery than any artist would have ventured upon, but yet so delicately touched that the likeness remained perfect. Malbone's miniature, though from the same original, was far inferior to Hepzibah's air-drawn picture, at which affection and sorrowful remembrance wrought together. Soft, mildly, and cheerfully contemplative, with full, red lips, just on the verge of a smile, which the eyes seemed to herald by a gentle kindling-up of their orbs! Feminine traits, molded inseparably with those of the other sex! The miniature, likewise, had this last peculiarity; so that you inevitably thought of the original as resembling his mother, and she a lovely and lovable woman, with perhaps some beautiful infirmity of character, that made it all the pleasanter to know and easier to love her.

"Yes," thought Hepzibah, with grief of which it was only the more tolerable portion that welled up from her heart to her eyelids, "they persecuted his mother in him! He never was a Pyncheon!"

But here the shop bell rang; it was like a sound from a remote distance, so far had Hepzibah descended into the sepulchral depths of her reminiscences. On entering the shop, she found an old man there, a humble resident of Pyncheon Street, and whom, for a great many years past, she had suffered to be a kind of familiar of the house. He was an immemorial personage, who seemed always to have had a white head and wrinkles, and never to have possessed but a single tooth, and that a half-decayed one, in the front of the upper jaw. Well advanced as Hepzibah was, she could not remember when Uncle Venner, as the neighborhood called him, had not gone up and down the street, stooping a little and drawing his feet heavily over the gravel or pavement. But still there was something tough and vigorous about him, that not only kept him in daily breath, but enabled him to fill a place which would else have been vacant in the apparently crowded world. To go on errands with his slow and shuffling gait, which made you doubt how he ever was to arrive anywhere; to saw a small household's foot or two of firewood, or knock to pieces an old barrel, or split up a pine board for kindling stuff; in summer, to dig the few yards of garden ground appertaining to a low-rented tenement, and share the produce of his labor at the halves; in winter, to shovel away the snow from the sidewalk, or open paths to the woodshed, or along the clothesline; such were some of the essential offices which Uncle Venner performed among at least a score of families. Within that circle, he claimed the same sort of privilege, and probably felt as much warmth of interest, as a clergyman does in the range of his parishioners. Not that he laid claim to the tithe pig; but, as an analogous mode of reverence, he went his rounds, every morning, to gather up the crumbs of the table and overflowings of the dinner pot, as food for a pig of his own.

In his younger days—for, after all, there was a dim tradition that he had been, not young, but younger—Uncle Venner was commonly regarded as rather deficient, than otherwise, in his wits. In truth, he had virtually pleaded guilty to the charge, by scarcely aiming at such success as other men seek, and by taking only that humble and modest part in the intercourse of life which belongs to the alleged deficiency. But now, in his extreme old age—whether it

were that his long and hard experience had actually brightened him, or that his decaying judgment rendered him less
capable of fairly measuring himself—the venerable man
made pretensions to no little wisdom, and really enjoyed
the credit of it. There was likewise, at times, a vein of something like poetry in him; it was the moss or wallflower of
his mind in its small dilapidation, and gave a charm to what
might have been vulgar and commonplace in his earlier
and middle life. Hepzibah had a regard for him, because
his name was ancient in the town and had formerly been
respectable. It was a still better reason for awarding him a
species of familiar reverence that Uncle Venner was himself the most ancient existence, whether of man or thing, in
Pyncheon Street, except the House of the Seven Gables,
and perhaps the elm that overshadowed it.

This patriarch now presented himself before Hepzibah,
clad in an old blue coat, which had a fashionable air, and
must have accrued to him from the cast-off wardrobe of
some dashing clerk. As for his trousers, they were of tow
cloth, very short in the legs, and bagging down strangely in
the rear, but yet having a suitableness to his figure which
his other garment entirely lacked. His hat had relation to
no other part of his dress, and but very little to the head
that wore it. Thus Uncle Venner was a miscellaneous old
gentleman, partly himself, but, in good measure, somebody
else; patched together, too, of different epochs; an epitome
of times and fashions.

"So, you have really begun trade," said he, "really begun
trade! Well, I'm glad to see it. Young people should never
live idle in the world, nor old ones neither, unless when
the rheumatize gets hold of them. It has given me warning already; and in two or three years longer, I shall think
of putting aside business and retiring to my farm. That's
yonder—the great brick house, you know—the workhouse,
most folks call it; but I mean to do my work first, and go
there to be idle and enjoy myself. And I'm glad to see you
beginning to do your work, Miss Hepzibah!"

"Thank you, Uncle Venner," said Hepzibah, smiling; for
she always felt kindly towards the simple and talkative old
man. Had he been an old woman, she might probably have

repelled the freedom, which she now took in good part. "It is time for me to begin work, indeed! Or, to speak the truth, I have just begun when I ought to be giving it up."

"Oh, never say that, Miss Hepzibah!" answered the old man. "You are a young woman yet. Why, I hardly thought myself younger than I am now, it seems so little while ago since I used to see you playing about the door of the old house, quite a small child! Oftener, though, you used to be sitting at the threshold, and looking gravely into the street; for you had always a grave kind of way with you—a grown-up air, when you were only the height of my knee. It seems as if I saw you now; and your grandfather with his red cloak, and his white wig, and his cocked hat, and his cane, coming out of the house, and stepping so grandly up the street! Those old gentlemen that grew up before the Revolution used to put on grand airs. In my young days, the great man of the town was commonly called King; and his wife, not Queen to be sure, but Lady. Nowadays, a man would not dare to be called King; and if he feels himself a little above common folks, he only stoops so much the lower to them. I met your cousin, the Judge, ten minutes ago; and, in my old tow-cloth trousers, as you see, the Judge raised his hat to me, I do believe! At any rate, the Judge bowed and smiled!"

"Yes," said Hepzibah, with something bitter stealing unawares into her tone. "My cousin Jaffrey is thought to have a very pleasant smile!"

"And so he has!" replied Uncle Venner. "And that's rather remarkable in a Pyncheon; for, begging your pardon, Miss Hepzibah, they never had the name of being an easy and agreeable set of folks. There was no getting close to them. But now, Miss Hepzibah, if an old man may be bold to ask, why don't Judge Pyncheon, with his great means, step forward, and tell his cousin to shut up her little shop at once? It's for your credit to be doing something, but it's not for the Judge's credit to let you!"

"We won't talk of this, if you please, Uncle Venner," said Hepzibah, coldly. "I ought to say, however, that, if I choose to earn bread for myself, it is not Judge Pyncheon's fault. Neither will he deserve the blame," added she, more kindly, remembering Uncle Venner's privileges of age and humble familiarity, "if I should, by and by, find it convenient to retire with you to your farm."

"And it's no bad place, either, that farm of mine!" cried the old man, cheerily, as if there were something positively delightful in the prospect. "No bad place is the great brick farmhouse, especially for them that will find a good many old cronies there, as will be my case. I quite long to be among them, sometimes, of the winter evenings; for it is but dull business for a lonesome elderly man, like me, to be nodding, by the hour together, with no company but his airtight stove. Summer or winter, there's a great deal to be said in favor of my farm! And, take it in the autumn, what can be pleasanter than to spend a whole day on the sunny side of a barn or a woodpile, chatting with somebody as old as one's self; or, perhaps, idling away the time with a natural-born simpleton, who knows how to be idle, because even our busy Yankees never have found out how to put him to any use? Upon my word, Miss Hepzibah, I doubt whether I've ever been so comfortable as I mean to be at my farm, which most folks call the workhouse. But you, you're a young woman yet; you never need go there! Something still better will turn up for you. I'm sure of it!"

Hepzibah fancied that there was something peculiar in her venerable friend's look and tone; insomuch, that she gazed into his face with considerable earnestness, endeavoring to discover what secret meaning, if any, might be lurking there. Individuals whose affairs have reached an utterly desperate crisis almost invariably keep themselves alive with hopes, so much the more airily magnificent as they have the less of solid matter within their grasp whereof to mold any judicious and moderate expectation of good. Thus, all the while Hepzibah was perfecting the scheme of her little shop, she had cherished an unacknowledged idea that some harlequin trick of fortune would intervene in her favor. For example, an uncle—who had sailed for India fifty years before, and never been heard of since— might yet return, and adopt her to be the comfort of his very extreme and decrepit age, and adorn her with pearls, diamonds, and Oriental shawls and turbans, and make her the ultimate heiress of his unreckonable riches. Or the member of Parliament, now at the head of the English branch of the family—with which the elder stock, on this side of the Atlantic, had held little or no intercourse for the last two centuries—this eminent gentleman might invite Hepzibah to quit the ruinous House of the Seven Gables, and come over to dwell with her kindred at Pyncheon Hall. But, for reasons the most imperative, she could not yield to his request. It was more probable, therefore, that the descendants of a Pyncheon who had emigrated to Virginia, in some past generation, and became a great planter there, hearing of Hepzibah's destitution, and impelled by the splendid generosity of character with which their Virginian mixture must have enriched the New England blood, would send her a remittance of a thousand dollars, with a hint of repeating the favor annually. Or—and, surely, anything so undeniably just could not be beyond the limits of reasonable anticipation—the great claim to the heritage of Waldo County might finally be decided in favor of the Pyncheons; so that, instead of keeping a cent shop, Hepzibah would build a palace, and look down from its highest tower on hill, dale, forest, field, and town, as her own share of the ancestral territory.

These were some of the fantasies which she had long dreamed about; and, aided by these, Uncle Venner's casual attempt at encouragement kindled a strange festal glory in the poor, bare, melancholy chambers of her brain, as if that inner world were suddenly lighted up with gas. But either he knew nothing of her castles in the air—as how should he?—or else her earnest scowl disturbed his recollection, as it might a more courageous man's. Instead of pursuing any weightier topic, Uncle Venner was pleased to favor Hepzibah with some sage counsel in her shopkeeping capacity.

"Give no credit!"—these were some of his golden maxims—"Never take paper money! Look well to your change! Ring the silver on the four-pound weight! Shove back all English halfpence and base copper tokens, such as are very plenty about town! At your leisure hours, knit children's woolen socks and mittens! Brew your own yeast, and make your own ginger beer!"

And while Hepzibah was doing her utmost to digest the hard little pellets of his already uttered wisdom, he gave vent to his final, and what he declared to be his all-important advice, as follows:

"Put on a bright face for your customers, and smile pleasantly as you hand them what they ask for! A stale article, if you dip it in a good, warm, sunny smile, will go off better than a fresh one that you've scowled upon."

To this last apothegm poor Hepzibah responded with a sigh so deep and heavy that it almost rustled Uncle Venner quite away, like a withered leaf—as he was—before an autumnal gale. Recovering himself, however, he bent forward, and, with a good deal of feeling in his ancient visage, beckoned her nearer to him.

"When do you expect him home?" whispered he.

"Whom do you mean?" asked Hepzibah, turning pale.

"Ah? You don't love to talk about it," said Uncle Venner. "Well, well! We'll say no more, though there's word of it all over town. I remember him, Miss Hepzibah, before he could run alone!"

During the remainder of the day, poor Hepzibah acquitted herself even less creditably, as a shopkeeper, than in her earlier efforts. She appeared to be walking in a dream; or, more truly, the vivid life and reality assumed by her emotions made all outward occurrences unsubstantial, like the teasing phantasms of a half-conscious slumber. She still responded, mechanically, to the frequent summons of the shop bell, and, at the demand of her customers, went prying with vague eyes about the shop, proffering them one article after another, and thrusting aside—perversely, as most of them supposed—the identical thing they asked for. There is sad confusion, indeed, when the spirit thus flits away into the past, or into the more awful future, or, in any manner, steps across the spaceless boundary betwixt its own region and the actual world; where the body remains to guide itself as best it may, with little more than the mechanism of animal life. It is like death, without death's quiet privilege—its freedom from mortal care. Worst of all, when the actual duties are comprised in such petty details as now vexed the brooding soul of the old gentlewoman. As the animosity of fate would have it, there was a great influx of custom in the course of the afternoon. Hepzibah blundered to and fro about her small place of business, committing the most unheard-of errors: now stringing up twelve, and now seven, tallow candles, instead of ten to the pound; selling ginger for Scotch snuff, pins for needles, and needles for pins; misreckoning her change, sometimes to the public detriment, and much oftener to her own; and thus she went on, doing her utmost to bring chaos back again, until, at the close of the day's labor, to her inexplicable astonishment, she found the money drawer almost destitute of coin. After all her painful traffic, the whole proceeds were perhaps half a dozen coppers, and a questionable ninepence which ultimately proved to be copper likewise.

At this price, or at whatever price, she rejoiced that the day had reached its end. Never before had she had such a sense of the intolerable length of time that creeps between dawn and sunset, and of the miserable irksomeness of having aught to do, and of the better wisdom that it would be to lie down at once, in sullen resignation, and let life, and its toils and vexations, trample over one's prostrate body as they may! Hepzibah's final operation was with the little devourer of Jim Crow and the elephant, who now proposed to eat a camel. In her bewilderment, she offered him first a wooden dragoon, and next a handful of marbles; neither of which being adapted to his else omnivorous appetite, she hastily held out her whole remaining stock of natural history in gingerbread, and huddled the small customer out of the shop. She then muffled the bell in an unfinished stocking, and put up the oaken bar across the door.

During the latter process, an omnibus came to a standstill under the branches of the elm tree. Hepzibah's heart was in her mouth. Remote and dusky, and with no sunshine on all the intervening space, was that region of the Past whence her only guest might be expected to arrive! Was she to meet him now?

Somebody, at all events, was passing from the farthest interior of the omnibus towards its entrance. A gentleman alighted; but it was only to offer his hand to a young girl, whose slender figure, nowise needing such assistance, now lightly descended the steps, and made an airy little jump from the final one to the sidewalk. She rewarded her cavalier with a smile, the cheery glow of which was seen reflected on his own face as he re-entered the vehicle. The girl then turned towards the House of the Seven Gables, to the door of which, meanwhile—not the shop door, but the antique portal—the omnibusman had carried a light trunk and a bandbox. First giving a sharp rap of the old iron knocker, he left his passenger and her luggage at the doorstep, and departed.

"Who can it be?" thought Hepzibah, who had been screwing her visual organs into the acutest focus of which they were capable. "The girl must have mistaken the house!"

She stole softly into the hall, and, herself invisible, gazed through the dusty side lights of the portal at the young, blooming, and very cheerful face, which presented itself for admittance into the gloomy old mansion. It was a face to which almost any door would have opened of its own accord.

The young girl, so fresh, so unconventional, and yet so orderly and obedient to common rules, as you at once recognized her to be, was widely in contrast, at that moment, with everything about her. The sordid and ugly luxuriance of gigantic weeds that grew in the angle of the house, and the heavy projection that overshadowed her, and the time-worn framework of the door—none of these things belonged to her sphere. But, even as a ray of sunshine, fall into what dismal place it may, instantaneously creates for itself a propriety in being there, so did it seem altogether fit that the girl should be standing at the threshold. It was no less evidently proper that the door should swing open to admit her. The maiden lady herself, sternly inhospitable in her first purposes, soon began to feel that the door ought to be shoved back, and the rusty key be turned in the reluctant lock.

"Can it be Phoebe?" questioned she within herself. "It must be little Phoebe, for it can be nobody else—and there is a look of her father about her, too! But what does she want here? And how like a country cousin, to come down upon a poor body in this way, without so much as a day's notice, or asking whether she would be welcome! Well; she must have a night's lodging, I suppose; and tomorrow the child shall go back to her mother!"

Phoebe, it must be understood, was that one little off-shoot of the Pyncheon race to whom we have already referred, as a native of a rural part of New England, where the old fashions and feelings of relationship are still partially kept up. In her own circle, it was regarded as by no means improper for kinsfolk to visit one another without invitation, or preliminary and ceremonious warning. Yet, in consideration of Miss Hepzibah's recluse way of life, a letter had actually been written and despatched, conveying information of Phoebe's projected visit. This epistle, for three or four days past, had been in the pocket of the penny-postman, who, happening to have no other business in Pyncheon Street, had not yet made it convenient to call at the House of the Seven Gables.

"No! She can stay only one night," said Hepzibah, unbolting the door. "If Clifford were to find her here, it might disturb him!"

❧5❧

May and November

PHOEBE PYNCHEON slept, on the night of her arrival, in a chamber that looked down on the garden of the old house. It fronted towards the east, so that at a very seasonable hour, a glow of crimson light came flooding through the window, and bathed the dingy ceiling and paper hangings in its own hue. There were curtains to Phoebe's bed; a dark, antique canopy, and ponderous festoons of a stuff which had been rich, and even magnificent, in its time; but which now brooded over the girl like a cloud, making a night in that one corner, while elsewhere it was beginning to be day. The morning light, however, soon stole into the aperture at the foot of the bed, betwixt those faded curtains. Finding the new guest there—with a bloom on her cheeks like the morning's own, and a gentle stir of departing slumber in her limbs, as when an early breeze moves the foliage—the dawn kissed her brow. It was the caress which a dewy maiden—such as the Dawn is, immortally—gives to her sleeping sister, partly from the impulse of irresistible fondness, and partly as a pretty hint that it is time now to unclose her eyes.

At the touch of those lips of light, Phoebe quietly awoke, and, for a moment, did not recognize where she was, nor how those heavy curtains chanced to be festooned around her. Nothing, indeed, was absolutely plain to her, except that it was now early morning, and that, whatever might happen next, it was proper, first of all, to get up and say her prayers. She was the more inclined to devotion from the grim aspect of the chamber and its furniture, especially the tall, stiff chairs; one of which stood close by her bedside, and looked as if some old-fashioned personage had been sitting there all night, and had vanished only just in season to escape discovery.

When Phoebe was quite dressed, she peeped out of the window, and saw a rosebush in the garden. Being a very tall one, and of luxuriant growth, it had been propped up against the side of the house, and was literally covered with a rare and very beautiful species of white rose. A large portion of them, as the girl afterwards discovered, had blight or mildew at their hearts; but, viewed at a fair distance, the whole rosebush looked as if it had been brought from Eden that very summer, together with the mold in which it grew. The truth was, nevertheless, that it had been planted by Alice Pyncheon—she was Phoebe's great-great-grand-aunt—in soil which, reckoning only its cultivation as a garden plat, was now unctuous with nearly two hundred years of vegetable decay. Growing as they did, however, out of the old earth, the flowers still sent a fresh and sweet incense up to their Creator; nor could it have been the less pure and acceptable because Phoebe's young breath mingled with it, as the fragrance floated past the window. Hastening down the creaking and carpetless staircase, she found her way into the garden, gathered some of the most perfect of the roses, and brought them to her chamber.

Little Phoebe was one of those persons who possess, as their exclusive patrimony, the gift of practical arrangement. It is a kind of natural magic that enables these favored ones to bring out the hidden capabilities of things around them; and particularly to give a look of comfort and habitableness to any place which, for however brief a period, may happen to be their home. A wild hut of underbrush, tossed together by wayfarers through the primitive forest, would acquire the home aspect by one night's lodging of such a woman, and would retain it long after her quiet figure had disappeared into the surrounding shade. No less a portion of such homely witchcraft was requisite to reclaim, as it were, Phoebe's waste, cheerless, and dusky chamber, which had been untenanted so long—except by spiders, and mice, and rats, and ghosts—that it was all overgrown with the desolation which watches to obliterate every trace of man's happier hours. What was precisely Phoebe's process we find it impossible to say. She appeared to have no preliminary design, but gave a touch here and another there; brought some articles of furniture to light and dragged others into the shadow; looped up or let down a window curtain; and, in the course of half an hour, had fully succeeded in throwing a kindly and hospitable smile over the apartment. No longer ago than the night before, it had resembled nothing so much as the old maid's heart; for there was neither sunshine nor household fire in one nor the other, and, save for ghosts and ghostly reminiscences, not a guest, for many years gone by, had entered the heart or the chamber.

There was still another peculiarity of this inscrutable charm. The bedchamber, no doubt, was a chamber of very great and varied experience, as a scene of human life: the joy of bridal nights had throbbed itself away here; new immortals had first drawn earthly breath here; and here old people had died. But—whether it were the white roses, or whatever the subtle influence might be—a person of delicate instinct would have known at once that it was now a maiden's bedchamber, and had been purified of all former evil and sorrow by her sweet breath and happy thoughts. Her dreams of the past night, being such cheerful ones, had exorcised the gloom, and now haunted the chamber in its stead.

After arranging matters to her satisfaction, Phoebe emerged from her chamber, with a purpose to descend again into the garden. Besides the rosebush, she had observed several other species of flowers growing there in a wilderness of neglect, and obstructing one another's development (as is often the parallel case in human society) by their uneducated entanglement and confusion. At the head of the stairs, however, she met Hepzibah, who, it being still early, invited her into a room which she would probably have called her boudoir, had her education embraced any such French phrase. It was strewn about with a few old books, and a workbasket, and a dusty writing desk;

and had, on one side, a large, black article of furniture, of
very strange appearance, which the old gentlewoman told
Phoebe was a harpsichord. It looked more like a coffin than
anything else; and, indeed—not having been played upon,
or opened, for years—there must have been a vast deal of
dead music in it, stifled for want of air. Human finger was
hardly known to have touched its chords since the days of
Alice Pyncheon, who had learned the sweet accomplishment of melody in Europe.

Hepzibah bade her young guest sit down, and, herself
taking a chair nearby, looked as earnestly at Phoebe's trim
little figure as if she expected to see right into its springs
and motive secrets.

"Cousin Phoebe," said she, at last, "I really can't see my
way clear to keep you with me."

These words, however, had not the inhospitable blunt-
ness with which they may strike the reader; for the two
relatives, in a talk before bedtime, had arrived at a certain
degree of mutual understanding. Hepzibah knew enough
to enable her to appreciate the circumstances (result-
ing from the second marriage of the girl's mother) which
made it desirable for Phoebe to establish herself in another
home. Nor did she misinterpret Phoebe's character, and the
genial activity pervading it—one of the most valuable traits
of the true New England woman—which had impelled her
forth, as might be said, to seek her fortune, but with a self-
respecting purpose to confer as much benefit as she could
anywise receive. As one of her nearest kindred, she had
naturally betaken herself to Hepzibah, with no idea of forcing herself on her cousin's protection, but only for a visit
of a week or two, which might be indefinitely extended,
should it prove for the happiness of both.

To Hepzibah's blunt observation, therefore, Phoebe replied, as frankly, and more cheerfully.

"Dear cousin, I cannot tell how it will be," said she. "But
I really think we may suit one another much better than
you suppose."

"You are a nice girl, I see it plainly," continued Hepzibah, "and it is not any question as to that point which
makes me hesitate. But, Phoebe, this house of mine is but a

melancholy place for a young person to be in. It lets in the wind and rain, and the snow, too, in the garret and upper chambers, in wintertime, but it never lets in the sunshine! And as for myself, you see what I am—a dismal and lonesome old woman (for I begin to call myself old, Phoebe), whose temper, I am afraid, is none of the best, and whose spirits are as bad as can be. I cannot make your life pleasant, Cousin Phoebe, neither can I so much as give you bread to eat."

"You will find me a cheerful little body," answered Phoebe, smiling, and yet with a kind of gentle dignity, "and I mean to earn my bread. You know I have not been brought up a Pyncheon. A girl learns many things in a New England village."

"Ah! Phoebe," said Hepzibah, sighing, "your knowledge would do but little for you here! And then it is a wretched thought that you should fling away your young days in a place like this. Those cheeks would not be so rosy after a month or two. Look at my face!"—and, indeed, the contrast was very striking. "You see how pale I am! It is my idea that the dust and continual decay of these old houses are unwholesome for the lungs."

"There is the garden, the flowers to be taken care of," observed Phoebe. "I should keep myself healthy with exercise in the open air."

"And, after all, child," exclaimed Hepzibah, suddenly rising, as if to dismiss the subject, "it is not for me to say who shall be a guest or inhabitant of the old Pyncheon House. Its master is coming."

"Do you mean Judge Pyncheon?" asked Phoebe, in surprise.

"Judge Pyncheon!" answered her cousin, angrily. "He will hardly cross the threshold while I live! No, no! But, Phoebe, you shall see the face of him I speak of."

She went in quest of the miniature already described, and returned with it in her hand. Giving it to Phoebe, she watched her features narrowly, and with a certain jealousy as to the mode in which the girl would show herself affected by the picture.

"How do you like the face?" asked Hepzibah.

"It is handsome—it is very beautiful!" said Phoebe, admiringly. "It is as sweet a face as a man's can be, or ought to be. It has something of a child's expression—and yet not childish—only one feels so very kindly towards him! He ought never to suffer anything. One would bear much for the sake of sparing him toil or sorrow. Who is it, Cousin Hepzibah?"

"Did you never hear," whispered her cousin, bending towards her, "of Clifford Pyncheon?"

"Never! I thought there were no Pyncheons left, except yourself and our cousin Jaffrey," answered Phoebe. "And yet I seem to have heard the name of Clifford Pyncheon. Yes—from my father or my mother; but has he not been a long while dead?"

"Well, well, child, perhaps he has!" said Hepzibah, with a sad, hollow laugh, "but, in old houses like this, you know, dead people are very apt to come back again! We shall see. And, Cousin Phoebe, since, after all that I have said, your courage does not fail you, we will not part so soon. You are welcome, my child, for the present, to such a home as your kinswoman can offer you."

With this measured, but not exactly cold assurance of a hospitable purpose, Hepzibah kissed her cheek.

They now went belowstairs, where Phoebe—not so much assuming the office as attracting it to herself, by the magnetism of innate fitness—took the most active part in preparing breakfast. The mistress of the house, meanwhile, as is usual with persons of her stiff and unmalleable cast, stood mostly aside; willing to lend her aid, yet conscious that her natural inaptitude would be likely to impede the business in hand. Phoebe, and the fire that boiled the tea-kettle, were equally bright, cheerful, and efficient, in their respective offices. Hepzibah gazed forth from her habitual sluggishness, the necessary result of long solitude, as from another sphere. She could not help being interested, however, and even amused, at the readiness with which her new inmate adapted herself to the circumstances, and brought the house, moreover, and all its rusty old appliances, into a suitableness for her purposes. Whatever she did, too, was done without conscious effort, and with frequent outbreaks of song, which were exceedingly pleasant to the ear. This natural tunefulness made Phoebe seem like a bird in a shadowy tree; or conveyed the idea that the stream of life warbled through her heart as a brook sometimes warbles through a pleasant little dell. It betokened the cheeriness of an active temperament, finding joy in its activity, and, therefore, rendering it beautiful; it was a New England trait—the stern old stuff of Puritanism with a gold thread in the web.

Hepzibah brought out some old silver spoons with the family crest upon them, and a china tea set painted over with grotesque figures of man, bird, and beast, in as grotesque a landscape. These pictured people were odd humorists, in a world of their own—a world of vivid brilliancy, so far as color went, and still unfaded, although the teapot and small cups were as ancient as the custom itself of tea-drinking.

"Your great-great-great-great-grandmother had these cups, when she was married," said Hepzibah to Phoebe. "She was a Davenport, of a good family. They were almost the first teacups ever seen in the colony; and if one of them were to be broken, my heart would break with it. But it is nonsense to speak so about a brittle teacup, when I remember what my heart has gone through without breaking."

The cups—not having been used, perhaps, since Hepzibah's youth—had contracted no small burden of dust, which Phoebe washed away with so much care and delicacy as to satisfy even the proprietor of this invaluable china.

"What a nice little housewife you are!" exclaimed the latter, smiling, and, at the same time, frowning so prodigiously that the smile was sunshine under a thundercloud. "Do you do other things as well? Are you as good at your book as you are at washing teacups?"

"Not quite, I am afraid," said Phoebe, laughing at the form of Hepzibah's question. "But I was schoolmistress for the little children in our district last summer, and might have been so still."

"Ah! 'tis all very well!" observed the maiden lady, drawing herself up. "But these things must have come to you with your mother's blood. I never knew a Pyncheon that had any turn for them."

It is very queer, but not the less true, that people are generally quite as vain, or even more so, of their deficiencies than of their available gifts; as was Hepzibah of this native inapplicability, so to speak, of the Pyncheons to any useful purpose. She regarded it as an hereditary trait; and so, perhaps, it was, but, unfortunately, a morbid one, such as is often generated in families that remain long above the surface of society.

Before they left the breakfast table, the shop bell rang sharply, and Hepzibah set down the remnant of her final cup of tea, with a look of sallow despair that was truly piteous to behold. In cases of distasteful occupation, the second day is generally worse than the first; we return to the rack with all the soreness of the preceding torture in our limbs. At all events, Hepzibah had fully satisfied herself of the impossibility of ever becoming wonted to this peevishly obstreperous little bell. Ring as often as it might, the sound always smote upon her nervous system rudely and suddenly. And especially now, while, with her crested teaspoons and antique china, she was flattering herself with ideas of gentility, she felt an unspeakable disinclination to confront a customer.

"Do not trouble yourself, dear cousin!" cried Phoebe, starting lightly up. "I am shopkeeper today."

"You, child!" exclaimed Hepzibah. "What can a little country girl know of such matters?"

"Oh, I have done all the shopping for the family at our village store," said Phoebe. "And I have had a table at a fancy fair, and made better sales than anybody. These things are not to be learnt; they depend upon a knack that comes, I suppose," added she, smiling, "with one's mother's blood. You shall see that I am as nice a little saleswoman as I am a housewife!"

The old gentlewoman stole behind Phoebe, and peeped from the passageway into the shop, to note how she would manage her undertaking. It was a case of some intricacy. A very ancient woman, in a white short gown and a green petticoat, with a string of gold beads about her neck, and what looked like a nightcap on her head, had brought a quantity of yarn to barter for the commodities of the shop. She was probably the very last person in town who still kept the time-honored spinning wheel in constant revolution. It was worth while to hear the croaking and hollow tones of the old lady, and the pleasant voice of Phoebe, mingling in one twisted thread of talk; and still better to contrast their figures—so light and bloomy, so decrepit and dusky—with only the counter betwixt them, in one sense, but more than three-score years, in another. As for the bargain, it was wrinkled slyness and craft pitted against native truth and sagacity.

"Was not that well done?" asked Phoebe, laughing, when the customer was gone.

"Nicely done, indeed, child!" answered Hepzibah. "I could not have gone through with it nearly so well. As you say, it must be a knack that belongs to you on the mother's side."

It is a very genuine admiration, that with which persons too shy or too awkward to take a due part in the bustling world regard the real actors in life's stirring scenes; so genuine, in fact, that the former are usually fain to make it palatable to their self-love, by assuming that these active and forcible qualities are incompatible with others, which they choose to deem higher and more important. Thus, Hepzibah was well content to acknowledge Phoebe's vastly superior gifts as a shopkeeper; she listened, with compliant ear, to her suggestion of various methods whereby the influx of trade might be increased, and rendered profitable, without a hazardous outlay of capital. She consented that the village maiden should manufacture yeast, both liquid and in cakes; and should brew a certain kind of beer, nectareous to the palate, and of rare stomachic virtues; and, moreover, should bake and exhibit for sale some little spice cakes, which whosoever tasted would longingly desire to taste again. All such proofs of a ready mind and skillful handiwork were highly acceptable to the aristocratic hucksteress, so long as she could murmur to herself with a grim smile, and a half-natural sigh, and a sentiment of mixed wonder, pity, and growing affection:

"What a nice little body she is! If she could only be a lady, too—but that's impossible! Phoebe is no Pyncheon. She takes everything from her mother."

As to Phoebe's not being a lady, or whether she were a lady or no, it was a point, perhaps, difficult to decide, but which could hardly have come up for judgment at all in any fair and healthy mind. Out of New England, it would be impossible to meet with a person combining so many ladylike attributes with so many others that form no necessary (if compatible) part of the character. She shocked no canon of taste; she was admirably in keeping with herself, and never jarred against surrounding circumstances. Her figure, to be sure—so small as to be almost childlike, and so elastic that motion seemed as easy or easier to it than rest—would hardly have suited one's idea of a countess. Neither did her face—with the brown ringlets on either side, and the slightly piquant nose, and the wholesome bloom, and the clear shade of tan, and the half a dozen freckles, friendly remembrancers of the April sun and breeze—precisely give us a right to call her beautiful. But there was both luster and depth in her eyes. She was very pretty; as graceful as a bird, and graceful much in the same way; as pleasant about the house as a gleam of sunshine falling on the floor through a shadow of twinkling leaves, or as a ray of firelight that dances on the wall while evening is drawing nigh. Instead of discussing her claim to rank among ladies, it would be preferable to regard Phoebe as the example of feminine grace and availability combined, in a state of society, if there were any such, where ladies did not exist. There it should be woman's office to move in the midst of practical affairs, and to gild them all, the very homeliest—were it even the scouring of pots and kettles—with an atmosphere of loveliness and joy.

Such was the sphere of Phoebe. To find the born and educated lady, on the other hand, we need look no farther than Hepzibah, our forlorn old maid, in her rustling and rusty silks, with her deeply cherished and ridiculous consciousness of long descent, her shadowy claims to princely territory, and, in the way of accomplishment, her recollections, it may be, of having formerly thrummed on a harpsichord, and walked a minuet, and worked an antique tapestry stitch on her sampler. It was a fair parallel between new Plebeianism and old Gentility.

It really seemed as if the battered visage of the House of the Seven Gables, black and heavy-browed as it still certainly looked, must have shown a kind of cheerfulness glimmering through its dusky windows as Phoebe passed to and fro in the interior. Otherwise, it is impossible to explain how the people of the neighborhood so soon became aware of the girl's presence. There was a great run of custom, setting steadily in, from about ten o'clock until towards noon; relaxing, somewhat, at dinnertime, but recommencing in the afternoon, and, finally, dying away a half an hour or so before the long day's sunset. One of the stanchest patrons was little Ned Higgins, the devourer of Jim Crow and the elephant, who today had signalized his omnivorous prowess by swallowing two dromedaries and a locomotive. Phoebe laughed, as she summed up her aggregate of sales upon the slate; while Hepzibah, first drawing on a pair of silk gloves, reckoned over the sordid accumulation of copper coin, not without silver intermixed, that had jingled into the till.

"We must renew our stock, Cousin Hepzibah!" cried the little saleswoman. "The gingerbread figures are all gone, and so are those Dutch wooden milkmaids, and most of our other playthings. There has been constant inquiry for cheap raisins, and a great cry for whistles, and trumpets, and jew's-harps; and at least a dozen little boys have asked for molasses candy. And we must contrive to get a peck of russet apples, late in the season as it is. But, dear cousin, what an enormous heap of copper! Positively a copper mountain!"

"Well done! well done! well done!" quoth Uncle Venner, who had taken occasion to shuffle in and out of the shop several times in the course of the day. "Here's a girl that will never end her days at my farm! Bless my eyes, what a brisk little soul!"

"Yes, Phoebe is a nice girl!" said Hepzibah, with a scowl of austere approbation. "But, Uncle Venner, you have known the family a great many years. Can you tell me whether there ever was a Pyncheon whom she takes after?"

"I don't believe there ever was," answered the venerable man. "At any rate, it never was my luck to see her like among them, nor, for that matter, anywhere else. I've seen a great deal of the world, not only in people's kitchens and back yards, but at the street corners, and on the wharves, and in other places where my business calls me; and I'm free to say, Miss Hepzibah, that I never knew a human creature do her work so much like one of God's angels as this child Phoebe does!"

Uncle Venner's eulogium, if it appear rather too high-strained for the person and occasion, had, nevertheless, a sense in which it was both subtile and true. There was a spiritual quality in Phoebe's activity. The life of the long and busy day—spent in occupations that might so easily have taken a squalid and ugly aspect—had been made pleasant, and even lovely, by the spontaneous grace with which these homely duties seemed to bloom out of her character; so that labor, while she dealt with it, had the easy and flexible charm of play. Angels do not toil, but let their good works grow out of them; and so did Phoebe.

The two relatives—the young maid and the old one—found time before nightfall, in the intervals of trade, to make rapid advances towards affection and confidence. A recluse, like Hepzibah, usually displays remarkable frankness, and at least temporary affability, on being absolutely cornered, and brought to the point of personal intercourse; like the angel whom Jacob wrestled with, she is ready to bless you when once overcome.

The old gentlewoman took a dreary and proud satisfaction in leading Phoebe from room to room of the house, and recounting the traditions with which, as we may say, the walls were lugubriously frescoed. She showed the indentations made by the lieutenant governor's sword hilt in the door panels of the apartment where old Colonel Pyncheon, a dead host, had received his affrighted visitors with an awful frown. The dusky terror of that frown, Hepzibah observed, was thought to be lingering ever since in the passageway. She bade Phoebe step into one of the tall chairs, and inspect the ancient map of the Pyncheon territory at the eastward. In a tract of land on which she laid her finger, there existed a silver mine, the locality of which was precisely pointed out in some memoranda of Colonel Pyncheon himself, but only to be made known when the family claim should be recognized by government. Thus it was for the interest of all New England that the Pyncheons should have justice done them. She told, too, how that there was undoubtedly an immense treasure of English guineas hidden somewhere about the house, or in the cellar, or possibly in the garden.

"If you should happen to find it, Phoebe," said Hepzibah, glancing aside at her with a grim yet kindly smile, "we will tie up the shop bell for good and all!"

"Yes, dear cousin," answered Phoebe, "but, in the meantime, I hear somebody ringing it!"

When the customer was gone, Hepzibah talked rather vaguely, and at great length, about a certain Alice Pyncheon, who had been exceedingly beautiful and accomplished in her lifetime, a hundred years ago. The fragrance of her rich and delightful character still lingered about the place where she had lived, as a dried rosebud scents the drawer where it has withered and perished. This lovely Alice had met with some great and mysterious calamity, and had grown thin and white, and gradually faded out of the world. But, even now, she was supposed to haunt the House of the Seven Gables, and, a great many times—especially when one of the Pyncheons was to die—she had been heard playing sadly and beautifully on the harpsichord. One of these tunes, just as it had sounded from her spiritual touch, had been written down by an amateur of music; it was so exquisitely mournful that nobody, to this day, could bear to hear it played, unless when a great sorrow had made them know the still profounder sweetness of it.

"Was it the same harpsichord that you showed me?" inquired Phoebe.

"The very same," said Hepzibah. "It was Alice Pyncheon's harpsichord. When I was learning music, my father would never let me open it. So, as I could only play on my teacher's instrument, I have forgotten all my music long ago."

Leaving these antique themes, the old lady began to talk about the daguerreotypist, whom, as he seemed to be a well-meaning and orderly young man, and in narrow circumstances, she had permitted to take up his residence in one of the seven gables. But, on seeing more of Mr. Holgrave, she hardly knew what to make of him. He had the strangest companions imaginable: men with long beards, and dressed in linen blouses, and other such newfangled and ill-fitting garments; reformers, temperance lecturers, and all manner of cross-looking philanthropists; community men, and come-outers, as Hepzibah believed, who acknowledged no law, and ate no solid food, but lived on the scent of other people's cookery, and turned up their noses at the fare. As for the daguerreotypist, she had read a paragraph in a penny paper, the other day, accusing him of making a speech full of wild and disorganizing matter, at a meeting of his banditti-like associates. For her own part, she had reason to believe that he practiced animal magnetism, and, if such things were in fashion nowadays, should be apt to suspect him of studying the Black Art up there in his lonesome chamber.

"But, dear cousin," said Phoebe, "if the young man is so dangerous, why do you let him stay? If he does nothing worse, he may set the house on fire!"

"Why, sometimes," answered Hepzibah, "I have seriously made it a question, whether I ought not to send him away. But, with all his oddities, he is a quiet kind of a person, and has such a way of taking hold of one's mind that, without exactly liking him (for I don't know enough of the young man), I should be sorry to lose sight of him entirely. A woman clings to slight acquaintances when she lives so much alone as I do."

"But if Mr. Holgrave is a lawless person!" remonstrated Phoebe, a part of whose essence it was to keep within the limits of law.

"Oh!" said Hepzibah, carelessly—for, formal as she was, still, in her life's experience, she had gnashed her teeth against human law, "I suppose he has a law of his own!"

❧ 6 ❧

Maule's Well

AFTER an early tea, the little country girl strayed into the garden. The enclosure had formerly been very extensive, but was now contracted within small compass, and hemmed about, partly by high wooden fences, and partly by the out-buildings of houses that stood on another street. In its center was a grass plat, surrounding a ruinous little structure, which showed just enough of its original design to indicate that it had once been a summerhouse. A hopvine, spring-ing from last year's root, was beginning to clamber over it, but would be long in covering the roof with its green mantle. Three of the seven gables either fronted or looked sideways, with a dark solemnity of aspect, down into the garden.

The black, rich soil had fed itself with the decay of a long period of time; such as fallen leaves, the petals of flow-ers, and the stalks and seed vessels of vagrant and lawless plants, more useful after their death than ever while flaunt-ing in the sun. The evil of these departed years would natu-rally have sprung up again, in such rank weeds (symbolic of the transmitted vices of society) as are always prone to root themselves about human dwellings. Phoebe saw, how-ever, that their growth must have been checked by a de-gree of careful labor, bestowed daily and systematically on the garden. The white double rosebush had evidently been propped up anew against the house since the commence-ment of the season; and a pear tree and three damson trees, which, except a row of currant bushes, constituted the only varieties of fruit, bore marks of the recent amputation of several superfluous or defective limbs. There were also a few species of antique and hereditary flowers, in no very flourishing condition, but scrupulously weeded; as if some person, either out of love or curiosity, had been anxious to bring them to such perfection as they were capable of attaining. The remainder of the garden presented a well-selected assortment of esculent vegetables, in a praiseworthy state of advancement. Summer squashes, almost in their golden blossom; cucumbers, now evincing a tendency to spread away from the main stock, and ramble far and wide; two or three rows of string beans, and as many more that were about to festoon themselves on poles; tomatoes, occupying a site so sheltered and sunny that the plants were already gigantic, and promised an early and abundant harvest.

Phoebe wondered whose care and toil it could have been that had planted these vegetables, and kept the soil so clean and orderly. Not surely her cousin Hepzibah's, who had no taste nor spirits for the ladylike employment of cultivating flowers, and—with her recluse habits, and tendency to shelter herself within the dismal shadow of the house—would hardly have come forth under the speck of open sky to weed and hoe among the fraternity of beans and squashes.

It being her first day of complete estrangement from rural objects, Phoebe found an unexpected charm in this little nook of grass, and foliage, and aristocratic flowers, and plebeian vegetables. The eye of heaven seemed to look down into it pleasantly, and with a peculiar smile, as if glad to perceive that nature, elsewhere overwhelmed, and driven out of the dusty town, had here been able to retain a breathing place. The spot acquired a somewhat wilder grace, and yet a very gentle one, from the fact that a pair of robins had built their nest in the pear tree, and were making themselves exceedingly busy and happy in the dark intricacy of its boughs. Bees, too—strange to say—had thought it worth their while to come hither, possibly from the range of hives beside some farmhouse miles away. How many aerial voyages might they have made, in quest of honey, or honeyladen, betwixt dawn and sunset! Yet, late as it now was, there still arose a pleasant hum out of one or two of the squash blossoms, in the depths of which these bees were plying their golden labor. There was one other object in the garden which Nature might fairly claim as her inalienable property, in spite of whatever man could do to render it his own. This was a fountain, set round with a rim of old mossy stones, and paved, in its bed, with what appeared to be a sort of mosaic work of variously colored pebbles. The play and slight agitation of the water, in its upward gush, wrought magically with these variegated pebbles, and made a continually shifting apparition of quaint figures, vanishing too suddenly to be definable. Thence, swelling over the rim of moss-grown stones, the water stole away under the fence, through what we regret to call a gutter, rather than a channel.

Nor must we forget to mention a hen coop of very reverend antiquity that stood in the farther corner of the garden, not a great way from the fountain. It now contained only Chanticleer, his two wives, and a solitary chicken. All of them were pure specimens of a breed which had been transmitted down as an heirloom in the Pyncheon family, and were said, while in their prime, to have attained almost the size of turkeys, and, on the score of delicate flesh, to be fit for a prince's table. In proof of the authenticity of this legendary renown, Hepzibah could have exhibited the shell of a great egg, which an ostrich need hardly have been ashamed of. Be that as it might, the hens were now scarcely larger than pigeons, and had a queer, rusty, withered aspect, and a gouty kind of movement, and a sleepy and melancholy tone throughout all the variations of their clucking and cackling. It was evident that the race had degenerated, like many a noble race besides, in consequence of too strict a watchfulness to keep it pure. These feathered people had existed too long in their distinct variety; a fact of which the present representatives, judging by their lugubrious deportment, seemed to be aware. They kept themselves alive, unquestionably, and laid now and then an egg, and hatched a chicken; not for any pleasure of their own, but that the world might not absolutely lose what had once been so admirable a breed of fowls. The distinguishing mark of the hens was a crest of lamentably scanty growth, in these latter days, but so oddly and wickedly analogous to Hepzibah's turban, that Phoebe—to the poignant distress of her conscience, but inevitably—was led to fancy a general resemblance betwixt these forlorn bipeds and her respectable relative.

The girl ran into the house to get some crumbs of bread, cold potatoes, and other such scraps as were suitable to the accommodating appetite of fowls. Returning, she gave a peculiar call, which they seemed to recognize. The chicken crept through the pales of the coop and ran, with some show of liveliness, to her feet, while Chanticleer and the ladies of his household regarded her with queer, sidelong glances, and then croaked one to another, as if communicating their sage opinions of her character. So wise, as well as antique, was their aspect, as to give color to the idea not merely that they were the descendants of a time-honored race, but that they had existed, in their individual capacity, ever since the House of the Seven Gables was founded, and were somehow mixed up with its destiny. They were a species of tutelary sprite, or Banshee; although winged and feathered differently from most other guardian angels.

"Here, you odd little chicken!" said Phoebe. "Here are some nice crumbs for you!"

The chicken, hereupon, though almost as venerable in appearance as its mother—possessing, indeed, the whole antiquity of its progenitors in miniature—mustered vivacity enough to flutter upward and alight on Phoebe's shoulder.

"That little fowl pays you a high compliment!" said a voice behind Phoebe.

Turning quickly, she was surprised at sight of a young man, who had found access into the garden by a door opening out of another gable than that whence she had emerged. He held a hoe in his hand, and, while Phoebe was gone in quest of the crumbs, had begun to busy himself with drawing up fresh earth about the roots of the tomatoes.

"The chicken really treats you like an old acquaintance," continued he, in a quiet way, while a smile made his face pleasanter than Phoebe at first fancied it. "Those venerable personages in the coop, too, seem very affably disposed. You are lucky to be in their good graces so soon! They have known me much longer, but never honor me with any familiarity, though hardly a day passes without my bringing them food. Miss Hepzibah, I suppose, will interweave the fact with her other traditions, and set it down that the fowls know you to be a Pyncheon!"

"The secret is," said Phoebe, smiling, "that I have learned how to talk with hens and chickens."

"Ah, but these hens," answered the young man, "these hens of aristocratic lineage would scorn to understand the vulgar language of a barnyard fowl. I prefer to think—and so would Miss Hepzibah—that they recognize the family tone. For you are a Pyncheon?"

"My name is Phoebe Pyncheon," said the girl, with a manner of some reserve; for she was aware that her new acquaintance could be no other than the daguerreotypist, of whose lawless propensities the old maid had given her a disagreeable idea. "I did not know that my cousin Hepzibah's garden was under another person's care."

"Yes," said Holgrave. "I dig, and hoe, and weed, in this black old earth, for the sake of refreshing myself with what little nature and simplicity may be left in it, after men have so long sown and reaped here. I turn up the earth by way of pastime. My sober occupation, so far as I have any, is with a lighter material. In short, I make pictures out of sunshine; and, not to be too much dazzled with my own trade, I have prevailed with Miss Hepzibah to let me lodge in one of these dusky gables. It is like a bandage over one's eyes, to come into it. But would you like to see a specimen of my productions?"

"A daguerreotype likeness, do you mean?" asked Phoebe, with less reserve; for, in spite of prejudice, her own youthfulness sprang forward to meet his. "I don't much like pictures of that sort—they are so hard and stern; besides dodging away from the eye, and trying to escape altogether. They are conscious of looking very unamiable, I suppose, and therefore hate to be seen."

"If you would permit me," said the artist, looking at Phoebe, "I should like to try whether the daguerreotype can bring out disagreeable traits on a perfectly amiable face. But there certainly is truth in what you have said. Most of my likenesses do look unamiable; but the very sufficient reason, I fancy, is because the originals are so. There is a wonderful insight in heaven's broad and simple sunshine. While we give it credit only for depicting the merest surface, it actually brings out the secret character with a truth that no painter would ever venture upon, even could he detect it. There is, at least, no flattery in my humble line of art. Now, here is a likeness which I have taken over and over again, and still with no better result. Yet the original wears, to common eyes, a very different expression. It would gratify me to have your judgment on this character."

He exhibited a daguerreotype miniature in a morocco case. Phoebe merely glanced at it, and gave it back.

"I know the face," she replied, "for its stern eye has been following me about all day. It is my Puritan ancestor, who hangs yonder in the parlor. To be sure, you have found some way of copying the portrait without its black velvet cap and gray beard, and have given him a modern coat and satin cravat, instead of his cloak and band. I don't think him improved by your alterations."

"You would have seen other differences had you looked a little longer," said Holgrave, laughing, yet apparently much struck. "I can assure you that this is a modern face, and one which you will very probably meet. Now, the remarkable point is, that the original wears, to the world's eye—and, for aught I know, to his most intimate friends—an exceedingly pleasant countenance, indicative of benevolence, openness of heart, sunny good humor, and other praiseworthy qualities of that cast. The sun, as you see, tells quite another story, and will not be coaxed out of it, after half a dozen patient attempts on my part. Here we have the man, sly, subtle, hard, imperious, and, withal, cold as ice. Look at that eye! Would you like to be at its mercy? At that mouth! Could it ever smile? And yet, if you could only see the benign smile of the original! It is so much the more unfortunate, as he is a public character of some eminence, and the likeness was intended to be engraved."

"Well, I don't wish to see it any more," observed Phoebe,

turning away her eyes. "It is certainly very like the old portrait. But my cousin Hepzibah has another picture, a miniature. If the original is still in the world, I think he might defy the sun to make him look stern and hard."

"You have seen that picture, then!" exclaimed the artist, with an expression of much interest. "I never did, but have a great curiosity to do so. And you judge favorably of the face?"

"There never was a sweeter one," said Phoebe. "It is almost too soft and gentle for a man's."

"Is there nothing wild in the eye?" continued Holgrave, so earnestly that it embarrassed Phoebe, as did also the quiet freedom with which he presumed on their so recent acquaintance. "Is there nothing dark or sinister anywhere? Could you not conceive the original to have been guilty of a great crime?"

"It is nonsense," said Phoebe, a little impatiently, "for us to talk about a picture which you have never seen. You mistake it for some other. A crime, indeed! Since you are a friend of my cousin Hepzibah's, you should ask her to show you the picture."

"It will suit my purpose still better to see the original," replied the daguerreotypist coolly. "As to his character, we need not discuss its points; they have already been settled by a competent tribunal, or one which called itself competent. But, stay! Do not go yet, if you please! I have a proposition to make you."

Phoebe was on the point of retreating, but turned back, with some hesitation; for she did not exactly comprehend his manner, although, on better observation, its feature seemed rather to be lack of ceremony than any approach to offensive rudeness. There was an odd kind of authority, too, in what he now proceeded to say, rather as if the garden were his own than a place to which he was admitted merely by Hepzibah's courtesy.

"If agreeable to you," he observed, "it would give me pleasure to turn over these flowers, and those ancient and respectable fowls, to your care. Coming fresh from country air and occupations, you will soon feel the need of some such out-of-door employment. My own sphere does not so much lie among flowers. You can trim and tend them, therefore, as you please; and I will ask only the least trifle of a blossom, now and then, in exchange for all the good, honest kitchen vegetables with which I propose to enrich Miss Hepzibah's table. So we will be fellow laborers, somewhat on the community system."

Silently, and rather surprised at her own compliance, Phoebe accordingly betook herself to weeding a flower bed, but busied herself still more with cogitations respecting this young man, with whom she so unexpectedly found herself on terms approaching to familiarity. She did not altogether like him. His character perplexed the little country girl, as it might a more practiced observer; for, while the tone of his conversation had generally been playful, the impression left on her mind was that of gravity, and, except as his youth modified it, almost sternness. She rebelled, as it were, against a certain magnetic element in the artist's nature, which he exercised towards her, possibly without being conscious of it.

After a little while, the twilight, deepened by the shadows of the fruit trees and the surrounding buildings, threw an obscurity over the garden.

"There," said Holgrave. "It is time to give over work! That last stroke of the hoe has cut off a bean stalk. Good night, Miss Phoebe Pyncheon! Any bright day, if you will put one of those rosebuds in your hair, and come to my rooms in Central Street, I will seize the purest ray of sunshine, and make a picture of the flower and its wearer."

He retired towards his own solitary gable, but turned his head, on reaching the door, and called to Phoebe, with a tone which certainly had laughter in it, yet which seemed to be more than half in earnest.

"Be careful not to drink at Maule's well!" said he. "Neither drink nor bathe your face in it!"

"Maule's well!" answered Phoebe. "Is that it with the rim of mossy stones? I have no thought of drinking there— but why not?"

"Oh," rejoined the daguerreotypist, "because, like an old lady's cup of tea, it is water bewitched!"

He vanished; and Phoebe, lingering a moment, saw a

glimmering light, and then the steady beam of a lamp, in a chamber of the gable. On returning into Hepzibah's apartment of the house, she found the low-studded parlor so dim and dusky that her eyes could not penetrate the interior. She was indistinctly aware, however, that the gaunt figure of the old gentlewoman was sitting in one of the straight-backed chairs, a little withdrawn from the window, the faint gleam of which showed the blanched paleness of her cheek, turned sideway towards a corner.

"Shall I light a lamp, Cousin Hepzibah?" she asked.

"Do, if you please, my dear child," answered Hepzibah. "But put it on the table in the corner of the passage. My eyes are weak; and I can seldom bear the lamplight on them."

What an instrument is the human voice! How wonderfully responsive to every emotion of the human soul! In Hepzibah's tone, at that moment, there was a certain rich depth and moisture, as if the words, commonplace as they were, had been steeped in the warmth of her heart. Again, while lighting the lamp in the kitchen, Phoebe fancied that her cousin spoke to her.

"In a moment, cousin!" answered the girl. "These matches just glimmer, and go out."

But, instead of a response from Hepzibah, she seemed to hear the murmur of an unknown voice. It was strangely indistinct, however, and less like articulate words than an unshaped sound, such as would be the utterance of feeling and sympathy, rather than of the intellect. So vague was it, that its impression or echo in Phoebe's mind was that of unreality. She concluded that she must have mistaken some other sound for that of the human voice; or else that it was altogether in her fancy.

She set the lighted lamp in the passage, and again entered the parlor. Hepzibah's form, though its sable outline mingled with the dusk, was now less imperfectly visible. In the remoter parts of the room, however, its walls being so ill adapted to reflect light, there was nearly the same obscurity as before.

"Cousin," said Phoebe, "did you speak to me just now?"

"No, child!" replied Hepzibah.

Fewer words than before, but with the same mysterious music in them! Mellow, melancholy, yet not mournful, the tone seemed to gush up out of the deep well of Hepzibah's heart, all steeped in its profoundest emotion. There was a tremor in it, too, that—as all strong feeling is electric— partly communicated itself to Phoebe. The girl sat silently for a moment. But soon, her senses being very acute, she became conscious of an irregular respiration in an obscure corner of the room. Her physical organization, moreover, being at once delicate and healthy, gave her a perception, operating with almost the effect of a spiritual medium, that somebody was near at hand.

"My dear cousin," asked she, overcoming an indefinable reluctance, "is there not someone in the room with us?"

"Phoebe, my dear little girl," said Hepzibah, after a moment's pause, "you were up betimes, and have been busy all day. Pray go to bed; for I am sure you must need rest. I will sit in the parlor awhile, and collect my thoughts. It has been my custom for more years, child, than you have lived!"

While thus dismissing her, the maiden lady stepped forward, kissed Phoebe, and pressed her to her heart, which beat against the girl's bosom with a strong, high, and tumultuous swell. How came there to be so much love in this desolate old heart, that it could afford to well over thus abundantly?

"Good night, cousin," said Phoebe, strangely affected by Hepzibah's manner. "If you begin to love me, I am glad!"

She retired to her chamber, but did not soon fall asleep, nor then very profoundly. At some uncertain period in the depths of night, and, as it were, through the thin veil of a dream, she was conscious of a footstep mounting the stairs heavily, but not with force and decision. The voice of Hepzibah, with a hush through it, was going up along with the footsteps; and, again, responsive to her cousin's voice, Phoebe heard that strange, vague murmur, which might be likened to an indistinct shadow of human utterance.

❧ 7 ❧

The Guest

WHEN Phoebe awoke—which she did with the early twittering of the conjugal couple of robins in the pear tree—she heard movements belowstairs, and, hastening down, found Hepzibah already in the kitchen. She stood by a window, holding a book in close contiguity to her nose, as if with the hope of gaining an olfactory acquaintance with its contents, since her imperfect vision made it not very easy to read them. If any volume could have manifested its essential wisdom in the mode suggested, it would certainly have been the one now in Hepzibah's hand; and the kitchen, in such an event, would forthwith have steamed with the fragrance of venison, turkeys, capons, larded partridges, puddings, cakes, and Christmas pies, in all manner of elaborate mixture and concoction. It was a cookery book, full of innumerable old fashions of English dishes, and illustrated with engravings, which represented the arrangements of the table at such banquets as it might have befitted a nobleman to give in the great hall of his castle. And, amid these rich and potent devices of the culinary art (not one of which, probably, had been tested, within the memory of any man's grandfather), poor Hepzibah was seeking for some nimble little titbit, which, with what skill she had, and such materials as were at hand, she might toss up for breakfast.

Soon, with a deep sigh, she put aside the savory volume, and inquired of Phoebe whether old Speckle, as she called one of the hens, had laid an egg the preceding day. Phoebe ran to see, but returned without the expected treasure in her hand. At that instant, however, the blast of a fish-dealer's conch was heard, announcing his approach along the street. With energetic raps at the shopwindow, Hepzibah summoned the man in, and made purchase of what he warranted as the finest mackerel in his cart, and as fat a one as ever he felt with his finger so early in the season. Requesting Phoebe to roast some coffee—which she casually observed was the real Mocha, and so long kept that each of the small berries ought to be worth its weight in gold—the maiden lady heaped fuel into the vast receptacle of the ancient fireplace in such quantity as soon to drive the lingering dusk out of the kitchen. The country girl, willing to give her utmost assistance, proposed to make an Indian cake, after her mother's peculiar method, of easy manufacture, and which she could vouch for as possessing a richness, and, if rightly prepared, a delicacy, unequaled by any other mode of breakfast cake. Hepzibah gladly assenting, the kitchen was soon the scene of savory preparation. Perchance, amid their proper element of smoke, which eddied forth from the ill-constructed chimney, the ghosts of departed cookmaids looked wonderingly on, or peeped down the great breadth of the flue, despising the simplicity of the projected meal, yet ineffectually pining to thrust their shadowy hands into each inchoate dish. The half-starved rats, at any rate, stole visibly out of their hiding places, and sat on their hind legs, snuffing the fumy atmosphere, and wistfully awaiting an opportunity to nibble.

Hepzibah had no natural turn for cookery, and, to say the truth, had fairly incurred her present meagerness by often choosing to go without her dinner rather than be attendant on the rotation of the spit, or ebullition of the pot. Her zeal over the fire, therefore, was quite an heroic test of sentiment. It was touching, and positively worthy of tears (if Phoebe, the only spectator, except the rats and ghosts aforesaid, had not been better employed than in shedding them), to see her rake out a bed of fresh and glowing coals, and proceed to broil the mackerel. Her usually pale cheeks were all ablaze with heat and hurry. She watched the fish with as much tender care and minuteness of attention as if—we know not how to express it otherwise—as if her own heart were on the gridiron, and her immortal happiness were involved in its being done precisely to a turn!

Life, within doors, has few pleasanter prospects than a neatly arranged and well-provisioned breakfast table. We come to it freshly, in the dewy youth of the day, and when our spiritual and sensual elements are in better accord than at a later period; so that the material delights of the morning meal are capable of being fully enjoyed, without any very grievous reproaches, whether gastric or conscientious, for yielding even a trifle overmuch to the animal department of our nature. The thoughts, too, that run around the ring of familiar guests have a piquancy and mirthfulness, and oftentimes a vivid truth, which more rarely find their way into the elaborate intercourse of dinner. Hepzibah's small and ancient table, supported on its slender and graceful legs, and covered with a cloth of the richest damask, looked worthy to be the scene and center of one of the cheerfulest of parties. The vapor of the broiled fish arose like incense from the shrine of a barbarian idol, while the fragrance of the Mocha might have gratified the nostrils of a tutelary Lar, or whatever power has scope over a modern breakfast table. Phoebe's Indian cakes were the sweetest offering of all—in their hue befitting the rustic altars of the innocent and golden age—or, so brightly yellow were they, resembling some of the bread which was changed to glistening gold when Midas tried to eat it. The butter must not be forgotten—butter which Phoebe herself had churned, in her own rural home, and brought it to her cousin as a propitiatory gift—smelling of clover blossoms, and diffusing the charm of pastoral scenery through the dark-paneled parlor. All this, with the quaint gorgeousness of the old china cups and saucers, and the crested spoons, and a silver cream jug (Hepzibah's only other article of plate, and shaped like the rudest porringer), set out a board at which the stateliest of old Colonel Pyncheon's guests need not have scorned to take his place. But the Puritan's face scowled down out of the picture, as if nothing on the table pleased his appetite.

By way of contributing what grace she could, Phoebe

gathered some roses and a few other flowers, possessing either scent or beauty, and arranged them in a glass pitcher, which, having long ago lost its handle, was so much the fitter for a flower vase. The early sunshine—as fresh as that which peeped into Eve's bower while she and Adam sat at breakfast there—came twinkling through the branches of the pear tree, and fell quite across the table. All was now ready. There were chairs and plates for three. A chair and plate for Hepzibah, the same for Phoebe—but what other guest did her cousin look for?

Throughout this preparation, there had been a constant tremor in Hepzibah's frame; an agitation so powerful that Phoebe could see the quivering of her gaunt shadow, as thrown by the firelight on the kitchen wall, or by the sunshine on the parlor floor. Its manifestations were so various, and agreed so little with one another, that the girl knew not what to make of it. Sometimes it seemed an ecstasy of delight and happiness. At such moments, Hepzibah would fling out her arms, and infold Phoebe in them, and kiss her cheek as tenderly as ever her mother had; she appeared to do so by an inevitable impulse, and as if her bosom were oppressed with tenderness, of which she must needs pour out a little, in order to gain breathing room. The next moment, without any visible cause for the change, her unwonted joy shrank back, appalled, as it were, and clothed itself in mourning; or it ran and hid itself, so to speak, in the dungeon of her heart, where it had long lain chained, while a cold, spectral sorrow took the place of the imprisoned joy, that was afraid to be enfranchised—a sorrow as black as that was bright. She often broke into a little, nervous, hysteric laugh, more touching than any tears could be; and forthwith, as if to try which was the most touching, a gush of tears would follow; or perhaps the laughter and tears came both at once, and surrounded our poor Hepzibah, in a moral sense, with a kind of pale, dim rainbow. Towards Phoebe, as we have said, she was affectionate— far tenderer than ever before, in their brief acquaintance, except for that one kiss on the preceding night—yet with a continually recurring pettishness and irritability. She would speak sharply to her; then, throwing aside all the starched reserve of her ordinary manner, ask pardon, and the next instant renew the just forgiven injury.

At last, when their mutual labor was all finished, she took Phoebe's hand in her own trembling one.

"Bear with me, my dear child," she cried, "for truly my heart is full to the brim! Bear with me; for I love you, Phoebe, though I speak so roughly! Think nothing of it, dearest child! By and by, I shall be kind, and only kind!"

"My dearest cousin, cannot you tell me what has happened?" asked Phoebe, with a sunny and tearful sympathy. "What is it that moves you so?"

"Hush! hush! He is coming!" whispered Hepzibah, hastily wiping her eyes. "Let him see you first, Phoebe; for you are young and rosy, and cannot help letting a smile break out whether or no. He always liked bright faces! And mine is old now, and the tears are hardly dry on it. He never could abide tears. There; draw the curtain a little, so that the shadow may fall across his side of the table! But let there be a good deal of sunshine, too; for he never was fond of gloom, as some people are. He has had but little sunshine in his life—poor Clifford—and, oh, what a black shadow! Poor, poor Clifford!"

Thus murmuring in an undertone, as if speaking rather to her own heart than to Phoebe, the old gentlewoman stepped on tiptoe about the room, making such arrangements as suggested themselves at the crisis.

Meanwhile, there was a step in the passageway abovestairs. Phoebe recognized it as the same which had passed upward, as through her dream, in the nighttime. The approaching guest, whoever it might be, appeared to pause at the head of the staircase; he paused twice or thrice in the descent; he paused again at the foot. Each time, the delay seemed to be without purpose, but rather from a forgetfulness of the purpose which had set him in motion, or as if the person's feet came involuntarily to a standstill because the motive power was too feeble to sustain his progress. Finally, he made a long pause at the threshold of the parlor. He took hold of the knob of the door; then loosened his grasp without opening it. Hepzibah, her hands convulsively clasped, stood gazing at the entrance.

"Dear Cousin Hepzibah, pray don't look so!" said Phoebe, trembling; for her cousin's emotion, and this mysteriously reluctant step, made her feel as if a ghost were coming into the room. "You really frighten me! Is something awful going to happen?"

"Hush!" whispered Hepzibah. "Be cheerful! Whatever may happen, be nothing but cheerful!"

The final pause at the threshold proved so long that Hepzibah, unable to endure the suspense, rushed forward, threw open the door, and led in the stranger by the hand. At the first glance, Phoebe saw an elderly personage, in an old-fashioned dressing gown of faded damask, and wearing his gray or almost white hair of an unusual length. It quite overshadowed his forehead, except when he thrust it back, and stared vaguely about the room. After a very brief inspection of his face, it was easy to conceive that his footstep must necessarily be such an one as that which, slowly, and with as indefinite an aim as a child's first journey across a floor, had just brought him hitherward. Yet there were no tokens that his physical strength might not have sufficed for a free and determined gait. It was the spirit of the man that could not walk. The expression of his countenance—while, notwithstanding, it had the light of reason in it—seemed to waver, and glimmer, and nearly to die away, and feebly to recover itself again. It was like a flame which we see twinkling among half-extinguished embers; we gaze at it more intently than if it were a positive blaze, gushing vividly upward—more intently, but with a certain impatience, as if it ought either to kindle itself into satisfactory splendor, or be at once extinguished.

For an instant after entering the room, the guest stood still, retaining Hepzibah's hand, instinctively, as a child does that of the grown person who guides it. He saw Phoebe, however, and caught an illumination from her youthful and pleasant aspect, which, indeed, threw a cheerfulness about the parlor, like the circle of reflected brilliancy around the glass vase of flowers that was standing in the sunshine. He made a salutation, or, to speak nearer the truth, an ill-defined, abortive attempt at courtesy. Imperfect as it was, however, it conveyed an idea, or, at least, gave a hint, of in-

describable grace, such as no practiced art of external manners could have attained. It was too slight to seize upon at
the instant; yet, as recollected afterwards, seemed to trans-
figure the whole man.

"Dear Clifford," said Hepzibah, in the tone with which
one soothes a wayward infant, "this is our cousin Phoebe—
little Phoebe Pyncheon—Arthur's only child, you know.
She has come from the country to stay with us awhile; for
our old house has grown to be very lonely now."

"Phoebe? Phoebe Pyncheon? Phoebe?" repeated the
guest, with a strange, sluggish, ill-defined utterance. "Arthur's child! Ah, I forget! No matter! She is very welcome!"

"Come, dear Clifford, take this chair," said Hepzibah,
leading him to his place. "Pray, Phoebe, lower the curtain a
very little more. Now let us begin breakfast."

The guest seated himself in the place assigned him, and
looked strangely around. He was evidently trying to grapple
with the present scene, and bring it home to his mind with a
more satisfactory distinctness. He desired to be certain, at
least, that he was here, in the low-studded, cross-beamed,
oaken-paneled parlor, and not in some other spot, which
had stereotyped itself into his senses. But the effort was too
great to be sustained with more than a fragmentary success.
Continually, as we may express it, he faded away out of his
place; or, in other words, his mind and consciousness took
their departure, leaving his wasted, gray, and melancholy
figure—a substantial emptiness, a material ghost—to occupy his seat at table. Again, after a blank moment, there
would be a flickering taper-gleam in his eyeballs. It betokened that his spiritual part had returned, and was doing
its best to kindle the heart's household fire, and light up
intellectual lamps in the dark and ruinous mansion, where
it was doomed to be a forlorn inhabitant.

At one of these moments of less torpid, yet still imperfect animation, Phoebe became convinced of what she had
at first rejected as too extravagant and startling an idea.
She saw that the person before her must have been the
original of the beautiful miniature in her cousin Hepzibah's
possession. Indeed, with a feminine eye for costume, she
had at once identified the damask dressing gown, which

enveloped him, as the same, in figure, material, and fashion, with that so elaborately represented in the picture.
This old, faded garment, with all its pristine brilliancy extinct, seemed, in some indescribable way, to translate the
wearer's untold misfortune, and make it perceptible to the
beholder's eye. It was the better to be discerned, by this exterior type, how worn and old were the soul's more immediate garments; that form and countenance, the beauty and
grace of which had almost transcended the skill of the most
exquisite of artists. It could the more adequately be known
that the soul of the man must have suffered some miserable wrong, from its earthly experience. There he seemed
to sit, with a dim veil of decay and ruin betwixt him and
the world, but through which, at flitting intervals, might be
caught the same expression, so refined, so softly imaginative, which Malbone—venturing a happy touch, with suspended breath—had imparted to the miniature! There had
been something so innately characteristic in this look, that
all the dusky years, and the burden of unfit calamity which
had fallen upon him, did not suffice utterly to destroy it.

Hepzibah had now poured out a cup of deliciously fragrant coffee, and presented it to her guest. As his eyes met
hers, he seemed bewildered and disquieted.

"Is this you, Hepzibah?" he murmured, sadly; then,
more apart, and perhaps unconscious that he was overheard, "How changed! how changed! And is she angry with
me? Why does she bend her brow so?"

Poor Hepzibah! It was that wretched scowl, which time
and her nearsightedness, and the fret of inward discomfort,
had rendered so habitual that any vehemence of mood
invariably evoked it. But at the indistinct murmur of his
words, her whole face grew tender, and even lovely, with
sorrowful affection; the harshness of her features disappeared, as it were, behind the warm and misty glow.

"Angry!" she repeated. "Angry with you, Clifford!"

Her tone, as she uttered the exclamation, had a plaintive
and really exquisite melody thrilling through it, yet without subduing a certain something which an obtuse auditor might still have mistaken for asperity. It was as if some
transcendent musician should draw a soul-thrilling sweet-

ness out of a cracked instrument, which makes its physical imperfection heard in the midst of ethereal harmony—so deep was the sensibility that found an organ in Hepzibah's voice!

"There is nothing but love here, Clifford," she added, "nothing but love! You are at home!"

The guest responded to her tone by a smile, which did not half light up his face. Feeble as it was, however, and gone in a moment, it had a charm of wonderful beauty. It was followed by a coarser expression; or one that had the effect of coarseness on the fine mold and outline of his countenance, because there was nothing intellectual to temper it. It was a look of appetite. He ate food with what might almost be termed voracity; and seemed to forget himself, Hepzibah, the young girl, and everything else around him, in the sensual enjoyment which the bountifully spread table afforded. In his natural system, though high-wrought and delicately refined, a sensibility to the delights of the palate was probably inherent. It would have been kept in check, however, and even converted into an accomplishment, and one of the thousand modes of intellectual culture, had his more ethereal characteristics retained their vigor. But as it existed now, the effect was painful and made Phoebe droop her eyes.

In a little while, the guest became sensible of the fragrance of the yet untasted coffee. He quaffed it eagerly. The subtle essence acted on him like a charmed draught, and caused the opaque substance of his animal being to grow transparent, or, at least, translucent; so that a spiritual gleam was transmitted through it, with a clearer luster than hitherto.

"More, more!" he cried, with nervous haste in his utterance, as if anxious to retain his grasp of what sought to escape him. "This is what I need! Give me more!"

Under this delicate and powerful influence, he sat more erect, and looked out from his eyes with a glance that took note of what it rested on. It was not so much that his expression grew more intellectual; this, though it had its share, was not the most peculiar effect. Neither was what we call the moral nature so forcibly awakened as to present itself in remarkable prominence. But a certain fine temper of being was now not brought out in full relief, but changeably and imperfectly betrayed, of which it was the function to deal with all beautiful and enjoyable things. In a character where it should exist as the chief attribute, it would bestow on its possessor an exquisite taste, and an enviable susceptibility of happiness. Beauty would be his life; his aspirations would all tend towards it; and, allowing his frame and physical organs to be in consonance, his own developments would likewise be beautiful. Such a man should have nothing to do with sorrow; nothing with strife; nothing with the martyrdom which, in an infinite variety of shapes, awaits those who have the heart, and will, and conscience, to fight a battle with the world. To these heroic tempers, such martyrdom is the richest meed in the world's gift. To the individual before us, it could only be a grief, intense in due proportion with the severity of the infliction. He had no right to be a martyr; and, beholding him so fit to be happy and so feeble for all other purposes, a generous, strong, and noble spirit would, methinks, have been ready to sacrifice what little enjoyment it might have planned for itself—it would have flung down the hopes, so paltry in its regard—if thereby the wintry blasts of our rude sphere might come tempered to such a man.

Not to speak it harshly or scornfully, it seemed Clifford's nature to be a sybarite. It was perceptible, even there, in the dark old parlor, in the inevitable polarity with which his eyes were attracted towards the quivering play of sunbeams through the shadowy foliage. It was seen in his appreciating notice of the vase of flowers, the scent of which he inhaled with a zest almost peculiar to a physical organization so refined that spiritual ingredients are molded in with it. It was betrayed in the unconscious smile with which he regarded Phoebe, whose fresh and maidenly figure was both sunshine and flowers—their essence, in a prettier and more agreeable mode of manifestation. Not less evident was this love and necessity for the Beautiful, in the instinctive caution with which, even so soon, his eyes turned away from his hostess, and wandered to any quarter rather than come back. It was Hepzibah's misfortune, not Clifford's fault. How could he—so yellow as she was, so wrinkled, so sad of mien, with that odd uncouthness of a turban on her head, and that most perverse of scowls contorting her brow—how could he love to gaze at her? But did he owe her no affection for so much as she had silently given? He owed her nothing. A nature like Clifford's can contract no debts of that kind. It is—we say it without censure, nor in diminution of the claim which it indefensibly possesses on beings of another mold—it is always selfish in its essence; and we must give it leave to be so, and heap up our heroic and disinterested love upon it so much the more, without a recompense. Poor Hepzibah knew this truth, or, at least, acted on the instinct of it. So long estranged from what was lovely as Clifford had been, she rejoiced—rejoiced, though with a present sigh, and a secret purpose to shed tears in her own chamber—that he had brighter objects now before his eyes than her aged and uncomely features. They never possessed a charm; and if they had, the canker of her grief for him would long since have destroyed it.

The guest leaned back in his chair. Mingled in his countenance with a dreamy delight, there was a troubled look of effort and unrest. He was seeking to make himself more fully sensible of the scene around him; or, perhaps, dreading it to be a dream, or a play of imagination, was vexing the fair moment with a struggle for some added brilliancy and more durable illusion.

"How pleasant! How delightful!" he murmured, but not as if addressing anyone. "Will it last? How balmy the atmosphere through that open window! An open window! How beautiful that play of sunshine! Those flowers, how very fragrant! That young girl's face, how cheerful, how blooming—a flower with the dew on it, and sunbeams in the dewdrops! Ah! This must be all a dream! A dream! A dream! But it has quite hidden the four stone walls!"

Then his face darkened, as if the shadow of a cavern or a dungeon had come over it; there was no more light in its expression than might have come through the iron grates of a prison window—still lessening, too, as if he were sinking farther into the depths. Phoebe (being of that quickness and activity of temperament that she seldom long refrained from taking a part, and generally a good one, in what was going forward) now felt herself moved to address the stranger.

"Here is a new kind of rose, which I found this morning in the garden," said she, choosing a small crimson one from among the flowers in the vase. "There will be but five or six on the bush this season. This is the most perfect of them all; not a speck of blight or mildew in it. And how sweet it is— sweet like no other rose! One can never forget that scent!"

"Ah! Let me see—let me hold it!" cried the guest, eagerly seizing the flower, which, by the spell peculiar to remembered odors, brought innumerable associations along with the fragrance that it exhaled. "Thank you! This has done me good. I remember how I used to prize this flower—long ago, I suppose, very long ago!—or was it only yesterday? It makes me feel young again! Am I young? Either this remembrance is singularly distinct, or this consciousness strangely dim! But how kind of the fair young girl! Thank you! Thank you!"

The favorable excitement derived from this little crimson rose afforded Clifford the brightest moment which he enjoyed at the breakfast table. It might have lasted longer, but that his eyes happened, soon afterwards, to rest on the face of the old Puritan, who, out of his dingy frame and lusterless canvas, was looking down on the scene like a ghost, and a most ill-tempered and ungenial one. The guest made an impatient gesture of the hand, and addressed Hepzibah with what might easily be recognized as the licensed irritability of a petted member of the family.

"Hepzibah! Hepzibah!" cried he with no little force and distinctness. "Why do you keep that odious picture on the wall? Yes, yes! That is precisely your taste! I have told you, a thousand times, that it was the evil genius of the house— my evil genius particularly! Take it down, at once!"

"Dear Clifford," said Hepzibah, sadly, "you know it cannot be!"

"Then, at all events," continued he, still speaking with some energy, "pray cover it with a crimson curtain, broad enough to hang in folds, and with a golden border and tassels. I cannot bear it! It must not stare me in the face!"

"Yes, dear Clifford, the picture shall be covered," said Hepzibah, soothingly. "There is a crimson curtain in a trunk abovestairs, a little faded and moth-eaten, I'm afraid, but Phoebe and I will do wonders with it."

"This very day, remember!" said he; and then added, in a low, self-communing voice, "Why should we live in this dismal house at all? Why not go to the South of France—to Italy—Paris, Naples, Venice, Rome? Hepzibah will say we have not the means. A droll idea that!"

He smiled to himself, and threw a glance of fine sarcastic meaning towards Hepzibah.

But the several moods of feeling, faintly as they were marked, through which he had passed, occurring in so brief an interval of time, had evidently wearied the stranger. He was probably accustomed to a sad monotony of life, not so much flowing in a stream, however sluggish, as stagnating in a pool around his feet. A slumberous veil diffused itself over his countenance, and had an effect, morally speaking, on its naturally delicate and elegant outline, like that which a brooding mist, with no sunshine in it, throws over the features of a landscape. He appeared to become grosser—almost cloddish. If aught of interest or beauty—even ruined beauty—had heretofore been visible in this man, the beholder might now begin to doubt it, and to accuse his own imagination of deluding him with whatever grace had flickered over that visage, and whatever exquisite luster had gleamed in those filmy eyes.

Before he had quite sunken away, however, the sharp and peevish tinkle of the shop bell made itself audible. Striking most disagreeably on Clifford's auditory organs and the characteristic sensibility of his nerves, it caused him to start upright out of his chair.

"Good heavens, Hepzibah! What horrible disturbance have we now in the house?" cried he, wreaking his resentful impatience—as a matter of course, and a custom of old—on the one person in the world that loved him. "I have never heard such a hateful clamor! Why do you permit it? In the name of all dissonance, what can it be?"

It was very remarkable into what prominent relief—even as if a dim picture should leap suddenly from its canvas—

Clifford's character was thrown by this apparently trifling annoyance. The secret was that an individual of his temper can always be pricked more acutely through his sense of the beautiful and harmonious than through his heart. It is even possible—for similar cases have often happened— that if Clifford, in his foregoing life, had enjoyed the means of cultivating his taste to its utmost perfectibility, that subtile attribute might, before this period, have completely eaten out or filed away his affections. Shall we venture to pronounce, therefore, that his long and black calamity may not have had a redeeming drop of mercy at the bottom?

"Dear Clifford, I wish I could keep the sound from your ears," said Hepzibah, patiently, but reddening with a painful suffusion of shame. "It is very disagreeable even to me. But, do you know, Clifford, I have something to tell you? This ugly noise—pray run, Phoebe, and see who is there!— this naughty little tinkle is nothing but our shop bell!"

"Shop bell!" repeated Clifford, with a bewildered stare.

"Yes, our shop bell," said Hepzibah, a certain natural dignity, mingled with deep emotion, now asserting itself in her manner. "For you must know, dearest Clifford, that we are very poor. And there was no other resource but either to accept assistance from a hand that I would push aside (and so would you!) were it to offer bread when we were dying for it—no help, save from him, or else to earn our subsistence with my own hands! Alone, I might have been content to starve. But you were to be given back to me! Do you think, then, dear Clifford," added she, with a wretched smile, "that I have brought an irretrievable disgrace on the old house, by opening a little shop in the front gable? Our great-great-grandfather did the same, when there was far less need! Are you ashamed of me?"

"Shame! Disgrace! Do you speak these words to me, Hepzibah?" said Clifford, not angrily, however; for when a man's spirit has been thoroughly crushed, he may be peevish at small offenses, but never resentful of great ones. So he spoke with only a grieved emotion. "It was not kind to say so, Hepzibah! What shame can befall me now?"

And then the unnerved man—he that had been born for enjoyment, but had met a doom so very wretched—burst into a woman's passion of tears. It was but of brief continuance, however; soon leaving him in a quiescent, and, to judge by his countenance, not an uncomfortable state. From this mood, too, he partially rallied for an instant, and looked at Hepzibah with a smile, the keen, half-derisory purport of which was a puzzle to her.

"Are we so very poor, Hepzibah?" said he.

Finally, his chair being deep and softly cushioned, Clifford fell asleep. Hearing the more regular rise and fall of his breath (which, however, even then, instead of being strong and full, had a feeble kind of tremor, corresponding with the lack of vigor in his character)—hearing these tokens of settled slumber, Hepzibah seized the opportunity to peruse his face more attentively than she had yet dared to do. Her heart melted away in tears; her profoundest spirit sent forth a moaning voice, low, gentle, but inexpressibly sad. In this depth of grief and pity, she felt that there was no irreverence in gazing at his altered, aged, faded, ruined face. But no sooner was she a little relieved than her conscience smote her for gazing curiously at him, now that he was so changed; and, turning hastily away, Hepzibah let down the curtain over the sunny window, and left Clifford to slumber there.

❧ 8 ❧

The Pyncheon of Today

PHOEBE, on entering the shop, beheld there the already familiar face of the little devourer—if we can reckon his mighty deeds aright—of Jim Crow, the elephant, the camel, the dromedaries, and the locomotive. Having expended his private fortune, on the two preceding days, in the purchase of the above unheard-of luxuries, the young gentleman's present errand was on the part of his mother, in quest of three eggs and half a pound of raisins. These articles Phoebe accordingly supplied, and, as a mark of gratitude for his previous patronage, and a slight superadded morsel after breakfast, put likewise into his hand a whale! The great fish, reversing his experience with the prophet of Nineveh, immediately began his progress down the same red pathway of fate whither so varied a caravan had preceded him. This remarkable urchin, in truth, was the very emblem of old Father Time, both in respect of his all-devouring appetite for men and things, and because he, as well as Time, after ingulfing thus much of creation, looked almost as youthful as if he had been just that moment made.

After partly closing the door, the child turned back, and mumbled something to Phoebe, which, as the whale was but half disposed of, she could not perfectly understand.

"What did you say, my little fellow?" asked she.

"Mother wants to know," repeated Ned Higgins, more distinctly, "how Old Maid Pyncheon's brother does? Folks say he has got home."

"My cousin Hepzibah's brother!" exclaimed Phoebe, surprised at this sudden explanation of the relationship between Hepzibah and her guest. "Her brother! And where can he have been?"

The little boy only put his thumb to his broad snub nose, with that look of shrewdness which a child, spending much of his time in the street, so soon learns to throw over his features, however unintelligent in themselves. Then, as Phoebe continued to gaze at him, without answering his mother's message, he took his departure.

As the child went down the steps, a gentleman ascended them, and made his entrance into the shop. It was the portly, and, had it possessed the advantage of a little more height, would have been the stately figure of a man considerably in the decline of life, dressed in a black suit of some thin stuff, resembling broadcloth as closely as possible. A gold-headed cane, of rare Oriental wood, added materially to the high respectability of his aspect, as did also a neck-cloth of the utmost snowy purity, and the conscientious polish of his boots. His dark, square countenance, with its almost shaggy depth of eyebrows, was naturally impressive, and would, perhaps, have been rather stern, had not the gentleman considerately taken upon himself to mitigate the harsh effect by a look of exceeding good humor and benevolence. Owing, however, to a somewhat massive accumulation of animal substance about the lower region of his face, the look was, perhaps, unctuous, rather than spiritual, and had, so to speak, a kind of fleshly effulgence, not altogether so satisfactory as he doubtless intended it to be. A susceptible observer, at any rate, might have regarded it as affording very little evidence of the general benignity of soul whereof it purported to be the outward reflection. And if the observer chanced to be ill-natured, as well as acute and susceptible, he would probably suspect that the smile on the gentleman's face was a good deal akin to the shine on his boots, and that each must have cost him and his bootblack, respectively, a good deal of hard labor to bring out and preserve them.

As the stranger entered the little shop, where the projection of the second story and the thick foliage of the elm tree, as well as the commodities at the window, created a sort of gray medium, his smile grew as intense as if he had set his heart on counteracting the whole gloom of the atmosphere (besides any moral gloom pertaining to Hepzibah and her inmates) by the unassisted light of his countenance. On perceiving a young rosebud of a girl, instead of the gaunt presence of the old maid, a look of surprise was manifest. He at first knit his brows; then smiled with more unctuous benignity than ever.

"Ah, I see how it is!" said he, in a deep voice—a voice which, had it come from the throat of an uncultivated man, would have been gruff, but, by dint of careful training, was now sufficiently agreeable. "I was not aware that Miss Hepzibah Pyncheon had commenced business under such favorable auspices. You are her assistant, I suppose?"

"I certainly am," answered Phoebe, and added, with a little air of ladylike assumption (for, civil as the gentleman was, he evidently took her to be a young person serving for wages), "I am a cousin of Miss Hepzibah, on a visit to her."

"Her cousin—and from the country? Pray pardon me, then," said the gentleman, bowing and smiling, as Phoebe never had been bowed to nor smiled on before. "In that case, we must be better acquainted; for, unless I am sadly mistaken, you are my own little kinswoman likewise! Let me see—Mary? Dolly? Phoebe? Yes, Phoebe is the name! Is it possible that you are Phoebe Pyncheon, only child of my dear cousin and classmate, Arthur? Ah, I see your father now, about your mouth! Yes, yes! We must be better acquainted! I am your kinsman, my dear. Surely you must have heard of Judge Pyncheon?"

As Phoebe courtesied in reply, the Judge bent forward, with the pardonable and even praiseworthy purpose—considering the nearness of blood, and the difference of age—of bestowing on his young relative a kiss of acknowledged kindred and natural affection. Unfortunately (without design, or only with such instinctive design as gives no account of itself to the intellect) Phoebe, just at the critical moment, drew back; so that her highly respectable kinsman, with his body bent over the counter, and his lips protruded, was betrayed into the rather absurd predicament of kissing the empty air. It was a modern parallel to the case of Ixion embracing a cloud, and was so much the more ridiculous, as the Judge prided himself on eschewing all airy matter, and never mistaking a shadow for a substance. The truth was—and it is Phoebe's only excuse—that, although Judge Pyncheon's glowing benignity might not be absolutely unpleasant to the feminine beholder, with the width of a street, or even an ordinary-sized room, interposed between, yet it became quite too intense, when this dark, full-fed physiognomy (so roughly bearded, too, that no razor could ever make it smooth) sought to bring itself into actual contact with the object of its regards. The man, the sex, somehow or other, was entirely too prominent in the Judge's demonstrations of that sort. Phoebe's eyes sank, and, without knowing why, she felt herself blushing deeply under his look. Yet she had been kissed before, and without any particular squeamishness, by perhaps half a dozen different cousins, younger as well as older than this dark-browed, grizzly-bearded, white-neckclothed, and unctuously benevolent Judge! Then, why not by him?

On raising her eyes, Phoebe was startled by the change in Judge Pyncheon's face. It was quite as striking, allowing for the difference of scale, as that betwixt a landscape under a broad sunshine and just before a thunderstorm; not that it had the passionate intensity of the latter aspect, but was cold, hard, immitigable, like a day-long brooding cloud.

"Dear me! What is to be done now?" thought the country girl to herself. "He looks as if there were nothing softer in him than a rock, nor milder than the east wind! I meant no harm! Since he is really my cousin, I would have let him kiss me, if I could!"

Then, all at once, it struck Phoebe that this very Judge Pyncheon was the original of the miniature which the daguerreotypist had shown her in the garden, and that the hard, stern, relentless look now on his face was the same that the sun had so inflexibly persisted in bringing out. Was it, therefore, no momentary mood, but, however skillfully concealed, the settled temper of his life? And not merely so, but was it hereditary in him, and transmitted down, as a precious heirloom, from that bearded ancestor in whose picture both the expression, and, to a singular degree, the features of the modern Judge were shown as by a kind of prophecy? A deeper philosopher than Phoebe might have found something very terrible in this idea. It implied that the weaknesses and defects, the bad passions, the mean tendencies, and the moral diseases which lead to crime are handed down from one generation to another, by a far surer process of transmission than human law has been able to establish in respect to the riches and honors which it seeks to entail upon posterity.

But, as it happened, scarcely had Phoebe's eyes rested again on the Judge's countenance than all its ugly sternness vanished; and she found herself quite overpowered by the sultry, dog-day heat, as it were, of benevolence, which this excellent man diffused out of his great heart into the surrounding atmosphere—very much like a serpent, which, as a preliminary to fascination, is said to fill the air with his peculiar odor.

"I like that, Cousin Phoebe!" cried he, with an emphatic nod of approbation. "I like it much, my little cousin! You are a good child, and know how to take care of yourself. A young girl—especially if she be a very pretty one—can never be too chary of her lips."

"Indeed, sir," said Phoebe, trying to laugh the matter off, "I did not mean to be unkind."

Nevertheless, whether or no it were entirely owing to the inauspicious commencement of their acquaintance, she still acted under a certain reserve, which was by no means customary to her frank and genial nature. The fantasy would not quit her, that the original Puritan, of whom she had heard so many somber traditions—the progenitor of the whole race of New England Pyncheons, the founder of the House of the Seven Gables, and who had died so strangely in it—had now stepped into the shop. In these days of offhand equipment, the matter was easily enough arranged. On his arrival from the other world, he had merely found it necessary to spend a quarter of an hour at a barber's, who had trimmed down the Puritan's full beard into a pair of grizzled whiskers; then, patronizing a ready-made clothing establishment, he had exchanged his velvet doublet and sable cloak, with the richly worked band under his chin, for a white collar and cravat, coat, vest, and pantaloons; and lastly, putting aside his steel-hilted broadsword to take up a gold-headed cane, the Colonel Pyncheon of two centuries ago steps forward as the Judge of the passing moment!

Of course, Phoebe was far too sensible a girl to entertain this idea in any other way than as matter for a smile. Possibly, also, could the two personages have stood together before her eye, many points of difference would have been perceptible, and perhaps only a general resemblance. The long lapse of intervening years, in a climate so unlike that which had fostered the ancestral Englishman, must inevitably have wrought important changes in the physical system of his descendant. The Judge's volume of muscle could hardly be the same as the Colonel's; there was undoubtedly less beef in him. Though looked upon as a weighty man among his contemporaries in respect of animal substance, and as favored with a remarkable degree of fundamental development, well adapting him for the judicial bench, we conceive that the modern Judge Pyncheon, if weighed in the same balance with his ancestor, would have required at least an old-fashioned fifty-six to keep the scale in *equilibrio*. Then, the Judge's face had lost the ruddy English hue that showed its warmth through all the duskiness of the Colonel's weather-beaten cheek, and had taken a sallow shade, the established complexion of his countrymen. If we mistake not, moreover, a certain quality of nervousness had become more or less manifest, even in so solid a specimen of Puritan descent as the gentleman now under discussion. As one of its effects, it bestowed on his countenance a quicker mobility than the old Englishman's had possessed, and keener vivacity, but at the expense of a sturdier something, on which these acute endowments seemed to act like dissolving acids. This process, for aught we know, may belong to the great system of human progress, which, with every ascending footstep, as it diminishes the necessity for animal force, may be destined gradually to spiritualize us, by refining away our grosser attributes of body. If so,

Judge Pyncheon could endure a century or two more of such refinement as well as most other men.

The similarity, intellectual and moral, between the Judge and his ancestor appears to have been at least as strong as the resemblance of mien and feature would afford reason to anticipate. In old Colonel Pyncheon's funeral discourse, the clergyman absolutely canonized his deceased parishioner, and opening, as it were, a vista through the roof of the church, and thence through the firmament above, showed him seated, harp in hand, among the crowned choristers of the spiritual world. On his tombstone, too, the record is highly eulogistic; nor does history, so far as he holds a place upon its page, assail the consistency and uprightness of his character. So also, as regards the Judge Pyncheon of today, neither clergyman, nor legal critic, nor inscriber of tombstones, nor historian of general or local politics, would venture a word against this eminent person's sincerity as a Christian, or respectability as a man, or integrity as a judge, or courage and faithfulness as the often-tried representative of his political party. But, besides these cold, formal, and empty words of the chisel that inscribes, the voice that speaks, and the pen that writes, for the public eye and for distant time—and which inevitably lose much of their truth and freedom by the fatal consciousness of so doing—there were traditions about the ancestor, and private diurnal gossip about the Judge, remarkably accordant in their testimony. It is often instructive to take the woman's, the private and domestic, view of a public man; nor can anything be more curious than the vast discrepancy between portraits intended for engraving and the pencil sketches that pass from hand to hand behind the original's back.

For example: tradition affirmed that the Puritan had been greedy of wealth; the Judge, too, with all the show of liberal expenditure, was said to be as close-fisted as if his gripe were of iron. The ancestor had clothed himself in a grim assumption of kindliness, a rough heartiness of word and manner, which most people took to be the genuine warmth of nature, making its way through the thick and inflexible hide of a manly character. His descendant, in compliance with the requirements of a nicer age, had etherealized this rude benevolence into that broad benignity of smile wherewith he shone like a noonday sun along the streets, or glowed like a household fire in the drawing rooms of his private acquaintance. The Puritan—if not belied by some singular stories, murmured, even at this day, under the narrator's breath—had fallen into certain transgressions to which men of his great animal development, whatever their faith or principles, must continue liable, until they put off impurity, along with the gross earthly substance that involves it. We must not stain our page with any contemporary scandal, to a similar purport, that may have been whispered against the Judge. The Puritan, again, an autocrat in his own household, had worn out three wives, and, merely by the remorseless weight and hardness of his character in the conjugal relation, had sent them, one after another, brokenhearted, to their graves. Here the parallel, in some sort, fails. The Judge had wedded but a single wife, and lost her in the third or fourth year of their marriage. There was a fable, however—for such we choose to consider it, though not impossibly typical of Judge Pyncheon's marital deportment—that the lady got her death blow in the honeymoon, and never smiled again, because her husband compelled her to serve him with coffee every morning at his bedside, in token of fealty to her liege lord and master.

But it is too fruitful a subject, this of hereditary resemblances, the frequent recurrence of which, in a direct line, is truly unaccountable, when we consider how large an accumulation of ancestry lies behind every man at the distance of one or two centuries. We shall only add, therefore, that the Puritan—so, at least, says chimney-corner tradition, which often preserves traits of character with marvelous fidelity—was bold, imperious, relentless, crafty; laying his purposes deep, and following them out with an inveteracy of pursuit that knew neither rest nor conscience; trampling on the weak, and, when essential to his ends, doing his utmost to beat down the strong. Whether the Judge in any degree resembled him, the further progress of our narrative may show.

Scarcely any of the items in the above-drawn parallel

occurred to Phoebe, whose country birth and residence, in truth, had left her pitifully ignorant of most of the family traditions, which lingered, like cobwebs and incrustations of smoke, about the rooms and chimney corners of the House of the Seven Gables. Yet there was a circumstance, very trifling in itself, which impressed her with an odd degree of horror. She had heard of the anathema flung by Maule, the executed wizard, against Colonel Pyncheon and his posterity—that God would give them blood to drink—and likewise of the popular notion that this miraculous blood might now and then be heard gurgling in their throats. The latter scandal—as became a person of sense, and, more especially, a member of the Pyncheon family—Phoebe had set down for the absurdity which it unquestionably was. But ancient superstitions, after being steeped in human hearts and embodied in human breath, and passing from lip to ear in manifold repetition, through a series of generations, become imbued with an effect of homely truth. The smoke of the domestic hearth has scented them through and through. By long transmission among household facts, they grow to look like them, and have such a familiar way of making themselves at home that their influence is usually greater than we suspect. Thus it happened that when Phoebe heard a certain noise in Judge Pyncheon's throat—rather habitual with him, not altogether voluntary, yet indicative of nothing, unless it were a slight bronchial complaint, or, as some people hinted, an apoplectic symptom—when the girl heard this queer and awkward ingurgitation (which the writer never did hear, and therefore cannot describe), she, very foolishly, started, and clasped her hands.

Of course, it was exceedingly ridiculous in Phoebe to be discomposed by such a trifle, and still more unpardonable to show her discomposure to the individual most concerned in it. But the incident chimed in so oddly with her previous fancies about the Colonel and the Judge that, for the moment, it seemed quite to mingle their identity.

"What is the matter with you, young woman?" said Judge Pyncheon, giving her one of his harsh looks. "Are you afraid of anything?"

"Oh, nothing, sir—nothing in the world!" answered

Phoebe, with a little laugh of vexation at herself. "But perhaps you wish to speak with my cousin Hepzibah. Shall I call her?"

"Stay a moment, if you please," said the Judge, again beaming sunshine out of his face. "You seem to be a little nervous this morning. The town air, Cousin Phoebe, does not agree with your good, wholesome country habits. Or has anything happened to disturb you—anything remarkable in Cousin Hepzibah's family? An arrival, eh? I thought so! No wonder you are out of sorts, my little cousin. To be an inmate with such a guest may well startle an innocent young girl!"

"You quite puzzle me, sir," replied Phoebe, gazing inquiringly at the Judge. "There is no frightful guest in the house, but only a poor, gentle, childlike man, whom I believe to be Cousin Hepzibah's brother. I am afraid (but you, sir, will know better than I) that he is not quite in his sound senses; but so mild and quiet he seems to be, that a mother might trust her baby with him; and I think he would play with the baby as if he were only a few years older than itself. He startle me! Oh, no indeed!"

"I rejoice to hear so favorable and so ingenuous an account of my cousin Clifford," said the benevolent Judge. "Many years ago, when we were boys and young men together, I had a great affection for him, and still feel a tender interest in all his concerns. You say, Cousin Phoebe, he appears to be weak-minded. Heaven grant him at least enough of intellect to repent of his past sins!"

"Nobody, I fancy," observed Phoebe, "can have fewer to repent of."

"And is it possible, my dear," rejoined the Judge, with a commiserating look, "that you have never heard of Clifford Pyncheon—that you know nothing of his history? Well, it is all right; and your mother has shown a very proper regard for the good name of the family with which she connected herself. Believe the best you can of this unfortunate person, and hope the best! It is a rule which Christians should always follow, in their judgments of one another; and especially is it right and wise among near relatives, whose characters have necessarily a degree of mutual dependence. But is Clifford in the parlor? I will just step in and see."

"Perhaps, sir, I had better call my cousin Hepzibah," said Phoebe; hardly knowing, however, whether she ought to obstruct the entrance of so affectionate a kinsman into the private regions of the house. "Her brother seemed to be just falling asleep after breakfast; and I am sure she would not like him to be disturbed. Pray, sir, let me give her notice!"

But the Judge showed a singular determination to enter unannounced; and as Phoebe, with the vivacity of a person whose movements unconsciously answer to her thoughts, had stepped towards the door, he used little or no ceremony in putting her aside.

"No, no, Miss Phoebe!" said Judge Pyncheon, in a voice as deep as a thunder growl, and with a frown as black as the cloud whence it issues. "Stay you here! I know the house, and know my cousin Hepzibah, and know her brother Clifford likewise! Nor need my little country cousin put herself to the trouble of announcing me!" In these latter words, by the by, there were symptoms of a change from his sudden harshness into his previous benignity of manner. "I am at home here, Phoebe, you must recollect, and you are the stranger. I will just step in, therefore, and see for myself how Clifford is, and assure him and Hepzibah of my kindly feelings and best wishes. It is right, at this juncture, that they should both hear from my own lips how much I desire to serve them. Ha! Here is Hepzibah herself!"

Such was the case. The vibrations of the Judge's voice had reached the old gentlewoman in the parlor, where she sat, with face averted, waiting on her brother's slumber. She now issued forth, as would appear, to defend the entrance, looking, we must needs say, amazingly like the dragon which, in fairy tales, is wont to be the guardian over an enchanted beauty. The habitual scowl of her brow was, undeniably, too fierce, at this moment, to pass itself off on the innocent score of nearsightedness; and it was bent on Judge Pyncheon in a way that seemed to confound, if not alarm him, so inadequately had he estimated the moral force of a deeply grounded antipathy. She made a repelling gesture with her hand, and stood a perfect picture of prohibition, at full length, in the dark frame of the doorway.

But we must betray Hepzibah's secret, and confess that the native timorousness of her character even now developed itself in a quick tremor, which, to her own perception, set each of her joints at variance with its fellows.

Possibly, the Judge was aware how little true hardihood lay behind Hepzibah's formidable front. At any rate, being a gentleman of steady nerves, he soon recovered himself, and failed not to approach his cousin with outstretched hand; adopting the sensible precaution, however, to cover his advance with a smile so broad and sultry that, had it been only half as warm as it looked, a trellis of grapes might at once have turned purple under its summer-like exposure. It may have been his purpose, indeed, to melt poor Hepzibah on the spot, as if she were a figure of yellow wax.

"Hepzibah, my beloved cousin, I am rejoiced!" exclaimed the Judge, most emphatically. "Now, at length, you have something to live for. Yes, and all of us, let me say, your friends and kindred, have more to live for than we had yesterday. I have lost no time in hastening to offer any assistance in my power towards making Clifford comfortable. He belongs to us all. I know how much he requires—how much he used to require—with his delicate taste, and his love of the beautiful. Anything in my house—pictures, books, wine, luxuries of the table—he may command them all! It would afford me most heartfelt gratification to see him! Shall I step in, this moment?"

"No," replied Hepzibah, her voice quivering too painfully to allow of many words. "He cannot see visitors!"

"A visitor, my dear cousin! Do you call me so?" cried the Judge, whose sensibility, it seems, was hurt by the coldness of the phrase. "Nay, then, let me be Clifford's host, and your own likewise. Come at once to my house. The country air, and all the conveniences—I may say luxuries—that I have gathered about me, will do wonders for him. And you and I, dear Hepzibah, will consult together, and watch together, and labor together, to make our dear Clifford happy. Come! Why should we make more words about what is both a duty and a pleasure on my part? Come to me at once!"

On hearing these so hospitable offers, and such generous recognition of the claims of kindred, Phoebe felt very much in the mood of running up to Judge Pyncheon, and giving him, of her own accord, the kiss from which she had so recently shrunk away. It was quite otherwise with Hepzibah; the Judge's smile seemed to operate on her acerbity of heart like sunshine upon vinegar, making it ten times sourer than ever.

"Clifford," said she, still too agitated to utter more than an abrupt sentence, "Clifford has a home here!"

"May heaven forgive you, Hepzibah," said Judge Pyncheon, reverently lifting his eyes towards that high court of equity to which he appealed, "if you suffer any ancient prejudice or animosity to weigh with you in this matter! I stand here with an open heart, willing and anxious to receive yourself and Clifford into it. Do not refuse my good offices, my earnest propositions for your welfare! They are such, in all respects, as it behooves your nearest kinsman to make. It will be a heavy responsibility, cousin, if you confine your brother to this dismal house and stifled air, when the delightful freedom of my country seat is at his command."

"It would never suit Clifford," said Hepzibah, as briefly as before.

"Woman!" broke forth the Judge, giving way to his resentment. "What is the meaning of all this? Have you other resources? Nay, I suspected as much! Take care, Hepzibah, take care! Clifford is on the brink of as black a ruin as ever befell him yet! But why do I talk with you, woman as you are? Make way! I must see Clifford!"

Hepzibah spread out her gaunt figure across the door, and seemed really to increase in bulk; looking the more terrible, also, because there was so much terror and agitation in her heart. But Judge Pyncheon's evident purpose of forcing a passage was interrupted by a voice from the inner room; a weak, tremulous, wailing voice, indicating helpless alarm, with no more energy for self-defense than belongs to a frightened infant.

"Hepzibah, Hepzibah!" cried the voice. "Go down on your knees to him! Kiss his feet! Entreat him not to come in! Oh, let him have mercy on me! Mercy! Mercy!"

For the instant, it appeared doubtful whether it were not the Judge's resolute purpose to set Hepzibah aside, and step across the threshold into the parlor, whence issued that broken and miserable murmur of entreaty. It was not pity that restrained him, for, at the first sound of the enfeebled voice, a red fire kindled in his eyes, and he made a quick pace forward, with something inexpressibly fierce and grim darkening forth, as it were, out of the whole man. To know Judge Pyncheon was to see him at that moment. After such a revelation, let him smile with what sultriness he would, he could much sooner turn grapes purple, or pumpkins yellow, than melt the iron-branded impression out of the beholder's memory. And it rendered his aspect not the less, but more frightful, that it seemed not to express wrath or hatred, but a certain hot fellness of purpose, which annihilated everything but itself.

Yet, after all, are we not slandering an excellent and amiable man? Look at the Judge now! He is apparently conscious of having erred, in too energetically pressing his deeds of loving-kindness on persons unable to appreciate them. He will await their better mood, and hold himself as ready to assist them then as at this moment. As he draws back from the door, an all-comprehensive benignity blazes from his visage, indicating that he gathers Hepzibah, little Phoebe, and the invisible Clifford, all three, together with the whole world besides, into his immense heart, and gives them a warm bath in its flood of affection.

"You do me great wrong, dear Cousin Hepzibah!" said he, first kindly offering her his hand, and then drawing on his glove preparatory to departure. "Very great wrong! But I forgive it, and will study to make you think better of me. Of course, our poor Clifford being in so unhappy a state of mind, I cannot think of urging an interview at present. But I shall watch over his welfare as if he were my own beloved brother; nor do I at all despair, my dear cousin, of constraining both him and you to acknowledge your injustice. When that shall happen, I desire no other revenge than your acceptance of the best offices in my power to do you."

With a bow to Hepzibah, and a degree of paternal benevolence in his parting nod to Phoebe, the Judge left the shop, and went smiling along the street. As is customary with the rich, when they aim at the honors of a republic, he

apologized, as it were, to the people, for his wealth, prosperity, and elevated station, by a free and hearty manner
towards those who knew him; putting off the more of his
dignity in due proportion with the humbleness of the man
whom he saluted, and thereby proving a haughty consciousness of his advantages as irrefragably as if he had marched
forth preceded by a troop of lackeys to clear the way. On
this particular forenoon, so excessive was the warmth of
Judge Pyncheon's kindly aspect that (such, at least, was the
rumor about town) an extra passage of the water carts was
found essential, in order to lay the dust occasioned by so
much extra sunshine!

No sooner had he disappeared than Hepzibah grew
deadly white, and, staggering towards Phoebe, let her head
fall on the young girl's shoulder.

"Oh, Phoebe!" murmured she. "That man has been the
horror of my life! Shall I never, never have the courage, will
my voice never cease from trembling long enough to let me
tell him what he is?"

"Is he so very wicked?" asked Phoebe. "Yet his offers
were surely kind!"

"Do not speak of them; he has a heart of iron!" rejoined
Hepzibah. "Go now, and talk to Clifford! Amuse and keep
him quiet! It would disturb him wretchedly to see me so
agitated as I am. There, go, dear child, and I will try to look
after the shop."

Phoebe went, accordingly, but perplexed herself, meanwhile, with queries as to the purport of the scene which she
had just witnessed, and also whether judges, clergymen, and
other characters of that eminent stamp and respectability
could really, in any single instance, be otherwise than just
and upright men. A doubt of this nature has a most disturbing influence, and, if shown to be a fact, comes with fearful and startling effect on minds of the trim, orderly, and
limit-loving class, in which we find our little country girl.
Dispositions more boldly speculative may derive a stern
enjoyment from the discovery, since there must be evil in
the world, that a high man is as likely to grasp his share
of it as a low one. A wider scope of view, and a deeper insight, may see rank, dignity, and station all proved illusory,

so far as regards their claim to human reverence, and yet not feel as if the universe were thereby tumbled headlong into chaos. But Phoebe, in order to keep the universe in its old place, was fain to smother, in some degree, her own intuitions as to Judge Pyncheon's character. And as for her cousin's testimony in disparagement of it, she concluded that Hepzibah's judgment was embittered by one of those family feuds which render hatred the more deadly by the dead and corrupted love that they intermingle with its native poison.

❧9❧

Clifford and Phoebe

TRULY was there something high, generous, and noble in the native composition of our poor old Hepzibah! Or else— and it was quite as probably the case—she had been en- riched by poverty, developed by sorrow, elevated by the strong and solitary affection of her life, and thus endowed with heroism, which never could have characterized her in what are called happier circumstances. Through dreary years, Hepzibah had looked forward—for the most part despairingly, never with any confidence of hope, but always with the feeling that it was her brightest possibility—to the very position in which she now found herself. In her own behalf, she had asked nothing of Providence but the oppor- tunity of devoting herself to this brother, whom she had so loved—so admired for what he was, or might have been— and to whom she had kept her faith, alone of all the world, wholly, unfalteringly, at every instant, and throughout life. And here, in his late decline, the lost one had come back out of his long and strange misfortune, and was thrown on her sympathy, as it seemed, not merely for the bread of his physical existence, but for everything that should keep him morally alive. She had responded to the call. She had come forward—our poor, gaunt Hepzibah, in her rusty silks, with her rigid joints, and the sad perversity of her scowl—ready to do her utmost; and with affection enough, if that were all, to do a hundred times as much! There could be few more tearful sights—and heaven forgive us if a smile insist on mingling with our conception of it!—few sights with truer pathos in them than Hepzibah presented on that first afternoon.

How patiently did she endeavor to wrap Clifford up in her great, warm love, and make it all the world to him, so that he should retain no torturing sense of the coldness and dreariness without! Her little efforts to amuse him! How pitiful, yet magnanimous, they were!

Remembering his early love of poetry and fiction, she unlocked a bookcase, and took down several books that had been excellent reading in their day. There was a volume of Pope, with *The Rape of the Lock* in it, and another of *The Tatler,* and an odd one of Dryden's *Miscellanies,* all with tarnished gilding on their covers, and thoughts of tarnished brilliancy inside. They had no success with Clifford. These, and all such writers of society, whose new works glow like the rich texture of a just-woven carpet, must be content to relinquish their charm, for every reader, after an age or two, and could hardly be supposed to retain any portion of it for a mind that had utterly lost its estimate of modes and manners. Hepzibah then took up *Rasselas,* and began to read of the Happy Valley, with a vague idea that some secret of a contented life had there been elaborated which might at least serve Clifford and herself for this one day. But the Happy Valley had a cloud over it. Hepzibah troubled her auditor, moreover, by innumerable sins of emphasis, which he seemed to detect, without any reference to the meaning; nor, in fact, did he appear to take much note of the sense of what she read, but evidently felt the tedium of the lecture, without harvesting its profit. His sister's voice, too, naturally harsh, had, in the course of her sorrowful lifetime, contracted a kind of croak, which, when it once gets into the human throat, is as ineradicable as sin. In both sexes, occasionally, this lifelong croak, accompanying each word of joy or sorrow, is one of the symptoms of a settled melancholy; and wherever it occurs, the whole history of misfortune is conveyed in its slightest accent. The effect is as if the voice had been dyed black; or—if we must use a more moderate simile—this miserable croak, running through all the variations of the voice, is like a black silken thread, on which the crystal beads of speech are strung, and whence they take their hue. Such voices have put on mourning for dead hopes; and they ought to die and be buried along with them!

Discerning that Clifford was not gladdened by her efforts, Hepzibah searched about the house for the means of more exhilarating pastime. At one time, her eyes chanced to rest on Alice Pyncheon's harpsichord. It was a moment of great peril; for—despite the traditionary awe that had gathered over this instrument of music, and the dirges which spiritual fingers were said to play on it—the devoted sister had solemn thoughts of thrumming on its chords for Clifford's benefit, and accompanying the performance with her voice. Poor Clifford! Poor Hepzibah! Poor harpsichord! All three would have been miserable together. By some good agency—possibly, by the unrecognized interposition of the long-buried Alice herself—the threatening calamity was averted.

But the worst of all—the hardest stroke of fate for Hepzibah to endure, and perhaps for Clifford, too—was his invincible distaste for her appearance. Her features, never the most agreeable, and now harsh with age and grief, and resentment against the world for his sake; her dress, and especially her turban; the queer and quaint manners, which had unconsciously grown upon her in solitude—such being the poor gentlewoman's outward characteristics, it is no great marvel, although the mournfulest of pities, that the instinctive lover of the Beautiful was fain to turn away his eyes. There was no help for it. It would be the latest impulse to die within him. In his last extremity, the expiring breath stealing faintly through Clifford's lips, he would doubtless press Hepzibah's hand, in fervent recognition of all her lavished love, and close his eyes—but not so much to die as to be constrained to look no longer on her face! Poor Hepzibah! She took counsel with herself what might be done, and thought of putting ribbons on her turban; but, by the instant rush of several guardian angels, was withheld from an experiment that could hardly have proved less than fatal to the beloved object of her anxiety.

To be brief, besides Hepzibah's disadvantages of person,

there was an uncouthness pervading all her deeds; a clumsy something that could but ill adapt itself for use, and not at all for ornament. She was a grief to Clifford, and she knew it. In this extremity, the antiquated virgin turned to Phoebe. No groveling jealousy was in her heart. Had it pleased heaven to crown the heroic fidelity of her life by making her personally the medium of Clifford's happiness, it would have rewarded her for all the past, by a joy with no bright tints, indeed, but deep and true, and worth a thousand gayer ecstasies. This could not be. She therefore turned to Phoebe, and resigned the task into the young girl's hands. The latter took it up cheerfully, as she did everything, but with no sense of a mission to perform, and succeeding all the better for that same simplicity.

By the involuntary effect of a genial temperament, Phoebe soon grew to be absolutely essential to the daily comfort, if not the daily life, of her two forlorn companions. The grime and sordidness of the House of the Seven Gables seemed to have vanished since her appearance there; the gnawing tooth of the dry rot was stayed among the old timbers of its skeleton frame; the dust had ceased to settle down so densely, from the antique ceilings, upon the floors and furniture of the rooms below—or, at any rate, there was a little housewife, as light-footed as the breeze that sweeps a garden walk, gliding hither and thither to brush it all away. The shadows of gloomy events that haunted the else lonely and desolate apartments; the heavy, breathless scent which death had left in more than one of the bed-chambers, ever since his visits of long ago—these were less powerful than the purifying influence scattered throughout the atmosphere of the household by the presence of one youthful, fresh, and thoroughly wholesome heart. There was no morbidness in Phoebe; if there had been, the old Pyncheon House was the very locality to ripen it into incurable disease. But now her spirit resembled, in its potency, a minute quantity of attar of rose in one of Hepzibah's huge, iron-bound trunks, diffusing its fragrance through the various articles of linen and wrought lace, kerchiefs, caps, stockings, folded dresses, gloves, and whatever else was treasured there. As every article in the great trunk was the sweeter for the rose scent, so did all the thoughts and emotions of Hepzibah and Clifford, somber as they might seem, acquire a subtle attribute of happiness from Phoebe's intermixture with them. Her activity of body, intellect, and heart impelled her continually to perform the ordinary little toils that offered themselves around her, and to think the thought proper for the moment, and to sympathize—now with the twittering gaiety of the robins in the pear tree, and now to such a depth as she could—with Hepzibah's dark anxiety, or the vague moan of her brother. This facile adaptation was at once the symptom of perfect health and its best preservative.

A nature like Phoebe's has invariably its due influence, but is seldom regarded with due honor. Its spiritual force, however, may be partially estimated by the fact of her having found a place for herself, amid circumstances so stern as those which surrounded the mistress of the house; and also by the effect which she produced on a character of so much more mass than her own. For the gaunt, bony frame and limbs of Hepzibah, as compared with the tiny lightsomeness of Phoebe's figure, were perhaps in some fit proportion with the moral weight and substance, respectively, of the woman and the girl.

To the guest, to Hepzibah's brother—or Cousin Clifford, as Phoebe now began to call him—she was especially necessary. Not that he could ever be said to converse with her, or often manifest, in any other very definite mode, his sense of a charm in her society. But if she were a long while absent, he became pettish and nervously restless, pacing the room to and fro with the uncertainty that characterized all his movements; or else would sit broodingly in his great chair, resting his head on his hands, and evincing life only by an electric sparkle of ill humor, whenever Hepzibah endeavored to arouse him. Phoebe's presence, and the contiguity of her fresh life to his blighted one, was usually all that he required. Indeed, such was the native gush and play of her spirit that she was seldom perfectly quiet and undemonstrative, any more than a fountain ever ceases to dimple and warble with its flow. She possessed the gift of song, and that, too, so naturally that you would as little think of inquiring whence she had caught it, or what master had taught her, as of asking the same questions about a bird, in whose small strain of music we recognize the voice of the Creator as distinctly as in the loudest accents of His thunder. So long as Phoebe sang, she might stray at her own will about the house. Clifford was content, whether the sweet, airy homeliness of her tones came down from the upper chambers, or along the passageway from the shop, or was sprinkled through the foliage of the pear tree, inward from the garden, with the twinkling sunbeams. He would sit quietly, with a gentle pleasure gleaming over his face, brighter now, and now a little dimmer, as the song happened to float near him, or was more remotely heard. It pleased him best, however, when she sat on a low footstool at his knee.

It is perhaps remarkable, considering her temperament, that Phoebe oftener chose a strain of pathos than of gaiety. But the young and happy are not ill pleased to temper their life with a transparent shadow. The deepest pathos of Phoebe's voice and song, moreover, came sifted through the golden texture of a cheery spirit, and was somehow so interfused with the quality thence acquired that one's heart felt all the lighter for having wept at it. Broad mirth, in the sacred presence of dark misfortune, would have jarred harshly and irreverently with the solemn symphony that rolled its undertone through Hepzibah's and her brother's life. Therefore, it was well that Phoebe so often chose sad themes, and not amiss that they ceased to be so sad while she was singing them.

Becoming habituated to her companionship, Clifford readily showed how capable of imbibing pleasant tints and gleams of cheerful light from all quarters his nature must originally have been. He grew youthful while she sat by him. A beauty—not precisely real, even in its utmost manifestation, and which a painter would have watched long to seize and fix upon his canvas, and, after all, in vain—beauty, nevertheless, that was not a mere dream would sometimes play upon and illuminate his face. It did more than to illuminate; it transfigured him with an expression that could only be interpreted as the glow of an exquisite and happy spirit. That gray hair, and those furrows—with their record of infinite sorrow so deeply written across his brow, and so compressed, as with a futile effort to crowd in all the tale, that the whole inscription was made illegible—these, for the moment, vanished. An eye, at once tender and acute, might have beheld in the man some shadow of what he was meant to be. Anon, as age came stealing, like a sad twilight, back over his figure, you would have felt tempted to hold an argument with Destiny, and affirm that either this being should not have been made mortal, or mortal existence should have been tempered to his qualities. There seemed no necessity for his having drawn breath at all; the world never wanted him; but, as he had breathed, it ought always to have been the balmiest of summer air. The same perplexity will invariably haunt us with regard to natures that tend to feed exclusively upon the Beautiful, let their earthly fate be as lenient as it may.

Phoebe, it is probable, had but a very imperfect comprehension of the character over which she had thrown so beneficent a spell. Nor was it necessary. The fire upon the hearth can gladden a whole semicircle of faces round about it, but need not know the individuality of one among them all. Indeed, there was something too fine and delicate in Clifford's traits to be perfectly appreciated by one whose sphere lay so much in the Actual as Phoebe's did. For Clifford, however, the reality, and simplicity, and thorough homeliness of the girl's nature were as powerful a charm as any that she possessed. Beauty, it is true, and beauty almost perfect in its own style, was indispensable. Had Phoebe been coarse in feature, shaped clumsily, of a harsh voice, and uncouthly mannered, she might have been rich with all good gifts, beneath this unfortunate exterior, and still, so long as she wore the guise of woman, she would have shocked Clifford, and depressed him by her lack of beauty. But nothing more beautiful—nothing prettier, at least—was ever made than Phoebe. And, therefore, to this man—whose whole poor and impalpable enjoyment of existence heretofore, and until both his heart and fancy died within him, had been a dream; whose images of women had more and more lost their warmth and substance, and been frozen, like the pictures of secluded artists, into the dullest ideality—to him, this little figure of the cheeriest household life was just what he required to bring him back into the breathing world. Persons who have wandered, or been expelled, out of the common track of things, even were it for a better system, desire nothing so much as to be led back. They shiver in their loneliness, be it on a mountaintop or in a dungeon. Now, Phoebe's presence made a home about her—that very sphere which the outcast, the prisoner, the potentate; the wretch beneath mankind, the wretch aside from it, or the wretch above it instinctively pines after—a home! She was real! Holding her hand, you felt something; a tender something; a substance, and a warm one—and so long as you should feel its grasp, soft as it was, you might be certain that your place was good in the whole sympathetic chain of human nature. The world was no longer a delusion.

By looking a little further in this direction, we might suggest an explanation of an often-suggested mystery. Why are poets so apt to choose their mates not for any similarity of poetic endowment, but for qualities which might make the happiness of the rudest handicraftsman as well as that of the ideal craftsman of the spirit? Because, probably, at his highest elevation, the poet needs no human intercourse; but he finds it dreary to descend, and be a stranger.

There was something very beautiful in the relation that grew up between this pair, so closely and constantly linked together, yet with such a waste of gloomy and mysterious years from his birthday to hers. On Clifford's part it was the feeling of a man naturally endowed with the liveliest sensibility to feminine influence, but who had never quaffed the cup of passionate love, and knew that it was now too late. He knew it, with the instinctive delicacy that had survived his intellectual decay. Thus, his sentiment for Phoebe, without being paternal, was not less chaste than if she had been his daughter. He was a man, it is true, and recognized her as a woman. She was his only representative of womankind. He took unfailing note of every charm that appertained to her sex, and saw the ripeness of her lips, and the virginal development of her bosom. All her little womanly ways, budding out of her like blossoms on a young fruit tree, had their effect on him, and sometimes caused his very heart to tingle with the keenest thrills of pleasure. At such moments—for the effect was seldom more than momentary—the half-torpid man would be full of harmonious life, just as a long-silent harp is full of sound, when the musician's fingers sweep across it. But, after all, it seemed rather a perception, or a sympathy, than a sentiment belonging to himself as an individual. He read Phoebe, as he would a sweet and simple story; he listened to her, as if she were a verse of household poetry, which God, in requital of his bleak and dismal lot, had permitted some angel, that most pitied him, to warble through the house. She was not an actual fact for him, but the interpretation of all that he had lacked on earth brought warmly home to his conception; so that this mere symbol, or lifelike picture, had almost the comfort of reality.

But we strive in vain to put the idea into words. No adequate expression of the beauty and profound pathos with which it impresses us is attainable. This being, made only for happiness, and heretofore so miserably failing to be happy—his tendencies so hideously thwarted that, some unknown time ago, the delicate springs of his character, never morally or intellectually strong, had given way, and he was now imbecile—this poor, forlorn voyager from the Islands of the Blest, in a frail bark, on a tempestuous sea, had been flung, by the last mountain wave of his shipwreck, into a quiet harbor. There, as he lay more than half lifeless on the strand, the fragrance of an earthly rosebud had come to his nostrils, and, as odors will, had summoned up reminiscences or visions of all the living and breathing beauty amid which he should have had his home. With his native susceptibility of happy influences, he inhales the slight, ethereal rapture into his soul, and expires!

And how did Phoebe regard Clifford? The girl's was not one of those natures which are most attracted by what is strange and exceptional in human character. The path which would best have suited her was the well-worn track of ordinary life; the companions in whom she would most have delighted were such as one encounters at every turn. The mystery which enveloped Clifford, so far as it affected her at all, was an annoyance, rather than the piquant charm which many women might have found in it. Still, her native kindliness was brought strongly into play, not by what was darkly picturesque in his situation, nor so much, even, by the finer graces of his character, as by the simple appeal of a heart so forlorn as his to one so full of genuine sympathy as hers. She gave him an affectionate regard, because he needed so much love, and seemed to have received so little. With a ready tact, the result of ever-active and wholesome sensibility, she discerned what was good for him, and did it. Whatever was morbid in his mind and experience she ignored; and thereby kept their intercourse healthy, by the incautious, but, as it were, heaven-directed freedom of her whole conduct. The sick in mind, and, perhaps, in body, are rendered more darkly and hopelessly so by the manifold reflection of their disease, mirrored back from all quarters in the deportment of those about them; they are compelled to inhale the poison of their own breath, in infinite repetition. But Phoebe afforded her poor patient a supply of purer air. She impregnated it, too, not with a wild-flower scent—for wildness was no trait of hers—but with the perfume of garden roses, pinks, and other blossoms of much sweetness, which nature and man have consented together in making grow from summer to summer, and from century to century. Such a flower was Phoebe, in her relation with Clifford, and such the delight that he inhaled from her.

Yet, it must be said, her petals sometimes drooped a little, in consequence of the heavy atmosphere about her. She grew more thoughtful than heretofore. Looking aside at Clifford's face, and seeing the dim, unsatisfactory elegance and the intellect almost quenched, she would try to inquire what had been his life. Was he always thus? Had this veil been over him from his birth—this veil under which far more of his spirit was hidden than revealed, and through which he so imperfectly discerned the actual world—or was its gray texture woven of some dark calamity? Phoebe loved no riddles, and would have been glad to escape the perplexity of this one. Nevertheless, there was so far a good result of her meditations on Clifford's character that, when her involuntary conjectures, together with the tendency of every strange circumstance to tell its own story, had gradually taught her the fact, it had no terrible effect upon her. Let the world have done him what vast wrong it might, she knew Cousin Clifford too well—or fancied so—ever to shudder at the touch of his thin, delicate fingers.

Within a few days after the appearance of this remarkable inmate, the routine of life had established itself with a good deal of uniformity in the old house of our narrative. In the morning, very shortly after breakfast, it was Clifford's custom to fall asleep in his chair; nor, unless accidentally disturbed, would he emerge from a dense cloud of slumber or the thinner mists that flitted to and fro, until well towards noonday. These hours of drowsihead were the season of the old gentlewoman's attendance on her brother, while Phoebe took charge of the shop; an arrangement which the public speedily understood, and evinced their decided preference of the younger shopwoman by the multiplicity of their calls during her administration of affairs. Dinner over, Hepzibah took her knitting work—a long stocking of gray yarn, for her brother's winter wear—and with a sigh, and a scowl of affectionate farewell to Clifford, and a gesture enjoining watchfulness on Phoebe, went to take her seat behind the counter. It was now the young girl's turn to be the nurse, the guardian, the playmate—or whatever is the fitter phrase—of the gray-haired man.

❧10❧

The Pyncheon Garden

CLIFFORD, except for Phoebe's more active instigation, would ordinarily have yielded to the torpor which had crept through all his modes of being, and which sluggishly counseled him to sit in his morning chair till eventide. But the girl seldom failed to propose a removal to the garden, where Uncle Venner and the daguerreotypist had made such repairs on the roof of the ruinous arbor, or summer-house, that it was now a sufficient shelter from sunshine and casual showers. The hopvine, too, had begun to grow luxuriantly over the sides of the little edifice, and made an interior of verdant seclusion, with innumerable peeps and glimpses into the wider solitude of the garden.

Here, sometimes, in this green play place of flickering light, Phoebe read to Clifford. Her acquaintance, the artist, who appeared to have a literary turn, had supplied her with works of fiction, in pamphlet form, and a few volumes of poetry, in altogether a different style and taste from those which Hepzibah selected for his amusement. Small thanks were due to the books, however, if the girl's readings were in any degree more successful than her elderly cousin's. Phoebe's voice had always a pretty music in it, and could either enliven Clifford by its sparkle and gaiety of tone, or soothe him by a continued flow of pebbly and brooklike cadences. But the fictions—in which the country girl, unused to works of that nature, often became deeply absorbed—interested her strange auditor very little, or not at all. Pictures of life, scenes of passion or sentiment, wit, humor, and pathos, were all thrown away, or worse than thrown away, on Clifford; either because he lacked an experience by which to test their truth, or because his own griefs were a touchstone of reality that few feigned emotions could withstand. When Phoebe broke into a peal of merry laughter at what she read, he would now and then laugh for sympathy, but oftener respond with a troubled, questioning look. If a tear—a maiden's sunshiny tear over imaginary woe— dropped upon some melancholy page, Clifford either took it as a token of actual calamity, or else grew peevish, and angrily motioned her to close the volume. And wisely, too! Is not the world sad enough, in genuine earnest, without making a pastime of mock sorrows?

With poetry it was rather better. He delighted in the swell and subsidence of the rhythm, and the happily recurring rhyme. Nor was Clifford incapable of feeling the sentiment of poetry—not, perhaps, where it was highest or deepest, but where it was most flitting and ethereal. It was impossible to foretell in what exquisite verse the awakening spell might lurk; but, on raising her eyes from the page to Clifford's face, Phoebe would be made aware, by the light breaking through it, that a more delicate intelligence than her own had caught a lambent flame from what she read. One glow of this kind, however, was often the precursor of gloom for many hours afterward; because, when the glow left him, he seemed conscious of a missing sense and power, and groped about for them, as if a blind man should go seeking his lost eyesight.

It pleased him more, and was better for his inward welfare, that Phoebe should talk, and make passing occurrences vivid to his mind by her accompanying description and remarks. The life of the garden offered topics enough for such discourse as suited Clifford best. He never failed to inquire what flowers had bloomed since yesterday. His feeling for flowers was very exquisite, and seemed not so much a taste as an emotion; he was fond of sitting with one in his hand, intently observing it, and looking from its petals into Phoebe's face, as if the garden flower were the sister of the household maiden. Not merely was there a delight in the flower's perfume, or pleasure in its beautiful form, and the delicacy or brightness of its hue; but Clifford's enjoyment was accompanied with a perception of life, character, and individuality that made him love these blossoms of the garden, as if they were endowed with sentiment and intelligence. This affection and sympathy for flowers is almost exclusively a woman's trait. Men, if endowed with it by nature, soon lose, forget, and learn to despise it, in their contact with coarser things than flowers. Clifford, too, had long forgotten it; but found it again now, as he slowly revived from the chill torpor of his life.

It is wonderful how many pleasant incidents continually came to pass in that secluded garden spot when once Phoebe had set herself to look for them. She had seen or heard a bee there, on the first day of her acquaintance with the place. And often—almost continually, indeed—since then, the bees kept coming thither, heaven knows why, or by what pertinacious desire, for far-fetched sweets, when, no doubt, there were broad clover fields, and all kinds of garden growth, much nearer home than this. Thither the bees came, however, and plunged into the squash blossoms, as if there were no other squash vines within a long day's flight, or as if the soil of Hepzibah's garden gave its productions just the very quality which these laborious little wizards wanted, in order to impart the Hymettus odor to their whole hive of New England honey. When Clifford heard their sunny, buzzing murmur, in the heart of the great yellow blossoms, he looked about him with a joyful sense of warmth, and blue sky, and green grass, and of God's free air in the whole height from earth to heaven. After all, there need be no question why the bees came to that one green nook in the dusty town. God sent them thither to gladden our poor Clifford. They brought the rich summer with them, in requital of a little honey.

When the bean vines began to flower on the poles, there was one particular variety which bore a vivid scarlet blossom. The daguerreotypist had found these beans in a garret, over one of the seven gables, treasured up in an old chest of drawers by some horticultural Pyncheon of days gone by, who, doubtless, meant to sow them the next sum-

mer, but was himself first sown in Death's garden ground.
By way of testing whether there were still a living germ in
such ancient seeds, Holgrave had planted some of them;
and the result of his experiment was a splendid row of
bean vines, clambering, early, to the full height of the poles,
and arraying them, from top to bottom, in a spiral profu-
sion of red blossoms. And, ever since the unfolding of the
first bud, a multitude of hummingbirds had been attracted
thither. At times, it seemed as if for every one of the hundred blossoms, there was one of these tiniest fowls of the
air—a thumb's bigness of burnished plumage, hovering
and vibrating about the bean poles. It was with indescribable interest, and even more than childish delight, that Clifford watched the hummingbirds. He used to thrust his head
softly out of the arbor to see them the better; all the while,
too, motioning Phoebe to be quiet, and snatching glimpses
of the smile upon her face, so as to heap his enjoyment up
the higher with her sympathy. He had not merely grown
young—he was a child again.

Hepzibah, whenever she happened to witness one of
these fits of miniature enthusiasm, would shake her head,
with a strange mingling of the mother and sister, and of
pleasure and sadness, in her aspect. She said that it had
always been thus with Clifford when the hummingbirds
came—always, from his babyhood—and that his delight
in them had been one of the earliest tokens by which he
showed his love for beautiful things. And it was a wonderful coincidence, the good lady thought, that the artist
should have planted these scarlet-flowering beans—which
the hummingbirds sought far and wide, and which had not
grown in the Pyncheon garden before for forty years—on
the very summer of Clifford's return.

Then would the tears stand in poor Hepzibah's eyes, or
overflow them with a too abundant gush, so that she was
fain to betake herself into some corner lest Clifford should
espy her agitation. Indeed, all the enjoyments of this period
were provocative of tears. Coming so late as it did, it was
a kind of Indian summer, with a mist in its balmiest sunshine, and decay and death in its gaudiest delight. The more
Clifford seemed to taste the happiness of a child, the sad-

der was the difference to be recognized. With a mysterious and terrible Past, which had annihilated his memory, and a blank Future before him, he had only this visionary and impalpable Now, which, if you once look closely at it, is nothing. He himself, as was perceptible by many symptoms, lay darkly behind his pleasure, and knew it to be a baby play, which he was to toy and trifle with, instead of thoroughly believing. Clifford saw, it may be, in the mirror of his deeper consciousness, that he was an example and representative of that great class of people whom an inexplicable Providence is continually putting at cross-purposes with the world: breaking what seems its own promise in their nature; withholding their proper food, and setting poison before them for a banquet; and thus—when it might so easily, as one would think, have been adjusted otherwise—making their existence a strangeness, a solitude, and torment. All his life long, he had been learning how to be wretched, as one learns a foreign tongue; and now, with the lesson thoroughly by heart, he could with difficulty comprehend his little airy happiness. Frequently, there was a dim shadow of doubt in his eyes. "Take my hand, Phoebe," he would say, "and pinch it hard with your little fingers! Give me a rose, that I may press its thorns, and prove myself awake by the sharp touch of pain!" Evidently, he desired this prick of a trifling anguish, in order to assure himself, by that quality which he best knew to be real, that the garden, and the seven weather-beaten gables, and Hepzibah's scowl, and Phoebe's smile, were real likewise. Without this signet in his flesh, he could have attributed no more substance to them than to the empty confusion of imaginary scenes with which he had fed his spirit, until even that poor sustenance was exhausted.

The author needs great faith in his reader's sympathy; else he must hesitate to give details so minute, and incidents apparently so trifling, as are essential to make up the idea of this garden life. It was the Eden of a thunder-smitten Adam, who had fled for refuge thither out of the same dreary and perilous wilderness into which the original Adam was expelled.

One of the available means of amusement, of which

Phoebe made the most in Clifford's behalf, was that feathered society, the hens, a breed of whom, as we have already said, was an immemorial heirloom in the Pyncheon family. In compliance with a whim of Clifford, as it troubled him to see them in confinement, they had been set at liberty, and now roamed at will about the garden; doing some little mischief but hindered from escape by buildings on three sides, and the difficult peaks of a wooden fence on the other. They spent much of their abundant leisure on the margin of Maule's well, which was haunted by a kind of snail, evidently a titbit to their palates; and the brackish water itself, however nauseous to the rest of the world, was so greatly esteemed by these fowls that they might be seen tasting, turning up their heads, and smacking their bills, with precisely the air of wine-bibbers round a probationary cask. Their generally quiet, yet often brisk, and constantly diversified talk, one to another, or sometimes in soliloquy—as they scratched worms out of the rich, black soil, or pecked at such plants as suited their taste—had such a domestic tone that it was almost a wonder why you could not establish a regular interchange of ideas about household matters, human and gallinaceous. All hens are well worth studying for the piquancy and rich variety of their manners; but by no possibility can there have been other fowls of such odd appearance and deportment as these ancestral ones. They probably embodied the traditionary peculiarities of their whole line of progenitors, derived through an unbroken succession of eggs; or else this individual Chanticleer and his two wives had grown to be humorists, and a little crack-brained withal, on account of their solitary way of life, and out of sympathy for Hepzibah, their lady patroness.

Queer, indeed, they looked! Chanticleer himself, though stalking on two stiltlike legs, with the dignity of interminable descent in all his gestures, was hardly bigger than an ordinary partridge; his two wives were about the size of quails; and as for the one chicken, it looked small enough to be still in the egg, and, at the same time, sufficiently old, withered, wizened, and experienced, to have been the founder of the antiquated race. Instead of being the youngest of the family, it rather seemed to have aggregated into itself the ages not only of these living specimens of the breed, but of all its forefathers and foremothers, whose united excellences and oddities were squeezed into its little body. Its mother evidently regarded it as the one chicken of the world, and as necessary, in fact, to the world's continuance, or, at any rate, to the equilibrium of the present system of affairs, whether in church or state. No lesser sense of the infant fowl's importance could have justified, even in a mother's eyes, the perseverance with which she watched over its safety, ruffling her small person to twice its proper size, and flying in everybody's face that so much as looked towards her hopeful progeny. No lower estimate could have vindicated the indefatigable zeal with which she scratched, and her unscrupulousness in digging up the choicest flower or vegetable, for the sake of the fat earthworm at its root. Her nervous cluck, when the chicken happened to be hidden in the long grass or under the squash leaves; her gentle croak of satisfaction, while sure of it beneath her wing; her note of ill-concealed fear and obstreperous defiance, when she saw her archenemy, a neighbor's cat, on the top of the high fence—one or other of these sounds was to be heard at almost every moment of the day. By degrees, the observer came to feel nearly as much interest in this chicken of illustrious race as the mother hen did.

Phoebe, after getting well acquainted with the old hen, was sometimes permitted to take the chicken in her hand, which was quite capable of grasping its cubic inch or two of body. While she curiously examined its hereditary marks—the peculiar speckle of its plumage, the funny tuft on its head, and a knob on each of its legs—the little biped, as she insisted, kept giving her a sagacious wink. The daguerreotypist once whispered her that these marks betokened the oddities of the Pyncheon family, and that the chicken itself was a symbol of the life of the old house, embodying its interpretation, likewise, although an unintelligible one, as such clues generally are. It was a feathered riddle; a mystery hatched out of an egg, and just as mysterious as if the egg had been addle!

The second of Chanticleer's two wives, ever since Phoebe's arrival, had been in a state of heavy despondency,

caused, as it afterwards appeared, by her inability to lay
an egg. One day, however, by her self-important gait, the
sideway turn of her head, and the cock of her eye, as she
pried into one and another nook of the garden—croaking
to herself, all the while, with inexpressible complacency—it
was made evident that this identical hen, much as mankind
undervalued her, carried something about her person the
worth of which was not to be estimated either in gold or
precious stones. Shortly after, there was a prodigious cackling and gratulation of Chanticleer and all his family, including the wizened chicken, who appeared to understand
the matter quite as well as did his sire, his mother, or his
aunt. That afternoon, Phoebe found a diminutive egg—not
in the regular nest, it was far too precious to be trusted
there—but cunningly hidden under the currant bushes, on
some dry stalks of last year's grass. Hepzibah, on learning
the fact, took possession of the egg and appropriated it to
Clifford's breakfast, on account of a certain delicacy of flavor, for which, as she affirmed, these eggs had always been
famous. Thus unscrupulously did the old gentlewoman
sacrifice the continuance, perhaps, of an ancient feathered
race, with no better end than to supply her brother with a
dainty that hardly filled the bowl of a teaspoon! It must
have been in reference to this outrage that Chanticleer, the
next day, accompanied by the bereaved mother of the egg,
took his post in front of Phoebe and Clifford, and delivered
himself of a harangue that might have proved as long as
his own pedigree, but for a fit of merriment on Phoebe's
part. Hereupon, the offended fowl stalked away on his long
stilts, and utterly withdrew his notice from Phoebe and the
rest of human nature, until she made her peace with an offering of spice cake, which, next to snails, was the delicacy
most in favor with his aristocratic taste.

We linger too long, no doubt, beside this paltry rivulet
of life that flowed through the garden of the Pyncheon
House. But we deem it pardonable to record these mean
incidents and poor delights, because they proved so greatly
to Clifford's benefit. They had the earth smell in them, and
contributed to give him health and substance. Some of his
occupations wrought less desirably upon him. He had a sin-

gular propensity, for example, to hang over Maule's well, and look at the constantly shifting phantasmagoria of figures produced by the agitation of the water over the mosaicwork of colored pebbles at the bottom. He said that faces looked upward to him there—beautiful faces, arrayed in bewitching smiles—each momentary face so fair and rosy, and every smile so sunny, that he felt wronged at its departure, until the same flitting witchcraft made a new one. But sometimes he would suddenly cry out, "The dark face gazes at me!" and be miserable the whole day afterwards. Phoebe, when she hung over the fountain by Clifford's side, could see nothing of all this—neither the beauty nor the ugliness— but only the colored pebbles, looking as if the gush of the waters shook and disarranged them. And the dark face, that so troubled Clifford, was no more than the shadow thrown from a branch of one of the damson trees, and breaking the inner light of Maule's well. The truth was, however, that his fancy—reviving faster than his will and judgment, and always stronger than they—created shapes of loveliness that were symbolic of his native character, and now and then a stern and dreadful shape that typified his fate.

On Sundays, after Phoebe had been at church—for the girl had a churchgoing conscience, and would hardly have been at ease had she missed either prayer, singing, sermon, or benediction—after churchtime, therefore, there was, ordinarily, a sober little festival in the garden. In addition to Clifford, Hepzibah, and Phoebe, two guests made up the company. One was the artist, Holgrave, who, in spite of his consociation with reformers, and his other queer and questionable traits, continued to hold an elevated place in Hepzibah's regard. The other, we are almost ashamed to say, was the venerable Uncle Venner, in a clean shirt, and a broadcloth coat, more respectable than his ordinary wear, inasmuch as it was neatly patched on each elbow, and might be called an entire garment, except for a slight inequality in the length of its skirts. Clifford, on several occasions, had seemed to enjoy the old man's intercourse, for the sake of his mellow, cheerful vein, which was like the sweet flavor of a frost-bitten apple, such as one picks up under the tree in December. A man at the very lowest point of the social

scale was easier and more agreeable for the fallen gentleman to encounter than a person at any of the intermedi-
ate degrees; and, moreover, as Clifford's young manhood
had been lost, he was fond of feeling himself comparatively
youthful, now, in apposition with the patriarchal age of
Uncle Venner. In fact, it was sometimes observable that
Clifford half willfully hid from himself the consciousness of
being stricken in years, and cherished visions of an earthly
future still before him; visions, however, too indistinctly
drawn to be followed by disappointment—though, doubtless, by depression—when any casual incident or recollection made him sensible of the withered leaf.

So this oddly composed little social party used to assemble under the ruinous arbor. Hepzibah—stately as ever at
heart, and yielding not an inch of her old gentility, but resting upon it so much the more, as justifying a princess-like
condescension—exhibited a not ungraceful hospitality. She
talked kindly to the vagrant artist, and took sage counsel—
lady as she was—with the wood-sawyer, the messenger of
everybody's petty errands, the patched philosopher. And
Uncle Venner, who had studied the world at street corners,
and other posts equally well adapted for just observation,
was as ready to give out his wisdom as a town pump to give
water.

"Miss Hepzibah, ma'am," said he once, after they had
all been cheerful together, "I really enjoy these quiet little
meetings of a Sabbath afternoon. They are very much like
what I expect to have after I retire to my farm!"

"Uncle Venner," observed Clifford, in a drowsy, inward
tone, "is always talking about his farm. But I have a better
scheme for him, by and by. We shall see!"

"Ah, Mr. Clifford Pyncheon!" said the man of patches.
"You may scheme for me as much as you please; but I'm not
going to give up this one scheme of my own, even if I never
bring it really to pass. It does seem to me that men make
a wonderful mistake in trying to heap up property upon
property. If I had done so, I should feel as if Providence was
not bound to take care of me; and, at all events, the city
wouldn't be! I'm one of those people who think that infinity
is big enough for us all—and eternity long enough."

"Why, so they are, Uncle Venner," remarked Phoebe, after a pause; for she had been trying to fathom the profundity and appositeness of this concluding apothegm. "But for this short life of ours, one would like a house and a moderate garden spot of one's own."

"It appears to me," said the daguerreotypist, smiling, "that Uncle Venner has the principles of Fourier at the bottom of his wisdom; only they have not quite so much distinctness, in his mind, as in that of the systematizing Frenchman."

"Come, Phoebe," said Hepzibah, "it is time to bring the currants."

And then, while the yellow richness of the declining sunshine still fell into the open space of the garden, Phoebe brought out a loaf of bread and a china bowl of currants, freshly gathered from the bushes, and crushed with sugar. These, with water—but not from the fountain of ill omen, close at hand—constituted all the entertainment. Meanwhile, Holgrave took some pains to establish an intercourse with Clifford, actuated, it might seem, entirely by an impulse of kindliness, in order that the present hour might be cheerfuler than most which the poor recluse had spent, or was destined yet to spend. Nevertheless, in the artist's deep, thoughtful, all-observant eyes, there was, now and then, an expression not sinister, but questionable; as if he had some other interest in the scene than a stranger, a youthful and unconnected adventurer, might be supposed to have. With great mobility of outward mood, however, he applied himself to the task of enlivening the party; and with so much success that even dark-hued Hepzibah threw off one tint of melancholy, and made what shift she could with the remaining portion. Phoebe said to herself, "How pleasant he can be!" As for Uncle Venner, as a mark of friendship and approbation, he readily consented to afford the young man his countenance in the way of his profession—not metaphorically, be it understood, but literally, by allowing a daguerreotype of his face, so familiar to the town, to be exhibited at the entrance of Holgrave's studio.

Clifford, as the company partook of their little banquet, grew to be the gayest of them all. Either it was one of those upquivering flashes of the spirit, to which minds in an abnormal state are liable, or else the artist had subtly touched some chord that made musical vibration. Indeed, what with the pleasant summer evening, and the sympathy of this little circle of not unkindly souls, it was perhaps natural that a character so susceptible as Clifford's should become animated, and show itself readily responsive to what was said around him. But he gave out his own thoughts, likewise, with an airy and fanciful glow; so that they glistened, as it were, through the arbor, and made their escape among the interstices of the foliage. He had been as cheerful, no doubt, while alone with Phoebe, but never with such tokens of acute, although partial, intelligence.

But, as the sunlight left the peaks of the Seven Gables, so did the excitement fade out of Clifford's eyes. He gazed vaguely and mournfully about him, as if he missed something precious, and missed it the more drearily for not knowing precisely what it was.

"I want my happiness!" at last he murmured, hoarsely and indistinctly, hardly shaping out the words. "Many, many years have I waited for it! It is late! It is late! I want my happiness!"

Alas, poor Clifford! You are old, and worn with troubles that ought never to have befallen you. You are partly crazy and partly imbecile; a ruin, a failure, as almost everybody is—though some in less degree, or less perceptibly, than their fellows. Fate has no happiness in store for you; unless your quiet home in the old family residence with the faithful Hepzibah, and your long summer afternoons with Phoebe, and these Sabbath festivals with Uncle Venner and the daguerreotypist deserve to be called happiness! Why not? If not the thing itself, it is marvelously like it, and the more so for that ethereal and intangible quality which causes it all to vanish at too close an introspection. Take it, therefore, while you may! Murmur not—question not—but make the most of it!

❦11❧

The Arched Window

FROM the inertness, or what we may term the vegetative character, of his ordinary mood, Clifford would perhaps have been content to spend one day after another, interminably—or, at least, throughout the summertime—in just the kind of life described in the preceding pages. Fancying, however, that it might be for his benefit occasionally to diversify the scene, Phoebe sometimes suggested that he should look out upon the life of the street. For this purpose, they used to mount the staircase together, to the second story of the house, where, at the termination of a wide entry, there was an arched window of uncommonly large dimensions, shaded by a pair of curtains. It opened above the porch, where there had formerly been a balcony, the balustrade of which had long since gone to decay, and been removed. At this arched window, throwing it open but keeping himself in comparative obscurity by means of the curtain, Clifford had an opportunity of witnessing such a portion of the great world's movement as might be supposed to roll through one of the retired streets of a not very populous city. But he and Phoebe made a sight as well worth seeing as any that the city could exhibit. The pale, gray, childish, aged, melancholy, yet often simply cheerful, and sometimes delicately intelligent aspect of Clifford, peering from behind the faded crimson of the curtain— watching the monotony of everyday occurrences with a kind of inconsequential interest and earnestness, and, at every petty throb of his sensibility, turning for sympathy to the eyes of the bright young girl!

If once he were fairly seated at the window, even Pyncheon Street would hardly be so dull and lonely but that, somewhere or other along its extent, Clifford might discover matter to occupy his eye, and titillate, if not engross, his observation. Things familiar to the youngest child that had begun its outlook at existence seemed strange to him. A cab; an omnibus, with its populous interior, dropping here and there a passenger, and picking up another, and thus typifying that vast rolling vehicle the world, the end of whose journey is everywhere and nowhere; these objects he followed eagerly with his eyes, but forgot them before the dust raised by the horses and wheels had settled along their track. As regarded novelties (among which cabs and omnibuses were to be reckoned), his mind appeared to have lost its proper gripe and retentiveness. Twice or thrice, for example, during the sunny hours of the day, a water cart went along by the Pyncheon House, leaving a broad wake of moistened earth, instead of the white dust that had risen at a lady's lightest footfall; it was like a summer shower, which the city authorities had caught and tamed, and compelled it into the commonest routine of their convenience. With the water cart Clifford could never grow familiar; it always affected him with just the same surprise as at first. His mind took an apparently sharp impression from it, but lost the recollection of this perambulatory shower, before its next reappearance, as completely as did the street itself, along which the heat so quickly strewed white dust again. It was the same with the railroad. Clifford could hear the obstreperous howl of the steam devil, and, by leaning a little way from the arched window, could catch a glimpse of the trains of cars, flashing a brief transit across the extremity of the street. The idea of terrible energy thus forced upon him was new at every recurrence, and seemed to affect him as disagreeably, and with almost as much surprise, the hundredth time as the first.

Nothing gives a sadder sense of decay than this loss or suspension of the power to deal with unaccustomed things, and to keep up with the swiftness of the passing moment. It can merely be a suspended animation; for, were the power actually to perish, there would be little use of immortality. We are less than ghosts, for the time being, whenever this calamity befalls us.

Clifford was indeed the most inveterate of conservatives. All the antique fashions of the street were dear to him; even such as were characterized by a rudeness that would naturally have annoyed his fastidious senses. He loved the old rumbling and jolting carts, the former track of which he still found in his long-buried remembrance, as the observer of today finds the wheel tracks of ancient vehicles in Herculaneum. The butcher's cart, with its snowy canopy, was an acceptable object; so was the fish cart, heralded by its horn; so, likewise, was the countryman's cart of vegetables, plodding from door to door, with long pauses of the patient horse, while his owner drove a trade in turnips, carrots, summer squashes, string beans, green peas, and new potatoes, with half the housewives of the neighborhood. The baker's cart, with the harsh music of its bells, had a pleasant effect on Clifford, because, as few things else did, it jingled the very dissonance of yore. One afternoon, a scissor-grinder chanced to set his wheel agoing under the Pyncheon Elm, and just in front of the arched window. Children came running with their mothers' scissors, or the carving knife, or the paternal razor, or anything else that lacked an edge (except, indeed, poor Clifford's wits), that the grinder might apply the article to his magic wheel, and give it back as good as new. Round went the busily revolving machinery, kept in motion by the scissor-grinder's foot, and wore away the hard steel against the hard stone, whence issued an intense and spiteful prolongation of a hiss as fierce as those emitted by Satan and his compeers in Pandemonium, though squeezed into smaller compass. It was an ugly, little, venomous serpent of a noise, as ever did petty violence to human ears. But Clifford listened with rapturous delight. The sound, however disagreeable, had very brisk life in it, and, together with the circle of curious children watching the revolutions of the wheel, appeared to give him a more vivid sense of active, bustling, and sunshiny existence than he had attained in almost any other way. Nevertheless, its

charm lay chiefly in the past; for the scissor-grinder's wheel
had hissed in his childish ears.

He sometimes made doleful complaint that there were
no stagecoaches nowadays. And he asked in an injured tone
what had become of all those old square-top chaises, with
wings sticking out on either side, that used to be drawn by
a plow horse, and driven by a farmer's wife and daughter,
peddling whortleberries and blackberries about the town.
Their disappearance made him doubt, he said, whether the
berries had not left off growing in the broad pastures and
along the shady country lanes.

But anything that appealed to the sense of beauty, in
however humble a way, did not require to be recommended
by these old associations. This was observable when one of
those Italian boys (who are rather a modern feature of our
streets) came along with his barrel organ, and stopped under the wide and cool shadows of the elm. With his quick
professional eye, he took note of the two faces watching
him from the arched window, and, opening his instrument,
began to scatter its melodies abroad. He had a monkey on
his shoulder, dressed in a Highland plaid; and, to complete
the sum of splendid attractions wherewith he presented
himself to the public, there was a company of little figures,
whose sphere and habitation was in the mahogany case of
his organ, and whose principle of life was the music which
the Italian made it his business to grind out. In all their
variety of occupation—the cobbler, the blacksmith, the soldier, the lady with her fan, the toper with his bottle, the
milkmaid sitting by her cow—this fortunate little society
might truly be said to enjoy a harmonious existence, and
to make life literally a dance. The Italian turned a crank;
and, behold! every one of these small individuals started
into the most curious vivacity. The cobbler wrought upon a
shoe; the blacksmith hammered his iron; the soldier waved
his glittering blade; the lady raised a tiny breeze with her
fan; the jolly toper swigged lustily at his bottle; a scholar
opened his book with eager thirst for knowledge, and
turned his head to and fro along the page; the milkmaid energetically drained her cow; and a miser counted gold into
his strongbox—all at the same turning of a crank. Yes; and,

moved by the selfsame impulse, a lover saluted his mistress on her lips! Possibly some cynic, at once merry and bitter, had desired to signify, in this pantomimic scene, that we mortals, whatever our business or amusement—however serious, however trifling—all dance to one identical tune, and, in spite of our ridiculous activity, bring nothing finally to pass. For the most remarkable aspect of the affair was that, at the cessation of the music, everybody was petrified, at once, from the most extravagant life into a dead torpor. Neither was the cobbler's shoe finished, nor the blacksmith's iron shaped out; nor was there a drop less of brandy in the toper's bottle, nor a drop more of milk in the milkmaid's pail, nor one additional coin in the miser's strongbox, nor was the scholar a page deeper in his book. All were precisely in the same condition as before they made themselves so ridiculous by their haste to toil, to enjoy, to accumulate gold, and to become wise. Saddest of all, moreover, the lover was none the happier for the maiden's granted kiss! But, rather than swallow this last too acrid ingredient, we reject the whole moral of the show.

The monkey, meanwhile, with a thick tail curling out into preposterous prolixity from beneath his tartans, took his station at the Italian's feet. He turned a wrinkled and abominable little visage to every passer-by, and to the circle of children that soon gathered round, and to Hepzibah's shop door, and upward to the arched window, whence Phoebe and Clifford were looking down. Every moment, also, he took off his Highland bonnet, and performed a bow and scrape. Sometimes, moreover, he made personal application to individuals, holding out his small black palm, and otherwise plainly signifying his excessive desire for whatever filthy lucre might happen to be in anybody's pocket. The mean and low, yet strangely manlike expression of his wilted countenance; the prying and crafty glance, that showed him ready to gripe at every miserable advantage; his enormous tail (too enormous to be decently concealed under his gabardine), and the deviltry of nature which it betokened—take this monkey just as he was, in short, and you could desire no better image of the Mammon of copper coin, symbolizing the grossest form of the love of money. Neither was there any possibility of satisfying the covetous little devil. Phoebe threw down a whole handful of cents, which he picked up with joyless eagerness, handed them over to the Italian for safekeeping, and immediately recommenced a series of pantomimic petitions for more.

Doubtless, more than one New Englander—or, let him be of what country he might, it is as likely to be the case—passed by, and threw a look at the monkey, and went on, without imagining how nearly his own moral condition was here exemplified. Clifford, however, was a being of another order. He had taken childish delight in the music, and smiled, too, at the figures which it set in motion. But, after looking a while at the long-tailed imp, he was so shocked by his horrible ugliness, spiritual as well as physical, that he actually began to shed tears; a weakness which men of merely delicate endowments, and destitute of the fiercer, deeper, and more tragic power of laughter, can hardly avoid, when the worst and meanest aspect of life happens to be presented to them.

Pyncheon Street was sometimes enlivened by spectacles of more imposing pretensions than the above, and which brought the multitude along with them. With a shivering repugnance at the idea of personal contact with the world, a powerful impulse still seized on Clifford, whenever the rush and roar of the human tide grew strongly audible to him. This was made evident, one day, when a political procession, with hundreds of flaunting banners, and drums, fifes, clarions, and cymbals, reverberating between the rows of buildings, marched all through town, and trailed its length of trampling footstep, and most infrequent uproar, past the ordinarily quiet House of the Seven Gables. As a mere object of sight, nothing is more deficient in picturesque features than a procession seen in its passage through narrow streets. The spectator feels it to be fool's play, when he can distinguish the tedious commonplace of each man's visage, with the perspiration and weary self-importance on it, and the very cut of his pantaloons, and the stiffness or laxity of his shirt collar, and the dust on the back of his black coat. In order to become majestic, it should be viewed from some vantage point, as it rolls its slow and long array through the center of a wide plain, or the stateliest public square of a city; for then, by its remoteness, it melts all the petty personalities, of which it is made up, into one broad mass of existence—one great life—one collected body of mankind, with a vast, homogeneous spirit animating it. But, on the other hand, if an impressible person, standing alone over the brink of one of these processions, should behold it, not in its atoms, but in its aggregate—as a mighty river of life, massive in its tide, and black with mystery, and, out of its depths, calling to the kindred depth within him—then the contiguity would add to the effect. It might so fascinate him that he would hardly be restrained from plunging into the surging stream of human sympathies.

So it proved with Clifford. He shuddered; he grew pale; he threw an appealing look at Hepzibah and Phoebe, who were with him at the window. They comprehended nothing of his emotions, and supposed him merely disturbed by the unaccustomed tumult. At last, with tremulous limbs, he started up, set his foot on the window sill, and in an instant more would have been in the unguarded balcony. As it was, the whole procession might have seen him, a wild, haggard figure, his gray locks floating in the wind that waved their banners; a lonely being, estranged from his race, but now feeling himself man again, by virtue of the irrepressible instinct that possessed him. Had Clifford attained the balcony, he would probably have leaped into the street; but whether impelled by the species of terror that sometimes urges its victim over the very precipice which he shrinks from, or by a natural magnetism, tending towards the great center of humanity, it were not easy to decide. Both impulses might have wrought on him at once.

But his companions, affrighted by his gesture—which was that of a man hurried away in spite of himself—seized Clifford's garment and held him back. Hepzibah shrieked. Phoebe, to whom all extravagance was a horror, burst into sobs and tears.

"Clifford, Clifford! Are you crazy?" cried his sister.

"I hardly know, Hepzibah," said Clifford, drawing a long breath. "Fear nothing—it is over now—but had I taken that plunge, and survived it, methinks it would have made me another man!"

Possibly, in some sense, Clifford may have been right. He needed a shock; or perhaps he required to take a deep, deep plunge into the ocean of human life, and to sink down and be covered by its profoundness, and then to emerge, sobered, invigorated, restored to the world and himself. Perhaps, again, he required nothing less than the great final remedy—death!

A similar yearning to renew the broken links of brotherhood with his kind sometimes showed itself in a milder form; and once it was made beautiful by the religion that lay even deeper than itself. In the incident now to be sketched, there was a touching recognition, on Clifford's part, of God's care and love towards him—towards this poor, forsaken man, who, if any mortal could, might have been pardoned for regarding himself as thrown aside, forgotten, and left to be the sport of some fiend, whose playfulness was an ecstasy of mischief.

It was the Sabbath morning; one of those bright, calm Sabbaths, with its own hallowed atmosphere, when heaven seems to diffuse itself over the earth's face in a solemn smile, no less sweet than solemn. On such a Sabbath morn, were we pure enough to be its medium, we should be conscious of the earth's natural worship ascending through our frames, on whatever spot of ground we stood. The church bells, with various tones, but all in harmony, were calling out, and responding to one another—"It is the Sabbath!— The Sabbath!—Yea; the Sabbath!"—and over the whole city the bells scattered the blessed sounds, now slowly, now with livelier joy, now one bell alone, now all the bells together, crying earnestly, "It is the Sabbath!" and flinging their accents afar off, to melt into the air, and pervade it with the holy word. The air, with God's sweetest and tenderest sunshine in it, was meet for mankind to breathe into their hearts, and send it forth again as the utterance of prayer.

Clifford sat at the window with Hepzibah, watching the neighbors as they stepped into the street. All of them, however unspiritual on other days, were transfigured by the

Sabbath influence; so that their very garments—whether it were an old man's decent coat, well brushed for the thousandth time, or a little boy's first sack and trousers, finished yesterday by his mother's needle—had somewhat of the quality of ascension robes. Forth, likewise, from the portal of the old house stepped Phoebe, putting up her small green sunshade, and throwing upward a glance and smile of parting kindness to the faces at the arched window. In her aspect there was a familiar gladness, and a holiness that you could play with, and yet reverence it as much as ever. She was like a prayer, offered up in the homeliest beauty of one's mother tongue. Fresh was Phoebe, moreover, and airy and sweet in her apparel; as if nothing that she wore— neither her gown, nor her small straw bonnet, nor her little kerchief, any more than her snowy stockings—had ever been put on before; or, if worn, were all the fresher for it, and with a fragrance as if they had lain among the rosebuds.

The girl waved her hand to Hepzibah and Clifford, and went up the street; a religion in herself, warm, simple, true, with a substance that could walk on earth, and a spirit that was capable of heaven.

"Hepzibah," asked Clifford, after watching Phoebe to the corner, "do you never go to church?"

"No, Clifford!" she replied. "Not these many, many years!"

"Were I to be there," he rejoined, "it seems to me that I could pray once more, when so many human souls were praying all around me!"

She looked into Clifford's face, and beheld there a soft natural effusion; for his heart gushed out, as it were, and ran over at his eyes, in delightful reverence for God, and kindly affection for his human brethren. The emotion communicated itself to Hepzibah. She yearned to take him by the hand, and go and kneel down, they two together—both so long separate from the world, and, as she now recognized, scarcely friends with Him above—to kneel down among the people, and be reconciled to God and man at once.

"Dear brother," said she, earnestly, "let us go! We belong nowhere. We have not a foot of space in any church to kneel upon; but let us go to some place of worship, even if we stand in the broad aisle. Poor and forsaken as we are, some pew door will be opened to us!"

So Hepzibah and her brother made themselves ready—as ready as they could in the best of their old-fashioned garments, which had hung on pegs, or been laid away in trunks, so long that the dampness and moldy smell of the past was on them—made themselves ready, in their faded bettermost, to go to church. They descended the staircase together—gaunt, sallow Hepzibah, and pale, emaciated, age-stricken Clifford! They pulled open the front door, and stepped across the threshold, and felt, both of them, as if they were standing in the presence of the whole world, and with mankind's great and terrible eye on them alone. The eye of their Father seemed to be withdrawn, and gave them no encouragement. The warm, sunny air of the street made them shiver. Their hearts quaked within them at the idea of taking one step farther.

"It cannot be, Hepzibah! It is too late," said Clifford, with deep sadness. "We are ghosts! We have no right among human beings—no right anywhere but in this old house, which has a curse on it, and which, therefore, we are doomed to haunt! And, besides," he continued, with a fastidious sensibility, inalienably characteristic of the man, "it would not be fit nor beautiful to go! It is an ugly thought that I should be frightful to my fellow beings, and that children would cling to their mothers' gowns at sight of me!"

They shrank back into the dusky passageway, and closed the door. But, going up the staircase again, they found the whole interior of the house tenfold more dismal, and the air closer and heavier, for the glimpse and breath of freedom which they had just snatched. They could not flee; their jailer had but left the door ajar in mockery, and stood behind it to watch them stealing out. At the threshold, they felt his pitiless gripe upon them. For, what other dungeon is so dark as one's own heart! What jailer so inexorable as one's self!

But it would be no fair picture of Clifford's state of mind were we to represent him as continually or prevailingly wretched. On the contrary, there was no other man in the city, we are bold to affirm, of so much as half his years, who enjoyed so many lightsome and griefless moments as himself. He had no burden of care upon him; there were none of those questions and contingencies with the future to be settled which wear away all other lives, and render them not worth having by the very process of providing for their support. In this respect he was a child—a child for the whole term of his existence, be it long or short. Indeed, his life seemed to be standing still at a period little in advance of childhood, and to cluster all his reminiscences about that epoch; just as, after the torpor of a heavy blow, the sufferer's reviving consciousness goes back to a moment considerably behind the accident that stupefied him. He sometimes told Phoebe and Hepzibah his dreams, in which he invariably played the part of a child, or a very young man. So vivid were they, in his relation of them, that he once held a dispute with his sister as to the particular figure or print of a chintz morning dress, which he had seen their mother wear, in the dream of the preceding night. Hepzibah, piquing herself on a woman's accuracy in such matters, held it to be slightly different from what Clifford described; but, producing the very gown from an old trunk, it proved to be identical with his remembrance of it. Had Clifford, every time that he emerged out of dreams so lifelike, undergone the torture of transformation from a boy into an old and broken man, the daily recurrence of the shock would have been too much to bear. It would have caused an acute agony to thrill from the morning twilight, all the day through, until bedtime; and even then would have mingled a dull, inscrutable pain, and pallid hue of misfortune, with the visionary bloom and adolescence of his slumber. But the nightly moonshine interwove itself with the morning mist, and enveloped him as in a robe, which he hugged about his person, and seldom let realities pierce through; he was not often quite awake, but slept open-eyed, and perhaps fancied himself most dreaming then.

Thus, lingering always so near his childhood, he had sympathies with children, and kept his heart the fresher thereby, like a reservoir into which rivulets were pouring not far from the fountainhead. Though prevented, by a subtile sense of propriety, from desiring to associate with them, he loved few things better than to look out of the arched window, and see a little girl driving her hoop along the sidewalk, or schoolboys at a game of ball. Their voices, also, were very pleasant to him, heard at a distance, all swarming and intermingling together as flies do in a sunny room.

Clifford would, doubtless, have been glad to share their sports. One afternoon, he was seized with an irresistible desire to blow soap bubbles; an amusement, as Hepzibah told Phoebe apart, that had been a favorite one with her brother when they were both children. Behold him, therefore, at the arched window, with an earthen pipe in his mouth! Behold him, with his gray hair, and a wan, unreal smile over his countenance, where still hovered a beautiful grace, which his worst enemy must have acknowledged to be spiritual and immortal, since it had survived so long! Behold him, scattering airy spheres abroad, from the window into the street! Little impalpable worlds were those soap bubbles, with the big world depicted, in hues bright as imagination, on the nothing of their surface. It was curious to see how the passers-by regarded these brilliant fantasies, as they came floating down, and made the dull atmosphere imaginative about them. Some stopped to gaze, and, perhaps, carried a pleasant recollection of the bubbles onward as far as the street corner; some looked angrily upward, as if poor Clifford wronged them by setting an image of beauty afloat so near their dusty pathway. A great many put out their fingers or their walking sticks to touch, withal; and were perversely gratified, no doubt, when the bubble, with all its pictured earth and sky scene, vanished as if it had never been.

At length, just as an elderly gentleman of very dignified presence happened to be passing, a large bubble sailed majestically down, and burst right against his nose! He looked up, at first with a stern, keen glance, which penetrated at once into the obscurity behind the arched window, then with a smile, which might be conceived as diffusing a dog-day sultriness for the space of several yards about him.

"Aha, Cousin Clifford!" cried Judge Pyncheon. "What! Still blowing soap bubbles!"

The tone seemed as if meant to be kind and soothing, but yet had a bitterness of sarcasm in it. As for Clifford, an absolute palsy of fear came over him. Apart from any definite cause of dread which his past experience might have given him, he felt that native and original horror of the excellent Judge which is proper to a weak, delicate, and apprehensive character in the presence of massive strength. Strength is incomprehensible by weakness, and, therefore, the more terrible. There is no greater bugbear than a strong-willed relative in the circle of his own connections.

❖12❖

The Daguerreotypist

It must not be supposed that the life of a personage naturally so active as Phoebe could be wholly confined within the precincts of the old Pyncheon House. Clifford's demands upon her time were usually satisfied, in those long days, considerably earlier than sunset. Quiet as his daily existence seemed, it nevertheless drained all the resources by which he lived. It was not physical exercise that overwearied him—for except that he sometimes wrought a little with a hoe, or paced the garden walk, or, in rainy weather, traversed a large, unoccupied room—it was his tendency to remain only too quiescent, as regarded any toil of the limbs and muscles. But, either there was a smoldering fire within him that consumed his vital energy, or the monotony that would have dragged itself with benumbing effect over a mind differently situated was no monotony to Clifford. Possibly, he was in a state of second growth and recovery, and was constantly assimilating nutriment for his spirit and intellect from sights, sounds, and events which passed as a perfect void to persons more practiced with the world. As all is activity and vicissitude to the new mind of a child, so might it be, likewise, to a mind that had undergone a kind of new creation, after its long-suspended life.

Be the cause what it might, Clifford commonly retired to rest, thoroughly exhausted, while the sunbeams were still melting through his window curtains, or were thrown with late luster on the chamber wall. And while he thus slept early, as other children do, and dreamed of childhood, Phoebe was free to follow her own tastes for the remainder of the day and evening.

This was a freedom essential to the health even of a character so little susceptible of morbid influences as that of Phoebe. The old house, as we have already said, had both the dry rot and the damp rot in its walls; it was not good to breathe no other atmosphere than that. Hepzibah, though she had her valuable and redeeming traits, had grown to be a kind of lunatic, by imprisoning herself so long in one place, with no other company than a single series of ideas, and but one affection, and one bitter sense of wrong. Clifford, the reader may perhaps imagine, was too inert to operate morally on his fellow creatures, however intimate and exclusive their relations with him. But the sympathy or magnetism among human beings is more subtile and universal than we think; it exists, indeed, among different classes of organized life, and vibrates from one to another. A flower, for instance, as Phoebe herself observed, always began to droop sooner in Clifford's hand, or Hepzibah's, than in her own; and by the same law, converting her whole daily life into a flower fragrance for these two sickly spirits, the blooming girl must inevitably droop and fade much sooner than if worn on a younger and happier breast. Unless she had now and then indulged her brisk impulses, and breathed rural air in a suburban walk, or ocean breezes along the shore; had occasionally obeyed the impulse of Nature, in New England girls, by attending a metaphysical or philosophical lecture, or viewing a seven-mile panorama, or listening to a concert; had gone shopping about the city, ransacking entire depots of splendid merchandise, and bringing home a ribbon; had employed, likewise, a little time to read the Bible in her chamber, and had stolen a little more to think of her mother and her native place—unless for such moral medicines as the above, we should soon have beheld our poor Phoebe grow thin and put on a bleached, unwholesome aspect, and assume strange, shy ways, prophetic of old-maidenhood and a cheerless future.

Even as it was, a change grew visible; a change partly to be regretted, although whatever charm it infringed upon was repaired by another, perhaps more precious. She was not so constantly gay, but had her moods of thought, which Clifford, on the whole, liked better than her former phase of unmingled cheerfulness; because now she understood him better and more delicately, and sometimes even interpreted him to himself. Her eyes looked larger, and darker, and deeper; so deep, at some silent moments, that they seemed like Artesian wells, down, down, into the infinite. She was less girlish than when we first beheld her alighting from the omnibus; less girlish, but more a woman.

The only youthful mind with which Phoebe had an opportunity of frequent intercourse was that of the daguerreotypist. Inevitably, by the pressure of the seclusion about them, they had been brought into habits of some familiarity. Had they met under different circumstances, neither of these young persons would have been likely to bestow much thought upon the other, unless, indeed, their extreme dissimilarity should have proved a principle of mutual attraction. Both, it is true, were characters proper to New England life, and possessing a common ground, therefore, in their more external developments; but as unlike, in their respective interiors, as if their native climes had been at worldwide distance. During the early part of their acquaintance, Phoebe had held back rather more than was customary with her frank and simple manners from Holgrave's not very marked advances. Nor was she yet satisfied that she knew him well, although they almost daily met and talked together, in a kind, friendly, and what seemed to be a familiar way.

The artist, in a desultory manner, had imparted to Phoebe something of his history. Young as he was, and had his career terminated at the point already attained, there had been enough of incident to fill, very creditably, an autobiographic volume. A romance on the plan of Gil Blas, adapted to American society and manners, would cease to be a romance. The experience of many individuals among us, who think it hardly worth the telling, would equal the vicissitudes of the Spaniard's earlier life; while their ultimate success, or the point whither they tend, may be incomparably higher than any that a novelist would imagine for his hero. Holgrave, as he told Phoebe somewhat proudly, could not boast of his origin, unless as being exceedingly humble, nor of his education, except that it had been the scantiest possible, and obtained by a few winter months' attendance at a district school. Left early to his own guidance, he had begun to be self-dependent while yet a boy; and it was a condition aptly suited to his natural force of will. Though now but twenty-two years old (lacking some months, which are years in such a life), he had already been, first, a country schoolmaster; next, a salesman in a country store; and either at the same time or afterwards, the political editor of a country newspaper. He had subsequently traveled New England and the Middle States, as a peddler, in the employment of a Connecticut manufactory of cologne water and other essences. In an episodical way, he had studied and practiced dentistry, and with very flattering success, especially in many of the factory towns along our inland streams. As a supernumerary official, of some kind or other, aboard a packet ship, he had visited Europe, and found means, before his return, to see Italy, and part of France and Germany. At a later period, he had spent some months in a community of Fourierists. Still more recently, he had been a public lecturer on Mesmerism, for which science (as he assured Phoebe, and, indeed, satisfactorily proved, by putting Chanticleer, who happened to be scratching nearby, to sleep) he had very remarkable endowments.

His present phase, as a daguerreotypist, was of no more importance in his own view, nor likely to be more permanent, than any of the preceding ones. It had been taken up with the careless alacrity of an adventurer, who had his bread to earn. It would be thrown aside as carelessly, whenever he should choose to earn his bread by some other equally digressive means. But what was most remarkable, and, perhaps, showed a more than common poise in the young man, was the fact that, amid all these personal vicissitudes, he had never lost his identity. Homeless as he had been—continually changing his whereabout, and, therefore, responsible neither to public opinion nor to individuals; putting off one exterior, and snatching up another, to be soon shifted for a third—he had never violated the innermost man, but had carried his conscience along with him. It was impossible to know Holgrave without recognizing this to be the fact. Hepzibah had seen it. Phoebe soon saw it, likewise, and gave him the sort of confidence which such a certainty inspires. She was startled, however, and sometimes repelled, not by any doubt of his integrity to whatever law he acknowledged, but by a sense that his law differed from her own. He made her uneasy, and seemed to unsettle everything around her, by his lack of reverence for what was fixed, unless, at a moment's warning, it could establish its right to hold its ground.

Then, moreover, she scarcely thought him affectionate in his nature. He was too calm and cool an observer. Phoebe felt his eye often; his heart, seldom or never. He took a certain kind of interest in Hepzibah and her brother, and Phoebe herself. He studied them attentively, and allowed no slightest circumstance of their individualities to escape him. He was ready to do them whatever good he might; but, after all, he never exactly made common cause with them, nor gave any reliable evidence that he loved them better in proportion as he knew them more. In his relations with them, he seemed to be in quest of mental food, not heart sustenance. Phoebe could not conceive what interested him so much in her friends and herself, intellectually, since he cared nothing for them, or, comparatively, so little, as objects of human affection.

Always, in his interviews with Phoebe, the artist made especial inquiry as to the welfare of Clifford, whom, except at the Sunday festival, he seldom saw.

"Does he still seem happy?" he asked one day.

"As happy as a child," answered Phoebe, "but—like a child, too—very easily disturbed."

"How disturbed?" inquired Holgrave. "By things without, or by thoughts within?"

"I cannot see his thoughts! How should I?" replied Phoebe, with simple piquancy. "Very often, his humor changes without any reason that can be guessed at, just as a cloud comes over the sun. Latterly, since I have begun to know him better, I feel it to be not quite right to look closely into his moods. He has had such a great sorrow that his heart is made all solemn and sacred by it. When he is cheerful—when the sun shines into his mind—then I venture to peep in, just as far as the light reaches, but no further. It is holy ground where the shadow falls!"

"How prettily you express this sentiment!" said the artist. "I can understand the feeling, without possessing it. Had I your opportunities, no scruples would prevent me from fathoming Clifford to the full depth of my plummet line!"

"How strange that you should wish it!" remarked Phoebe, involuntarily. "What is Cousin Clifford to you?"

"Oh, nothing—of course, nothing!" answered Holgrave, with a smile. "Only this is such an odd and incomprehensible world! The more I look at it, the more it puzzles me, and I begin to suspect that a man's bewilderment is the measure of his wisdom. Men and women, and children, too, are such strange creatures that one never can be certain that he really knows them; nor ever guess what they have been, from what he sees them to be now. Judge Pyncheon! Clifford! What a complex riddle—a complexity of complexities—do they present! It requires intuitive sympathy, like a young girl's, to solve it. A mere observer, like myself (who never have any intuitions, and am, at best, only subtile and acute), is pretty certain to go astray."

The artist now turned the conversation to themes less dark than that which they had touched upon. Phoebe and he were young together; nor had Holgrave, in his premature experience of life, wasted entirely that beautiful spirit of youth, which, gushing forth from one small heart and fancy, may diffuse itself over the universe, making it all as bright as on the first day of creation. Man's own youth is the world's youth; at least, he feels as if it were, and imagines that the earth's granite substance is something not yet hardened, and which he can mold into whatever shape he likes. So it was with Holgrave. He could talk sagely about the world's old age, but never actually believed what he said; he was a young man still, and therefore looked upon the world—that gray-bearded and wrinkled profligate, decrepit without being venerable—as a tender stripling, capable of being improved into all that it ought to be, but scarcely yet had shown the remotest promise of becoming.

He had that sense, or inward prophecy—which a young man had better never have been born than not to have, and a mature man had better die at once than utterly to relinquish—that we are not doomed to creep on forever in the old bad way, but that, this very now, there are the harbingers abroad of a golden era, to be accomplished in his own lifetime. It seemed to Holgrave—as doubtless it has seemed to the hopeful of every century since the epoch of Adam's grandchildren—that in this age, more than ever before, the moss-grown and rotten Past is to be torn down, and lifeless institutions to be thrust out of the way, and their dead corpses buried, and everything to begin anew.

As to the main point—may we never live to doubt it!— as to the better centuries that are coming, the artist was surely right. His error lay in supposing that this age, more than any past or future one, is destined to see the tattered garments of Antiquity exchanged for a new suit, instead of gradually renewing themselves by patchwork; in applying his own little life span as the measure of an interminable achievement; and, more than all, in fancying that it mattered anything to the great end in view whether he himself should contend for it or against it. Yet it was well for him to think so. This enthusiasm, infusing itself through the calmness of his character, and thus taking an aspect of settled thought and wisdom, would serve to keep his youth pure, and make his aspirations high. And when, with the years settling down more weightily upon him, his early faith should be modified by inevitable experience, it would be with no harsh and sudden revolution of his sentiments. He would still have faith in man's brightening destiny, and perhaps love him all the better, as he should recognize his helplessness in his own behalf; and the haughty faith, with which he began life, would be well bartered for a far humbler one at its close, in discerning that man's best-directed effort accomplishes a kind of dream, while God is the sole worker of realities.

Holgrave had read very little, and that little in passing through the thoroughfare of life, where the mystic language of his books was necessarily mixed up with the babble of the multitude, so that both one and the other were apt to lose any sense that might have been properly their own. He considered himself a thinker, and was certainly of a thoughtful turn, but, with his own path to discover, had perhaps hardly yet reached the point where an educated man begins to think. The true value of his character lay in that deep consciousness of inward strength, which made all his past vicissitudes seem merely like a change of garments; in that enthusiasm, so quiet that he scarcely knew of its existence, but which gave a warmth to everything that he laid his hand on; in that personal ambition, hidden— from his own as well as other eyes—among his more generous impulses, but in which lurked a certain efficacy, that might solidify him from a theorist into the champion of some practicable cause. Altogether, in his culture and want of culture—in his crude, wild, and misty philosophy, and the practical experience that counteracted some of its tendencies; in his magnanimous zeal for man's welfare, and his recklessness of whatever the ages had established in man's behalf; in his faith, and in his infidelity; in what he had, and in what he lacked—the artist might fitly enough stand forth as the representative of many compeers in his native land.

His career it would be difficult to prefigure. There appeared to be qualities in Holgrave such as, in a country where everything is free to the hand that can grasp it, could hardly fail to put some of the world's prizes within his reach. But these matters are delightfully uncertain. At almost every step in life, we meet with young men of just about Holgrave's age, for whom we anticipate wonderful things, but of whom, even after much and careful inquiry, we never happen to hear another word. The effervescence of youth and passion, and the fresh gloss of the intellect and imagination, endow them with a false brilliancy, which makes fools of themselves and other people. Like certain chintzes, calicoes, and ginghams, they show finely in their first newness, but cannot stand the sun and rain, and assume a very sober aspect after washing day.

But our business is with Holgrave as we find him on this particular afternoon, and in the arbor of the Pyncheon garden. In that point of view, it was a pleasant sight to behold this young man, with so much faith in himself, and so fair an appearance of admirable powers—so little harmed, too, by the many tests that had tried his metal—it was pleasant to see him in his kindly intercourse with Phoebe. Her thought had scarcely done him justice when it pronounced him cold; or, if so, he had grown warmer now. Without such purpose on her part, and unconsciously on his, she made the House of the Seven Gables like a home to him, and the garden a familiar precinct. With the insight on which he prided himself, he fancied that he could look through Phoebe, and all around her, and could read her off like a page of a child's storybook. But these transparent natures are often deceptive in their depth; those pebbles at the bottom of the fountain are farther from us than we think. Thus the artist, whatever he might judge of Phoebe's capacity, was beguiled, by some silent charm of hers, to talk freely of what he dreamed of doing in the world. He poured himself out as to another self. Very possibly, he forgot Phoebe while he talked to her, and was moved only by the inevitable tendency of thought, when rendered sympathetic by enthusiasm and emotion, to flow into the first safe reservoir which it finds. But, had you peeped at them through the chinks of the garden fence, the young man's earnestness and heightened color might have led you to suppose that he was making love to the young girl!

At length, something was said by Holgrave that made it apposite for Phoebe to inquire what had first brought him acquainted with her cousin Hepzibah, and why he now chose to lodge in the desolate old Pyncheon House. Without directly answering her, he turned from the Future, which had heretofore been the theme of his discourse, and began to speak of the influences of the Past. One subject, indeed, is but the reverberation of the other.

"Shall we never, never get rid of this Past?" cried he, keeping up the earnest tone of his preceding conversation. "It lies upon the Present like a giant's dead body! In fact, the case is just as if a young giant were compelled to waste all his strength in carrying about the corpse of the old giant, his grandfather, who died a long while ago, and only needs to be decently buried. Just think a moment, and it

will startle you to see what slaves we are to bygone times—
to Death, if we give the matter the right word!"

"But I do not see it," observed Phoebe.

"For example, then," continued Holgrave. "A dead man,
if he happen to have made a will, disposes of wealth no
longer his own; or, if he die intestate, it is distributed in accordance with the notions of men much longer dead than
he. A dead man sits on all our judgment seats; and living
judges do but search out and repeat his decisions. We read
in dead men's books! We laugh at dead men's jokes, and
cry at dead men's pathos! We are sick of dead men's diseases, physical and moral, and die of the same remedies
with which dead doctors killed their patients! We worship
the living Deity according to dead men's forms and creeds.
Whatever we seek to do, of our own free motion, a dead
man's icy hand obstructs us! Turn our eyes to what point
we may, a dead man's white, immitigable face encounters
them, and freezes our very heart! And we must be dead
ourselves before we can begin to have our proper influence
on our own world, which will then be no longer our world,
but the world of another generation, with which we shall
have no shadow of a right to interfere. I ought to have said,
too, that we live in dead men's houses; as, for instance, in
this of the Seven Gables!"

"And why not," said Phoebe, "so long as we can be comfortable in them?"

"But we shall live to see the day, I trust," went on the
artist, "when no man shall build his house for posterity.
Why should he? He might just as reasonably order a durable suit of clothes—leather, or gutta-percha, or whatever
else lasts longest—so that his great-grandchildren should
have the benefit of them, and cut precisely the same figure
in the world that he himself does. If each generation were
allowed and expected to build its own houses, that single
change, comparatively unimportant in itself, would imply
almost every reform which society is now suffering for. I
doubt whether even our public edifices—our capitols, state
houses, courthouses, city halls, and churches—ought to be
built of such permanent materials as stone or brick. It were
better that they should crumble to ruin once in twenty

years, or thereabouts, as a hint to the people to examine
into and reform the institutions which they symbolize."

"How you hate everything old!" said Phoebe, in dismay.
"It makes me dizzy to think of such a shifting world!"

"I certainly love nothing moldy," answered Holgrave.
"Now, this old Pyncheon House! Is it a wholesome place
to live in, with its black shingles, and the green moss that
shows how damp they are; its dark, low-studded rooms; its
grime and sordidness, which are the crystallization on its
walls of the human breath that has been drawn and exhaled here in discontent and anguish? The house ought to
be purified with fire—purified till only its ashes remain!"

"Then why do you live in it?" asked Phoebe, a little
piqued.

"Oh, I am pursuing my studies here; not in books, however," replied Holgrave. "The house, in my view, is expressive of that odious and abominable Past, with all its bad
influences, against which I have just been declaiming. I
dwell in it for a while, that I may know the better how to
hate it. By the by, did you ever hear the story of Maule, the
wizard, and what happened between him and your immea-
surably great-grandfather?"

"Yes, indeed!" said Phoebe. "I heard it long ago, from
my father, and two or three times from my cousin Hepzibah, in the month that I have been here. She seems to
think that all the calamities of the Pyncheons began from
that quarrel with the wizard, as you call him. And you, Mr.
Holgrave, look as if you thought so, too! How singular that
you should believe what is so very absurd, when you reject
many things that are a great deal worthier of credit!"

"I do believe it," said the artist, seriously, "not as a superstition, however, but as proved by unquestionable facts,
and as exemplifying a theory. Now, see: under those seven
gables, at which we now look up—and which old Colonel Pyncheon meant to be the house of his descendants,
in prosperity and happiness, down to an epoch far beyond
the present—under that roof, through a portion of three
centuries, there has been perpetual remorse of conscience,
a constantly defeated hope, strife amongst kindred, various
misery, a strange form of death, dark suspicion, unspeak-

able disgrace—all or most of which calamity I have the means of tracing to the old Puritan's inordinate desire to plant and endow a family. To plant a family! This idea is at the bottom of most of the wrong and mischief which men do. The truth is, that, once in every half century, at longest, a family should be merged into the great, obscure mass of humanity, and forget all about its ancestors. Human blood, in order to keep its freshness, should run in hidden streams, as the water of an aqueduct is conveyed in subterranean pipes. In the family existence of these Pyncheons, for instance—forgive me, Phoebe; but I cannot think of you as one of them—in their brief New England pedigree, there has been time enough to infect them all with one kind of lunacy or another!"

"You speak very unceremoniously of my kindred," said Phoebe, debating with herself whether she ought to take offense.

"I speak true thoughts to a true mind!" answered Holgrave, with a vehemence which Phoebe had not before witnessed in him. "The truth is as I say! Furthermore, the original perpetrator and father of this mischief appears to have perpetuated himself, and still walks the street—at least, his very image, in mind and body—with the fairest prospect of transmitting to posterity as rich and as wretched an inheritance as he has received! Do you remember the daguerreotype, and its resemblance to the old portrait?"

"How strangely in earnest you are!" exclaimed Phoebe, looking at him with surprise and perplexity; half alarmed and partly inclined to laugh. "You talk of the lunacy of the Pyncheons; is it contagious?"

"I understand you!" said the artist, coloring and laughing. "I believe I am a little mad. This subject has taken hold of my mind with the strangest tenacity of clutch since I have lodged in yonder old gable. As one method of throwing it off, I have put an incident of the Pyncheon family history, with which I happen to be acquainted, into the form of a legend, and mean to publish it in a magazine."

"Do you write for the magazines?" inquired Phoebe.

"Is it possible you did not know it?" cried Holgrave. "Well, such is literary fame! Yes, Miss Phoebe Pyncheon, among the multitude of my marvelous gifts I have that of writing stories; and my name has figured, I can assure you, on the covers of *Graham* and *Godey,* making as respectable an appearance, for aught I could see, as any of the canonized beadroll with which it was associated. In the humorous line, I am thought to have a very pretty way with me; and as for pathos, I am as provocative of tears as an onion. But shall I read you my story?"

"Yes, if it is not very long," said Phoebe, and added laughingly, "nor very dull."

As this latter point was one which the daguerreotypist could not decide for himself, he forthwith produced his roll of manuscript, and, while the late sunbeams gilded the seven gables, began to read.

❖ 13 ❖

Alice Pyncheon

THERE was a message brought, one day, from the worshipful Gervayse Pyncheon to young Matthew Maule, the carpenter, desiring his immediate presence at the House of the Seven Gables.

"And what does your master want with me?" said the carpenter to Mr. Pyncheon's black servant. "Does the house need any repair? Well it may, by this time; and no blame to my father who built it, neither! I was reading the old Colonel's tombstone, no longer ago than last Sabbath; and, reckoning from that date, the house has stood seven and thirty years. No wonder if there should be a job to do on the roof."

"Don't know what massa wants," answered Scipio. "The house is a berry good house, and old Colonel Pyncheon think so, too, I reckon; else why the old man haunt it so, and frighten a poor nigga, as he does?"

"Well, well, friend Scipio; let your master know that I'm coming," said the carpenter, with a laugh. "For a fair, workmanlike job, he'll find me his man. And so the house is haunted, is it? It will take a tighter workman than I am to keep the spirits out of the Seven Gables. Even if the Colonel would be quiet," he added, muttering to himself, "my old grandfather, the wizard, will be pretty sure to stick to the Pyncheons as long as their walls hold together."

"What's that you mutter to yourself, Matthew Maule?" asked Scipio. "And what for do you look so black at me?"

"No matter, darky!" said the carpenter. "Do you think nobody is to look black but yourself? Go tell your master I'm coming; and if you happen to see Mistress Alice, his daughter, give Matthew Maule's humble respects to her. She has brought a fair face from Italy—fair, and gentle, and proud—has that same Alice Pyncheon!"

"He talk of Mistress Alice!" cried Scipio, as he returned from his errand. "The low carpenter man! He no business so much as to look at her a great way off!"

This young Matthew Maule, the carpenter, it must be observed, was a person little understood, and not very generally liked, in the town where he resided; not that anything could be alleged against his integrity, or his skill and diligence in the handicraft which he exercised. The aversion (as it might justly be called) with which many persons regarded him was partly the result of his own character and deportment, and partly an inheritance.

He was the grandson of a former Matthew Maule, one of the early settlers of the town, and who had been a famous and terrible wizard in his day. This old reprobate was one of the sufferers when Cotton Mather, and his brother ministers, and the learned judges, and other wise men, and Sir William Phipps, the sagacious governor, made such laudable efforts to weaken the great enemy of souls, by sending a multitude of his adherents up the rocky pathway of Gallows Hill. Since those days, no doubt, it had grown to be suspected that, in consequence of an unfortunate overdoing of a work praiseworthy in itself, the proceedings against the witches had proved far less acceptable to the Beneficent Father than to that very Archenemy whom they were intended to distress and utterly overwhelm. It is not the less certain, however, that awe and terror brooded over the memories of those who died for this horrible crime of witchcraft. Their graves, in the crevices of the rocks, were supposed to be incapable of retaining the occupants who had been so hastily thrust into them. Old Matthew Maule, especially, was known to have as little hesitation or difficulty in rising out of his grave as an ordinary man in getting out of bed, and was as often seen at midnight as living people at noonday. This pestilent wizard (in whom his just punishment seemed to have wrought no manner of amendment) had an inveterate habit of haunting a certain mansion, styled the House of the Seven Gables, against the owner of which he pretended to hold an unsettled claim for ground rent. The ghost, it appears—with the pertinacity which was one of his distinguishing characteristics while alive—insisted that he was the rightful proprietor of the site upon which the house stood. His terms were that either the aforesaid ground rent, from the day when the cellar began to be dug, should be paid down, or the mansion itself given up; else he, the ghostly creditor, would have his finger in all the affairs of the Pyncheons, and make everything go wrong with them, though it should be a thousand years after his death. It was a wild story, perhaps, but seemed not altogether so incredible to those who could remember what an inflexibly obstinate old fellow this wizard Maule had been.

Now, the wizard's grandson, the young Matthew Maule of our story, was popularly supposed to have inherited some of his ancestor's questionable traits. It is wonderful how many absurdities were promulgated in reference to the young man. He was fabled, for example, to have a strange power of getting into people's dreams, and regulating matters there according to his own fancy, pretty much like the stage manager of a theatre. There was a great deal of talk among the neighbors, particularly the petticoated ones, about what they called the witchcraft of Maule's eye. Some said that he could look into people's minds; others, that, by the marvelous power of this eye, he could draw people into his own mind, or send them, if he pleased, to do errands to his grandfather, in the spiritual world; others, again, that it was what is termed an Evil Eye, and possessed the valuable faculty of blighting corn, and drying children into mummies with the heartburn. But, after all, what worked most to the young carpenter's disadvantage was, first, the reserve and sternness of his natural disposition, and next, the fact of his not being a church communicant, and the suspicion of his holding heretical tenets in matters of religion and polity.

After receiving Mr. Pyncheon's message, the carpenter

merely tarried to finish a small job, which he happened to have in hand, and then took his way towards the House of the Seven Gables. This noted edifice, though its style might be getting a little out of fashion, was still as respectable a family residence as that of any gentleman in town. The present owner, Gervayse Pyncheon, was said to have contracted a dislike to the house, in consequence of a shock to his sensibility, in early childhood, from the sudden death of his grandfather. In the very act of running to climb Colonel Pyncheon's knee, the boy had discovered the old Puritan to be a corpse! On arriving at manhood, Mr. Pyncheon had visited England, where he married a lady of fortune, and had subsequently spent many years, partly in the mother country, and partly in various cities on the continent of Europe. During this period, the family mansion had been consigned to the charge of a kinsman, who was allowed to make it his home for the time being, in consideration of keeping the premises in thorough repair. So faithfully had this contract been fulfilled, that now, as the carpenter approached the house, his practiced eye could detect nothing to criticize in its condition. The peaks of the seven gables rose up sharply; the shingled roof looked thoroughly watertight; and the glittering plasterwork entirely covered the exterior walls, and sparkled in the October sun, as if it had been new only a week ago.

The house had that pleasant aspect of life which is like the cheery expression of comfortable activity in the human countenance. You could see, at once, that there was the stir of a large family within it. A huge load of oak wood was passing through the gateway, towards the outbuildings in the rear; the fat cook—or probably it might be the housekeeper—stood at the side door, bargaining for some turkeys and poultry, which a countryman had brought for sale. Now and then a maidservant, neatly dressed, and now the shining sable face of a slave, might be seen bustling across the windows, in the lower part of the house. At an open window of a room in the second story, hanging over some pots of beautiful and delicate flowers—exotics, but which had never known a more genial sunshine than that of the New England autumn—was the figure of a young lady, an exotic, like the flowers, and beautiful and delicate as they. Her presence imparted an indescribable grace and faint witchery to the whole edifice. In other respects, it was a substantial, jolly-looking mansion, and seemed fit to be the residence of a patriarch, who might establish his own headquarters in the front gable and assign one of the remainder to each of his six children, while the great chimney in the center should symbolize the old fellow's hospitable heart, which kept them all warm, and made a great whole of the seven smaller ones.

There was a vertical sundial on the front gable; and as the carpenter passed beneath it, he looked up and noted the hour.

"Three o'clock!" said he to himself. "My father told me that dial was put up only an hour before the old Colonel's death. How truly it has kept time these seven and thirty years past! The shadow creeps and creeps, and is always looking over the shoulder of the sunshine!"

It might have befitted a craftsman, like Matthew Maule, on being sent for to a gentleman's house, to go to the back door, where servants and workpeople were usually admitted; or at least to the side entrance, where the better class of tradesmen made application. But the carpenter had a great deal of pride and stiffness in his nature; and, at this moment, moreover, his heart was bitter with the sense of hereditary wrong, because he considered the great Pyncheon House to be standing on soil which should have been his own. On this very site, beside a spring of delicious water, his grandfather had felled the pine trees and built a cottage, in which children had been born to him; and it was only from a dead man's stiffened fingers that Colonel Pyncheon had wrested away the title deeds. So young Maule went straight to the principal entrance, beneath a portal of carved oak, and gave such a peal of the iron knocker that you would have imagined the stern old wizard himself to be standing at the threshold.

Black Scipio answered the summons in a prodigious hurry; but showed the whites of his eyes, in amazement, on beholding only the carpenter.

"Lord-a-mercy! what a great man he be, this carpenter

fellow!" mumbled Scipio, down in his throat. "Anybody think he beat on the door with his biggest hammer!"

"Here I am!" said Maule, sternly. "Show me the way to your master's parlor!"

As he stepped into the house, a note of sweet and melancholy music thrilled and vibrated along the passageway, proceeding from one of the rooms abovestairs. It was the harpsichord which Alice Pyncheon had brought with her from beyond the sea. The fair Alice bestowed most of her maiden leisure between flowers and music, although the former were apt to droop, and the melodies were often sad. She was of foreign education, and could not take kindly to the New England modes of life, in which nothing beautiful had ever been developed.

As Mr. Pyncheon had been impatiently awaiting Maule's arrival, black Scipio, of course, lost no time in ushering the carpenter into his master's presence. The room in which this gentleman sat was a parlor of moderate size, looking out upon the garden of the house, and having its windows partly shadowed by the foliage of fruit trees. It was Mr. Pyncheon's peculiar apartment, and was provided with furniture, in an elegant and costly style, principally from Paris; the floor (which was unusual at that day) being covered with a carpet, so skillfully and richly wrought that it seemed to glow as with living flowers. In one corner stood a marble woman, to whom her own beauty was the sole and sufficient garment. Some pictures—that looked old, and had a mellow tinge diffused through all their artful splendor—hung on the walls. Near the fireplace was a large and very beautiful cabinet of ebony, inlaid with ivory—a piece of antique furniture, which Mr. Pyncheon had bought in Venice, and which he used as the treasure place for medals, ancient coins, and whatever small and valuable curiosities he had picked up on his travels. Through all this variety of decoration, however, the room showed its original characteristics—its low stud, its crossbeam, its chimney piece, with the old-fashioned Dutch tiles—so that it was the emblem of a mind industriously stored with foreign ideas, and elaborated into artificial refinement, but neither larger, nor, in its proper self, more elegant than before.

There were two objects that appeared rather out of place in this very handsomely furnished room. One was a large map, or surveyor's plan, of a tract of land, which looked as if it had been drawn a good many years ago, and was now dingy with smoke, and soiled, here and there, with the touch of fingers. The other was a portrait of a stern old man, in a Puritan garb, painted roughly, but with a bold effect, and a remarkably strong expression of character.

At a small table, before a fire of English sea coal, sat Mr. Pyncheon, sipping coffee, which had grown to be a very favorite beverage with him in France. He was a middle-aged and really handsome man, with a wig flowing down upon his shoulders; his coat was of blue velvet, with lace on the borders and at the buttonholes; and the firelight glistened on the spacious breadth of his waistcoat, which was flowered all over with gold. On the entrance of Scipio, ushering in the carpenter, Mr. Pyncheon turned partly round, but resumed his former position, and proceeded deliberately to finish his cup of coffee, without immediate notice of the guest whom he had summoned to his presence. It was not that he intended any rudeness or improper neglect—which, indeed, he would have blushed to be guilty of—but it never occurred to him that a person in Maule's station had a claim on his courtesy, or would trouble himself about it one way or the other.

The carpenter, however, stepped at once to the hearth, and turned himself about, so as to look Mr. Pyncheon in the face.

"You sent for me," said he. "Be pleased to explain your business, that I may go back to my own affairs."

"Ah! Excuse me," said Mr. Pyncheon, quietly. "I did not mean to tax your time without a recompense. Your name, I think, is Maule—Thomas or Matthew Maule—a son or grandson of the builder of this house?"

"Matthew Maule," replied the carpenter, "son of him who built the house, grandson of the rightful proprietor of the soil."

"I know the dispute to which you allude," observed Mr. Pyncheon, with undisturbed equanimity. "I am well aware that my grandfather was compelled to resort to a suit at law, in order to establish his claim to the foundation site of this edifice. We will not, if you please, renew the discussion. The matter was settled at the time, and by the competent authorities—equitably, it is to be presumed, and, at all events, irrevocably. Yet, singularly enough, there is an incidental reference to this very subject in what I am now about to say to you. And this same inveterate grudge—excuse me, I mean no offense—this irritability, which you have just shown, is not entirely aside from the matter."

"If you can find anything for your purpose, Mr. Pyncheon," said the carpenter, "in a man's natural resentment for the wrongs done to his blood, you are welcome to it!"

"I take you at your word, Goodman Maule," said the owner of the Seven Gables, with a smile, "and will proceed to suggest a mode in which your hereditary resentments—justifiable, or otherwise—may have had a bearing on my affairs. You have heard, I suppose, that the Pyncheon family, ever since my grandfather's days, have been prosecuting a still unsettled claim to a very large extent of territory at the eastward?"

"Often," replied Maule, and it is said that a smile came over his face, "very often—from my father!"

"This claim," continued Mr. Pyncheon, after pausing a moment, as if to consider what the carpenter's smile might mean, "appeared to be on the very verge of a settlement and full allowance, at the period of my grandfather's decease. It was well known, to those in his confidence, that he anticipated neither difficulty nor delay. Now, Colonel Pyncheon, I need hardly say, was a practical man, well acquainted with public and private business, and not at all the person to cherish ill-founded hopes, or to attempt the following out of an impracticable scheme. It is obvious to conclude, therefore, that he had grounds, not apparent to his heirs, for his confident anticipation of success in the matter of this Eastern claim. In a word, I believe—and my legal advisers coincide in the belief, which, moreover, is authorized, to a certain extent, by the family traditions—that my grandfather was in possession of some deed, or other document, essential to this claim, but which has since disappeared."

"Very likely," said Matthew Maule, and again, it is said, there was a dark smile on his face, "but what can a poor carpenter have to do with the grand affairs of the Pyncheon family?"

"Perhaps nothing," returned Mr. Pyncheon, "possibly much!"

Here ensued a great many words between Matthew Maule and the proprietor of the Seven Gables, on the subject which the latter had thus broached. It seems (although Mr. Pyncheon had some hesitation in referring to stories so exceedingly absurd in their aspect) that the popular belief pointed to some mysterious connection and dependence, existing between the family of the Maules and these vast unrealized possessions of the Pyncheons. It was an ordinary saying that the old wizard, hanged though he was, had obtained the best end of the bargain in his contest with Colonel Pyncheon; inasmuch as he had got possession of the great Eastern claim, in exchange for an acre or two of garden ground. A very aged woman, recently dead, had often used the metaphorical expression, in her fireside talk, that miles and miles of the Pyncheon lands had been shoveled into Maule's grave; which, by the by, was but a very shallow nook, between two rocks, near the summit of Gallows Hill. Again, when the lawyers were making inquiry for the missing document, it was a byword that it would never be found, unless in the wizard's skeleton hand. So much weight had the shrewd lawyers assigned to these fables, that (but Mr. Pyncheon did not see fit to inform the carpenter of the fact) they had secretly caused the wizard's grave to be searched. Nothing was discovered, however, except that, unaccountably, the right hand of the skeleton was gone.

Now, what was unquestionably important, a portion of these popular rumors could be traced, though rather doubtfully and indistinctly, to chance words and obscure hints of the executed wizard's son, and the father of this present Matthew Maule. And here Mr. Pyncheon could bring an item of his own personal evidence into play. Though but a child at the time, he either remembered or fancied that Matthew's father had had some job to perform, on the day before, or possibly the very morning of the Colonel's decease, in the private room where he and the carpenter were at this moment talking. Certain papers belonging to Colonel Pyncheon, as his grandson distinctly recollected, had been spread out on the table.

Matthew Maule understood the insinuated suspicion.

"My father," he said, but still there was that dark smile, making a riddle of his countenance, "my father was an honester man than the bloody old Colonel! Not to get his rights back again would he have carried off one of those papers!"

"I shall not bandy words with you," observed the foreign-bred Mr. Pyncheon, with haughty composure. "Nor will it become me to resent any rudeness towards either my grandfather or myself. A gentleman, before seeking intercourse with a person of your station and habits, will first consider whether the urgency of the end may compensate for the disagreeableness of the means. It does so in the present instance."

He then renewed the conversation, and made great pecuniary offers to the carpenter, in case the latter should give information leading to the discovery of the lost document, and the consequent success of the Eastern claim. For a long time, Matthew Maule is said to have turned a cold ear to these propositions. At last, however, with a strange kind of laugh, he inquired whether Mr. Pyncheon would make over to him the old wizard's homestead ground, together with the House of the Seven Gables, now standing on it, in requital of the documentary evidence so urgently required.

The wild, chimney-corner legend (which, without copying all its extravagances, my narrative essentially follows) here gives an account of some very strange behavior on the part of Colonel Pyncheon's portrait. This picture, it must be understood, was supposed to be so intimately connected with the fate of the house, and so magically built into its walls, that, if once it should be removed, that very instant the whole edifice would come thundering down in a heap of dusty ruin. All through the foregoing conversation between Mr. Pyncheon and the carpenter, the portrait had been frowning, clenching its fist, and giving many such proofs of excessive discomposure, but without attracting the notice of either of the two colloquists. And finally, at Matthew Maule's audacious suggestion of a transfer of the seven-gabled structure, the ghostly portrait is averred to have lost all patience, and to have shown itself on the point of descending bodily from its frame. But such incredible incidents are merely to be mentioned aside.

"Give up this house!" exclaimed Mr. Pyncheon, in amazement at the proposal. "Were I to do so, my grandfather would not rest quiet in his grave!"

"He never has, if all stories are true," remarked the carpenter, composedly. "But that matter concerns his grandson more than it does Matthew Maule. I have no other terms to propose."

Impossible as he at first thought it to comply with Maule's conditions, still, on a second glance, Mr. Pyncheon was of opinion that they might at least be made matter of discussion. He himself had no personal attachment for the house, nor any pleasant associations connected with his childish residence in it. On the contrary, after seven and thirty years, the presence of his dead grandfather seemed still to pervade it, as on that morning when the affrighted boy had beheld him, with so ghastly an aspect, stiffening in his chair. His long abode in foreign parts, moreover, and familiarity with many of the castles and ancestral halls of England, and the marble palaces of Italy, had caused him to look contemptuously at the House of the Seven Gables, whether in point of splendor or convenience. It was a mansion exceedingly inadequate to the style of living which it would be incumbent on Mr. Pyncheon to support, after realizing his territorial rights. His steward might deign to occupy it, but never, certainly, the great landed proprietor himself. In the event of success, indeed, it was his purpose to return to England; nor, to say the truth, would he recently have quitted that more congenial home, had not his own fortune, as well as his deceased wife's, begun to give symptoms of exhaustion. The Eastern claim once fairly settled, and put upon the firm basis of actual possession, Mr. Pyncheon's property—to be measured by miles, not acres—would be worth an earldom, and would reasonably entitle him to solicit, or enable him to purchase, that elevated dignity from the British monarch. Lord Pyncheon! Or the Earl of Waldo! How could such a magnate be expected to contract his grandeur within the pitiful compass of seven shingled gables?

In short, on an enlarged view of the business, the carpenter's terms appeared so ridiculously easy that Mr. Pyncheon could scarcely forbear laughing in his face. He was quite ashamed, after the foregoing reflections, to propose any diminution of so moderate a recompense for the immense service to be rendered.

"I consent to your proposition, Maule," cried he. "Put me in possession of the document essential to establish my rights, and the House of the Seven Gables is your own!"

According to some versions of the story, a regular contract to the above effect was drawn up by a lawyer, and signed and sealed in the presence of witnesses. Others say that Matthew Maule was contented with a private written agreement, in which Mr. Pyncheon pledged his honor and integrity to the fulfillment of the terms concluded upon. The gentleman then ordered wine, which he and the carpenter drank together, in confirmation of their bargain. During the whole preceding discussion and subsequent formalities, the old Puritan's portrait seems to have persisted in its shadowy gestures of disapproval; but without effect, except that, as Mr. Pyncheon set down the emptied glass, he thought he beheld his grandfather frown.

"This sherry is too potent a wine for me; it has affected my brain already," he observed, after a somewhat startled look at the picture. "On returning to Europe, I shall confine myself to the more delicate vintages of Italy and France, the best of which will not bear transportation."

"My Lord Pyncheon may drink what wine he will, and wherever he pleases," replied the carpenter, as if he had been privy to Mr. Pyncheon's ambitious projects. "But first, sir, if you desire tidings of this lost document, I must crave the favor of a little talk with your fair daughter Alice."

"You are mad, Maule!" exclaimed Mr. Pyncheon, haughtily; and now, at last, there was anger mixed up with his pride. "What can my daughter have to do with a business like this?"

Indeed, at this new demand on the carpenter's part, the proprietor of the Seven Gables was even more thunderstruck than at the cool proposition to surrender his house. There was, at least, an assignable motive for the first stipulation; there appeared to be none whatever for the last. Nevertheless, Matthew Maule sturdily insisted on the young lady being summoned, and even gave her father to understand, in a mysterious kind of explanation—which made the matter considerably darker than it looked before— that the only chance of acquiring the requisite knowledge was through the clear, crystal medium of a pure and virgin intelligence, like that of the fair Alice. Not to encumber our story with Mr. Pyncheon's scruples, whether of conscience, pride, or fatherly affection, he at length ordered his daughter to be called. He well knew that she was in her chamber, and engaged in no occupation that could not readily be laid aside; for, as it happened, ever since Alice's name had been spoken, both her father and the carpenter had heard the sad and sweet music of her harpsichord, and the airier melancholy of her accompanying voice.

So Alice Pyncheon was summoned and appeared. A portrait of this young lady, painted by a Venetian artist, and left by her father in England, is said to have fallen into the hands of the present Duke of Devonshire, and to be now preserved at Chatsworth; not on account of any associations with the original, but for its value as a picture, and the high character of beauty in the countenance. If ever there was a lady born, and set apart from the world's vulgar mass by a certain gentle and cold stateliness, it was this very Alice Pyncheon. Yet there was the womanly mixture in her; the tenderness, or, at least, the tender capabilities. For the sake of that redeeming quality, a man of generous nature would have forgiven all her pride, and have been content, almost, to lie down in her path, and let Alice set her slender foot upon his heart. All that he would have required was simply the acknowledgment that he was indeed a man, and a fellow being, molded of the same elements as she.

As Alice came into the room, her eyes fell upon the carpenter, who was standing near its center, clad in a green woolen jacket, a pair of loose breeches, open at the knees, and with a long pocket for his rule, the end of which protruded; it was as proper a mark of the artisan's calling as Mr. Pyncheon's full-dress sword of that gentleman's aristocratic pretensions. A glow of artistic approval brightened over Alice Pyncheon's face; she was struck with admiration—which she made no attempt to conceal—of the remarkable comeliness, strength, and energy of Maule's figure. But that admiring glance (which most other men, perhaps, would have cherished as a sweet recollection, all through life) the carpenter never forgave. It must have been the devil himself that made Maule so subtile in his perception.

"Does the girl look at me as if I were a brute beast?" thought he, setting his teeth. "She shall know whether I have a human spirit; and the worse for her, if it prove stronger than her own!"

"My father, you sent for me," said Alice, in her sweet and harplike voice. "But, if you have business with this young man, pray let me go again. You know I do not love this room, in spite of that Claude, with which you try to bring back sunny recollections."

"Stay a moment, young lady, if you please!" said Matthew Maule. "My business with your father is over. With yourself, it is now to begin!"

Alice looked towards her father in surprise and inquiry.

"Yes, Alice," said Mr. Pyncheon, with some disturbance and confusion. "This young man—his name is Matthew Maule—professes, so far as I can understand him, to be able to discover, through your means, a certain paper or parchment, which was missing long before your birth. The importance of the document in question renders it advisable to neglect no possible, even if improbable, method of regaining it. You will therefore oblige me, my dear Alice, by answering this person's inquiries, and complying with his lawful and reasonable requests, so far as they may appear to have the aforesaid object in view. As I shall remain in the room, you need apprehend no rude nor unbecoming deportment, on the young man's part; and, at your slightest wish, of course, the investigation, or whatever we may call it, shall immediately be broken off."

"Mistress Alice Pyncheon," remarked Matthew Maule,

with the utmost deference, but yet a half-hidden sarcasm in his look and tone, "will no doubt feel herself quite safe in her father's presence, and under his all-sufficient protection."

"I certainly shall entertain no manner of apprehension, with my father at hand," said Alice, with maidenly dignity. "Neither do I conceive that a lady, while true to herself, can have aught to fear from whomsoever, or in any circumstances!"

Poor Alice! By what unhappy impulse did she thus put herself at once on terms of defiance against a strength which she could not estimate?

"Then, Mistress Alice," said Matthew Maule, handing a chair—gracefully enough, for a craftsman, "will it please you only to sit down, and do me the favor (though altogether beyond a poor carpenter's deserts) to fix your eyes on mine!"

Alice complied. She was very proud. Setting aside all advantages of rank, this fair girl deemed herself conscious of a power—combined of beauty, high, unsullied purity, and the preservative force of womanhood—that could make her sphere impenetrable, unless betrayed by treachery within. She instinctively knew, it may be, that some sinister or evil potency was now striving to pass her barriers; nor would she decline the contest. So Alice put woman's might against man's might; a match not often equal on the part of woman.

Her father meanwhile had turned away, and seemed absorbed in the contemplation of a landscape by Claude, where a shadowy and sun-streaked vista penetrated so remotely into an ancient wood that it would have been no wonder if his fancy had lost itself in the picture's bewildering depths. But, in truth, the picture was no more to him at that moment than the blank wall against which it hung. His mind was haunted with the many and strange tales which he had heard, attributing mysterious if not supernatural endowments to these Maules, as well the grandson here present as his two immediate ancestors. Mr. Pyncheon's long residence abroad, and intercourse with men of wit and fashion—courtiers, worldlings, and free-thinkers—had done much towards obliterating the grim Puritan superstitions which no man of New England birth at that early period could entirely escape. But, on the other hand, had not a whole community believed Maule's grandfather to be a wizard? Had not the crime been proved? Had not the wizard died for it? Had he not bequeathed a legacy of hatred against the Pyncheons to this only grandson, who, as it appeared, was now about to exercise a subtle influence over the daughter of his enemy's house? Might not this influence be the same that was called witchcraft?

Turning half around, he caught a glimpse of Maule's figure in the looking glass. At some paces from Alice, with his arms uplifted in the air, the carpenter made a gesture as if directing downward a slow, ponderous, and invisible weight upon the maiden.

"Stay, Maule!" exclaimed Mr. Pyncheon, stepping forward. "I forbid your proceeding further!"

"Pray, my dear father, do not interrupt the young man," said Alice, without changing her position. "His efforts, I assure you, will prove very harmless."

Again Mr. Pyncheon turned his eyes towards the Claude. It was then his daughter's will, in opposition to his own, that the experiment should be fully tried. Henceforth, therefore, he did but consent, not urge it. And was it not for her sake far more than for his own that he desired its success? That lost parchment once restored, the beautiful Alice Pyncheon, with the rich dowry which he could then bestow, might wed an English duke or a German reigning prince, instead of some New England clergyman or lawyer! At the thought, the ambitious father almost consented, in his heart, that, if the devil's power were needed to the accomplishment of this great object, Maule might evoke him. Alice's own purity would be her safeguard.

With his mind full of imaginary magnificence, Mr. Pyncheon heard a half-uttered exclamation from his daughter. It was very faint and low; so indistinct that there seemed but half a will to shape out the words, and too undefined a purport to be intelligible. Yet it was a call for help—his conscience never doubted it—and, little more than a whisper to his ear, it was a dismal shriek, and long re-echoed so, in the region round his heart! But this time the father did not turn.

After a further interval, Maule spoke.

"Behold your daughter!" said he.

Mr. Pyncheon came hastily forward. The carpenter was standing erect in front of Alice's chair, and pointing his finger towards the maiden with an expression of triumphant power the limits of which could not be defined, as, indeed, its scope stretched vaguely towards the unseen and the infinite. Alice sat in an attitude of profound repose, with the long brown lashes drooping over her eyes.

"There she is!" said the carpenter. "Speak to her!"

"Alice! My daughter!" exclaimed Mr. Pyncheon. "My own Alice!"

She did not stir.

"Louder!" said Maule, smiling.

"Alice! Awake!" cried her father. "It troubles me to see you thus! Awake!"

He spoke loudly, with terror in his voice, and close to that delicate ear which had always been so sensitive to every discord. But the sound evidently reached her not. It is indescribable what a sense of remote, dim, unattainable distance, betwixt himself and Alice, was impressed on the father by this impossibility of reaching her with his voice.

"Best touch her!" said Matthew Maule. "Shake the girl, and roughly, too! My hands are hardened with too much use of ax, saw, and plane—else I might help you!"

Mr. Pyncheon took her hand, and pressed it with the earnestness of startled emotion. He kissed her, with so great a heartthrob in the kiss that he thought she must needs feel it. Then, in a gust of anger at her insensibility, he shook her maiden form with a violence which, the next moment, it affrighted him to remember. He withdrew his encircling arms, and Alice—whose figure, though flexible, had been wholly impassive—relapsed into the same attitude as before these attempts to arouse her. Maule having shifted his position, her face was turned towards him slightly, but with what seemed to be a reference of her very slumber to his guidance.

Then it was a strange sight to behold how the man of

conventionalities shook the powder out of his periwig; how the reserved and stately gentleman forgot his dignity; how the gold-embroidered waistcoat flickered and glistened in the firelight with the convulsion of rage, terror, and sorrow in the human heart that was beating under it.

"Villain!" cried Mr. Pyncheon, shaking his clenched fist at Maule. "You and the fiend together have robbed me of my daughter! Give her back, spawn of the old wizard, or you shall climb Gallows Hill in your grandfather's footsteps!"

"Softly, Mr. Pyncheon!" said the carpenter, with scornful composure. "Softly, an it please your worship, else you will spoil those rich lace ruffles at your wrists! Is it my crime if you have sold your daughter for the mere hope of getting a sheet of yellow parchment into your clutch? There sits Mistress Alice quietly asleep! Now let Matthew Maule try whether she be as proud as the carpenter found her awhile since."

He spoke, and Alice responded, with a soft, subdued, inward acquiescence, and a bending of her form towards him, like the flame of a torch when it indicates a gentle draught of air. He beckoned with his hand, and, rising from her chair—blindly, but undoubtingly, as tending to her sure and inevitable center—the proud Alice approached him. He waved her back, and, retreating, Alice sank again into her seat.

"She is mine!" said Matthew Maule. "Mine, by the right of the strongest spirit!"

In the further progress of the legend, there is a long, grotesque, and occasionally awe-striking account of the carpenter's incantations (if so they are to be called), with a view of discovering the lost document. It appears to have been his object to convert the mind of Alice into a kind of telescopic medium, through which Mr. Pyncheon and himself might obtain a glimpse into the spiritual world. He succeeded, accordingly, in holding an imperfect sort of intercourse, at one remove, with the departed personages in whose custody the so much valued secret had been carried beyond the precincts of earth. During her trance, Alice described three figures as being present to her spiritualized perception. One was an aged, dignified, stern-looking gentleman, clad as for a solemn festival in grave and costly attire, but with a great bloodstain on his richly wrought band; the second, an aged man, meanly dressed, with a dark and malign countenance, and a broken halter about his neck; the third, a person not so advanced in life as the former two, but beyond the middle age, wearing a coarse woolen tunic and leather breeches, and with a carpenter's rule sticking out of his side pocket. These three visionary characters possessed a mutual knowledge of the missing document. One of them, in truth—it was he with the bloodstain on his band—seemed, unless his gestures were misunderstood, to hold the parchment in his immediate keeping, but was prevented, by his two partners in the mystery, from disburdening himself of the trust. Finally, when he showed a purpose of shouting forth the secret, loudly enough to be heard from his own sphere into that of mortals, his companions struggled with him, and pressed their hands over his mouth; and forthwith—whether that he were choked by it, or that the secret itself was of a crimson hue—there was a fresh flow of blood upon his band. Upon this, the two meanly dressed figures mocked and jeered at the much-abashed old dignitary, and pointed their fingers at the stain.

At this juncture, Maule turned to Mr. Pyncheon.

"It will never be allowed," said he. "The custody of this secret, that would so enrich his heirs, makes part of your grandfather's retribution. He must choke with it until it is no longer of any value. And keep you the House of the Seven Gables! It is too dear-bought an inheritance, and too heavy with the curse upon it, to be shifted yet awhile from the Colonel's posterity!"

Mr. Pyncheon tried to speak, but—what with fear and passion—could make only a gurgling murmur in his throat. The carpenter smiled.

"Aha, worshipful sir! So, you have old Maule's blood to drink!" said he, jeeringly.

"Fiend in man's shape! Why dost thou keep dominion over my child?" cried Mr. Pyncheon, when his choked utterance could make way. "Give me back my daughter! Then go thy ways; and may we never meet again!"

"Your daughter!" said Matthew Maule. "Why, she is

fairly mine! Nevertheless, not to be too hard with fair Mistress Alice, I will leave her in your keeping: but I do not warrant you that she shall never have occasion to remember Maule, the carpenter."

He waved his hands with an upward motion; and, after a few repetitions of similar gestures, the beautiful Alice Pyncheon awoke from her strange trance. She awoke, without the slightest recollection of her visionary experience; but as one losing herself in a momentary reverie, and returning to the consciousness of actual life, in almost as brief an interval as the down-sinking flame of the hearth should quiver again up the chimney. On recognizing Matthew Maule, she assumed an air of somewhat cold but gentle dignity, the rather as there was a certain peculiar smile on the carpenter's visage that stirred the native pride of the fair Alice. So ended, for that time, the quest for the lost title deed of the Pyncheon territory at the eastward; nor, though often subsequently renewed, has it ever yet befallen a Pyncheon to set his eye upon that parchment.

But, alas for the beautiful, the gentle, yet too haughty Alice! A power that she little dreamed of had laid its grasp upon her maiden soul. A will, most unlike her own, constrained her to do its grotesque and fantastic bidding. Her father, as it proved, had martyred his poor child to an inordinate desire for measuring his land by miles instead of acres. And, therefore, while Alice Pyncheon lived, she was Maule's slave, in a bondage more humiliating, a thousand-fold, than that which binds its chain around the body. Seated by his humble fireside, Maule had but to wave his hand; and, wherever the proud lady chanced to be—whether in her chamber, or entertaining her father's stately guests, or worshiping at church—whatever her place or occupation, her spirit passed from beneath her own control, and bowed itself to Maule. "Alice, laugh!" the carpenter, beside his hearth, would say; or perhaps intensely will it, without a spoken word. And, even were it prayer time, or at a funeral, Alice must break into wild laughter. "Alice, be sad!" and, at the instant, down would come her tears, quenching all the mirth of those around her like sudden rain upon a bonfire. "Alice, dance!" and dance she would, not in such courtlike measures as she had learned abroad, but some high-paced jig, or hop-skip rigadoon, befitting the brisk lasses at a rustic merrymaking. It seemed to be Maule's impulse not to ruin Alice, nor to visit her with any black or gigantic mischief, which would have crowned her sorrows with the grace of tragedy, but to wreak a low, ungenerous scorn upon her. Thus all the dignity of life was lost. She felt herself too much abased, and longed to change natures with some worm!

One evening, at a bridal party (but not her own; for, so lost from self-control, she would have deemed it sin to marry), poor Alice was beckoned forth by her unseen despot, and constrained, in her gossamer white dress and satin slippers, to hasten along the street to the mean dwelling of a laboring man. There was laughter and good cheer within; for Matthew Maule, that night, was to wed the laborer's daughter, and had summoned proud Alice Pyncheon to wait upon his bride. And so she did; and when the twain were one, Alice awoke out of her enchanted sleep. Yet, no longer proud—humbly, and with a smile all steeped in sadness—she kissed Maule's wife, and went her way. It was an inclement night; the southeast wind drove the mingled snow and rain into her thinly sheltered bosom; her satin slippers were wet through and through, as she trod the muddy sidewalks. The next day, a cold; soon, a settled cough; anon, a hectic cheek, a wasted form, that sat beside the harpsichord, and filled the house with music! Music, in which a strain of the heavenly choristers was echoed! Oh, joy! For Alice had borne her last humiliation! Oh, greater joy! For Alice was penitent of her one earthly sin, and proud no more!

The Pyncheons made a great funeral for Alice. The kith and kin were there, and the whole respectability of the town besides. But, last in the procession, came Matthew Maule, gnashing his teeth, as if he would have bitten his own heart in twain—the darkest and woefulest man that ever walked behind a corpse! He meant to humble Alice, not to kill her; but he had taken a woman's delicate soul into his rude gripe, to play with—and she was dead!

⇥14⇤

Phoebe's Good-by

HOLGRAVE, plunging into his tale with the energy and absorption natural to a young author, had given a good deal of action to the parts capable of being developed and exemplified in that manner. He now observed that a certain remarkable drowsiness (wholly unlike that with which the reader possibly feels himself affected) had been flung over the senses of his auditress. It was the effect, unquestionably, of the mystic gesticulations by which he had sought to bring bodily before Phoebe's perception the figure of the mesmerizing carpenter. With the lids drooping over her eyes—now lifted for an instant, and drawn down again as with leaden weights—she leaned slightly towards him, and seemed almost to regulate her breath by his. Holgrave gazed at her, as he rolled up his manuscript, and recognized an incipient stage of that curious psychological condition which, as he had himself told Phoebe, he possessed more than an ordinary faculty of producing. A veil was beginning to be muffled about her, in which she could behold only him, and live only in his thoughts and emotions. His glance, as he fastened it on the young girl, grew involuntarily more concentrated; in his attitude there was the consciousness of power, investing his hardly mature figure with a dignity that did not belong to its physical manifestation. It was evident, that, with but one wave of his hand and a corresponding effort of his will, he could complete his mastery over Phoebe's yet free and virgin spirit: he could establish an influence over this good, pure, and simple child as dangerous, and perhaps as disastrous, as that which the carpenter of his legend had acquired and exercised over the ill-fated Alice.

To a disposition like Holgrave's, at once speculative and active, there is no temptation so great as the opportunity of acquiring empire over the human spirit; nor any idea more seductive to a young man than to become the arbiter of a young girl's destiny. Let us, therefore—whatever his defects of nature and education, and in spite of his scorn for creeds and institutions—concede to the daguerreotypist the rare and high quality of reverence for another's individuality. Let us allow him integrity, also, forever after to be confided in; since he forbade himself to twine that one link more which might have rendered his spell over Phoebe indissoluble.

He made a slight gesture upward with his hand.

"You really mortify me, my dear Miss Phoebe!" he exclaimed, smiling half-sarcastically at her. "My poor story, it is but too evident, will never do for *Godey* or *Graham*! Only think of your falling asleep at what I hoped the newspaper critics would pronounce a most brilliant, powerful, imaginative, pathetic, and original winding up! Well, the manuscript must serve to light lamps with—if, indeed, being so imbued with my gentle dullness, it is any longer capable of flame!"

"Me asleep! How can you say so?" answered Phoebe, as unconscious of the crisis through which she had passed as an infant of the precipice to the verge of which it has rolled. "No, no! I consider myself as having been very attentive; and, though I don't remember the incidents quite distinctly, yet I have an impression of a vast deal of trouble and calamity—so, no doubt, the story will prove exceedingly attractive."

By this time, the sun had gone down, and was tinting the clouds towards the zenith with those bright hues which are not seen there until some time after sunset, and when the horizon has quite lost its richer brilliancy. The moon, too, which had long been climbing overhead, and unobtrusively melting its disk into the azure—like an ambitious demagogue, who hides his aspiring purpose by assuming the prevalent hue of popular sentiment—now began to shine out, broad and oval, in its middle pathway. These silvery beams were already powerful enough to change the character of the lingering daylight. They softened and embellished the aspect of the old house; although the shadows fell deeper into the angles of its many gables, and lay brooding under the projecting story, and within the half-open door. With the lapse of every moment, the garden grew more picturesque; the fruit trees, shrubbery, and flower bushes had a dark obscurity among them. The commonplace characteristics—which, at noontide, it seemed to have taken a century of sordid life to accumulate—were now transfigured by a charm of romance. A hundred mysterious years were whispering among the leaves, whenever the slight sea breeze found its way thither and stirred them. Through the foliage that roofed the little summerhouse, the moonlight flickered to and fro, and fell silvery white on the dark floor, the table, and the circular bench, with a continual shift and play, according as the chinks and wayward crevices among the twigs admitted or shut out the glimmer.

So sweetly cool was the atmosphere, after all the feverish day, that the summer eve might be fancied as sprinkling dews and liquid moonlight, with a dash of icy temper in them, out of a silver vase. Here and there, a few drops of this freshness were scattered on a human heart, and gave it youth again, and sympathy with the eternal youth of nature. The artist chanced to be one on whom the reviving influence fell. It made him feel—what he sometimes almost forgot, thrust so early as he had been into the rude struggle of man with man—how youthful he still was.

"It seems to me," he observed, "that I never watched the coming of so beautiful an eve, and never felt anything so very much like happiness as at this moment. After all, what a good world we live in! How good, and beautiful! How young it is, too, with nothing really rotten or age-worn in it! This old house, for example, which sometimes has positively oppressed my breath with its smell of decaying timber! And this garden, where the black mold always clings to my spade, as if I were a sexton delving in a graveyard!

Could I keep the feeling that now possesses me, the garden would every day be virgin soil, with the earth's first freshness in the flavor of its beans and squashes; and the house! It would be like a bower in Eden, blossoming with the earliest roses that God ever made. Moonlight, and the sentiment in man's heart responsive to it, are the greatest of renovators and reformers. And all other reform and renovation, I suppose, will prove to be no better than moonshine!"

"I have been happier than I am now; at least, much gayer," said Phoebe, thoughtfully. "Yet I am sensible of a great charm in this brightening moonlight; and I love to watch how the day, tired as it is, lags away reluctantly, and hates to be called yesterday so soon. I never cared much about moonlight before. What is there, I wonder, so beautiful in it tonight?"

"And you have never felt it before?" inquired the artist, looking earnestly at the girl through the twilight.

"Never," answered Phoebe. "And life does not look the same, now that I have felt it so. It seems as if I had looked at everything, hitherto, in broad daylight, or else in the ruddy light of a cheerful fire, glimmering and dancing through a room. Ah, poor me!" she added, with a half-melancholy laugh. "I shall never be so merry as before I knew Cousin Hepzibah and poor Cousin Clifford. I have grown a great deal older, in this little time. Older, and, I hope, wiser, and—not exactly sadder, but, certainly, with not half so much lightness in my spirits! I have given them my sunshine, and have been glad to give it; but, of course, I cannot both give and keep it. They are welcome, notwithstanding!"

"You have lost nothing, Phoebe, worth keeping, nor which it was possible to keep," said Holgrave, after a pause. "Our first youth is of no value; for we are never conscious of it until after it is gone. But sometimes—always, I suspect, unless one is exceedingly unfortunate—there comes a sense of second youth, gushing out of the heart's joy at being in love; or, possibly, it may come to crown some other grand festival in life, if any other such there be. This bemoaning of one's self (as you do now) over the first careless, shallow gaiety of youth departed, and this profound happiness at youth regained—so much deeper and richer than that we lost—are essential to the soul's development. In some cases, the two states come almost simultaneously, and mingle the sadness and the rapture in one mysterious emotion."

"I hardly think I understand you," said Phoebe.

"No wonder," replied Holgrave, smiling. "For I have told you a secret which I hardly began to know before I found myself giving it utterance. Remember it, however; and when the truth becomes clear to you, then think of this moonlight scene!"

"It is entirely moonlight now, except only a little flush of faint crimson, upward from the west, between those buildings," remarked Phoebe. "I must go in. Cousin Hepzibah is not quick at figures, and will give herself a headache over the day's accounts, unless I help her."

But Holgrave detained her a little longer.

"Miss Hepzibah tells me," observed he, "that you return to the country in a few days."

"Yes, but only for a little while," answered Phoebe, "for I look upon this as my present home. I go to make a few arrangements, and to take a more deliberate leave of my mother and friends. It is pleasant to live where one is much desired and very useful; and I think I may have the satisfaction of feeling myself so here."

"You surely may, and more than you imagine," said the artist. "Whatever health, comfort, and natural life exists in the house is embodied in your person. These blessings came along with you, and will vanish when you leave the threshold. Miss Hepzibah, by secluding herself from society, has lost all true relation with it, and is, in fact, dead; although she galvanizes herself into a semblance of life, and stands behind her counter, afflicting the world with a greatly-to-be-deprecated scowl. Your poor cousin Clifford is another dead and long-buried person, on whom the governor and council have wrought a necromantic miracle. I should not wonder if he were to crumble away, some morning, after you are gone, and nothing be seen of him more, except a heap of dust. Miss Hepzibah, at any rate, will lose what little flexibility she has. They both exist by you."

"I should be very sorry to think so," answered Phoebe,

gravely. "But it is true that my small abilities were precisely what they needed; and I have a real interest in their welfare—an odd kind of motherly sentiment—which I wish you would not laugh at! And let me tell you frankly, Mr. Holgrave, I am sometimes puzzled to know whether you wish them well or ill."

"Undoubtedly," said the daguerreotypist, "I do feel an interest in this antiquated, poverty-stricken old maiden lady, and this degraded and shattered gentleman—this abortive lover of the beautiful. A kindly interest, too, helpless old children that they are! But you have no conception what a different kind of heart mine is from your own. It is not my impulse, as regards these two individuals, either to help or hinder; but to look on, to analyze, to explain matters to myself, and to comprehend the drama which, for almost two hundred years, has been dragging its slow length over the ground where you and I now tread. If permitted to witness the close, I doubt not to derive a moral satisfaction from it, go matters how they may. There is a conviction within me that the end draws nigh. But, though Providence sent you hither to help, and sends me only as a privileged and meet spectator, I pledge myself to lend these unfortunate beings whatever aid I can!"

"I wish you would speak more plainly," cried Phoebe, perplexed and displeased, "and, above all, that you would feel more like a Christian and a human being! How is it possible to see people in distress, without desiring, more than anything else, to help and comfort them? You talk as if this old house were a theater; and you seem to look at Hepzibah's and Clifford's misfortunes, and those of generations before them, as a tragedy, such as I have seen acted in the hall of a country hotel, only the present one appears to be played exclusively for your amusement. I do not like this. The play costs the performers too much, and the audience is too coldhearted."

"You are severe," said Holgrave, compelled to recognize a degree of truth in this piquant sketch of his own mood.

"And then," continued Phoebe, "what can you mean by your conviction, which you tell me of, that the end is drawing near? Do you know of any new trouble hanging over my poor relatives? If so, tell me at once, and I will not leave them!"

"Forgive me, Phoebe!" said the daguerreotypist, holding out his hand, to which the girl was constrained to yield her own. "I am somewhat of a mystic, it must be confessed. The tendency is in my blood, together with the faculty of mesmerism, which might have brought me to Gallows Hill, in the good old times of witchcraft. Believe me, if I were really aware of any secret the disclosure of which would benefit your friends—who are my own friends, likewise—you should learn it before we part. But I have no such knowledge."

"You hold something back!" said Phoebe.

"Nothing—no secrets but my own," answered Holgrave. "I can perceive, indeed, that Judge Pyncheon still keeps his eye on Clifford, in whose ruin he had so large a share. His motives and intentions, however, are a mystery to me. He is a determined and relentless man, with the genuine character of an inquisitor; and had he any object to gain by putting Clifford to the rack, I verily believe that he would wrench his joints from their sockets, in order to accomplish it. But, so wealthy and eminent as he is—so powerful in his own strength, and in the support of society on all sides—what can Judge Pyncheon have to hope or fear from the imbecile, branded, half-torpid Clifford?"

"Yet," urged Phoebe, "you did speak as if misfortune were impending!"

"Oh, that was because I am morbid!" replied the artist. "My mind has a twist aside, like almost everybody's mind, except your own. Moreover, it is so strange to find myself an inmate of this old Pyncheon House, and sitting in this old garden (hark, how Maule's well is murmuring!) that, were it only for this one circumstance, I cannot help fancying that Destiny is arranging its fifth act for a catastrophe."

"There!" cried Phoebe with renewed vexation; for she was by nature as hostile to mystery as the sunshine to a dark corner. "You puzzle me more than ever!"

"Then let us part friends!" said Holgrave, pressing her hand. "Or, if not friends, let us part before you entirely hate me. You, who love everybody else in the world!"

"Good-by, then," said Phoebe, frankly. "I do not mean to be angry a great while, and should be sorry to have you think so. There has Cousin Hepzibah been standing in the shadow of the doorway, this quarter of an hour past! She thinks I stay too long in the damp garden. So, good night, and good-by!"

On the second morning thereafter, Phoebe might have been seen, in her straw bonnet, with a shawl on one arm and a little carpetbag on the other, bidding adieu to Hepzibah and Cousin Clifford. She was to take a seat in the next train of cars, which would transport her to within half a dozen miles of her country village.

The tears were in Phoebe's eyes; a smile, dewy with affectionate regret, was glimmering around her pleasant mouth. She wondered how it came to pass that her life of a few weeks, here in this heavyhearted old mansion, had taken such hold of her, and so melted into her associations, as now to seem a more important center point of remembrance than all which had gone before. How had Hepzibah—grim, silent, and irresponsive to her overflow of cordial sentiment—contrived to win so much love? And Clifford—in his abortive decay, with the mystery of fearful crime upon him, and the close prison atmosphere yet lurking in his breath—how had he transformed himself into the simplest child, whom Phoebe felt bound to watch over, and be, as it were, the providence of his unconsidered hours! Everything, at that instant of farewell, stood out prominently to her view. Look where she would, lay her hand on what she might, the object responded to her consciousness, as if a moist human heart were in it.

She peeped from the window into the garden, and felt herself more regretful at leaving this spot of black earth, vitiated with such an agelong growth of weeds, than joyful at the idea of again scenting her pine forests and fresh clover fields. She called Chanticleer, his two wives, and the venerable chicken, and threw them some crumbs of bread from the breakfast table. These being hastily gobbled up, the chicken spread its wings, and alighted close by Phoebe on the windowsill, where it looked gravely into her face and vented its emotions in a croak. Phoebe bade it be a good old chicken during her absence, and promised to bring it a little bag of buckwheat.

"Ah, Phoebe!" remarked Hepzibah. "You do not smile so naturally as when you came to us! Then, the smile chose to shine out; now, you choose it should. It is well that you are going back, for a little while, into your native air. There has been too much weight on your spirits. The house is too gloomy and lonesome; the shop is full of vexations; and as for me, I have no faculty of making things look brighter than they are. Dear Clifford has been your only comfort!"

"Come hither, Phoebe," suddenly cried her cousin Clifford, who had said very little all the morning. "Close—closer—and look me in the face!"

Phoebe put one of her small hands on each elbow of his chair, and leaned her face towards him, so that he might peruse it as carefully as he would. It is probable that the latent emotions of this parting hour had revived, in some degree, his bedimmed and enfeebled faculties. At any rate, Phoebe soon felt that, if not the profound insight of a seer, yet a more than feminine delicacy of appreciation was making her heart the subject of its regard. A moment before, she had known nothing which she would have sought to hide. Now, as if some secret were hinted to her own consciousness through the medium of another's perception, she was fain to let her eyelids droop beneath Clifford's gaze. A blush, too—the redder because she strove hard to keep it down—ascended higher and higher, in a tide of fitful progress, until even her brow was all suffused with it.

"It is enough, Phoebe," said Clifford, with a melancholy smile. "When I first saw you, you were the prettiest little maiden in the world; and now you have deepened into beauty! Girlhood has passed into womanhood; the bud is a bloom! Go, now! I feel lonelier than I did."

Phoebe took leave of the desolate couple, and passed through the shop, twinkling her eyelids to shake off a dewdrop; for—considering how brief her absence was to be, and therefore the folly of being cast down about it—she would not so far acknowledge her tears as to dry them with her handkerchief. On the doorstep, she met the little urchin whose marvelous feats of gastronomy have been recorded in the earlier pages of our narrative. She took from the window some specimen or other of natural history—her eyes being too dim with moisture to inform her accurately whether it was a rabbit or a hippopotamus—put it into the child's hand, as a parting gift, and went her way. Old Uncle Venner was just coming out of his door, with a wood horse and saw on his shoulder; and, trudging along the street, he scrupled not to keep company with Phoebe so far as their paths lay together; nor, in spite of his patched coat and rusty beaver, and the curious fashion of his tow-cloth trousers, could she find it in her heart to outwalk him.

"We shall miss you, next Sabbath afternoon," observed the street philosopher. "It is unaccountable how little while it takes some folks to grow just as natural to a man as his own breath; and, begging your pardon, Miss Phoebe (though there can be no offense in an old man's saying it), that's just what you've grown to me! My years have been a great many, and your life is but just beginning; and yet, you are somehow as familiar to me as if I had found you at my mother's door, and you had blossomed, like a running vine, all along my pathway since. Come back soon, or I shall be gone to my farm; for I begin to find these wood-sawing jobs a little too tough for my backache."

"Very soon, Uncle Venner," replied Phoebe.

"And let it be all the sooner, Phoebe, for the sake of those poor souls yonder," continued her companion. "They can never do without you now—never, Phoebe, never!—no more than if one of God's angels had been living with them, and making their dismal house pleasant and comfortable! Don't it seem to you they'd be in a sad case, if, some pleasant summer morning like this, the angel should spread his wings, and fly to the place he came from? Well, just so they feel, now that you're going home by the railroad! They can't bear it, Miss Phoebe; so be sure to come back!"

"I am no angel, Uncle Venner," said Phoebe, smiling, as she offered him her hand at the street corner. "But, I suppose, people never feel so much like angels as when they are doing what little good they may. So I shall certainly come back!"

Thus parted the old man and the rosy girl; and Phoebe took the wings of the morning, and was soon flitting almost as rapidly away as if endowed with the aerial locomotion of the angels to whom Uncle Venner had so graciously compared her.

❧15❧

The Scowl and Smile

SEVERAL days passed over the Seven Gables, heavily and drearily enough. In fact (not to attribute the whole gloom of sky and earth to the one inauspicious circumstance of Phoebe's departure), an easterly storm had set in, and indefatigably applied itself to the task of making the black roof and walls of the old house look more cheerless than ever before. Yet was the outside not half so cheerless as the interior. Poor Clifford was cut off, at once, from all his scanty resources of enjoyment. Phoebe was not there; nor did the sunshine fall upon the floor. The garden, with its muddy walks, and the chill, dripping foliage of its summerhouse, was an image to be shuddered at. Nothing flourished in the cold, moist, pitiless atmosphere, drifting with the brackish scud of sea breezes, except the moss along the joints of the shingle roof, and the great bunch of weeds, that had lately been suffering from drought, in the angle between the two front gables.

As for Hepzibah, she seemed not merely possessed with the east wind, but to be, in her very person, only another phase of this gray and sullen spell of weather—the east wind itself, grim and disconsolate, in a rusty black silk gown, and with a turban of cloud wreaths on its head. The custom of the shop fell off, because a story got abroad that she soured her small beer and other damageable commodities, by scowling on them. It is, perhaps, true that the public had something reasonably to complain of in her deportment; but towards Clifford she was neither ill-tempered nor unkind, nor felt less warmth of heart than always, had it been possible to make it reach him. The inutility of her best efforts, however, palsied the poor old gentlewoman. She could do little else than sit silently in a corner of the room, when the wet pear-tree branches, sweeping across the small windows, created a noonday dusk, which Hepzibah unconsciously darkened with her woebegone aspect. It was no fault of Hepzibah's. Everything—even the old chairs and tables, that had known what weather was for three or four such lifetimes as her own—looked as damp and chill as if the present were their worst experience. The picture of the Puritan Colonel shivered on the wall. The house itself shivered, from every attic of its seven gables, down to the great kitchen fireplace, which served all the better as an emblem of the mansion's heart, because, though built for warmth, it was now so comfortless and empty.

Hepzibah attempted to enliven matters by a fire in the parlor. But the storm demon kept watch above, and, whenever a flame was kindled, drove the smoke back again, choking the chimney's sooty throat with its own breath. Nevertheless, during four days of this miserable storm, Clifford wrapped himself in an old cloak, and occupied his customary chair. On the morning of the fifth, when summoned to breakfast, he responded only by a brokenhearted murmur, expressive of a determination not to leave his bed. His sister made no attempt to change his purpose. In fact, entirely as she loved him, Hepzibah could hardly have borne any longer the wretched duty—so impracticable by her few and rigid faculties—of seeking pastime for a still sensitive but ruined mind, critical and fastidious, without force or volition. It was, at least, something short of positive despair that, today, she might sit shivering alone, and not suffer continually a new grief, and unreasonable pang of remorse, at every fitful sigh of her fellow sufferer.

But Clifford, it seemed, though he did not make his appearance belowstairs, had, after all, bestirred himself in quest of amusement. In the course of the forenoon, Hepzibah heard a note of music, which (there being no other tuneful contrivance in the House of the Seven Gables) she knew must proceed from Alice Pyncheon's harpsichord. She was aware that Clifford, in his youth, had possessed a cultivated taste for music, and a considerable degree of skill in its practice. It was difficult, however, to conceive of his retaining an accomplishment to which daily exercise is so essential, in the measure indicated by the sweet, airy, and delicate, though most melancholy strain that now stole upon her ear. Nor was it less marvelous that the long-silent instrument should be capable of so much melody. Hepzibah involuntarily thought of the ghostly harmonies, prelusive of death in the family, which were attributed to the legendary Alice. But it was, perhaps, proof of the agency of other than spiritual fingers that, after a few touches, the chords seemed to snap asunder with their own vibrations, and the music ceased.

But a harsher sound succeeded to the mysterious notes; nor was the easterly day fated to pass without an event sufficient in itself to poison, for Hepzibah and Clifford, the balmiest air that ever brought the hummingbirds along with it. The final echoes of Alice Pyncheon's performance (or Clifford's, if his we must consider it) were driven away by no less vulgar a dissonance than the ringing of the shop bell. A foot was heard scraping itself on the threshold, and thence somewhat ponderously stepping on the floor. Hepzibah delayed a moment, while muffling herself in a faded shawl which had been her defensive armor in a forty years' warfare against the east wind. A characteristic sound, however—neither a cough nor a hem, but a kind of rumbling and reverberating spasm in somebody's capacious depth of chest—impelled her to hurry forward, with that aspect of fierce faintheartedness so common to women in cases of perilous emergency. Few of her sex, on such occasions, have ever looked so terrible as our poor scowling Hepzibah. But the visitor quietly closed the shop door behind him, stood up his umbrella against the counter, and turned a visage of composed benignity, to meet the alarm and anger which his appearance had excited.

Hepzibah's presentiment had not deceived her. It was no other than Judge Pyncheon, who, after in vain trying the front door, had now effected his entrance into the shop.

"How do you do, Cousin Hepzibah? And how does this most inclement weather affect our poor Clifford?" began the Judge; and wonderful it seemed, indeed, that the easterly storm was not put to shame, or, at any rate, a little mollified, by the genial benevolence of his smile. "I could not rest without calling to ask, once more, whether I can in any manner promote his comfort, or your own."

"You can do nothing," said Hepzibah, controlling her agitation as well as she could. "I devote myself to Clifford. He has every comfort which his situation admits of."

"But allow me to suggest, dear cousin," rejoined the Judge, "you err—in all affection and kindness, no doubt, and with the very best intentions—but you do err, nevertheless, in keeping your brother so secluded. Why insulate him thus from all sympathy and kindness? Clifford, alas, has had too much of solitude. Now let him try society—the society, that is to say, of kindred and old friends. Let me, for instance, but see Clifford, and I will answer for the good effect of the interview."

"You cannot see him," answered Hepzibah. "Clifford has kept his bed since yesterday."

"What! How! Is he ill?" exclaimed Judge Pyncheon, starting with what seemed to be angry alarm; for the very frown of the old Puritan darkened through the room as he spoke. "Nay, then, I must and will see him! What if he should die?"

"He is in no danger of death," said Hepzibah, and added, with bitterness that she could repress no longer, "none; unless he shall be persecuted to death, now, by the same man who long ago attempted it!"

"Cousin Hepzibah," said the Judge, with an impressive earnestness of manner, which grew even to tearful pathos as he proceeded, "is it possible that you do not perceive how unjust, how unkind, how unchristian, is this constant, this long-continued bitterness against me, for a part which I was constrained by duty and conscience, by the force of law, and at my own peril, to act? What did I do, in detriment to Clifford, which it was possible to leave undone? How could you, his sister—if, for your never-ending sorrow, as it has been for mine, you had known what I did—have shown greater tenderness? And do you think, cousin, that it has cost me no pang? That it has left no anguish in my bosom, from that day to this, amidst all the prosperity with which heaven has blessed me? Or that I do not now rejoice, when it is deemed consistent with the dues of public justice and the welfare of society that this dear kinsman, this early friend, this nature so delicately and beautifully constituted—so unfortunate, let us pronounce him, and forbear to say, so guilty—that our own Clifford, in fine, should be given back to life, and its possibilities of enjoyment? Ah, you little know me, Cousin Hepzibah! You little know this heart! It now throbs at the thought of meeting him! There lives not the human being (except yourself—and you not more than I) who has shed so many tears for Clifford's calamity! You behold some of them now. There is none who would so delight to promote his happiness! Try me, Hepzibah—try me, cousin—try the man whom you have treated as your enemy and Clifford's—try Jaffrey Pyncheon, and you shall find him true, to the heart's core!"

"In the name of heaven," cried Hepzibah, provoked only to intenser indignation by this outgush of the inestimable tenderness of a stern nature, "in God's name, whom you insult—and whose power I could almost question, since he hears you utter so many false words without palsying your tongue—give over, I beseech you, this loathsome pretense of affection for your victim! You hate him! Say so, like a man! You cherish, at this moment, some black purpose against him in your heart! Speak it out, at once! Or, if you hope so to promote it better, hide it till you can triumph in its success! But never speak again of your love for my poor brother! I cannot bear it! It will drive me beyond a woman's decency! It will drive me mad! Forbear! Not another word! It will make me spurn you!"

For once, Hepzibah's wrath had given her courage. She had spoken. But, after all, was this unconquerable distrust of Judge Pyncheon's integrity, and this utter denial, apparently, of his claim to stand in the ring of human sympathies—were they founded in any just perception of his character, or merely the offspring of a woman's unreasonable prejudice, deduced from nothing?

The Judge, beyond all question, was a man of eminent respectability. The church acknowledged it; the state acknowledged it. It was denied by nobody. In all the very extensive sphere of those who knew him, whether in his public or private capacities, there was not an individual—except Hepzibah, and some lawless mystic, like the daguerreotypist, and, possibly, a few political opponents—who would have dreamed of seriously disputing his claim to a high and honorable place in the world's regard. Nor (we must do him the further justice to say) did Judge Pyncheon himself, probably, entertain many or very frequent doubts that his enviable reputation accorded with his deserts. His conscience, therefore, usually considered the surest witness to a man's integrity—his conscience, unless it might be for the little space of five minutes in the twenty-four hours, or, now and then, some black day in the whole year's circle—his conscience bore an accordant testimony with the world's laudatory voice. And yet, strong as this evidence may seem to be, we should hesitate to peril our own conscience on the assertion that the Judge and the consenting world were right, and that poor Hepzibah, with her solitary prejudice, was wrong. Hidden from mankind—forgotten by himself, or buried so deeply under a sculptured and ornamented pile of ostentatious deeds that his daily life could take no note of it—there may have lurked some evil and unsightly thing. Nay, we could almost venture to say, further, that a daily guilt might have been acted by him, continually renewed, and reddening forth afresh, like the miraculous bloodstain of a murder, without his necessarily and at every moment being aware of it.

Men of strong minds, great force of character, and a hard texture of the sensibilities are very capable of falling into mistakes of this kind. They are ordinarily men to whom forms are of paramount importance. Their field of action lies among the external phenomena of life. They possess vast ability in grasping, and arranging, and appropriating to themselves the big, heavy, solid unrealities, such as gold, landed estate, offices of trust and emolument, and public honors. With these materials, and with deeds of goodly aspect, done in the public eye, an individual of this class builds up, as it were, a tall and stately edifice, which, in the view of other people, and ultimately in his own view, is no other than the man's character, or the man himself. Behold, therefore, a palace! Its splendid halls, and suites of spacious apartments, are floored with a mosaicwork of costly marbles; its windows, the whole height of each room, admit the sunshine through the most transparent of plate glass; its high cornices are gilded, and its ceilings gorgeously painted; and a lofty dome—through which, from the central pavement, you may gaze up to the sky, as with no obstructing medium between—surmounts the whole. With what fairer and nobler emblem could any man desire to shadow forth his character? Ah, but in some low and obscure nook—some narrow closet on the ground floor, shut, locked and bolted, and the key flung away; or beneath the marble pavement, in a stagnant water puddle, with the richest pattern of mosaicwork above—may lie a corpse, half decayed, and still decaying, and diffusing its death scent all through the palace! The inhabitant will not be conscious of it, for it has long been his daily breath! Neither will the visitors, for they smell only the rich odors which the master sedulously scatters through the palace, and the incense which they bring, and delight to burn before him! Now and then, perchance, comes in a seer, before whose sadly gifted eye the whole structure melts into thin air, leaving only the hidden nook, the bolted closet, with the cobwebs festooned over its forgotten door, or the deadly hole under the pavement, and the decaying corpse within. Here, then, we are to seek the true emblem of the man's character, and of the deed that gives whatever reality it possesses to his life. And, beneath the show of a marble palace, that pool of stagnant water, foul with many impurities, and, perhaps, tinged with blood—that secret abomination, above which, possibly, he may say his prayers, without remembering it—is this man's miserable soul!

To apply this train of remark somewhat more closely to Judge Pyncheon: we might say (without in the least imputing crime to a personage of his eminent respectability) that there was enough of splendid rubbish in his life to cover up and paralyze a more active and subtile conscience than the Judge was ever troubled with. The purity of his judicial character, while on the bench; the faithfulness of his public service in subsequent capacities; his devotedness to his party, and the rigid consistency with which he had adhered to its principles, or, at all events, kept pace with its organized movements; his remarkable zeal as president of a Bible society; his unimpeachable integrity as treasurer of a widow's and orphan's fund; his benefits to horticulture, by producing two much-esteemed varieties of the pear, and to agriculture, through the agency of the famous Pyncheon bull; the cleanliness of his moral deportment, for a great many years past; the severity with which he had frowned upon, and finally cast off, an expensive and dissipated son, delaying forgiveness until within the final quarter of an hour of the young man's life; his prayers at morning and eventide, and graces at mealtime; his efforts in furtherance of the temperance cause; his confining himself, since the last attack of the gout, to five diurnal glasses of old sherry wine; the snowy whiteness of his linen, the polish of his boots, the handsomeness of his gold-headed cane, the square and roomy fashion of his coat, and the fineness of its material, and, in general, the studied propriety of his dress and equipment; the scrupulousness with which he paid public notice, in the street, by a bow, a lifting of the hat, a nod, or a motion of the hand, to all and sundry of his acquaintances, rich or poor; the smile of broad benevolence wherewith he made it a point to gladden the whole world—what room could possibly be found for darker traits in a portrait made up of these? This proper face was what he beheld in the looking glass. This admirably arranged life was what he was conscious of in the progress of every day. Then might not he claim to be its result and sum, and say to himself and the community, "Behold Judge Pyncheon there"?

And allowing that many, many years ago, in his early and reckless youth, he had committed some one wrong act—or that, even now, the inevitable force of circumstances should occasionally make him do one questionable deed among a thousand praiseworthy, or, at least, blameless ones—would you characterize the Judge by that one necessary deed, and that half-forgotten act, and let it overshadow the fair aspect of a lifetime? What is there so ponderous in evil that a thumb's bigness of it should outweigh the mass of things not evil which were heaped into the other scale! This scale-and-balance system is a favorite one with people of Judge Pyncheon's brotherhood. A hard, cold man, thus unfortunately situated, seldom or never looking inward, and resolutely taking his idea of himself from what purports to be his image as reflected in the mirror of public opinion, can scarcely arrive at true self-knowledge, except through loss of property and reputation. Sickness will not always help him do it; not always the death hour!

But our affair now is with Judge Pyncheon as he stood confronting the fierce outbreak of Hepzibah's wrath. Without premeditation, to her own surprise, and indeed terror, she had given vent, for once, to the inveteracy of her resentment, cherished against this kinsman for thirty years.

Thus far the Judge's countenance had expressed mild forbearance—grave and almost gentle deprecation of his cousin's unbecoming violence, free and Christian-like forgiveness of the wrong inflicted by her words. But when those words were irrevocably spoken, his look assumed sternness, the sense of power, and immitigable resolve; and this with so natural and imperceptible a change that it seemed as if the iron man had stood there from the first, and the meek man not at all. The effect was as when the light, vapory clouds, with their soft coloring, suddenly vanish from the stony brow of a precipitous mountain, and leave there the frown which you at once feel to be eternal. Hepzibah almost adopted the insane belief that it was her old Puritan ancestor, and not the modern Judge, on whom she had just been wreaking the bitterness of her heart. Never did a man show stronger proof of the lineage attributed to him than Judge Pyncheon, at this crisis, by his unmistakable resemblance to the picture in the inner room.

"Cousin Hepzibah," said he, very calmly, "it is time to have done with this."

"With all my heart!" answered she. "Then, why do you persecute us any longer? Leave poor Clifford and me in peace. Neither of us desires anything better!"

"It is my purpose to see Clifford before I leave this

house," continued the Judge. "Do not act like a madwoman, Hepzibah! I am his only friend, and an all-powerful one. Has it never occurred to you—are you so blind as not to have seen—that, without not merely my consent, but my efforts, my representations, the exertion of my whole influence, political, official, personal, Clifford would never have been what you call free? Did you think his release a triumph over me? Not so, my good cousin; not so, by any means! The furthest possible from that! No; but it was the accomplishment of a purpose long entertained on my part. I set him free!"

"You!" answered Hepzibah. "I never will believe it! He owed his dungeon to you; his freedom to God's providence!"

"I set him free!" reaffirmed Judge Pyncheon, with the calmest composure. "And I came hither now to decide whether he shall retain his freedom. It will depend upon himself. For this purpose, I must see him."

"Never! It would drive him mad!" exclaimed Hepzibah, but with an irresoluteness sufficiently perceptible to the keen eye of the Judge; for, without the slightest faith in his good intentions, she knew not whether there was most to dread in yielding or resistance. "And why should you wish to see this wretched, broken man, who retains hardly a fraction of his intellect, and will hide even that from an eye which has no love in it?"

"He shall see love enough in mine, if that be all!" said the Judge, with well-grounded confidence in the benignity of his aspect. "But, Cousin Hepzibah, you confess a great deal, and very much to the purpose. Now, listen, and I will frankly explain my reasons for insisting on this interview. At the death, thirty years since, of our uncle Jaffrey, it was found—I know not whether the circumstance ever attracted much of your attention, among the sadder interests that clustered round that event—but it was found that his visible estate, of every kind, fell far short of any estimate ever made of it. He was supposed to be immensely rich. Nobody doubted that he stood among the weightiest men of his day. It was one of his eccentricities, however—and not altogether a folly, neither—to conceal the amount of his property by making distant and foreign investments, perhaps under other names than his own, and by various means familiar enough to capitalists, but unnecessary here to be specified. By Uncle Jaffrey's last will and testament, as you are aware, his entire property was bequeathed to me, with the single exception of a life interest to yourself in this old family mansion, and the strip of patrimonial estate remaining attached to it."

"And do you seek to deprive us of that?" asked Hepzibah, unable to restrain her bitter contempt. "Is this your price for ceasing to persecute poor Clifford?"

"Certainly not, my dear cousin!" answered the Judge, smiling benevolently. "On the contrary, as you must do me the justice to own, I have constantly expressed my readiness to double or treble your resources, whenever you should make up your mind to accept any kindness of that nature at the hands of your kinsman. No, no! But here lies the gist of the matter. Of my uncle's unquestionably great estate, as I have said, not the half—no, not one third, as I am fully convinced—was apparent after his death. Now, I have the best possible reasons for believing that your brother Clifford can give me a clue to the recovery of the remainder."

"Clifford! Clifford know of any hidden wealth? Clifford have it in his power to make you rich?" cried the old gentlewoman, affected with a sense of something like ridicule at the idea. "Impossible! You deceive yourself! It is really a thing to laugh at!"

"It is as certain as that I stand here!" said Judge Pyncheon, striking his gold-headed cane on the floor, and at the same time stamping his foot, as if to express his conviction the more forcibly by the whole emphasis of his substantial person. "Clifford told me so himself!"

"No, no!" exclaimed Hepzibah, incredulously. "You are dreaming, Cousin Jaffrey!"

"I do not belong to the dreaming class of men," said the Judge, quietly. "Some months before my uncle's death, Clifford boasted to me of the possession of the secret of incalculable wealth. His purpose was to taunt me, and excite my curiosity. I know it well. But, from a pretty distinct recollection of the particulars of our conversation, I am thoroughly

convinced that there was truth in what he said. Clifford,
at this moment, if he chooses—and choose he must!—can
inform me where to find the schedule, the documents, the
evidences, in whatever shape they exist, of the vast amount
of Uncle Jaffrey's missing property. He has the secret. His
boast was no idle word. It had a directness, an emphasis,
a particularity, that showed a backbone of solid meaning
within the mystery of his expression."

"But what could have been Clifford's object," asked
Hepzibah, "in concealing it so long?"

"It was one of the bad impulses of our fallen nature,"
replied the Judge, turning up his eyes. "He looked upon
me as his enemy. He considered me as the cause of his
overwhelming disgrace, his imminent peril of death, his irretrievable ruin. There was no great probability, therefore,
of his volunteering information, out of his dungeon, that
should elevate me still higher on the ladder of prosperity.
But the moment has now come when he must give up his
secret."

"And what if he should refuse?" inquired Hepzibah.
"Or—as I steadfastly believe—what if he has no knowledge of this wealth?"

"My dear cousin," said Judge Pyncheon, with a quietude
which he had the power of making more formidable than
any violence, "since your brother's return, I have taken the
precaution (a highly proper one in the near kinsman and
natural guardian of an individual so situated) to have his
deportment and habits constantly and carefully overlooked.
Your neighbors have been eyewitnesses to whatever has
passed in the garden. The butcher, the baker, the fish-
monger, some of the customers of your shop, and many a
prying old woman have told me several of the secrets of
your interior. A still larger circle—I myself, among the
rest—can testify to his extravagances at the arched window.
Thousands beheld him, a week or two ago, on the point of
flinging himself thence into the street. From all this testimony, I am led to apprehend—reluctantly, and with deep
grief—that Clifford's misfortunes have so affected his intellect, never very strong, that he cannot safely remain at
large. The alternative, you must be aware—and its adoption

will depend entirely on the decision which I am now about to make—the alternative is his confinement, probably for the remainder of his life, in a public asylum for persons in his unfortunate state of mind."

"You cannot mean it!" shrieked Hepzibah.

"Should my cousin Clifford," continued Judge Pyncheon, wholly undisturbed, "from mere malice, and hatred of one whose interests ought naturally to be dear to him—a mode of passion that, as often as any other, indicates mental disease—should he refuse me the information so important to myself, and which he assuredly possesses, I shall consider it the one needed jot of evidence to satisfy my mind of his insanity. And, once sure of the course pointed out by conscience, you know me too well, Cousin Hepzibah, to entertain a doubt that I shall pursue it."

"Oh, Jaffrey, Cousin Jaffrey!" cried Hepzibah, mournfully, not passionately. "It is you that are diseased in mind, not Clifford! You have forgotten that a woman was your mother—that you have had sisters, brothers, children of your own—or that there ever was affection between man and man, or pity from one man to another, in this miserable world! Else, how could you have dreamed of this? You are not young, Cousin Jaffrey—no, nor middle-aged—but already an old man! The hair is white upon your head! How many years have you to live? Are you not rich enough for that little time? Shall you be hungry—shall you lack clothes, or a roof to shelter you—between this point and the grave? No! But, with the half of what you now possess, you could revel in costly food and wines, and build a house twice as splendid as you now inhabit, and make a far greater show to the world—and yet leave riches to your only son, to make him bless the hour of your death! Then, why should you do this cruel, cruel thing? So mad a thing, that I know not whether to call it wicked! Alas, Cousin Jaffrey, this hard and grasping spirit has run in our blood these two hundred years. You are but doing over again, in another shape, what your ancestor before you did, and sending down to your posterity the curse inherited from him!"

"Talk sense, Hepzibah, for heaven's sake!" exclaimed the Judge, with the impatience natural to a reasonable man, on hearing anything so utterly absurd as the above, in a discussion about matters of business. "I have told you my determination. I am not apt to change. Clifford must give up his secret or take the consequences. And let him decide quickly; for I have several affairs to attend to this morning, and an important dinner engagement with some political friends."

"Clifford has no secret!" answered Hepzibah. "And God will not let you do the thing you meditate!"

"We shall see," said the unmoved Judge. "Meanwhile, choose whether you will summon Clifford, and allow this business to be amicably settled by an interview between two kinsmen, or drive me to harsher measures, which I should be most happy to feel myself justified in avoiding. The responsibility is altogether on your part."

"You are stronger than I," said Hepzibah, after a brief consideration, "and you have no pity in your strength! Clifford is not now insane; but the interview which you insist upon may go far to make him so. Nevertheless, knowing you as I do, I believe it to be my best course to allow you to judge for yourself as to the improbability of his possessing any valuable secret. I will call Clifford. Be merciful in your dealings with him—be far more merciful than your heart bids you be—for God is looking at you, Jaffrey Pyncheon!"

The Judge followed his cousin from the shop, where the foregoing conversation had passed, into the parlor, and flung himself heavily into the great ancestral chair. Many a former Pyncheon had found repose in its capacious arms: rosy children, after their sports; young men, dreamy with love; grown men, weary with cares; old men, burdened with winters—they had mused, and slumbered, and departed to a yet profounder sleep. It had been a long tradition, though a doubtful one, that this was the very chair, seated in which the earliest of the Judge's New England forefathers—he whose picture still hung upon the wall—had given a dead man's silent and stern reception to the throng of distinguished guests. From that hour of evil omen until the present, it may be—though we know not the secret of his heart—but it may be that no wearier and sadder man had ever sunk into the chair than this same Judge Pyncheon, whom we have just beheld so immitigably hard and resolute. Surely, it must have been at no slight cost that he had thus fortified his soul with iron. Such calmness is a mightier effort than the violence of weaker men. And there was yet a heavy task for him to do. Was it a little matter—a trifle to be prepared for in a single moment, and to be rested from in another moment—that he must now, after thirty years, encounter a kinsman risen from a living tomb, and wrench a secret from him, or else consign him to a living tomb again?

"Did you speak?" asked Hepzibah, looking in from the threshold of the parlor; for she imagined that the Judge had uttered some sound which she was anxious to interpret as a relenting impulse. "I thought you called me back."

"No, no!" gruffly answered Judge Pyncheon, with a harsh frown, while his brow grew almost a black purple, in the shadow of the room. "Why should I call you back? Time flies! Bid Clifford come to me!"

The Judge had taken his watch from his vest pocket and now held it in his hand, measuring the interval which was to ensue before the appearance of Clifford.

❧16❧

Clifford's Chamber

NEVER had the old house appeared so dismal to poor Hepzibah as when she departed on that wretched errand. There was a strange aspect in it. As she trod along the footworn passages, and opened one crazy door after another, and ascended the creaking staircase, she gazed wistfully and fearfully around. It would have been no marvel, to her excited mind, if, behind or beside her, there had been the rustle of dead people's garments, or pale visages awaiting her on the landing place above. Her nerves were set all ajar by the scene of passion and terror through which she had just struggled. Her colloquy with Judge Pyncheon, who so perfectly represented the person and attributes of the founder of the family, had called back the dreary past. It weighed upon her heart. Whatever she had heard, from legendary aunts and grandmothers, concerning the good or evil fortunes of the Pyncheons—stories which had heretofore been kept warm in her remembrance by the chimney-corner glow that was associated with them—now recurred to her, somber, ghastly, cold, like most passages of family history, when brooded over in melancholy mood. The whole seemed little else but a series of calamity, reproducing itself in successive generations, with one general hue, and varying in little, save the outline. But Hepzibah now felt as if the Judge, and Clifford, and herself—they three together—were on the point of adding another incident to the annals of the house, with a bolder relief of wrong and sorrow, which would cause it to stand out from all the rest. Thus it is that the grief of the passing moment takes upon itself an individuality, and a character of climax, which it is destined to lose after a while, and to fade into the dark gray tissue common to the grave or glad events of many years ago. It is but for a moment, comparatively, that anything looks strange or startling—a truth that has the bitter and the sweet in it.

But Hepzibah could not rid herself of the sense of something unprecedented at that instant passing and soon to be accomplished. Her nerves were in a shake. Instinctively she paused before the arched window, and looked out upon the street, in order to seize its permanent objects with her mental grasp, and thus to steady herself from the reel and vibration which affected her more immediate sphere. It brought her up, as we may say, with a kind of shock, when she beheld everything under the same appearance as the day before, and numberless preceding days, except for the difference between sunshine and sullen storm. Her eyes traveled along the street, from doorstep to doorstep, noting the wet sidewalks, with here and there a puddle in hollows that had been imperceptible until filled with water. She screwed her dim optics to their acutest point, in the hope of making out, with greater distinctness, a certain window, where she half saw, half guessed, that a tailor's seamstress was sitting at her work. Hepzibah flung herself upon that unknown woman's companionship, even thus far off. Then she was attracted by a chaise rapidly passing, and watched its moist and glistening top, and its splashing wheels, until it had turned the corner, and refused to carry any further her idly trifling, because appalled and overburdened, mind. When the vehicle had disappeared, she allowed herself still another loitering moment; for the patched figure of good Uncle Venner was now visible, coming slowly from the head of the street downward, with a rheumatic limp, because the east wind had got into his joints. Hepzibah wished that he would pass yet more slowly, and befriend her shivering solitude a little longer. Anything that would take her out of the grievous present, and interpose human beings betwixt herself and what was nearest to her: whatever would defer, for an instant, the inevitable errand on which she was bound—all such impediments were welcome. Next to the lightest heart, the heaviest is apt to be most playful.

Hepzibah had little hardihood for her own proper pain and far less for what she must inflict on Clifford. Of so slight a nature, and so shattered by his previous calamities, it could not well be short of utter ruin to bring him face to face with the hard, relentless man who had been his evil destiny through life. Even had there been no bitter recollections, nor any hostile interest now at stake between them, the mere natural repugnance of the more sensitive system to the massive, weighty, and unimpressible one must, in itself, have been disastrous to the former. It would be like flinging a porcelain vase, with already a crack in it, against a granite column. Never before had Hepzibah so adequately estimated the powerful character of her cousin Jaffrey—powerful by intellect, energy of will, the long habit of acting among men, and, as she believed, by his unscrupulous pursuit of selfish ends through evil means. It did but increase the difficulty that Judge Pyncheon was under a delusion as to the secret which he supposed Clifford to possess. Men of his strength of purpose, and customary sagacity, if they chance to adopt a mistaken opinion in practical matters, so wedge it and fasten it among things known to be true, that to wrench it out of their minds is hardly less difficult than pulling up an oak. Thus, as the Judge required an impossibility of Clifford, the latter, as he could not perform it, must needs perish. For what, in the grasp of a man like this, was to become of Clifford's soft, poetic nature, that never should have had a task more stubborn than to set a life of beautiful enjoyment to the flow and rhythm of musical cadences! Indeed, what had become of it already? Broken! Blighted! All but annihilated! Soon to be wholly so!

For a moment, the thought crossed Hepzibah's mind whether Clifford might not really have such knowledge of their deceased uncle's vanished estate as the Judge imputed to him. She remembered some vague intimations, on her brother's part, which—if the supposition were not essentially preposterous—might have been so interpreted. There had been schemes of travel and residence abroad, daydreams of brilliant life at home, and splendid castles in the air, which it would have required boundless wealth to build and realize. Had this wealth been in her power, how gladly would Hepzibah have bestowed it all upon her ironhearted kinsman, to buy for Clifford the freedom and seclusion of the desolate old house! But she believed that her brother's schemes were as destitute of actual substance and purpose as a child's pictures of its future life, while sitting in a little chair by its mother's knee. Clifford had none but shadowy gold at his command; and it was not the stuff to satisfy Judge Pyncheon!

Was there no help, in their extremity? It seemed strange that there should be none, with a city round about her. It would be so easy to throw up the window, and send forth a shriek, at the strange agony of which everybody would come hastening to the rescue, well understanding it to be the cry of a human soul at some dreadful crisis! But how wild, how almost laughable, the fatality—and yet how continually it comes to pass, thought Hepzibah, in this dull delirium of a world—that whosoever, and with however kindly a purpose, should come to help, they would be sure to help the strongest side! Might and wrong combined, like iron magnetized, are endowed with irresistible attraction. There would be Judge Pyncheon—a person eminent in the public view, of high station and great wealth, a philanthropist, a member of Congress and of the church, and intimately associated with whatever else bestows good name—so imposing, in these advantageous lights, that Hepzibah herself could hardly help shrinking from her own conclusions as to his hollow integrity. The Judge, on one side! And who, on the other? The guilty Clifford! Once a byword! Now, an indistinctly remembered ignominy!

Nevertheless, in spite of this perception that the Judge would draw all human aid to his own behalf, Hepzibah was so unaccustomed to act for herself that the least word of counsel would have swayed her to any mode of action. Little Phoebe Pyncheon would at once have lighted up the whole scene, if not by any available suggestion, yet simply by the warm vivacity of her character. The idea of the artist occurred to Hepzibah. Young and unknown, mere vagrant adventurer as he was, she had been conscious of a force in Holgrave which might well adapt him to be the champion of a crisis. With this thought in her mind, she unbolted a door, cobwebbed and long disused, but which had served as a former medium of communication between her own part of the house and the gable where the wandering daguerreotypist had now established his temporary home. He was not there. A book, face downward, on the table, a roll of manuscript, a half-written sheet, a newspaper, some tools of his present occupation, and several rejected daguerreotypes conveyed an impression as if he were close at hand. But, at this period of the day, as Hepzibah might have anticipated, the artist was at his public rooms. With an impulse of idle curiosity, that flickered among her heavy thoughts, she looked at one of the daguerreotypes, and beheld Judge Pyncheon frowning at her. Fate stared her in the face. She turned back from her fruitless quest, with a heart-sinking sense of disappointment. In all her years of seclusion, she had never felt, as now, what it was to be alone. It seemed as if the house stood in a desert, or, by some spell, was made invisible to those who dwelt around, or passed beside it; so that any mode of misfortune, miserable accident, or crime might happen in it without the possibility of aid. In her grief and wounded pride, Hepzibah had spent her life in divesting herself of friends; she had willfully cast off the support which God has ordained his creatures to need from one another; and it was now her punishment that Clifford and herself would fall the easier victims to their kindred enemy.

Returning to the arched window, she lifted her eyes—scowling, poor, dim-sighted Hepzibah, in the face of heaven!—and strove hard to send up a prayer through the dense gray pavement of clouds. Those mists had gathered, as if to symbolize a great, brooding mass of human trouble, doubt, confusion, and chill indifference, between earth and the better regions. Her faith was too weak; the prayer too heavy to be thus uplifted. It fell back, a lump of lead, upon her heart. It smote her with the wretched conviction that Providence intermeddled not in these petty wrongs of one individual to his fellow, nor had any balm for these little agonies of a solitary soul; but shed its justice, and its mercy, in a broad, sunlike sweep, over half the universe at once. Its vastness made it nothing. But Hepzibah did not see that, just as there comes a warm sunbeam into every cottage window, so comes a lovebeam of God's care and pity for every separate need.

At last, finding no other pretext for deferring the torture that she was to inflict on Clifford—her reluctance to which was the true cause of her loitering at the window, her search for the artist, and even her abortive prayer— dreading, also, to hear the stern voice of Judge Pyncheon from belowstairs, chiding her delay, she crept slowly, a pale, grief-stricken figure, a dismal shape of woman, with almost torpid limbs, slowly to her brother's door, and knocked!

There was no reply!

And how should there have been? Her hand, tremulous with the shrinking purpose which directed it, had smitten so feebly against the door that the sound could hardly have gone inward. She knocked again. Still, no response! Nor was it to be wondered at. She had struck with the entire force of her heart's vibration, communicating, by some subtle magnetism, her own terror to the summons. Clifford would turn his face to the pillow, and cover his head beneath the bedclothes, like a startled child at midnight. She knocked a third time, three regular strokes, gentle, but perfectly distinct, and with meaning in them; for, modulate it with what cautious art we will, the hand cannot help playing some tune of what we feel, upon the senseless wood.

Clifford returned no answer.

"Clifford! Dear brother!" said Hepzibah. "Shall I come in?"

A silence.

Two or three times, and more, Hepzibah repeated his name, without result; till, thinking her brother's sleep unwontedly profound, she undid the door, and entering, found the chamber vacant. How could he have come forth, and when, without her knowledge? Was it possible that, in spite of the stormy day, and worn out with the irksomeness within doors, he had betaken himself to his customary haunt in the garden, and was now shivering under the

cheerless shelter of the summerhouse? She hastily threw
up a window, thrust forth her turbaned head and the half of
her gaunt figure, and searched the whole garden through,
as completely as her dim vision would allow. She could see
the interior of the summerhouse, and its circular seat, kept
moist by the droppings of the roof. It had no occupant. Clifford was not thereabouts; unless, indeed, he had crept for
concealment (as, for a moment, Hepzibah fancied might be
the case) into a great, wet mass of tangled and broad-leaved
shadow, where the squash vines were clambering tumultu-
ously upon an old wooden framework, set casually aslant
against the fence. This could not be, however; he was not
there; for, while Hepzibah was looking, a strange grimalkin
stole forth from the very spot, and picked his way across
the garden. Twice he paused to snuff the air, and then anew
directed his course towards the parlor window. Whether it
was only on account of the stealthy, prying manner common to the race, or that this cat seemed to have more than
ordinary mischief in his thoughts, the old gentlewoman, in
spite of her much perplexity, felt an impulse to drive the animal away, and accordingly flung down a window stick. The
cat stared up at her, like a detected thief or murderer, and,
the next instant, took to flight. No other living creature was
visible in the garden. Chanticleer and his family had either
not left their roost, disheartened by the interminable rain,
or had done the next wisest thing, by seasonably returning
to it. Hepzibah closed the window.

But where was Clifford? Could it be that, aware of the
presence of his Evil Destiny, he had crept silently down
the staircase, while the Judge and Hepzibah stood talking
in the shop, and had softly undone the fastenings of the
outer door, and made his escape into the street? With that
thought, she seemed to behold his gray, wrinkled, yet childlike aspect, in the old-fashioned garments which he wore
about the house; a figure such as one sometimes imagines
himself to be, with the world's eye upon him, in a troubled
dream. This figure of her wretched brother would go wandering through the city, attracting all eyes, and everybody's
wonder and repugnance, like a ghost, the more to be shuddered at because visible at noontide. To incur the ridicule of

the younger crowd, that knew him not—the harsher scorn
and indignation of a few old men, who might recall his once
familiar features! To be the sport of boys, who, when old
enough to run about the streets, have no more reverence
for what is beautiful and holy, nor pity for what is sad—no
more sense of sacred misery, sanctifying the human shape
in which it embodies itself—than if Satan were the father
of them all! Goaded by their taunts, their loud, shrill cries,
and cruel laughter, insulted by the filth of the public ways,
which they would fling upon him—or, as it might well be,
distracted by the mere strangeness of his situation, though
nobody should afflict him with so much as a thoughtless
word—what wonder if Clifford were to break into some
wild extravagance which was certain to be interpreted as
lunacy? Thus Judge Pyncheon's fiendish scheme would be
ready accomplished to his hands!

Then Hepzibah reflected that the town was almost completely water-girdled. The wharves stretched out towards
the center of the harbor, and, in this inclement weather,
were deserted by the ordinary throng of merchants, laborers, and seafaring men; each wharf a solitude, with the vessels moored stem and stern, along its misty length. Should
her brother's aimless footsteps stray thitherward, and he
but bend, one moment, over the deep, black tide, would he
not bethink himself that here was the sure refuge within his
reach, and that, with a single step, or the slightest overbal-
ance of his body, he might be forever beyond his kinsman's
gripe? Oh, the temptation! To make of his ponderous sorrow a security! To sink, with its leaden weight upon him,
and never rise again!

The horror of this last conception was too much for
Hepzibah. Even Jaffrey Pyncheon must help her now! She
hastened down the staircase, shrieking as she went.

"Clifford is gone!" she cried. "I cannot find my brother!
Help, Jaffrey Pyncheon! Some harm will happen to him!"

She threw open the parlor door. But, what with the shade
of branches across the windows, and the smoke-blackened
ceiling, and the dark oak paneling of the walls, there was
hardly so much daylight in the room that Hepzibah's imperfect sight could accurately distinguish the Judge's fig-

ure. She was certain, however, that she saw him sitting in the ancestral armchair, near the center of the floor, with his face somewhat averted, and looking towards a window. So firm and quiet is the nervous system of such men as Judge Pyncheon, that he had perhaps stirred not more than once since her departure, but, in the hard composure of his temperament, retained the position into which accident had thrown him.

"I tell you, Jaffrey," cried Hepzibah, impatiently, as she turned from the parlor door to search other rooms, "my brother is not in his chamber! You must help me seek him!"

But Judge Pyncheon was not the man to let himself be startled from an easy chair with haste ill-befitting either the dignity of his character or his broad personal basis, by the alarm of an hysteric woman. Yet, considering his own interest in the matter, he might have bestirred himself with a little more alacrity.

"Do you hear me, Jaffrey Pyncheon?" screamed Hepzibah, as she again approached the parlor door, after an ineffectual search elsewhere. "Clifford is gone!"

At this instant, on the threshold of the parlor, emerging from within, appeared Clifford himself! His face was preternaturally pale; so deadly white, indeed, that, through all the glimmering indistinctness of the passageway, Hepzibah could discern his features, as if a light fell on them alone. Their vivid and wild expression seemed likewise sufficient to illuminate them; it was an expression of scorn and mockery, coinciding with the emotions indicated by his gesture. As Clifford stood on the threshhold, partly turning back, he pointed his finger within the parlor, and shook it slowly as though he would have summoned not Hepzibah alone, but the whole world, to gaze at some object inconceivably ridiculous. This action, so ill-timed and extravagant—accompanied, too, with a look that showed more like joy than any other kind of excitement—compelled Hepzibah to dread that her stern kinsman's ominous visit had driven her poor brother to absolute insanity. Nor could she otherwise account for the Judge's quiescent mood than by supposing him craftily on the watch, while Clifford developed these symptoms of a distracted mind.

"Be quiet, Clifford!" whispered his sister, raising her hand to impress caution. "Oh, for heaven's sake, be quiet!"

"Let him be quiet! What can he do better?" answered Clifford, with a still wilder gesture, pointing into the room which he had just quitted. "As for us, Hepzibah, we can dance now—we can sing, laugh, play, do what we will! The weight is gone, Hepzibah! It is gone off this weary old world, and we may be as lighthearted as little Phoebe herself!"

And, in accordance with his words, he began to laugh, still pointing his finger at the object, invisible to Hepzibah, within the parlor. She was seized with a sudden intuition of some horrible thing. She thrust herself past Clifford, and disappeared into the room; but almost immediately returned, with a cry choking in her throat. Gazing at her brother with an affrighted glance of inquiry, she beheld him all in a tremor and a quake, from head to foot, while, amid these commoted elements of passion or alarm, still flickered his gusty mirth.

"My God! What is to become of us?" gasped Hepzibah.

"Come!" said Clifford, in a tone of brief decision, most unlike what was usual with him. "We stay here too long! Let us leave the old house to our cousin Jaffrey! He will take good care of it!"

Hepzibah now noticed that Clifford had on a cloak—a garment of long ago—in which he had constantly muffled himself during these days of easterly storm. He beckoned with his hand, and intimated, so far as she could comprehend him, his purpose that they should go together from the house. There are chaotic, blind, or drunken moments, in the lives of persons who lack real force of character— moments of test, in which courage would most assert itself—but where these individuals, if left to themselves, stagger aimlessly along, or follow implicitly whatever guidance may befall them, even if it be a child's. No matter how preposterous or insane, a purpose is a godsend to them. Hepzibah had reached this point. Unaccustomed to action or responsibility—full of horror at what she had seen, and afraid to inquire, or almost to imagine, how it had come to pass—affrighted at the fatality which seemed to pursue her brother—stupefied by the dim, thick, stifling atmosphere of dread, which filled the house as with a death smell, and obliterated all definiteness of thought—she yielded without a question, and on the instant, to the will which Clifford expressed. For herself, she was like a person in a dream, when the will always sleeps. Clifford, ordinarily so destitute of this faculty, had found it in the tension of the crisis.

"Why do you delay so?" cried he, sharply. "Put on your cloak and hood, or whatever it pleases you to wear! No matter what; you cannot look beautiful nor brilliant, my poor Hepzibah! Take your purse, with money in it, and come along!"

Hepzibah obeyed these instructions, as if nothing else were to be done or thought of. She began to wonder, it is true, why she did not wake up, and at what still more intolerable pitch of dizzy trouble her spirit would struggle out of the maze, and make her conscious that nothing of all this had actually happened. Of course it was not real; no such black, easterly day as this had yet begun to be; Judge Pyncheon had not talked with her; Clifford had not laughed, pointed, beckoned her away with him; but she had merely been afflicted—as lonely sleepers often are—with a great deal of unreasonable misery, in a morning dream!

"Now—now—I shall certainly awake!" thought Hepzibah, as she went to and fro, making her little preparations. "I can bear it no longer! I must wake up now!"

But it came not, that awakening moment! It came not, even when, just before they left the house, Clifford stole to the parlor door, and made a parting obeisance to the sole occupant of the room.

"What an absurd figure the old fellow cuts now!" whispered he to Hepzibah. "Just when he fancied he had me completely under his thumb! Come, come; make haste, or he will start up, like Giant Despair in pursuit of Christian and Hopeful, and catch us yet!"

As they passed into the street, Clifford directed Hepzibah's attention to something on one of the posts of the front door. It was merely the initials of his own name, which, with somewhat of his characteristic grace about the forms of the letters, he had cut there when a boy. The brother and sister departed, and left Judge Pyncheon sitting in the old home of his forefathers, all by himself; so heavy and lumpish that we can liken him to nothing better than a defunct nightmare, which had perished in the midst of its wickedness, and left its flabby corpse on the breast of the tormented one, to be gotten rid of as it might!

❧17❧

The Flight of Two Owls

Summer as it was, the east wind set poor Hepzibah's few remaining teeth chattering in her head, as she and Clifford faced it, on their way up Pyncheon Street, and towards the center of the town. Not merely was it the shiver which this pitiless blast brought to her frame (although her feet and hands, especially, had never seemed so death-a-cold as now), but there was a moral sensation, mingling itself with the physical chill, and causing her to shake more in spirit than in body. The world's broad, bleak atmosphere was all so comfortless! Such, indeed, is the impression which it makes on every new adventurer, even if he plunge into it while the warmest tide of life is bubbling through his veins. What, then, must it have been to Hepzibah and Clifford—so time-stricken as they were, yet so like children in their inexperience—as they left the doorstep, and passed from beneath the wide shelter of the Pyncheon Elm! They were wandering all abroad, on precisely such a pilgrimage as a child often meditates, to the world's end, with perhaps a sixpence and a biscuit in his pocket. In Hepzibah's mind, there was the wretched consciousness of being adrift. She had lost the faculty of self-guidance; but, in view of the difficulties around her, felt it hardly worth an effort to regain it, and was, moreover, incapable of making one.

As they proceeded on their strange expedition, she now and then cast a look sidelong at Clifford, and could not but observe that he was possessed and swayed by a powerful excitement. It was this, indeed, that gave him the control which he had at once, and so irresistibly, established over his movements. It not a little resembled the exhilaration of wine. Or, it might more fancifully be compared to a joyous piece of music, played with wild vivacity, but upon a disordered instrument. As the cracked, jarring note might always be heard, and as it jarred loudest amid the loftiest exultation of the melody, so was there a continual quake through Clifford, causing him most to quiver while he wore a triumphant smile, and seemed almost under a necessity to skip in his gait.

They met few people abroad, even on passing from the retired neighborhood of the House of the Seven Gables into what was ordinarily the more thronged and busier portion of the town. Glistening sidewalks, with little pools of rain, here and there, along their unequal surface; umbrellas displayed ostentatiously in the shopwindows, as if the life of trade had concentered itself in that one article; wet leaves of the horse chestnut or elm trees, torn off untimely by the blast and scattered along the public way; an unsightly accumulation of mud in the middle of the street, which perversely grew the more unclean for its long and laborious washing—these were the more definable points of a very somber picture. In the way of movement, and human life, there was the hasty rattle of a cab or coach, its driver protected by a waterproof cap over his head and shoulders; the forlorn figure of an old man, who seemed to have crept out of some subterranean sewer, and was stooping along the kennel, and poking the wet rubbish with a stick, in quest of rusty nails; a merchant or two, at the door of the post office, together with an editor, and a miscellaneous politician, awaiting a dilatory mail; a few visages of retired sea captains at the window of an insurance office, looking out vacantly at the vacant street, blaspheming at the weather, and fretting at the dearth as well of public news as local gossip. What a treasure trove to these venerable quidnuncs, could they have guessed the secret which Hepzibah and Clifford were carrying along with them! But their two figures attracted hardly so much notice as that of a young girl, who passed at the same instant, and happened to raise her skirt a trifle too high above her ankles. Had it been a sunny and cheerful day, they could hardly have gone through the streets without making themselves obnoxious to remark. Now, probably, they were felt to be in keeping with the dismal and bitter weather, and therefore did not stand out in strong relief; as if the sun were shining on them, but melted into the gray gloom and were forgotten as soon as gone.

Poor Hepzibah! Could she have understood this fact, it would have brought her some little comfort; for, to all her other troubles—strange to say!—there was added the womanish and old-maiden-like misery arising from a sense of unseemliness in her attire. Thus, she was fain to shrink deeper into herself, as it were, as if in the hope of making people suppose that here was only a cloak and hood, threadbare and woefully faded, taking an airing in the midst of the storm, without any wearer!

As they went on, the feeling of indistinctness and unreality kept dimly hovering round about her, and so diffusing itself into her system that one of her hands was hardly palpable to the touch of the other. Any certainty would have been preferable to this. She whispered to herself, again and again, "Am I awake? Am I awake?" and sometimes exposed her face to the chill spatter of the wind, for the sake of its rude assurance that she was. Whether it was Clifford's purpose, or only chance, had led them thither, they now found themselves passing beneath the arched entrance of a large structure of gray stone. Within, there was a spacious breadth, and an airy height from floor to roof, now partially filled with smoke and steam, which eddied voluminously upward and formed a mimic cloud region over their heads. A train of cars was just ready for a start; the locomotive was fretting and fuming, like a steed impatient for a headlong rush; and the bell rang out its hasty peal, so well expressing the brief summons which life vouchsafes to us in its hurried career. Without question or delay—with the irresistible decision, if not rather to be called recklessness, which had so strangely taken possession of him, and through him of Hepzibah—Clifford impelled her towards the cars, and assisted her to enter. The signal was given; the engine puffed forth its short, quick breaths; the train began its movement;

and, along with a hundred other passengers, these two unwonted travelers sped onward like the wind.

At last, therefore, and after so long estrangement from everything that the world acted or enjoyed, they had been drawn into the great current of human life, and were swept away with it, as by the suction of fate itself.

Still haunted with the idea that not one of the past incidents, inclusive of Judge Pyncheon's visit, could be real, the recluse of the Seven Gables murmured in her brother's ear:

"Clifford! Clifford! Is not this a dream?"

"A dream, Hepzibah!" repeated he, almost laughing in her face. "On the contrary, I have never been awake before!"

Meanwhile, looking from the window, they could see the world racing past them. At one moment, they were rattling through a solitude; the next, a village had grown up around them; a few breaths more, and it had vanished, as if swallowed by an earthquake. The spires of meeting houses seemed set adrift from their foundations; the broad-based hills glided away. Everything was unfixed from its agelong rest, and moving at whirlwind speed in a direction opposite to their own.

Within the car, there was the usual interior life of the railroad, offering little to the observation of other passengers, but full of novelty for this pair of strangely enfranchised prisoners. It was novelty enough, indeed, that there were fifty human beings in close relation with them, under one long and narrow roof, and drawn onward by the same mighty influence that had taken their two selves into its grasp. It seemed marvelous how all these people could remain so quietly in their seats, while so much noisy strength was at work in their behalf. Some, with tickets in their hats (long travelers these, before whom lay a hundred miles of railroad), had plunged into the English scenery and adventures of pamphlet novels, and were keeping company with dukes and earls. Others, whose briefer span forbade their devoting themselves to studies so abstruse, beguiled the little tedium of the way with penny papers. A party of girls, and one young man, on opposite sides of the car,

found huge amusement in a game of ball. They tossed it
to and fro, with peals of laughter that might be measured
by mile lengths; for, faster than the nimble ball could fly,
the merry players fled unconsciously along, leaving the trail
of their mirth afar behind, and ending their game under
another sky than had witnessed its commencement. Boys,
with apples, cakes, candy, and rolls of variously tinctured
lozenges—merchandise that reminded Hepzibah of her
deserted shop—appeared at each momentary stopping
place, doing up their business in a hurry, or breaking it
short off, lest the market should ravish them away with it.
New people continually entered. Old acquaintances—for
such they soon grew to be, in this rapid current of affairs—
continually departed. Here and there, amid the rumble and
the tumult, sat one asleep. Sleep; sport; business; graver or
lighter study; and the common and inevitable movement
onward! It was life itself!

Clifford's naturally poignant sympathies were all
aroused. He caught the color of what was passing about
him, and threw it back more vividly than he received it,
but mixed, nevertheless, with a lurid and portentous hue.
Hepzibah, on the other hand, felt herself more apart from
humankind than even in the seclusion which she had just
quitted.

"You are not happy, Hepzibah!" said Clifford, apart,
in a tone of reproach. "You are thinking of that dismal
old house, and of Cousin Jaffrey"—here came the quake
through him—"and of Cousin Jaffrey sitting there, all by
himself! Take my advice—follow my example—and let such
things slip aside. Here we are, in the world, Hepzibah—in
the midst of life—in the throng of our fellow beings! Let
you and I be happy! As happy as that youth, and those
pretty girls, at their game of ball!"

"Happy!" thought Hepzibah, bitterly conscious, at the
word, of her dull and heavy heart, with the frozen pain in it.
"Happy! He is mad already; and, if I could once feel myself
broad awake, I should go mad, too!"

If a fixed idea be madness, she was perhaps not remote
from it. Fast and far as they had rattled and clattered along
the iron track, they might just as well, as regarded Hep-

zibah's mental images, have been passing up and down Pyncheon Street. With miles and miles of varied scenery between, there was no scene for her, save the seven old gable peaks, with their moss, and the tuft of weeds in one of the angles, and the shopwindow, and a customer shaking the door, and compelling the little bell to jingle fiercely, but without disturbing Judge Pyncheon! This one old house was everywhere! It transported its great, lumbering bulk with more than railroad speed, and set itself phlegmatically down on whatever spot she glanced at. The quality of Hepzibah's mind was too unmalleable to take new impressions so readily as Clifford's. He had a winged nature; she was rather of the vegetable kind, and could hardly be kept long alive, if drawn up by the roots. Thus it happened that the relation heretofore existing between her brother and herself was changed. At home, she was his guardian; here, Clifford had become hers, and seemed to comprehend whatever belonged to their new position with a singular rapidity of intelligence. He had been startled into manhood and intellectual vigor; or, at least, into a condition that resembled them, though it might be both diseased and transitory.

The conductor now applied for their tickets; and Clifford, who had made himself the purse bearer, put a bank note into his hand, as he had observed others do.

"For the lady and yourself?" asked the conductor. "And how far?"

"As far as that will carry us," said Clifford. "It is no great matter. We are riding for pleasure merely!"

"You choose a strange day for it, sir!" remarked a gimlet-eyed old gentleman, on the other side of the car, looking at Clifford and his companion, as if curious to make them out. "The best chance of pleasure, in an easterly rain, I take it, is in a man's own house, with a nice little fire in the chimney."

"I cannot precisely agree with you," said Clifford, courteously bowing to the old gentleman, and at once taking up the clue of conversation which the latter had proffered. "It had just occurred to me, on the contrary, that this admirable invention of the railroad—with the vast and inevitable improvements to be looked for, both as to speed and convenience—is destined to do away with those stale ideas of home and fireside, and substitute something better."

"In the name of common sense," asked the old gentleman, rather testily, "what can be better for a man than his own parlor and chimney corner?"

"These things have not the merit which many good people attribute to them," replied Clifford. "They may be said, in few and pithy words, to have ill served a poor purpose. My impression is that our wonderfully increased and still increasing facilities of locomotion are destined to bring us round again to the nomadic state. You are aware, my dear sir—you must have observed it in your own experience— that all human progress is in a circle; or, to use a more accurate and beautiful figure, in an ascending spiral curve. While we fancy ourselves going straight forward, and attaining, at every step, an entirely new position of affairs, we do actually return to something long ago tried and abandoned, but which we now find etherealized, refined, and perfected to its ideal. The past is but a coarse and sensual prophecy of the present and the future. To apply this truth to the topic now under discussion: in the early epochs of our race, men dwelt in temporary huts, of bowers of branches, as easily constructed as a bird's nest, and which they built—if it should be called building, when such sweet homes of a summer solstice rather grew than were made with hands— which Nature, we will say, assisted them to rear where fruit abounded, where fish and game were plentiful, or, most especially, where the sense of beauty was to be gratified by a lovelier shade than elsewhere, and a more exquisite arrangement of lake, wood, and hill. This life possessed a charm, which, ever since man quitted it, has vanished from existence. And it typified something better than itself. It had its drawbacks; such as hunger and thirst, inclement weather, hot sunshine, and weary and foot-blistering marches over barren and ugly tracts, that lay between the sites desirable for their fertility and beauty. But in our ascending spiral, we escape all this. These railroads—could but the whistle be made musical, and the rumble and the jar got rid of—are positively the greatest blessing that the ages have wrought out for us. They give us wings; they annihilate the toil and dust of pilgrimage; they spiritualize travel! Transition being so facile, what can be any man's inducement to tarry in one spot? Why, therefore, should he build a more cumbrous habitation than can readily be carried off with him? Why should he make himself a prisoner for life in brick, and stone, and old worm-eaten timber, when he may just as easily dwell, in one sense, nowhere—in a better sense, wherever the fit and beautiful shall offer him a home?"

Clifford's countenance glowed, as he divulged this theory; a youthful character shone out from within, converting the wrinkles and pallid duskiness of age into an almost transparent mask. The merry girls let their ball drop upon the floor, and gazed at him. They said to themselves, perhaps, that, before his hair was gray and the crow's feet tracked his temples, this now decaying man must have stamped the impress of his features on many a woman's heart. But, alas! No woman's eye had seen his face while it was beautiful.

"I should scarcely call it an improved state of things," observed Clifford's new acquaintance, "to live everywhere and nowhere!"

"Would you not?" exclaimed Clifford, with singular energy. "It is as clear to me as sunshine—were there any in the sky—that the greatest possible stumbling blocks in the path of human happiness and improvement are these heaps of bricks and stones, consolidated with mortar, or hewn timber, fastened together with spike nails, which men painfully contrive for their own torment, and call them house and home! The soul needs air; a wide sweep and frequent change of it. Morbid influences, in a thousandfold variety, gather about hearths, and pollute the life of households. There is no such unwholesome atmosphere as that of an old home, rendered poisonous by one's defunct forefathers and relatives. I speak of what I know. There is a certain house within my familiar recollection, one of those peaked-gable (there are seven of them), projecting-storied edifices, such as you occasionally see in our older towns—a rusty, crazy, creaky, dry-rotted, damp-rotted, dingy, dark, and miserable old dungeon, with an arched window over the porch, and a little shop door on one side, and a great, melancholy

elm before it! Now sir, whenever my thoughts recur to this
seven-gabled mansion (the fact is so very curious that I
must needs mention it), immediately I have a vision or image of an elderly man, of remarkably stern countenance,
sitting in an oaken elbowchair, dead, stone dead, with an
ugly flow of blood upon his shirt bosom! Dead, but with
open eyes! He taints the whole house, as I remember it. I
could never flourish there, nor be happy, nor do nor enjoy
what God meant me to do and enjoy!"

His face darkened, and seemed to contract, and shrivel
itself up, and wither into age.

"Never, sir!" he repeated. "I could never draw cheerful
breath there!"

"I should think not," said the old gentleman, eying Clifford earnestly, and rather apprehensively. "I should conceive not, sir, with that notion in your head!"

"Surely not," continued Clifford, "and it were a relief to
me if that house could be torn down, or burnt up, and so
the earth be rid of it, and grass be sown abundantly over its
foundation. Not that I should ever visit its site again! For,
sir, the farther I get away from it, the more does the joy, the
lightsome freshness, the heart leap, the intellectual dance,
the youth, in short—yes, my youth, my youth!—the more
does it come back to me. No longer ago than this morning,
I was old. I remember looking in the glass, and wondering at my own gray hair, and the wrinkles, many and deep,
right across my brow, and the furrows down my cheeks, and
the prodigious trampling of crow's feet about my temples!
It was too soon! I could not bear it! Age had no right to
come! I had not lived! But now do I look old? If so, my
aspect belies me strangely; for—a great weight being off
my mind—I feel in the very heyday of my youth, with the
world and my best days before me!"

"I trust you may find it so," said the old gentleman, who
seemed rather embarrassed, and desirous of avoiding the
observation which Clifford's wild talk drew on them both.
"You have my best wishes for it."

"For heaven's sake, dear Clifford, be quiet!" whispered
his sister. "They think you mad."

"Be quiet yourself, Hepzibah!" returned her brother.

"No matter what they think! I am not mad. For the first time in thirty years, my thoughts gush up and find words ready for them. I must talk, and I will!"

He turned again towards the old gentleman, and renewed the conversation.

"Yes, my dear sir," said he, "it is my firm belief and hope that these terms of roof and hearthstone, which have so long been held to embody something sacred, are soon to pass out of men's daily use, and be forgotten. Just imagine, for a moment, how much of human evil will crumble away, with this one change! What we call real estate—the solid ground to build a house on—is the broad foundation on which nearly all the guilt of this world rests. A man will commit almost any wrong—he will heap up an immense pile of wickedness, as hard as granite, and which will weigh as heavily upon his soul, to eternal ages—only to build a great, gloomy, dark-chambered mansion, for himself to die in, and for his posterity to be miserable in. He lays his own dead corpse beneath the underpinning, as one may say, and hangs his frowning picture on the wall, and, after thus converting himself into an evil destiny, expects his remotest great-grandchildren to be happy there! I do not speak wildly. I have just such a house in my mind's eye!"

"Then, sir," said the old gentleman, getting anxious to drop the subject, "you are not to blame for leaving it."

"Within the lifetime of the child already born," Clifford went on, "all this will be done away. The world is growing too ethereal and spiritual to bear these enormities a great while longer. To me—though, for a considerable period of time, I have lived chiefly in retirement, and know less of such things than most men—even to me, the harbingers of a better era are unmistakable. Mesmerism, now! Will that effect nothing, think you, towards purging away the grossness out of human life?"

"All a humbug!" growled the old gentleman.

"These rapping spirits, that little Phoebe told us of, the other day," said Clifford, "what are these but the messengers of the spiritual world, knocking at the door of substance? And it shall be flung wide open!"

"A humbug, again!" cried the old gentleman, growing

more and more testy, at these glimpses of Clifford's meta-physics. "I should like to rap with a good stick on the empty pates of the dolts who circulate such nonsense!"

"Then there is electricity—the demon, the angel, the mighty physical power, the all-pervading intelligence!" exclaimed Clifford. "Is that a humbug, too? Is it a fact—or have I dreamt it—that, by means of electricity, the world of matter has become a great nerve, vibrating thousands of miles in a breathless point of time? Rather, the round globe is a vast head, a brain, instinct with intelligence! Or, shall we say, it is itself a thought, nothing but thought, and no longer the substance which we deemed it!"

"If you mean the telegraph," said the old gentleman, glancing his eye toward its wire, alongside the rail track, "it is an excellent thing—that is, of course, if the speculators in cotton and politics don't get possession of it. A great thing, indeed, sir, particularly as regards the detection of bank robbers and murderers."

"I don't quite like it, in that point of view," replied Clifford. "A bank robber, and what you call a murderer, likewise, has his rights, which men of enlightened humanity and conscience should regard in so much the more liberal spirit, because the bulk of society is prone to controvert their existence. An almost spiritual medium, like the electric telegraph, should be consecrated to high, deep, joyful, and holy missions. Lovers, day by day—hour by hour, if so often moved to do it—might send their heartthrobs from Maine to Florida, with some such words as these: 'I love you forever!' 'My heart runs over with love!' 'I love you more than I can!' and, again, at the next message, 'I have lived an hour longer, and love you twice as much!' Or, when a good man has departed, his distant friend should be conscious of an electric thrill, as from the world of happy spirits, telling him, 'Your dear friend is in bliss!' Or, to an absent husband, should come tidings thus, 'An immortal being, of whom you are the father, has this moment come from God!' and immediately its little voice would seem to have reached so far, and to be echoing in his heart. But for these poor rogues, the bank robbers, who, after all, are about as honest as nine people in ten, except that they disregard certain formalities, and prefer to transact business at midnight rather than 'Change hours, and for these murderers, as you phrase it, who are often excusable in the motives of their deed, and deserve to be ranked among public benefactors, if we consider only its result—for unfortunate individuals like these, I really cannot applaud the enlistment of an immaterial and miraculous power in the universal world hunt at their heels!"

"You can't, hey?" cried the old gentleman, with a hard look.

"Positively, no!" answered Clifford. "It puts them too miserably at disadvantage. For example, sir, in a dark, low, cross-beamed, paneled room of an old house, let us suppose a dead man, sitting in an armchair, with a bloodstain on his shirt bosom; and let us add to our hypothesis another man, issuing from the house, which he feels to be overfilled with the dead man's presence; and let us lastly imagine him fleeing, heaven knows whither, at the speed of a hurricane, by railroad! Now, sir, if the fugitive alight in some distant town, and find all the people babbling about that selfsame dead man, whom he has fled so far to avoid the sight and thought of, will you not allow that his natural rights have been infringed? He has been deprived of his city of refuge, and, in my humble opinion, has suffered infinite wrong!"

"You are a strange man, sir!" said the old gentleman, bringing his gimlet eye to a point on Clifford, as if determined to bore right into him. "I can't see through you!"

"No, I'll be bound you can't!" cried Clifford, laughing. "And yet, my dear sir, I am as transparent as the water of Maule's well! But come, Hepzibah! We have flown far enough for once. Let us alight, as the birds do, and perch ourselves on the nearest twig, and consult whither we shall fly next!"

Just then, as it happened, the train reached a solitary way station. Taking advantage of the brief pause, Clifford left the car, and drew Hepzibah along with him. A moment afterwards, the train—with all the life of its interior, amid which Clifford had made himself so conspicuous an object—was gliding away in the distance, and rapidly lessening to a point, which, in another moment, vanished. The world had fled away from these two wanderers. They gazed drearily about them. At a little distance stood a wooden church, black with age, and in a dismal state of ruin and decay, with broken windows, a great rift through the main body of the edifice, and a rafter dangling from the top of the square tower. Farther off was a farmhouse, in the old style, as venerably black as the church, with a roof sloping downward from the three-story peak, to within a man's height of the ground. It seemed uninhabited. There were the relics of a woodpile, indeed, near the door, but with grass sprouting up among the chips and scattered logs. The small raindrops came down aslant; the wind was not turbulent, but sullen, and full of chilly moisture.

Clifford shivered from head to foot. The wild effervescence of his mood—which had so readily supplied thoughts, fantasies, and a strange aptitude of words, and impelled him to talk from the mere necessity of giving vent to this bubbling-up gush of ideas—had entirely subsided. A powerful excitement had given him energy and vivacity. Its operation over, he forthwith began to sink.

"You must take the lead now, Hepzibah!" murmured he, with a torpid and reluctant utterance. "Do with me as you will!"

She knelt down upon the platform where they were standing and lifted her clasped hands to the sky. The dull, gray weight of clouds made it invisible; but it was no hour for disbelief—no juncture this to question that there was a sky above, and an Almighty Father looking from it!

"O God!" ejaculated poor, gaunt Hepzibah, then paused a moment, to consider what her prayer should be—"O God—our Father—are we not thy children? Have mercy on us!"

❦18❧

Governor Pyncheon

JUDGE PYNCHEON, while his two relatives have fled away with such ill-considered haste, still sits in the old parlor, keeping house, as the familiar phrase is, in the absence of its ordinary occupants. To him, and to the venerable House of the Seven Gables, does our story now betake itself, like an owl, bewildered in the daylight, and hastening back to his hollow tree.

The Judge has not shifted his position for a long while now. He has not stirred hand or foot, nor withdrawn his eyes so much as a hairbreadth from their fixed gaze towards the corner of the room, since the footsteps of Hepzibah and Clifford creaked along the passage, and the outer door was closed cautiously behind their exit. He holds his watch in his left hand, but clutched in such a manner that you cannot see the dial plate. How profound a fit of meditation! Or, supposing him asleep, how infantile a quietude of conscience, and what wholesome order in the gastric region, are betokened by slumber so entirely undisturbed with starts, cramp, twitches, muttered dream talk, trumpet blasts through the nasal organ, or any slightest irregularity of breath! You must hold your own breath, to satisfy yourself whether he breathes at all. It is quite inaudible. You hear the ticking of his watch; his breath you do not hear. A most refreshing slumber, doubtless! And yet, the Judge cannot be asleep. His eyes are open! A veteran politician, such as he, would never fall asleep with wide-open eyes, lest some enemy or mischief-maker, taking him thus at unawares, should peep through these windows into his consciousness, and make strange discoveries among the reminiscences, projects, hopes, apprehensions, weaknesses, and strong points which he has heretofore shared with nobody. A cautious man is proverbially said to sleep with one eye open. That may be wisdom. But not with both; for this were heedlessness! No, no! Judge Pyncheon cannot be asleep.

It is odd, however, that a gentleman so burdened with engagements—and noted, too, for punctuality—should linger thus in an old, lonely mansion, which he has never seemed very fond of visiting. The oaken chair, to be sure, may tempt him with its roominess. It is, indeed, a spacious, and, allowing for the rude age that fashioned it, a moderately easy seat, with capacity enough, at all events, and offering no restraint to the Judge's breadth of beam. A bigger man might find ample accommodation in it. His ancestor, now pictured upon the wall, with all his English beef about him, used hardly to present a front extending from elbow to elbow of this chair, or a base that would cover its whole cushion. But there are better chairs than this—mahogany, black-walnut, rosewood, spring-seated and damask-cushioned, with varied slopes, and innumerable artifices to make them easy, and obviate the irksomeness of too tame an ease—a score of such might be at Judge Pyncheon's service. Yes! in a score of drawing rooms he would be more than welcome. Mama would advance to meet him, with outstretched hand; the virgin daughter, elderly as he has now got to be—an old widower, as he smilingly describes himself—would shake up the cushion for the Judge, and do her pretty little utmost to make him comfortable. For the Judge is a prosperous man. He cherishes his schemes, moreover, like other people, and reasonably brighter than most others; or did so, at least, as he lay abed this morning, in an agreeable half-drowse, planning the business of the day, and speculating on the probabilities of the next fifteen years. With his firm health, and the little inroad that age has made upon him, fifteen years or twenty— yes, or perhaps five and twenty!—are no more than he may

fairly call his own. Five and twenty years for the enjoyment
of his real estate in town and country, his railroad, bank,
and insurance shares, his United States stock—his wealth,
in short, however invested, now in possession, or soon to be
acquired, together with the public honors that have fallen
upon him, and the weightier ones that are yet to fall! It is
good! It is excellent! It is enough!

Still lingering in the old chair! If the Judge has a little
time to throw away, why does not he visit the insurance office, as is his frequent custom, and sit awhile in one of their
leathern-cushioned armchairs, listening to the gossip of
the day, and dropping some deeply designed chance word,
which will be certain to become the gossip of tomorrow!
And have not the bank directors a meeting at which it was
the Judge's purpose to be present, and his office to preside?
Indeed they have; and the hour is noted on a card, which is,
or ought to be, in Judge Pyncheon's right vest pocket. Let
him go thither, and loll at ease upon his moneybags! He has
lounged long enough in the old chair!

This was to have been such a busy day! In the first place,
the interview with Clifford. Half an hour, by the Judge's
reckoning, was to suffice for that; it would probably be less,
but—taking into consideration that Hepzibah was first to
be dealt with, and that these women are apt to make many
words where a few would do much better—it might be
safest to allow half an hour. Half an hour? Why, Judge, it
is already two hours, by your own undeviatingly accurate
chronometer! Glance your eye down at it and see! Ah! He
will not give himself the trouble either to bend his head,
or elevate his hand, so as to bring the faithful timekeeper
within his range of vision! Time, all at once, appears to have
become a matter of no moment with the Judge!

And has he forgotten all the other items of his memoranda? Clifford's affair arranged, he was to meet a State
Street broker, who has undertaken to procure a heavy per-
centage, and the best of paper, for a few loose thousands
which the Judge happens to have by him, uninvested. The
wrinkled note-shaver will have taken his railroad trip in
vain. Half an hour later, in the street next to this, there was
to be an auction of real estate, including a portion of the

old Pyncheon property, originally belonging to Maule's garden ground. It has been alienated from the Pyncheons these fourscore years; but the Judge had kept it in his eye, and had set his heart on reannexing it to the small demesne still left around the Seven Gables; and now, during this odd fit of oblivion, the fatal hammer must have fallen, and transferred our ancient patrimony to some alien possessor! Possibly, indeed, the sale may have been postponed till fairer weather. If so, will the Judge make it convenient to be present, and favor the auctioneer with his bid, on the proximate occasion?

The next affair was to buy a horse for his own driving. The one heretofore his favorite stumbled, this very morning, on the road to town, and must be at once discarded. Judge Pyncheon's neck is too precious to be risked on such a contingency as a stumbling steed. Should all the above business be seasonably got through with, he might attend the meeting of a charitable society; the very name of which, however, in the multiplicity of his benevolence, is quite forgotten; so that this engagement may pass unfulfilled, and no great harm done. And if he have time, amid the press of more urgent matters, he must take measures for the renewal of Mrs. Pyncheon's tombstone, which, the sexton tells him, has fallen on its marble face, and is cracked quite in twain. She was a praiseworthy woman enough, thinks the Judge, in spite of her nervousness, and the tears that she was so oozy with, and her foolish behavior about the coffee; and as she took her departure so seasonably, he will not grudge the second tombstone. It is better, at least, than if she had never needed any! The next item on his list was to give orders for some fruit trees, of a rare variety, to be deliverable at his country-seat, in the ensuing autumn. Yes, buy them, by all means; and may the peaches be luscious in your mouth, Judge Pyncheon! After this comes something more important. A committee of his political party has besought him for a hundred or two of dollars, in addition to his previous disbursements, towards carrying on the fall campaign. The Judge is a patriot; the fate of the country is staked on the November election; and besides, as will be shadowed forth in another paragraph, he has no trifling stake of his own in the same great game. He will do what the committee asks; nay, he will be liberal beyond their expectations; they shall have a check for five hundred dollars, and more anon, if it be needed. What next? A decayed widow, whose husband was Judge Pyncheon's early friend, has laid her case of destitution before him, in a very moving letter. She and her fair daughter have scarcely bread to eat. He partly intends to call on her, today—perhaps so, perhaps not—accordingly as he may happen to have leisure, and a small bank note.

Another business, which, however, he puts no great weight on (it is well, you know, to be heedful, but not over-anxious, as respects one's personal health)—another business, then, was to consult his family physician. About what, for heaven's sake? Why, it is rather difficult to describe the symptoms. A mere dimness of sight and dizziness of brain, was it—or a disagreeable choking, or stifling, or gurgling, or bubbling, in the region of the thorax, as the anatomists say—or was it a pretty severe throbbing and kicking of the heart, rather creditable to him than otherwise, as showing that the organ had not been left out of the Judge's physical contrivance? No matter what it was. The doctor, probably, would smile at the statement of such trifles to his professional ear; the Judge would smile in his turn; and meeting one another's eyes, they would enjoy a hearty laugh together! But a fig for medical advice! The Judge will never need it.

Pray, pray, Judge Pyncheon, look at your watch, now! What—not a glance! It is within ten minutes of the dinner hour! It surely cannot have slipped your memory that the dinner of today is to be the most important, in its consequences, of all the dinners you ever ate. Yes, precisely the most important; although, in the course of your somewhat eminent career, you have been placed high towards the head of the table, at splendid banquets, and have poured out your festive eloquence to ears yet echoing with Webster's mighty organ tones. No public dinner this, however. It is merely a gathering of some dozen or so of friends from several districts of the State; men of distinguished character and influence, assembling, almost casually, at the house of a common friend, likewise distinguished, who will make

them welcome to a little better than his ordinary fare.
Nothing in the way of French cookery, but an excellent dinner nevertheless. Real turtle, we understand, and salmon,
tautog, canvasbacks, pig, English mutton, good roast beef,
or dainties of that serious kind, fit for substantial country
gentlemen, as these honorable persons mostly are. The del-
icacies of the season, in short, and flavored by a brand of
old Madeira which has been the pride of many seasons. It is
the Juno brand; a glorious wine, fragrant, and full of gentle
might; a bottled-up happiness, put by for use; a golden liquid, worth more than liquid gold; so rare and admirable,
that veteran wine-bibbers count it among their epochs to
have tasted it! It drives away the heartache, and substitutes
no headache! Could the Judge but quaff a glass, it might
enable him to shake off the unaccountable lethargy which
(for the ten intervening minutes, and five to boot, are already past) has made him such a laggard at this momentous dinner. It would all but revive a dead man! Would you
like to sip it now, Judge Pyncheon?

Alas, this dinner! Have you really forgotten its true object? Then let us whisper it, that you may start at once out
of the oaken chair, which really seems to be enchanted,
like the one in Comus, or that in which Moll Pitcher imprisoned your own grandfather. But ambition is a talisman
more powerful than witchcraft. Start up, then, and, hurry-
ing through the streets, burst in upon the company, that
they may begin before the fish is spoiled! They wait for
you; and it is little for your interest that they should wait.
These gentlemen—need you be told it?—have assembled,
not without purpose, from every quarter of the State. They
are practiced politicians, every man of them, and skilled
to adjust those preliminary measures which steal from the
people, without its knowledge, the power of choosing its
own rulers. The popular voice, at the next gubernatorial
election, though loud as thunder, will be really but an echo
of what these gentlemen shall speak, under their breath, at
your friend's festive board. They meet to decide upon their
candidate. This little knot of subtle schemers will control
the convention, and, through it, dictate to the party. And
what worthier candidate—more wise and learned, more

noted for philanthropic liberality, truer to safe principles, tried oftener by public trusts, more spotless in private character, with a larger stake in the common welfare, and deeper grounded, by hereditary descent, in the faith and practice of the Puritans—what man can be presented by the suffrage of the people so eminently combining all these claims to the chief-rulership as Judge Pyncheon here before us?

Make haste, then! Do your part! The meed for which you have toiled, and fought, and climbed, and crept, is ready for your grasp! Be present at this dinner—drink a glass or two of that noble wine—make your pledges in as low a whisper as you will—and you rise up from table virtually governor of the glorious old State! Governor Pyncheon of Massachusetts!

And is there no potent and exhilarating cordial in a certainty like this? It has been the grand purpose of half your lifetime to obtain it. Now, when there needs little more than to signify your acceptance, why do you sit so lumpishly in your great-great-grandfather's oaken chair, as if preferring it to the gubernatorial one? We have all heard of King Log; but, in these jostling times, one of that royal kindred will hardly win the race for an elective chief magistracy.

Well! It is absolutely too late for dinner! Turtle, salmon, tautog, woodcock, boiled turkey, Southdown mutton, pig, roast beef have vanished, or exist only in fragments, with lukewarm potatoes, and gravies crusted over with cold fat. The Judge, had he done nothing else, would have achieved wonders with his knife and fork. It was he, you know, of whom it used to be said, in reference to his ogre-like appetite, that his Creator made him a great animal, but that the dinner hour made him a great beast. Persons of his large sensual endowments must claim indulgence, at their feeding time. But, for once, the Judge is entirely too late for dinner! Too late, we fear, even to join the party at their wine! The guests are warm and merry; they have given up the Judge; and, concluding that the Free-Soilers have him, they will fix upon another candidate. Were our friend now to stalk in among them, with that wide-open stare, at once wild and stolid, his ungenial presence would be apt to change their

cheer. Neither would it be seemly in Judge Pyncheon, generally so scrupulous in his attire, to show himself at a dinner
table with that crimson stain upon his shirt bosom. By the
by, how came it there? It is an ugly sight, at any rate; and the
wisest way for the Judge is to button his coat closely over
his breast, and, taking his horse and chaise from the livery
stable, to make all speed to his own house. There, after a
glass of brandy and water, and a mutton chop, a beefsteak,
a broiled fowl, or some such hasty little dinner and supper
all in one, he had better spend the evening by the fireside.
He must toast his slippers a long while, in order to get rid
of the chilliness which the air of this vile old house has sent
curdling through his veins.

Up, therefore, Judge Pyncheon, up! You have lost a day.
But tomorrow will be here anon. Will you rise, betimes, and
make the most of it? Tomorrow! Tomorrow! Tomorrow!
We, that are live, may rise betimes tomorrow. As for him
that has died today, his morrow will be the resurrection
morn.

Meanwhile, the twilight is glooming upward out of the
corners of the room. The shadows of the tall furniture grow
deeper, and at first become more definite; then, spreading
wider, they lose their distinctness of outline in the dark
gray tide of oblivion, as it were, that creeps slowly over
the various objects, and the one human figure sitting in the
midst of them. The gloom has not entered from without; it
has brooded here all day, and now, taking its own inevitable
time, will possess itself of everything. The Judge's face, indeed, rigid, and singularly white, refuses to melt into this
universal solvent. Fainter and fainter grows the light. It is as
if another double handful of darkness had been scattered
through the air. Now it is no longer gray, but sable. There
is still a faint appearance at the window; neither a glow,
nor a gleam, nor a glimmer—any phrase of light would express something far brighter than this doubtful perception,
or sense, rather, that there is a window there. Has it yet
vanished? No! Yes! Not quite! And there is still the swarthy whiteness—we shall venture to marry these ill-agreeing
words—the swarthy whiteness of Judge Pyncheon's face.
The features are all gone: there is only the paleness of them

left. And how looks it now? There is no window! There is no face! An infinite, inscrutable blackness has annihilated sight! Where is our universe? All crumbled away from us; and we, adrift in chaos, may hearken to the gusts of home-less wind, that go sighing and murmuring about, in quest of what was once a world!

Is there no other sound? One other, and a fearful one. It is the ticking of the Judge's watch, which, ever since Hep-zibah left the room in search of Clifford, he has been hold-ing in his hand. Be the cause what it may, this little, quiet, never-ceasing throb of Time's pulse, repeating its small strokes with such busy regularity, in Judge Pyncheon's mo-tionless hand, has an effect of terror, which we do not find in any other accompaniment of the scene.

But, listen! That puff of the breeze was louder; it had a tone unlike the dreary and sullen one which has bemoaned itself, and afflicted all mankind with miserable sympa-thy, for five days past. The wind has veered about! It now comes boisterously from the northwest, and, taking hold of the aged framework of the Seven Gables, gives it a shake, like a wrestler that would try strength with his antagonist. Another and another sturdy tussle with the blast! The old house creaks again, and makes a vociferous but somewhat unintelligible bellowing in its sooty throat (the big flue, we mean, of its wide chimney), partly in complaint at the rude wind, but rather, as befits their century and a half of hostile intimacy, in tough defiance. A rumbling kind of a bluster roars behind the fireboard. A door has slammed abovestairs. A window, perhaps, has been left open, or else is driven in by an unruly gust. It is not to be conceived, beforehand, what wonderful wind instruments are these old timber mansions, and how haunted with the strangest noises, which immediately begin to sing, and sigh, and sob, and shriek—and to smite with sledge hammers, airy but ponderous, in some distant chamber—and to tread along the entries as with stately footsteps, and rustle up and down the staircase, as with silks miraculously stiff—whenever the gale catches the house with a window open, and gets fairly into it. Would that we were not an attendant spirit here! It is too awful! This clamor of the wind through the lonely house; the Judge's quietude, as he sits invisible; and that pertinacious ticking of his watch!

As regards Judge Pyncheon's invisibility, however, that matter will soon be remedied. The northwest wind has swept the sky clear. The window is distinctly seen. Through its panes, moreover, we dimly catch the sweep of the dark, clustering foliage, outside, fluttering with a constant irregularity of movement, and letting in a peep of starlight, now here, now there. Oftener than any other object, these glimpses illuminate the Judge's face. But here comes more effectual light. Observe that silvery dance upon the upper branches of the pear tree, and now a little lower, and now on the whole mass of boughs, while, through their shifting intricacies, the moonbeams fall aslant into the room. They play over the Judge's figure and show that he has not stirred throughout the hours of darkness. They follow the shadows, in changeful sport, across his unchanging features. They gleam upon his watch. His grasp conceals the dial plate; but we know that the faithful hands have met; for one of the city clocks tells midnight.

A man of sturdy understanding, like Judge Pyncheon, cares no more for twelve o'clock at night than for the corresponding hour of noon. However just the parallel drawn, in some of the preceding pages, between his Puritan ancestor and himself, it fails in this point. The Pyncheon of two centuries ago, in common with most of his contemporaries, professed his full belief in spiritual ministrations, although reckoning them chiefly of a malignant character. The Pyncheon of tonight, who sits in yonder armchair, believes in no such nonsense. Such, at least, was his creed, some few hours since. His hair will not bristle, therefore, at the stories which—in times when chimney corners had benches in them, where old people sat poking into the ashes of the past, and raking out traditions like live coals—used to be told about this very room of his ancestral house. In fact, these tales are too absurd to bristle even childhood's hair. What sense, meaning, or moral, for example, such as even ghost stories should be susceptible of, can be traced in the ridiculous legend that, at midnight, all the dead Pyncheons are bound to assemble in this parlor? And, pray, for what?

Why, to see whether the portrait of their ancestor still keeps its place upon the wall, in compliance with his testamentary directions! Is it worth while to come out of their graves for that?

We are tempted to make a little sport with the idea. Ghost stories are hardly to be treated seriously, any longer. The family party of the defunct Pyncheons, we presume, goes off in this wise.

First comes the ancestor himself, in his black cloak, steeple hat, and trunk breeches, girt about the waist with a leathern belt, in which hangs his steel-hilted sword; he has a long staff in his hand, such as gentlemen in advanced life used to carry, as much for the dignity of the thing as for the support to be derived from it. He looks up at the portrait; a thing of no substance, gazing at its own painted image! All is safe. The picture is still there. The purpose of his brain has been kept sacred thus long after the man himself has sprouted up in graveyard grass. See! He lifts his ineffectual hand, and tries the frame. All safe! But is that a smile? Is it not, rather, a frown of deadly import, that darkens over the shadow of his features? The stout Colonel is dissatisfied! So decided is his look of discontent as to impart additional distinctness to his features; through which, nevertheless, the moonlight passes, and flickers on the wall beyond. Something has strangely vexed the ancestor! With a grim shake of the head, he turns away. Here come other Pyncheons, the whole tribe, in their half a dozen generations, jostling and elbowing one another, to reach the picture. We behold aged men and grandames, a clergyman with the Puritanic stiffness still in his garb and mien, and a red-coated officer of the old French war; and there comes the shopkeeping Pyncheon of a century ago, with the ruffles turned back from his wrists; and there the periwigged and brocaded gentleman of the artist's legend, with the beautiful and pensive Alice, who brings no pride out of her virgin grave. All try the picture frame. What do these ghostly people seek? A mother lifts her child, that his little hands may touch it! There is evidently a mystery about the picture, that perplexes these poor Pyncheons when they ought to be at rest. In a corner, meanwhile, stands the figure of an elderly man, in a leather jerkin and breeches, with a carpenter's rule sticking out of his side pocket; he points his finger at the bearded Colonel and his descendants, nodding, jeering, mocking, and finally bursting into obstreperous though inaudible laughter.

Indulging our fancy in this freak, we have partly lost the power of restraint and guidance. We distinguish an unlooked-for figure in our visionary scene. Among those ancestral people there is a young man, dressed in the very fashion of today: he wears a dark frock coat, almost destitute of skirts, gray pantaloons, gaiter boots of patent leather, and has a finely wrought gold chain across his breast, and a little silver-headed whalebone stick in his hand. Were we to meet this figure at noonday, we should greet him as young Jaffrey Pyncheon, the Judge's only surviving child, who has been spending the last two years in foreign travel. If still in life, how comes his shadow hither? If dead, what a misfortune! The old Pyncheon property, together with the great estate acquired by the young man's father, would devolve on whom? On poor, foolish Clifford, gaunt Hepzibah, and rustic little Phoebe! But another and a greater marvel greets us! Can we believe our eyes? A stout, elderly gentleman has made his appearance; he has an aspect of eminent respectability, wears a black coat and pantaloons, of roomy width, and might be pronounced scrupulously neat in his attire, but for a broad crimson stain across his snowy neckcloth and down his shirt bosom. Is it the Judge, or no? How can it be Judge Pyncheon? We discern his figure, as plainly as the flickering moonbeams can show us anything, still seated in the oaken chair! Be the apparition whose it may, it advances to the picture, seems to seize the frame, tries to peep behind it, and turns away, with a frown as black as the ancestral one.

The fantastic scene just hinted at must by no means be considered as forming an actual portion of our story. We were betrayed into this brief extravagance by the quiver of the moonbeams; they dance hand in hand with shadows, and are reflected in the looking glass, which, you are aware, is always a kind of window or doorway into the spiritual world. We needed relief, moreover, from our too long and exclusive contemplation of that figure in the chair. This wild wind, too, has tossed our thoughts into strange confusion, but without tearing them away from their one determined center. Yonder leaden Judge sits immovably upon our soul. Will he never stir again? We shall go mad unless he stirs! You may the better estimate his quietude by the fearlessness of a little mouse, which sits on its hind legs, in a streak of moonlight, close by Judge Pyncheon's foot, and seems to meditate a journey of exploration over this great black bulk. Ha! What has startled the nimble little mouse? It is the visage of grimalkin, outside of the window, where he appears to have posted himself for a deliberate watch. This grimalkin has a very ugly look. Is it a cat watching for a mouse, or the devil for a human soul? Would we could scare him from the window!

Thank heaven, the night is well-nigh past! The moonbeams have no longer so silvery a gleam, nor contrast so strongly with the blackness of the shadows among which they fall. They are paler now; the shadows look gray, not black. The boisterous wind is hushed. What is the hour? Ah! The watch has at last ceased to tick; for the Judge's forgetful fingers neglected to wind it up, as usual, at ten o'clock, being half an hour or so before his ordinary bedtime, and it has run down, for the first time in five years. But the great world clock of Time still keeps its beat. The dreary night—for, oh, how dreary seems its haunted waste, behind us!—gives place to a fresh, transparent, cloudless morn. Blessed, blessed radiance! The day beam—even what little of it finds its way into this always dusky parlor—seems part of the universal benediction, annulling evil, and rendering all goodness possible, and happiness attainable. Will Judge Pyncheon now rise up from his chair? Will he go forth, and receive the early sunbeams on his brow? Will he begin this new day—which God has smiled upon, and blessed, and given to mankind—will he begin it with better purposes than the many that have been spent amiss? Or are all the deep-laid schemes of yesterday as stubborn in his heart, and as busy in his brain, as ever?

In this latter case, there is much to do. Will the Judge still insist with Hepzibah on the interview with Clifford? Will he buy a safe, elderly gentleman's horse? Will he persuade the purchaser of the old Pyncheon property to relinquish the bargain, in his favor? Will he see his family physician, and obtain a medicine that shall preserve him, to be an honor and blessing to his race, until the utmost term of patriarchal longevity? Will Judge Pyncheon, above all, make due apologies to that company of honorable friends, and satisfy them that his absence from the festive board was unavoidable, and so fully retrieve himself in their good opinion that he shall yet be Governor of Massachusetts? And all these great purposes accomplished, will he walk the streets again, with that dog-day smile of elaborate benevolence, sultry enough to tempt flies to come and buzz in it? Or will he, after the tomb-like seclusion of the past day and night, go forth a humbled and repentant man, sorrowful, gentle, seeking no profit, shrinking from worldly honor, hardly daring to love God, but bold to love his fellow man, and to do him what good he may? Will he bear about with him no odious grin of feigned benignity, insolent in its pretense, and loathsome in its falsehood, but the tender sadness of a contrite heart, broken, at last, beneath its own weight of sin? For it is our belief, whatever show of honor he may have piled upon it, that there was heavy sin at the base of this man's being.

Rise up, Judge Pyncheon! The morning sunshine glimmers through the foliage, and, beautiful and holy as it is, shuns not to kindle up your face. Rise up, thou subtle, worldly, selfish, ironhearted hypocrite, and make thy choice whether still to be subtle, worldly, selfish, ironhearted, and hypocritical, or to tear these sins out of thy nature, though they bring the lifeblood with them! The Avenger is upon thee! Rise up, before it be too late!

What! Thou art not stirred by this last appeal? No, not a jot! And there we see a fly—one of your common houseflies, such as are always buzzing on the windowpane—which has smelt out Governor Pyncheon, and alights, now on his forehead, now on his chin, and now, heaven help us! is creeping over the bridge of his nose, towards the would-be chief magistrate's wide-open eyes! Canst thou not brush the fly away? Art thou too sluggish? Thou man, that hadst so many busy projects yesterday! Art thou too weak, that wast so powerful? Not brush away a fly? Nay, then, we give thee up!

And hark! The shop bell rings. After hours like these latter ones, through which we have borne our heavy tale, it is good to be made sensible that there is a living world, and that even this old, lonely mansion retains some manner of connection with it. We breathe more freely, emerging from Judge Pyncheon's presence into the street before the Seven Gables.

❧19❧

Alice's Posies

UNCLE VENNER, trundling a wheelbarrow, was the earliest person stirring in the neighborhood the day after the storm.

Pyncheon Street, in front of the House of the Seven Gables, was a far pleasanter scene than a by-lane, confined by shabby fences, and bordered with wooden dwellings of the meaner class, could reasonably be expected to present. Nature made sweet amends, that morning, for the five unkindly days which had preceded it. It would have been enough to live for, merely to look up at the wide benediction of the sky, or as much of it as was visible between the houses, genial once more with sunshine. Every object was agreeable, whether to be gazed at in the breadth, or examined more minutely. Such, for example, were the well-washed pebbles and gravel of the sidewalk; even the sky-reflecting pools in the center of the street; and the grass, now freshly verdant, that crept along the base of the fences, on the other side of which, if one peeped over, was seen the multifarious growth of gardens. Vegetable productions, of whatever kind, seemed more than negatively happy, in the juicy warmth and abundance of their life. The Pyncheon Elm, throughout its great circumference, was all alive, and full of the morning sun and a sweet-tempered little breeze, which lingered within this verdant sphere, and set a thousand leafy tongues awhispering all at once. This aged tree appeared to have suffered nothing from the gale. It had kept its boughs unshattered, and its full complement of leaves; and the whole in perfect verdure, except a single branch, that, by the earlier change with which the elm tree sometimes prophesies the autumn, had been transmuted to bright gold. It was like the golden branch that gained Aeneas and the Sibyl admittance into Hades.

This one mystic branch hung down before the main entrance of the Seven Gables, so nigh the ground that any passer-by might have stood on tiptoe and plucked it off. Presented at the door, it would have been a symbol of his right to enter, and be made acquainted with all the secrets of the house. So little faith is due to external appearance that there was really an inviting aspect over the venerable edifice, conveying an idea that its history must be a decorous and happy one, and such as would be delightful for a fireside tale. Its windows gleamed cheerfully in the slanting sunlight. The lines and tufts of green moss, here and there, seemed pledges of familiarity and sisterhood with Nature; as if this human dwelling place, being of such old date, had established its prescriptive title among primeval oaks and whatever other objects, by virtue of their long continuance, have acquired a gracious right to be. A person of imaginative temperament, while passing by the house, would turn, once and again, and peruse it well: its many peaks, consenting together in the clustered chimneys; the deep projection over its basement story; the arched window, imparting a look, if not of grandeur, yet of antique gentility, to the broken portal over which it opened; the luxuriance of gigantic burdocks, near the threshold; he would note all these characteristics, and be conscious of something deeper than he saw. He would conceive the mansion to have been the residence of the stubborn old Puritan, Integrity, who, dying in some forgotten generation, had left a blessing in all its rooms and chambers, the efficacy of which was to be seen in the religion, honesty, moderate competence, or upright poverty and solid happiness, of his descendants, to this day.

One object, above all others, would take root in the imaginative observer's memory. It was the great tuft of flowers—weeds you would have called them, only a week

ago—the tuft of crimson-spotted flowers, in the angle between the two front gables. The old people used to give
them the name of Alice's Posies, in remembrance of fair
Alice Pyncheon, who was believed to have brought their
seeds from Italy. They were flaunting in rich beauty and full
bloom today, and seemed, as it were, a mystic expression
that something within the house was consummated.

It was but little after sunrise, when Uncle Venner made
his appearance, as aforesaid, impelling a wheelbarrow along
the street. He was going his matutinal rounds to collect
cabbage leaves, turnip tops, potato skins, and the miscellaneous refuse of the dinner pot, which the thrifty housewives of the neighborhood were accustomed to put aside,
as fit only to feed a pig. Uncle Venner's pig was fed entirely,
and kept in prime order, on these eleemosynary contri-
butions; insomuch that the patched philosopher used to
promise that, before retiring to his farm, he would make
a feast of the portly grunter, and invite all his neighbors to
partake of the joints and spare ribs which they had helped
to fatten. Miss Hepzibah Pyncheon's housekeeping had so
greatly improved, since Clifford became a member of the
family, that her share of the banquet would have been no
lean one; and Uncle Venner, accordingly, was a good deal
disappointed not to find the large earthen pan, full of fragmentary eatables, that ordinarily awaited his coming at the
back doorstep of the Seven Gables.

"I never knew Miss Hepzibah so forgetful before,"
said the patriarch to himself. "She must have had a dinner
yesterday—no question of that! She always has one, nowadays. So where's the pot liquor and potato skins? I ask.
Shall I knock, and see if she's stirring yet? No, no, 'twont
do! If little Phoebe was about the house, I should not mind
knocking; but Miss Hepzibah, likely as not, would scowl
down at me out of the window, and look cross, even if she
felt pleasantly. So, I'll come back at noon."

With these reflections, the old man was shutting the gate
of the little back yard. Creaking on its hinges, however, like
every other gate and door about the premises, the sound
reached the ears of the occupant of the northern gable, one
of the windows of which had a side view towards the gate.

"Good morning, Uncle Venner!" said the daguerreo-typist, leaning out of the window. "Do you hear nobody stirring?"

"Not a soul," said the man of patches. "But that's no wonder. 'Tis barely half an hour past sunrise, yet. But I'm really glad to see you, Mr. Holgrave! There's a strange, lone-some look about this side of the house; so that my heart misgave me, somehow or other, and I felt as if there was nobody alive in it. The front of the house looks a good deal cheerier; and Alice's Posies are blooming there beautifully; and if I were a young man, Mr. Holgrave, my sweetheart should have one of those flowers in her bosom, though I risked my neck climbing for it! Well, and did the wind keep you awake last night?"

"It did, indeed!" answered the artist, smiling. "If I were a believer in ghosts—and I don't quite know whether I am or not—I should have concluded that all the old Pyncheons were running riot in the lower rooms, especially in Miss Hepzibah's part of the house. But it is very quiet now."

"Yes, Miss Hepzibah will be apt to oversleep herself, af-ter being disturbed, all night, with the racket," said Uncle Venner. "But it would be odd, now, wouldn't it, if the Judge had taken both his cousins into the country along with him? I saw him go into the shop yesterday."

"At what hour?" inquired Holgrave.

"Oh, along in the forenoon," said the old man. "Well, well! I must go my rounds, and so must my wheelbarrow. But I'll be back here at dinnertime; for my pig likes a din-ner as well as a breakfast. No mealtime, and no sort of vict-uals, ever seems to come amiss to my pig. Good morning to you! And, Mr. Holgrave, if I were a young man, like you, I'd get one of Alice's posies, and keep it in water till Phoebe comes back."

"I have heard," said the daguerreotypist, as he drew in his head, "that the water of Maule's well suits these flowers best."

Here the conversation ceased, and Uncle Venner went on his way. For half an hour longer, nothing disturbed the repose of the Seven Gables; nor was there any visitor, ex-cept a carrier boy, who, as he passed the front doorstep, threw down one of his newspapers; for Hepzibah, of late, had regularly taken it in. After a while, there came a fat woman, making prodigious speed, and stumbling as she ran up the steps of the shop door. Her face glowed with fire heat, and, it being a pretty warm morning, she bubbled and hissed, as it were, as if all afry with chimney warmth, and summer warmth, and the warmth of her own corpulent velocity. She tried the shop door; it was fast. She tried it again, with so angry a jar that the bell tinkled angrily back at her.

"The deuce take Old Maid Pyncheon!" muttered the irascible housewife. "Think of her pretending to set up a cent shop, and then lying abed till noon! These are what she calls gentlefolk's airs, I suppose! But I'll either start her ladyship, or break the door down!"

She shook it accordingly, and the bell, having a spiteful little temper of its own, rang obstreperously, making its remonstrances heard—not, indeed, by the ears for which they were intended—but by a good lady on the opposite side of the street. She opened her window, and addressed the impatient applicant.

"You'll find nobody there, Mrs. Gubbins."

"But I must and will find somebody here!" cried Mrs. Gubbins, inflicting another outrage on the bell. "I want a half pound of pork, to fry some first-rate flounders, for Mr. Gubbins's breakfast; and, lady or not, Old Maid Pyncheon shall get up and serve me with it!"

"But do hear reason, Mrs. Gubbins!" responded the lady opposite. "She, and her brother, too, have both gone to their cousin, Judge Pyncheon's, at his country seat. There's not a soul in the house, but that young daguerreotype man that sleeps in the north gable. I saw old Hepzibah and Clifford go away yesterday; and a queer couple of ducks they were, paddling through the mud puddles! They're gone, I'll assure you."

"And how do you know they're gone to the Judge's?" asked Mrs. Gubbins. "He's a rich man; and there's been a quarrel between him and Hepzibah, this many a day, because he won't give her a living. That's the main reason of her setting up a cent shop."

"I know that well enough," said the neighbor. "But

they're gone—that's one thing certain. And who but a blood relation, that couldn't help himself, I ask you, would take in that awful-tempered old maid, and that dreadful Clifford? That's it, you may be sure."

Mrs. Gubbins took her departure, still brimming over with hot wrath against the absent Hepzibah. For another half hour, or, perhaps, considerably more, there was almost as much quiet on the outside of the house as within. The elm, however, made a pleasant, cheerful, sunny sigh, responsive to the breeze that was elsewhere imperceptible; a swarm of insects buzzed merrily under its drooping shadow, and became specks of light whenever they darted into the sunshine; a locust sang, once or twice, in some inscrutable seclusion of the tree; and a solitary little bird, with plumage of pale gold, came and hovered about Alice's Posies.

At last, our small acquaintance, Ned Higgins, trudged up the street, on his way to school; and happening, for the first time in a fortnight, to be the possessor of a cent, he could by no means get past the shop door of the Seven Gables. But it would not open. Again and again, however, and half a dozen other agains, with the inexorable pertinacity of a child intent upon some object important to itself, did he renew his efforts for admittance. He had, doubtless, set his heart upon an elephant; or, possibly, with Hamlet, he meant to eat a crocodile. In response to his more violent attacks, the bell gave, now and then, a moderate tinkle, but could not be stirred into clamor by any exertion of the little fellow's childish and tiptoe strength. Holding by the door handle, he peeped through a crevice of the curtain, and saw that the inner door, communicating with the passage towards the parlor, was closed.

"Miss Pyncheon!" screamed the child, rapping on the windowpane. "I want an elephant!"

There being no answer to several repetitions of the summons, Ned began to grow impatient; and his little pot of passion quickly boiling over, he picked up a stone, with a naughty purpose to fling it through the window; at the same time blubbering and sputtering with wrath. A man—one of two who happened to be passing by—caught the urchin's arm.

"What's the trouble, old gentleman?" he asked.

"I want old Hepzibah, or Phoebe, or any of them!" answered Ned, sobbing. "They won't open the door; and I can't get my elephant!"

"Go to school, you little scamp!" said the man. "There's another cent shop round the corner. 'Tis very strange, Dixey," added he to his companion, "what's become of all these Pyncheons! Smith, the livery-stable keeper, tells me Judge Pyncheon put his horse up yesterday, to stand till after dinner, and has not taken him away yet. And one of the Judge's hired men has been in, this morning, to make inquiry about him. He's a kind of person, they say, that seldom breaks his habits, or stays out o' nights."

"Oh, he'll turn up safe enough!" said Dixey. "And as for Old Maid Pyncheon, take my word for it, she has run in debt, and gone off from her creditors. I foretold, you remember, the first morning she set up shop, that her devilish scowl would frighten away customers. They couldn't stand it!"

"I never thought she'd make it go," remarked his friend. "This business of cent shops is overdone among the women-folks. My wife tried it, and lost five dollars on her outlay!"

"Poor business!" said Dixey, shaking his head. "Poor business!"

In the course of the morning, there were various other attempts to open a communication with the supposed inhabitants of this silent and impenetrable mansion. The man of root beer came, in his neatly painted wagon, with a couple of dozen full bottles, to be exchanged for empty ones; the baker, with a lot of crackers which Hepzibah had ordered for her retail custom; the butcher, with a nice titbit which he fancied she would be eager to secure for Clifford. Had any observer of these proceedings been aware of the fearful secret hidden within the house, it would have affected him with a singular shape and modification of horror, to see the current of human life making this small eddy hereabouts—whirling sticks, straws, and all such trifles, round and round, right over the black depth where a dead corpse lay unseen!

The butcher was so much in earnest with his sweetbread

of lamb, or whatever the dainty might be, that he tried every accessible door of the Seven Gables, and at length came round again to the shop, where he ordinarily found admittance.

"It's a nice article, and I know the old lady would jump at it," said he to himself. "She can't be gone away! In fifteen years that I have driven my cart through Pyncheon Street, I've never known her to be away from home; though often enough, to be sure, a man might knock all day without bringing her to the door. But that was when she'd only herself to provide for."

Peeping through the same crevice of the curtain where, only a little while before, the urchin of elephantine appetite had peeped, the butcher beheld the inner door, not closed, as the child had seen it, but ajar, and almost wide open. However it might have happened, it was the fact. Through the passageway there was a dark vista into the lighter but still obscure interior of the parlor. It appeared to the butcher that he could pretty clearly discern what seemed to be the stalwart legs, clad in black pantaloons, of a man sitting in a large oaken chair, the back of which concealed all the remainder of his figure. This contemptuous tranquillity on the part of an occupant of the house, in response to the butcher's indefatigable efforts to attract notice, so piqued the man of flesh that he determined to withdraw.

"So," thought he, "there sits Old Maid Pyncheon's bloody brother, while I've been giving myself all this trouble! Why, if a hog hadn't more manners, I'd stick him! I call it demeaning a man's business to trade with such people; and from this time forth, if they want a sausage or an ounce of liver, they shall run after the cart for it!"

He tossed the titbit angrily into his cart, and drove off in a pet.

Not a great while afterwards, there was a sound of music turning the corner, and approaching down the street, with several intervals of silence, and then a renewed and nearer outbreak of brisk melody. A mob of children was seen moving onward, or stopping, in unison with the sound, which appeared to proceed from the center of the throng; so that they were loosely bound together by slender strains of harmony, and drawn along captive; with ever and anon an accession of some little fellow in an apron and straw hat, capering forth from door or gateway. Arriving under the shadow of the Pyncheon Elm, it proved to be the Italian boy, who, with his monkey and show of puppets, had once before played his hurdy-gurdy beneath the arched window. The pleasant face of Phoebe—and doubtless, too, the liberal recompense which she had flung him—still dwelt in his remembrance. His expressive features kindled up, as he recognized the spot where this trifling incident of his erratic life had chanced. He entered the neglected yard (now wilder than ever, with its growth of hogweed and burdock), stationed himself on the doorstep of the main entrance, and, opening his show box, began to play. Each individual of the automatic community forthwith set to work, according to his or her proper vocation: the monkey, taking off his Highland bonnet, bowed and scraped to the bystanders most obsequiously, with ever an observant eye to pick up a stray cent; and the young foreigner himself, as he turned the crank of his machine, glanced upward to the arched window, expectant of a presence that would make his music the livelier and sweeter. The throng of children stood near; some on the sidewalk; some within the yard; two or three establishing themselves on the very doorsteps; and one squatting on the threshold. Meanwhile, the locust kept singing in the great old Pyncheon Elm.

"I don't hear anybody in the house," said one of the children to another. "The monkey won't pick up anything here."

"There is somebody at home," affirmed the urchin on the threshold. "I heard a step!"

Still the young Italian's eye turned sidelong upward; and it really seemed as if the touch of genuine, though slight and almost playful, emotion communicated a juicier sweetness to the dry, mechanical process of his minstrelsy. These wanderers are readily responsive to any natural kindness—be it no more than a smile, or a word itself not understood, but only a warmth in it—which befalls them on the roadside of life. They remember these things, because they are the little enchantments which, for the instant—for the space that reflects a landscape in a soap bubble—build up a home about them. Therefore, the Italian boy would not be discouraged by the heavy silence with which the old house seemed resolute to clog the vivacity of his instrument. He persisted in his melodious appeals; he still looked upward, trusting that his dark, alien countenance would soon be brightened by Phoebe's sunny aspect. Neither could he be willing to depart without again beholding Clifford, whose sensibility, like Phoebe's smile, had talked a kind of heart's language to the foreigner. He repeated all his music over and over again, until his auditors were getting weary. So were the little wooden people in his show box, and the monkey most of all. There was no response, save the singing of the locust.

"No children live in this house," said a schoolboy, at last. "Nobody lives here but an old maid and an old man. You'll get nothing here! Why don't you go along?"

"You fool, you, why do you tell him?" whispered a shrewd little Yankee, caring nothing for the music, but a good deal for the cheap rate at which it was had. "Let him play as long as he likes! If there's nobody to pay him, that's his own lookout!"

Once more, however, the Italian ran over his round of melodies. To the common observer—who could understand nothing of the case, except the music and the sunshine on the hither side of the door—it might have been amusing to watch the pertinacity of the street performer. Will he succeed at last? Will that stubborn door be suddenly flung open? Will a group of joyous children, the young ones of the house, come dancing, shouting, laughing, into the open air, and cluster round the show box, looking with eager merriment at the puppets, and tossing each a copper for long-tailed Mammon, the monkey, to pick up?

But to us, who know the inner heart of the Seven Gables as well as its exterior face, there is a ghastly effect in this repetition of light popular tunes at its doorstep. It would be an ugly business, indeed, if Judge Pyncheon (who would not have cared a fig for Paganini's fiddle in his most harmonious mood) should make his appearance at the door, with a bloody shirt bosom, and a grim frown on his swarthily white visage, and motion the foreign vagabond away! Was ever before such a grinding out of jigs and waltzes, where nobody was in the queue to dance? Yes, very often. This contrast, or intermingling of tragedy with mirth, happens daily, hourly, momently. The gloomy and desolate old house, deserted of life, and with awful Death sitting sternly in its solitude, was the emblem of many a human heart, which, nevertheless, is compelled to hear the thrill and echo of the world's gaiety around it.

Before the conclusion of the Italian's performance, a couple of men happened to be passing, on their way to dinner.

"I say, you young French fellow!" called out one of them. "Come away from that doorstep, and go somewhere else with your nonsense! The Pyncheon family live there; and they are in great trouble, just about this time. They don't feel musical today. It is reported all over town that Judge Pyncheon, who owns the house, has been murdered; and the city marshal is going to look into the matter. So be off with you, at once!"

As the Italian shouldered his hurdy-gurdy, he saw on the doorstep a card, which had been covered, all the morning, by the newspaper that the carrier had flung upon it, but was now shuffled into sight. He picked it up, and perceiving something written in pencil, gave it to the man to read. In fact, it was an engraved card of Judge Pyncheon's with certain penciled memoranda on the back, referring to various businesses which it had been his purpose to transact during the preceding day. It formed a prospective epitome of the day's history; only that affairs had not turned out altogether in accordance with the program. The card must have been lost from the Judge's vest pocket, in his preliminary attempt to gain access by the main entrance of the house. Though well soaked with rain, it was still partially legible.

"Look here, Dixey!" cried the man. "This has something to do with Judge Pyncheon. See! Here's his name printed on it; and here, I suppose, is some of his handwriting."

"Let's go to the city marshal with it!" said Dixey. "It may give him just the clue he wants. After all," whispered he in his companion's ear, "it would be no wonder if the

Judge has gone into that door and never come out again!
A certain cousin of his may have been at his old tricks. And
Old Maid Pyncheon having got herself in debt by the cent
shop—and the Judge's pocketbook being well filled—and
bad blood amongst them already! Put all these things together and see what they make!"

"Hush, hush!" whispered the other. "It seems like a sin
to be the first to speak of such a thing. But I think, with you,
that we had better go to the city marshal."

"Yes, yes!" said Dixey. "Well! I always said there was
something devilish in that woman's scowl!"

The men wheeled about, accordingly, and retraced their
steps up the street. The Italian, also, made the best of his
way off, with a parting glance up at the arched window. As
for the children, they took to their heels, with one accord,
and scampered as if some giant or ogre were in pursuit,
until, at a good distance from the house, they stopped as
suddenly and simultaneously as they had set out. Their susceptible nerves took an indefinite alarm from what they
had overheard. Looking back at the grotesque peaks and
shadowy angles of the old mansion, they fancied a gloom
diffused about it which no brightness of the sunshine could
dispel. An imaginary Hepzibah scowled and shook her finger at them, from several windows at the same moment.
An imaginary Clifford—for (and it would have deeply
wounded him to know it) he had always been a horror to
these small people—stood behind the unreal Hepzibah,
making awful gestures, in a faded dressing gown. Children
are even more apt, if possible, than grown people to catch
the contagion of a panic terror. For the rest of the day, the
more timid went whole streets about, for the sake of avoiding the Seven Gables; while the bolder signalized their
hardihood by challenging their comrades to race past the
mansion at full speed.

It could not have been more than half an hour after the
disappearance of the Italian boy, with his unseasonable
melodies, when a cab drove down the street. It stopped beneath the Pyncheon Elm; the cabman took a trunk, a canvas
bag, and a bandbox from the top of his vehicle, and depos-
ited them on the doorstep of the old house; a straw bonnet,

and then the pretty figure of a young girl came into view from the interior of the cab. It was Phoebe! Though not altogether so blooming as when she first tripped into our story—for, in the few intervening weeks, her experiences had made her graver, more womanly, and deeper-eyed, in token of a heart that had begun to suspect its depths—still there was the quiet glow of natural sunshine over her. Neither had she forfeited her proper gift of making things look real, rather than fantastic, within her sphere. Yet we feel it to be a questionable venture, even for Phoebe, at this juncture, to cross the threshold of the Seven Gables. Is her healthful presence potent enough to chase away the crowd of pale, hideous, and sinful phantoms that have gained admittance there since her departure? Or will she, likewise, fade, sicken, sadden, and grow into deformity, and be only another pallid phantom, to glide noiselessly up and down the stairs, and affright children as she pauses at the window?

At least, we would gladly forewarn the unsuspecting girl that there is nothing in human shape or substance to receive her, unless it be the figure of Judge Pyncheon, who—wretched spectacle that he is, and frightful in our remembrance, since our night-long vigil with him!—still keeps his place in the oaken chair.

Phoebe first tried the shop door. It did not yield to her hand; and the white curtain, drawn across the window which formed the upper section of the door, struck her quick perceptive faculty as something unusual. Without making another effort to enter here, she betook herself to the great portal, under the arched window. Finding it fastened, she knocked. A reverberation came from the emptiness within. She knocked again, and a third time; and, listening intently, fancied that the floor creaked, as if Hepzibah were coming, with her ordinary tiptoe movement, to admit her. But so dead a silence ensued upon this imaginary sound, that she began to question whether she might not have mistaken the house, familiar as she thought herself with its exterior.

Her notice was now attracted by a child's voice, at some distance. It appeared to call her name. Looking in the direction whence it proceeded, Phoebe saw little Ned Higgins, a good way down the street, stamping, shaking his head violently, making deprecatory gestures with both hands, and shouting to her at mouth-wide screech.

"No, no, Phoebe!" he screamed. "Don't you go in! There's something wicked there! Don't—don't—don't go in!"

But, as the little personage could not be induced to approach near enough to explain himself, Phoebe concluded that he had been frightened, on some of his visits to the shop, by her cousin Hepzibah; for the good lady's manifestations, in truth, ran about an equal chance of scaring children out of their wits, or compelling them to unseemly laughter. Still, she felt the more, for this incident, how unaccountably silent and impenetrable the house had become. As her next resort, Phoebe made her way into the garden, where on so warm and bright a day as the present, she had little doubt of finding Clifford, and perhaps Hepzibah also, idling away the noontide in the shadow of the arbor. Immediately on her entering the garden gate, the family of hens half ran, half flew, to meet her; while a strange grimalkin, which was prowling under the parlor window, took to his heels, clambered hastily over the fence, and vanished. The arbor was vacant and its floor, table, and circular bench were still damp, and bestrewn with twigs and the disarray of the past storm. The growth of the garden seemed to have got quite out of bounds; the weeds had taken advantage of Phoebe's absence, and the long-continued rain, to run rampant over the flowers and kitchen vegetables. Maule's well had overflowed its stone border, and made a pool of formidable breadth in that corner of the garden.

The impression of the whole scene was that of a spot where no human foot had left its print for many preceding days—probably not since Phoebe's departure—for she saw a side comb of her own under the table of the arbor, where it must have fallen on the last afternoon when she and Clifford sat there.

The girl knew that her two relatives were capable of far greater oddities than that of shutting themselves up in their old house, as they appeared now to have done. Nevertheless, with indistinct misgivings of something amiss, and apprehensions to which she could not give shape, she approached the door that formed the customary communication between the house and garden. It was secured within, like the two which she had already tried. She knocked, however; and immediately, as if the application had been expected, the door was drawn open, by a considerable exertion of some unseen person's strength, not wide, but far enough to afford her a sidelong entrance. As Hepzibah, in order not to expose herself to inspection from without, invariably opened a door in this manner, Phoebe necessarily concluded that it was her cousin who now admitted her.

Without hesitation, therefore, she stepped across the threshold, and had no sooner entered than the door closed behind her.

❧20❧

The Flower of Eden

PHOEBE, coming so suddenly from the sunny daylight, was altogether bedimmed in such density of shadow as lurked in most of the passages of the old house. She was not at first aware by whom she had been admitted. Before her eyes had adapted themselves to the obscurity, a hand grasped her own, with a firm but gentle and warm pressure, thus imparting a welcome which caused her heart to leap and thrill with an indefinable shiver of enjoyment. She felt herself drawn along, not towards the parlor, but into a large and unoccupied apartment, which had formerly been the grand reception room of the Seven Gables. The sunshine came freely into all the uncurtained windows of this room, and fell upon the dusty floor; so that Phoebe now clearly saw— what, indeed, had been no secret, after the encounter of a warm hand with hers—that it was not Hepzibah nor Clifford, but Holgrave, to whom she owed her reception. The subtile, intuitive communication, or, rather, the vague and formless impression of something to be told, had made her yield unresistingly to his impulse. Without taking away her hand, she looked eagerly in his face, not quick to forebode evil, but unavoidably conscious that the state of the family had changed since her departure, and therefore anxious for an explanation.

The artist looked paler than ordinary; there was a thoughtful and severe contraction of his forehead, tracing a deep, vertical line between the eyebrows. His smile, however, was full of genuine warmth, and had in it a joy, by far the most vivid expression that Phoebe had ever witnessed, shining out of the New England reserve with which Holgrave habitually masked whatever lay near his heart. It was the look wherewith a man, brooding alone over some fearful object, in a dreary forest, or illimitable desert, would recognize the familiar aspect of his dearest friend, bringing up all the peaceful ideas that belong to home, and the gentle current of everyday affairs. And yet, as he felt the necessity of responding to her look of inquiry, the smile disappeared.

"I ought not to rejoice that you have come, Phoebe," said he. "We meet at a strange moment!"

"What has happened?" she exclaimed. "Why is the house so deserted? Where are Hepzibah and Clifford?"

"Gone! I cannot imagine where they are!" answered Holgrave. "We are alone in the house!"

"Hepzibah and Clifford gone?" cried Phoebe. "It is not possible! And why have you brought me into this room, instead of the parlor? Ah, something terrible has happened! I must run and see!"

"No, no, Phoebe!" said Holgrave, holding her back. "It is as I have told you. They are gone, and I know not whither. A terrible event has, indeed, happened, but not to them, nor, as I undoubtingly believe, through any agency of theirs. If I read your character rightly, Phoebe," he continued, fixing his eyes on hers, with stern anxiety, intermixed with tenderness, "gentle as you are, and seeming to have your sphere among common things, you yet possess remarkable strength. You have wonderful poise, and a faculty which, when tested, will prove itself capable of dealing with matters that fall far out of the ordinary rule."

"Oh, no, I am very weak!" replied Phoebe, trembling. "But tell me what has happened!"

"You are strong!" persisted Holgrave. "You must be both strong and wise; for I am all astray, and need your counsel. It may be you can suggest the one right thing to do!"

"Tell me—tell me!" said Phoebe, all in a tremble. "It oppresses—it terrifies me—this mystery! Anything else I can bear!"

The artist hesitated. Notwithstanding what he had just said, and most sincerely, in regard to the self-balancing power with which Phoebe impressed him, it still seemed almost wicked to bring the awful secret of yesterday to her knowledge. It was like dragging a hideous shape of death into the cleanly and cheerful space before a household fire, where it would present all the uglier aspect, amid the decorousness of everything about it. Yet it could not be concealed from her; she must needs know it.

"Phoebe," said he, "do you remember this?"

He put into her hand a daguerreotype; the same that he had shown her at their first interview in the garden, and which so strikingly brought out the hard and relentless traits of the original.

"What has this to do with Hepzibah and Clifford?" asked Phoebe, with impatient surprise that Holgrave should so trifle with her at such a moment. "It is Judge Pyncheon! You have shown it to me before!"

"But here is the same face, taken within this half hour," said the artist, presenting her with another miniature. "I had just finished it, when I heard you at the door."

"This is death!" shuddered Phoebe, turning very pale. "Judge Pyncheon dead!"

"Such as there represented," said Holgrave, "he sits in the next room. The Judge is dead, and Clifford and Hepzibah have vanished! I know no more. All beyond is conjecture. On returning to my solitary chamber, last evening, I noticed no light, either in the parlor, or Hepzibah's room, or Clifford's; no stir nor footstep about the house. This morning, there was the same deathlike quiet. From my window, I overheard the testimony of a neighbor that your relatives were seen leaving the house, in the midst of yesterday's storm. A rumor reached me, too, of Judge Pyncheon being missed. A feeling which I cannot describe—an indefinite sense of some catastrophe, or consummation—impelled me to make my way into this part of the house, where I discovered what you see. As a point of evidence that may be useful to Clifford, and also as a memorial valuable to myself—for, Phoebe, there are hereditary reasons that connect me strangely with that man's fate—I used the means at my disposal to preserve this pictorial record of Judge Pyncheon's death."

Even in her agitation, Phoebe could not help remarking the calmness of Holgrave's demeanor. He appeared, it is true, to feel the whole awfulness of the Judge's death, yet had received the fact into his mind without any mixture of surprise, but as an event preordained, happening inevitably, and so fitting itself into past occurrences that it could almost have been prophesied.

"Why have you not thrown open the doors, and called in witnesses?" inquired she, with a painful shudder. "It is terrible to be here alone!"

"But Clifford!" suggested the artist. "Clifford and Hepzibah! We must consider what is best to be done in their behalf. It is a wretched fatality that they should have disappeared! Their flight will throw the worst coloring over this event of which it is susceptible. Yet how easy is the explanation, to those who know them! Bewildered and terror-stricken by the similarity of this death to a former one, which was attended with such disastrous consequences to Clifford, they have had no idea but of removing themselves from the scene. How miserably unfortunate! Had Hepzibah but shrieked aloud—had Clifford flung wide the door, and proclaimed Judge Pyncheon's death—it would have been, however awful in itself, an event fruitful of good consequences to them. As I view it, it would have gone far towards obliterating the black stain on Clifford's character."

"And how," asked Phoebe, "could any good come from what is so very dreadful?"

"Because," said the artist, "if the matter can be fairly considered and candidly interpreted, it must be evident that Judge Pyncheon could not have come unfairly to his end. This mode of death has been an idiosyncrasy with his family, for generations past; not often occurring, indeed, but, when it does occur, usually attacking individuals about the Judge's time of life, and generally in the tension of some mental crisis, or, perhaps, in an access of wrath. Old Maule's prophecy was probably founded on a knowledge of this physical predisposition in the Pyncheon race. Now, there is a minute and almost exact similarity in the appearances connected with the death that occurred yesterday and those recorded of the death of Clifford's uncle thirty years ago. It is true, there was a certain arrangement of circumstances, unnecessary to be recounted, which made it possible—nay, as men look at these things, probable, or even certain—that old Jaffrey Pyncheon came to a violent death, and by Clifford's hands."

"Whence came those circumstances?" exclaimed Phoebe, "he being innocent, as we know him to be!"

"They were arranged," said Holgrave, "at least, such has long been my conviction—they were arranged after the uncle's death, and before it was made public, by the man who sits in yonder parlor. His own death, so like that former one, yet attended by none of those suspicious circumstances, seems the stroke of God upon him, at once a punishment for his wickedness, and making plain the innocence of Clifford. But this flight—it distorts everything! He may be in concealment, near at hand. Could we but bring him back before the discovery of the Judge's death, the evil might be rectified."

"We must not hide this thing a moment longer!" said Phoebe. "It is dreadful to keep it so closely in our hearts. Clifford is innocent. God will make it manifest! Let us throw open the doors, and call all the neighborhood to see the truth!"

"You are right, Phoebe," rejoined Holgrave. "Doubtless you are right."

Yet the artist did not feel the horror, which was proper to Phoebe's sweet and order-loving character, at thus finding herself at issue with society, and brought in contact with an event that transcended ordinary rules. Neither was he in haste, like her, to betake himself within the precincts of common life. On the contrary, he gathered a wild enjoyment—as it were, a flower of strange beauty, growing in a desolate spot, and blossoming in the wind—such a flower of momentary happiness he gathered from his present position. It separated Phoebe and himself from the world, and bound them to each other, by their exclusive knowledge of Judge Pyncheon's mysterious death, and the counsel which they were forced to hold respecting it. The secret, so long as it should continue such, kept them within the circle of a spell, a solitude in the midst of men, a remoteness as entire as that of an island in midocean; once divulged, the ocean would flow betwixt them, standing on its widely sundered shores. Meanwhile, all the circumstances of their situation seemed to draw them together; they were like two children who go hand in hand, pressing closely to one another's side, through a shadow-haunted passage. The image of awful Death, which filled the house, held them united by his stiffened grasp.

These influences hastened the development of emotions that might not otherwise have flowered so. Possibly, indeed, it had been Holgrave's purpose to let them die in their undeveloped germs.

"Why do we delay so?" asked Phoebe. "This secret takes away my breath! Let us throw open the doors!"

"In all our lives there can never come another moment like this!" said Holgrave. "Phoebe, is it all terror—nothing but terror? Are you conscious of no joy, as I am, that has made this the only point of life worth living for?"

"It seems a sin," replied Phoebe, trembling, "to think of joy at such a time!"

"Could you but know, Phoebe, how it was with me the hour before you came!" exclaimed the artist. "A dark, cold, miserable hour! The presence of yonder dead man threw a great black shadow over everything; he made the universe, so far as my perception could reach, a scene of guilt and retribution more dreadful than the guilt. The sense of it took away my youth. I never hoped to feel young again! The world looked strange, wild, evil, hostile; my past life, so lonesome and dreary; my future, a shapeless gloom, which I must mold into gloomy shapes! But, Phoebe, you crossed the threshold; and hope, warmth, and joy came in with you! The black moment became at once a blissful one. It must not pass without the spoken word. I love you!"

"How can you love a simple girl like me?" asked Phoebe, compelled by his earnestness to speak. "You have many, many thoughts, with which I should try in vain to sympathize. And I—I, too—I have tendencies with which you would sympathize as little. That is less matter. But I have not scope enough to make you happy."

"You are my only possibility of happiness!" answered Holgrave. "I have no faith in it, except as you bestow it on me!"

"And then—I am afraid!" continued Phoebe, shrinking towards Holgrave, even while she told him so frankly the doubts with which he affected her. "You will lead me out of my own quiet path. You will make me strive to follow you where it is pathless. I cannot do so. It is not my nature. I shall sink down and perish!"

"Ah, Phoebe!" exclaimed Holgrave, with almost a sigh, and a smile that was burdened with thought. "It will be far otherwise than as you forebode. The world owes all its on-ward impulses to men ill at ease. The happy man inevitably confines himself within ancient limits. I have a presenti-ment that, hereafter, it will be my lot to set out trees, to make fences—perhaps, even, in due time, to build a house for another generation—in a word, to conform myself to laws, and the peaceful practice of society. Your poise will be more powerful than any oscillating tendency of mine."

"I would not have it so!" said Phoebe, earnestly.

"Do you love me?" asked Holgrave. "If we love one another, the moment has room for nothing more. Let us pause upon it, and be satisfied. Do you love me, Phoebe?"

"You look into my heart," said she, letting her eyes drop. "You know I love you!"

And it was in this hour, so full of doubt and awe, that the one miracle was wrought without which every human existence is a blank. The bliss which makes all things true, beautiful, and holy shone around this youth and maiden. They were conscious of nothing sad nor old. They trans-figured the earth, and made it Eden again, and themselves the two first dwellers in it. The dead man, so close beside them, was forgotten. At such a crisis, there is no death; for immortality is revealed anew, and embraces everything in its hallowed atmosphere.

But how soon the heavy earth dream settled down again!

"Hark!" whispered Phoebe. "Somebody is at the street door!"

"Now let us meet the world!" said Holgrave. "No doubt,

the rumor of Judge Pyncheon's visit to this house, and the flight of Hepzibah and Clifford, is about to lead to the investigation of the premises. We have no way but to meet it. Let us open the door at once."

But, to their surprise, before they could reach the street door—even before they quitted the room in which the foregoing interview had passed—they heard footsteps in the farther passage. The door, therefore, which they supposed to be securely locked—which Holgrave, indeed, had seen to be so, and at which Phoebe had vainly tried to enter—must have been opened from without. The sound of footsteps was not harsh, bold, decided, and intrusive, as the gait of strangers would naturally be, making authoritative entrance into a dwelling where they knew themselves unwelcome. It was feeble, as of persons either weak or weary; there was the mingled murmur of two voices, familiar to both the listeners.

"Can it be?" whispered Holgrave.

"It is they!" answered Phoebe. "Thank God! Thank God!"

And then, as if in sympathy with Phoebe's whispered ejaculation, they heard Hepzibah's voice, more distinctly.

"Thank God, my brother, we are at home!"

"Well! Yes! Thank God!" responded Clifford. "A dreary home, Hepzibah! But you have done well to bring me hither! Stay! That parlor door is open. I cannot pass by it! Let me go and rest me in the arbor, where I used—oh, very long ago, it seems to me, after what has befallen us—where I used to be so happy with little Phoebe!"

But the house was not altogether so dreary as Clifford imagined it. They had not made many steps—in truth, they were lingering in the entry, with the listlessness of an accomplished purpose, uncertain what to do next—when Phoebe ran to meet them. On beholding her, Hepzibah burst into tears. With all her might, she had staggered onward beneath the burden of grief and responsibility, until now that it was safe to fling it down. Indeed, she had not energy to fling it down, but had ceased to uphold it, and suffered it to press her to the earth. Clifford appeared the stronger of the two.

"It is our own little Phoebe! Ah, and Holgrave with her," exclaimed he, with a glance of keen and delicate insight, and a smile, beautiful, kind, but melancholy. "I thought of you both, as we came down the street, and beheld Alice's Posies in full bloom. And so the flower of Eden has bloomed, likewise, in this old, darksome house today."

⊰21⊱

The Departure

THE sudden death of so prominent a member of the social world as the Honorable Judge Jaffrey Pyncheon created a sensation (at least, in the circles more immediately connected with the deceased), which had hardly quite subsided in a fortnight.

It may be remarked, however, that, of all the events which constitute a person's biography, there is scarcely one—none, certainly, of anything like a similar importance—to which the world so easily reconciles itself as to his death. In most other cases and contingencies, the individual is present among us, mixed up with the daily revolution of affairs, and affording a definite point for observation. At his decease, there is only a vacancy, and a momentary eddy—very small, as compared with the apparent magnitude of the ingurgitated object—and a bubble or two, ascending out of the black depth and bursting at the surface. As regarded Judge Pyncheon, it seemed probable, at first blush, that the mode of his final departure might give him a larger and longer posthumous vogue than ordinarily attends the memory of a distinguished man. But when it came to be understood, on the highest professional authority, that the event was a natural, and—except for some unimportant particulars, denoting a slight idiosyncrasy—by no means an unusual form of death, the public, with its customary alacrity, proceeded to forget that he had ever lived. In short, the honorable Judge was beginning to be a stale subject before half the county newspapers had found time to put their columns in mourning, and publish his exceedingly eulogistic obituary.

Nevertheless, creeping darkly through the places which this excellent person had haunted in his lifetime, there was a hidden stream of private talk, such as it would have shocked all decency to speak loudly at the street corners. It is very singular how the fact of a man's death often seems to give people a truer idea of his character, whether for good or evil, than they have ever possessed while he was living and acting among them. Death is so genuine a fact that it excludes falsehood, or betrays its emptiness; it is a touchstone that proves the gold, and dishonors the baser metal. Could the departed, whoever he may be, return in a week after his decease, he would almost invariably find himself at a higher or lower point than he had formerly occupied, on the scale of public appreciation. But the talk, or scandal, to which we now allude had reference to matters of no less old a date than the supposed murder, thirty or forty years ago, of the late Judge Pyncheon's uncle. The medical opinion, with regard to his own recent and regretted decease, had almost entirely obviated the idea that a murder was committed in the former case. Yet, as the record showed, there were circumstances irrefragably indicating that some person had gained access to old Jaffrey Pyncheon's private apartments, at or near the moment of his death. His desk and private drawers, in a room contiguous to his bedchamber, had been ransacked; money and valuable articles were missing; there was a bloody handprint on the old man's linen; and, by a powerfully welded chain of deductive evidence, the guilt of the robbery and apparent murder had been fixed on Clifford, then residing with his uncle in the House of the Seven Gables.

Whencesoever originating, there now arose a theory that undertook so to account for these circumstances as to exclude the idea of Clifford's agency. Many persons affirmed that the history and elucidation of the facts, long so mysterious, had been obtained by the daguerreotypist from one of those mesmerical seers, who, nowadays, so strangely perplex the aspect of human affairs, and put everybody's natural vision to the blush, by the marvels which they see with their eyes shut.

According to this version of the story, Judge Pyncheon, exemplary as we have portrayed him in our narrative, was, in his youth, an apparently irreclaimable scapegrace. The brutish, the animal instincts, as is often the case, had been developed earlier than the intellectual qualities and the force of character, for which he was afterwards remarkable. He had shown himself wild, dissipated, addicted to low pleasures, little short of ruffianly in his propensities, and recklessly expensive, with no other resources than the bounty of his uncle. This course of conduct had alienated the old bachelor's affection, once strongly fixed upon him. Now it is averred—but whether on authority available in a court of justice, we do not pretend to have investigated—that the young man was tempted by the devil, one night, to search his uncle's private drawers, to which he had unsuspected means of access. While thus criminally occupied, he was startled by the opening of the chamber door. There stood old Jaffrey Pyncheon, in his nightclothes! The surprise of such a discovery, his agitation, alarm, and horror, brought on the crisis of a disorder to which the old bachelor had an hereditary liability; he seemed to choke with blood, and fell upon the floor, striking his temple a heavy blow against the corner of a table. What was to be done? The old man was surely dead! Assistance would come too late! What a misfortune, indeed, should it come too soon, since his reviving consciousness would bring the recollection of the ignominious offense which he had beheld his nephew in the very act of committing!

But he never did revive. With the cool hardihood that always pertained to him, the young man continued his search of the drawers, and found a will, of recent date, in favor of Clifford, which he destroyed, and an older one, in his own favor, which he suffered to remain. But before retiring, Jaffrey bethought himself of the evidence, in these ransacked drawers, that someone had visited the chamber with sinister purposes. Suspicion, unless averted, might fix upon the real offender. In the very presence of the dead man, therefore, he laid a scheme that should free himself at the expense

of Clifford, his rival, for whose character he had at once a
contempt and a repugnance. It is not probable, be it said,
that he acted with any set purpose of involving Clifford
in a charge of murder. Knowing that his uncle did not die
by violence, it may not have occurred to him, in the hurry
of the crisis, that such an inference might be drawn. But,
when the affair took this darker aspect, Jaffrey's previous
steps had already pledged him to those which remained.
So craftily had he arranged the circumstances that, at Clifford's trial, his cousin hardly found it necessary to swear
to anything false, but only to withhold the one decisive explanation, by refraining to state what he had himself done
and witnessed.

Thus Jaffrey Pyncheon's inward criminality, as regarded
Clifford, was, indeed, black and damnable; while its mere
outward show and positive commission was the smallest
that could possibly consist with so great a sin. This is just
the sort of guilt that a man of eminent respectability finds
it easiest to dispose of. It was suffered to fade out of sight or
be reckoned a venial matter, in the Honorable Judge Pyncheon's long subsequent survey of his own life. He shuffled
it aside, among the forgotten and forgiven frailties of his
youth, and seldom thought of it again.

We leave the Judge to his repose. He could not be styled
fortunate at the hour of death. Unknowingly, he was a
childless man, while striving to add more wealth to his only
child's inheritance. Hardly a week after his decease, one
of the Cunard steamers brought intelligence of the death,
by cholera, of Judge Pyncheon's son, just at the point of
embarkation for his native land. By this misfortune, Clifford became rich; so did Hepzibah; so did our little village
maiden, and, through her, that sworn foe of wealth and all
manner of conservatism, the wild reformer—Holgrave!

It was now far too late in Clifford's life for the good
opinion of society to be worth the trouble and anguish of
a formal vindication. What he needed was the love of a
very few; not the admiration, or even the respect, of the
unknown many. The latter might probably have been won
for him, had those on whom the guardianship of his welfare had fallen deemed it advisable to expose Clifford to

a miserable resuscitation of past ideas, when the condition of whatever comfort he might expect lay in the calm of forgetfulness. After such wrong as he had suffered, there is no reparation. The pitiable mockery of it, which the world might have been ready enough to offer, coming so long after the agony had done its utmost work, would have been fit only to provoke bitterer laughter than poor Clifford was ever capable of. It is a truth (and it would be a very sad one but for the higher hopes which it suggests) that no great mistake, whether acted or endured, in our mortal sphere, is ever really set right. Time, the continual vicissitude of circumstances, and the invariable inopportunity of death render it impossible. If, after long lapse of years, the right seems to be in our power, we find no niche to set it in. The better remedy is for the sufferer to pass on, and leave what he once thought his irreparable ruin far behind him.

The shock of Judge Pyncheon's death had a permanently invigorating and ultimately beneficial effect on Clifford. That strong and ponderous man had been Clifford's nightmare. There was no free breath to be drawn, within the sphere of so malevolent an influence. The first effect of freedom, as we have witnessed in Clifford's aimless flight, was a tremulous exhilaration. Subsiding from it, he did not sink into his former intellectual apathy. He never, it is true, attained to nearly the full measure of what might have been his faculties. But he recovered enough of them partially fo light up his character, to display some outline of the marvelous grace that was abortive in it, and to make him the object of no less deep, although less melancholy interest than heretofore. He was evidently happy. Could we pause to give another picture of his daily life, with all the appliances now at command to gratify his instinct for the beautiful, the garden scenes, that seemed so sweet to him, would look mean and trivial in comparison.

Very soon after their change of fortune, Clifford, Hepzibah, and little Phoebe, with the approval of the artist, concluded to remove from the dismal old House of the Seven Gables, and take up their abode, for the present, at the elegant country seat of the late Judge Pyncheon. Chanticleer and his family had already been transported thither, where the two hens had forthwith begun an indefatigable process of egg-laying, with an evident design, as a matter of duty and conscience, to continue their illustrious breed under better auspices than for a century past. On the day set for their departure, the principal personages of our story, including good Uncle Venner, were assembled in the parlor.

"The country house is certainly a very fine one, so far as the plan goes," observed Holgrave, as the party were discussing their future arrangements. "But I wonder that the late Judge—being so opulent, and with a reasonable prospect of transmitting his wealth to descendants of his own—should not have felt the propriety of embodying so excellent a piece of domestic architecture in stone, rather than in wood. Then, every generation of the family might have altered the interior, to suit its own taste and convenience; while the exterior, through the lapse of years, might have been adding venerableness to permanence, which I consider essential to the happiness of any one moment."

"Why," cried Phoebe, gazing into the artist's face with infinite amazement, "how wonderfully your ideas are changed! A house of stone, indeed! It is but two or three weeks ago that you seemed to wish people to live in something as fragile and temporary as a bird's nest!"

"Ah, Phoebe, I told you how it would be!" said the artist, with a half-melancholy laugh. "You find me a conservative already! Little did I think ever to become one. It is especially unpardonable in this dwelling of so much hereditary misfortune, and under the eye of yonder portrait of a model conservative, who, in that very character, rendered himself so long the evil destiny of his race."

"That picture!" said Clifford, seeming to shrink from its stern glance. "Whenever I look at it, there is an old dreamy recollection haunting me, but keeping just beyond the grasp of my mind. Wealth, it seems to say—boundless wealth—unimaginable wealth! I could fancy that, when I was a child, or a youth, that portrait had spoken, and told me a rich secret, or had held forth its hand, with the written record of hidden opulence. But those old matters are so dim with me, nowadays! What could this dream have been?"

"Perhaps I can recall it," answered Holgrave. "See! There are a hundred chances to one that no person, unacquainted with the secret, would ever touch this spring."

"A secret spring!" cried Clifford. "Ah, I remember now! I did discover it, one summer afternoon, when I was idling and dreaming about the house, long, long ago. But the mystery escapes me."

The artist put his finger on the contrivance to which he had referred. In former days, the effect would probably have been to cause the picture to start forward. But, in so long a period of concealment, the machinery had been eaten through with rust; so that at Holgrave's pressure, the portrait, frame and all, tumbled suddenly from its position, and lay face downward on the floor. A recess in the wall was thus brought to light, in which lay an object so covered with a century's dust that it could not immediately be recognized as a folded sheet of parchment. Holgrave opened it, and displayed an ancient deed, signed with the hieroglyphics of several Indian sagamores, and conveying to Colonel Pyncheon and his heirs, forever, a vast extent of territory at the eastward.

"This is the very parchment the attempt to recover which cost the beautiful Alice Pyncheon her happiness and life," said the artist, alluding to his legend. "It is what the Pyncheons sought in vain, while it was valuable; and now that they find the treasure, it has long been worthless."

"Poor Cousin Jaffrey! This is what deceived him," exclaimed Hepzibah. "When they were young together, Clifford probably made a kind of fairy tale of this discovery. He was always dreaming hither and thither about the house, and lighting up its dark corners with beautiful stories. And poor Jaffrey, who took hold of everything as if it were real, thought my brother had found out his uncle's wealth. He died with this delusion in his mind!"

"But," said Phoebe, apart to Holgrave, "how came you to know the secret?"

"My dearest Phoebe," said Holgrave, "how will it please you to assume the name of Maule? As for the secret, it is the only inheritance that has come down to me from my ancestors. You should have known sooner (only that I was afraid of frightening you away) that, in this long drama of wrong and retribution, I represent the old wizard, and am probably as much a wizard as ever he was. The son of the executed Matthew Maule, while building this house, took the opportunity to construct that recess, and hide away the Indian deed, on which depended the immense land claim of the Pyncheons. Thus they bartered their Eastern territory for Maule's garden ground."

"And now," said Uncle Venner, "I suppose their whole claim is not worth one man's share in my farm yonder!"

"Uncle Venner," cried Phoebe, taking the patched philosopher's hand, "you must never talk any more about your farm! You shall never go there, as long as you live! There is a cottage in our new garden—the prettiest little yellowish-brown cottage you ever saw; and the sweetest-looking place, for it looks just as if it were made of gingerbread—and we are going to fit it up and furnish it, on purpose for you. And you shall do nothing but what you choose, and shall be as happy as the day is long, and shall keep Cousin Clifford in spirits with the wisdom and pleasantness which is always dropping from your lips!"

"Ah, my dear child," quoth good Uncle Venner, quite overcome, "if you were to speak to a young man as you do to an old one, his chance of keeping his heart another minute would not be worth one of the buttons on my waistcoat! And—soul alive!—that great sigh, which you made me heave, has burst off the very last of them! But, never mind! It was the happiest sigh I ever did heave; and it seems as if I must have drawn in a gulp of heavenly breath, to make it with. Well, well, Miss Phoebe! They'll miss me in the gardens hereabouts, and round by the back doors; and Pyncheon Street, I'm afraid, will hardly look the same without old Uncle Venner, who remembers it with a mowing field on one side, and the garden of the Seven Gables on the other. But either I must go to your country seat, or you must come to my farm—that's one of two things certain; and I leave you to choose which!"

"Oh, come with us, by all means, Uncle Venner!" said Clifford, who had a remarkable enjoyment of the old man's mellow, quiet, and simple spirit. "I want you always to be

within five minutes' saunter of my chair. You are the only
philosopher I ever knew of whose wisdom has not a drop
of bitter essence at the bottom!"

"Dear me!" cried Uncle Venner, beginning partly to realize what manner of man he was. "And yet folks used to
set me down among the simple ones, in my younger days!
But I suppose I am like a Roxbury russet—a great deal
the better, the longer I can be kept. Yes; and my words of
wisdom, that you and Phoebe tell me of, are like the golden
dandelions, which never grow in the hot months, but may
be seen glistening among the withered grass, and under the
dry leaves, sometimes as late as December. And you are
welcome, friends, to my mess of dandelions, if there were
twice as many!"

A plain, but handsome, dark-green barouche had now
drawn up in front of the ruinous portal of the old mansion house. The party came forth, and (with the exception
of good Uncle Venner, who was to follow in a few days)
proceeded to take their places. They were chatting and
laughing very pleasantly together; and—as proves to be often the case, at moments when we ought to palpitate with
sensibility—Clifford and Hepzibah bade a final farewell
to the abode of their forefathers with hardly more emotion than if they had made it their arrangement to return
thither at teatime. Several children were drawn to the spot
by so unusual a spectacle as the barouche and pair of gray
horses. Recognizing little Ned Higgins among them, Hepzibah put her hand into her pocket, and presented the urchin,
her earliest and staunchest customer, with silver enough to
people the Domdaniel cavern of his interior with as various
a procession of quadrupeds as passed into the ark.

Two men were passing, just as the barouche drove off.

"Well, Dixey," said one of them, "what do you think of
this? My wife kept a cent shop three months, and lost five
dollars on her outlay. Old Maid Pyncheon has been in trade
just about as long, and rides off in her carriage with a couple
of hundred thousand—reckoning her share, and Clifford's,
and Phoebe's—and some say twice as much! If you choose
to call it luck, it is all very well; but if we are to take it as the
will of Providence, why, I can't exactly fathom it!"

"Pretty good business!" quoth the sagacious Dixey. "Pretty good business!"

Maule's well, all this time, though left in solitude, was throwing up a succession of kaleidoscopic pictures in which a gifted eye might have seen foreshadowed the coming fortunes of Hepzibah and Clifford, and the descendant of the legendary wizard, and the village maiden, over whom he had thrown Love's web of sorcery. The Pyncheon Elm, moreover, with what foliage the September gale had spared to it, whispered unintelligible prophecies. And wise Uncle Venner, passing slowly from the ruinous porch, seemed to hear a strain of music, and fancied that sweet Alice Pyncheon—after witnessing these deeds, this bygone woe and this present happiness, of her kindred mortals—had given one farewell touch of a spirit's joy upon her harpsichord, as she floated heavenward from the House of the Seven Gables!

AFTERWORD

WHEN he finished *The House of the Seven Gables,* Hawthorne decided he preferred it to *The Scarlet Letter,* the sleek tale of crime and punishment that had stirred so many hearts just a year before, hurling its author to literary fame. Its grand conclusion sent Mrs. Hawthorne to bed with a headache—a sure sign of the book's success. This new novel he liked even better, judging it "a more natural and healthy product of my mind," a cheery story, he said, though he admitted the past cast its dark shadow over the book. His neighbor in the Berkshire mountains of Massachusetts, esteemed writer Catharine Sedgwick, sniffed, "The book is an affliction," she said. "It affects one like a passage through the wards of an insane asylum."

Neither lighthearted nor gloomy, though a bit of both, *The House of the Seven Gables* struck another Berkshire confederate, the redoubtable Herman Melville, like a fine old chamber where "the curtains are more drawn; the sun comes in more; genialities peep out more." Plus, everywhere he went, people were talking about Hawthorne and the new novel. "So upon the whole," declared Melville, "I say to myself, 'this N. H. is in the ascendant.'"

He was. Just a few years earlier, Edgar Allan Poe had nominated Hawthorne as "the example, par excellence, in this country, of the privately-admired and publicly underappreciated man of genius." No more. Published in the spring of 1851, *The House of the Seven Gables* outsold *The Scarlet*

Letter in its first year, and a friend in England reported that the novel caused as much ruckus as *Jane Eyre*. Swabbed in success, Hawthorne reckoned that soon he might afford to buy a house of his own—by the sea, he hoped.

Though Hawthorne had been moored in hill country since the spring of 1850, his thoughts still wandered back to his natal city, Salem, Massachusetts, from which he bolted after losing his job at the Custom House, where he'd worked for three years as surveyor. Vowing never more to return, he naturally did not forget the place that bestowed as much as it took—quite the opposite. And though he told his readers his new novel had "a great deal more to do with the clouds overhead than with any portion of the actual soil of the County of Essex," he fooled no one. The setting for *The House of the Seven Gables* is vintage Salem, so much so that amateur literary sleuths, especially anyone steeped in New England lore, quickly identified Hawthorne's imaginary house as the antique structure on Turner Street.

Hawthorne's second cousin, Susannah Ingersoll, who lived under its low beams, told him as early as 1840 that the place once sported seven gables. Intrigued, he peeped into nooks and crannies and pored over documents, gathering material for future use. Ingersoll, herself an eccentric character, had, after her parents' death, fended off a rapacious uncle who tried to confiscate her house, which would have left her homeless and a pauper. Afterward, she became something of a hermit, though she admitted Hawthorne into her parlor, regaling him with stories of property and wills he'd someday weave into his work.

Hawthorne had brooded over family history since boyhood, those days when he'd been called Nat Hathorne. (The "w" came later, a tribute to his English ancestors and a slap at his American ones.) Local celebrities of an equivocal sort, the Hawthornes were among the oldest English settlers in New England. Hawthorne's renowned ancestor, Colonel John Hathorne, had meted out death to the poor souls accused of witchcraft during the Salem delusion of 1692. Witness to the first of the mass executions, this patriarch of granite doubtless heard the malediction uttered by Sarah Good when Reverend Nicholas Noyes called her a witch. "I'm no more a witch than you're a wizard!" she cried. "And if you take my life God will give you blood to drink!"

Along with his reputation for obdurate cruelty, Colonel Hathorne had supposedly acquired nine thousand acres of land in eastern Maine, though no one could substantiate the claim. Relatives whispered among themselves that a curse—much like Sarah Good's, much like Matthew Maule's—had robbed them of their patrimony. "The impalpable claim, therefore, resulted in nothing more solid than to cherish, from generation to generation, an absurd delusion of family importance," Hawthorne explained in his novel, as if writing directly of his own family and their pretensions to a grandeur never quite realized.

What better image than a house to represent family pride and dishonor, the tainted legacies passed down to heirs like a congenital disease: "What we call real estate—the solid ground to build a house on—is the broad foundation on which nearly all the guilt of this world rests," cries Clifford Pyncheon. For Hawthorne, houses possessed a boundless metaphorical value, their garrets chock-full of heirlooms, cellars stuffed with secrets, closets locked, timbers moist, and joints built to shelter a family, a government, a fantasy of permanence. Hawthorne's revised volume of *Twice-Told Tales* (1842) included four "Legends of the Province-house" about the historic site where royal governors held masked balls and ruled the colonists with myopic insouciance. And from the Province-house rose the house of the seven gables, another mansion of aristocratic pretension perched precariously in the more modern world of telegrams and anger.

One of the most pitiful inhabitants of the old Province-house is Esther Dudley, destitute relic from a once-noble family, baking gingerbread stamped with a royal crown for the children of democratic upstarts. Surely she is mother to Hepzibah Pyncheon. Poor Hepzibah Pyncheon: this sallow, gaunt, nearsighted woman is one of the most striking heroines of American literature, more remarkable, in many ways, even than Hester Prynne, for Hepzibah is neither young nor beautiful nor a victim of desire, except perhaps a passion of ancestral pride and an ungrudging devotion to her hapless brother, Clifford.

Hawthorne begins his history of the hidden life of property with Hepzibah on that terrible morning "when the patrician lady is to be transformed into the plebeian woman." Humiliated and terrified, this shabby gentlewoman barely swallows her pride to open a cent shop, the only resource, Hawthorne notes, of a woman in circumstances as diminished as hers. For Hawthorne tells a story not just of inheritance and place but of class. When Hepzibah notices an elegant woman in a costly dress swaying down the street, she vents "that feeling of hostility," Hawthorne explains, "which is the only real abasement of the poor, in the presence of the rich. 'For what good end, in the wisdom of Providence, does that woman live! Must the whole world toil, that the palms of her hands may be kept white and delicate?'"

Poor Hepzibah clumsily drops her gingerbread elephants and scatters a tumbler of marbles all over the shop floor, every creaky movement an index to her state of mind. The narrator surveying her barely suppresses his laughter, for much as he condemns the arrogance of pedigree, Hawthorne deeply pities this woman, so much like relatives of his own and out of step with modern America, that rapacious place "where everything is free to the hand that can grasp it." Hepzibah may be a parched anachronism, but democratic America is a place of roiling insecurity.

"In this republican country," writes Hawthorne, "amid the fluctuating waves of our social life, somebody is always at the drowning point." Recognizing antebellum America as a land of expansion, prosperity, and technological advance, he also acknowledges regional strife, market unrest, urban poverty, and sexual inequality as well as the acrid debate over property that included the ownership of human beings. (The Compromise of 1850 purported to eliminate slavery as a political issue, but it didn't abolish slavery per se, as Hepzibah's Jim Crow cookies all too tellingly suggest.) Moreover, America was not hospitable to its artists; as Emerson noted, "they are lonely." Only by ransacking the past could Hawthorne exercise his talent, observed T. S. Eliot, "his present being so narrowly barren."

But Hawthorne tries to connect America's past with "the very present that is flitting away from us." Such is the office of a romance, he explains in the preface to *The House of the Seven Gables,* declaring himself, as romancer, free to "manage his atmospherical medium as to bring out or mellow the lights and deepen and enrich the shadows." Though he hoped to finish many of his book's passages "with the minuteness of a Dutch picture," he told his zealous publisher, James T. Fields, he also wished to exercise his imagination untrammeled, probing beneath the surface of things to what lies beneath.

In a sense, Hawthorne impersonates the daguerreotypist Holgrave, the itinerant artist well-versed in present-day technology who eschews simple representation in order to reveal people's characters, not simply their looks. His art is a kind of contemporary sorcery that uses—or, as Holgrave quips, misuses—sunshine for effects "that no painter would ever venture upon, even could he detect it." As a daguerreotypist, Holgrave stops time, or records instants of it, the better to discover its secrets.

The best example of Hawthorne's—and Holgrave's—method lies in the incomparable Chapter 18, "Governor Pyncheon," where Judge Jaffrey Pyncheon, the story's villain, sits motionless, watch in hand, dial facing inward. "Time, all at once, appears to have become a matter of no moment with the Judge!" Hawthorne's narrator outrageously puns while glancing about the room. The Judge does not move. Eyes open, face rigid, features disappearing into nothingness, he remains suspended in space, a model of absorption, self-contained, static, terrifying. Night and day pass before him; he is indifferent, implacable, frozen. But the narrator's mobile consciousness ranges far, resisting death even as it embraces its horrid, incontrovertible reality. "There is no window! There is no face! An infinite, inscrutable blackness has annihilated sight! Where is our universe?" Then the shop bell rings, pulling the reader back into the flitting, consoling present.

In this singular novelistic hiatus—rare in literature and a tour de force—Hawthorne's extraordinary chapter registers the awful transition from life to death, stopping for a moment, as it were, in the interval between. Emily Dickinson, a Hawthorne fan, clearly borrowed several of the chapter's most chilling images: the perky fly, for instance, that alights on the Judge's face. "I heard a Fly buzz—" Dickinson writes with the cold illumination of Hawthorne, "when I died—" And this evocative, humorous, and terrifying chapter bears comparison with Virginia Woolf's more modernist version in the "Time Passes" section of *To the Lighthouse,* in which the Ramsey house, quiet and vacant, sinks slowly to naught.

At the last moment, a bustle of movement will rescue the Ramsey house—much as Holgrave will rescue Clifford from an accusation of the Judge's murder with his daguerreotype of (what else?) the dead Pyncheon. Yet, if Holgrave is Hawthorne's Keatsian sylvan artist, balancing art and life, past and present, Holgrave also teeters between two worlds. The supposed wizard Matthew Maule's descendant, Holgrave plants himself in the house of seven gables—privileged spectator, he calls himself—to nurse ancestral wounds. "I dwell in it for awhile, that I may know the better how to hate it," he tells Phoebe Pyncheon, claiming nonetheless that he wants to chuck the past to free himself of its encumbrance.

"Shall we never, never get rid of this Past?" Holgrave wails as he launches into the plaint Hawthorne copied almost verbatim from his own notebooks: "A dead man sits on all our judgment seats; and living judges do but search out and repeat his decisions. We read in dead men's books! We laugh at dead men's jokes, and cry at dead men's pathos! We are sick of dead men's diseases, physical and moral, and die of the same remedies with which dead doctors killed their patients. . . . And we must be dead ourselves before we can begin to have our proper influence on our own world, which will then be no longer our world, but the world of another generation, with which we shall have no shadow of a right to interfere." Regardless, Holgrave's raison d'être is the ancient feud of Pyncheon and Maule.

Predictably, Holgrave's romantic republicanism, though genuine, is short-lived—a function of youth, suggests Hawthorne, inevitably forsaken, like youth itself. (Ten years

earlier, Hawthorne had been a charter member of the
socialist experiment at Brook Farm, though his enthusiasm waned almost immediately.) Besides, you can't leap-
frog the past, as Fitzgerald's Nick Carraway reminds that
twentieth-century romantic, Jay Gatsby. Holgrave does
not yet understand that the fugitive present actually becomes the past right before our eyes. And no one makes
this grim truth more palpable than gentle, decrepit Clifford
Pyncheon, himself something of an exile chained to the decrepit house, or body, he now inhabits. An old man, his eyes
filmy with age, Clifford cannot flee himself or his past, and
all the newfangled appurtenances of the modern world—
railroads and electricity and telegraphs—will not check
time's relentless progress or undo what's been done. Time
is the great theme of Hawthorne's romance—time and its
human counterpart, age.

Holgrave is not a younger version of Clifford Pyncheon.
Despite his various occupations, pastimes, and the sedi-
tious ideas they share, Holgrave exerts a force of person-
ality that Clifford lacks: Holgrave "had never violated the
innermost man, but had carried his conscience with him."
By contrast, Clifford Pyncheon, archetypal victim, almost
surrenders to his destiny, partly because of those nefarious
"feminine traits" that render him poetic, delicate, soft, even
voluptuous, and remind the reader of Hawthorne's Owen
Warfield in "The Artist of the Beautiful." Clifford, like
Owen, is not a manly man; he is an aesthete displaced in a
crude world of getting and spending, a culture less forgiv-
ing of Clifford's tenderness than of the calumnies of Jaffrey
Pyncheon.

Unctuous and aggressive, Jaffrey Pyncheon is Clifford's
obverse, a man of concentrated purpose who eschews all
airy matter, never mistaking shadow for substance. A con-
summate materialist, in public he beams his sticky hypocritical smile; in private he breaks his wife's spirit on their
honeymoon. (His country-bred cousin Phoebe instinctively
recoils from his kiss.) Victim and victimizer, idealist and
materialist, the two Pyncheon heirs, both cursed, conjugate
manhood for Hawthorne, who regards them with a jaun-
diced eye. Fastidious Clifford in his damask dressing gown,

well-upholstered Judge Jaffrey with his gold-headed cane, the Pyncheon men are impaled by the patrimonial heritage they each in similar ways represent.

Enter Holgrave, the great reconciler. Ardent, youthful, radical, he embodies qualities that the decaying, corrupt Pyncheons lack. With an ability to march to his own drummer, as Hepzibah astutely observes, Holgrave resembles Hawthorne's ultimate outsider, Hester Prynne, another character who eventually makes her peace with society, more or less, as Holgrave the radical will by story's end. For though he insists "that, once in every half century, at longest, a family should be merged into the great, obscure mass of humanity, and forget all about its ancestors," he falls in love with the fresh-faced Phoebe Pyncheon, utterly ignoring his own declamations about self-reliance and reform. Tamed by the morally neat, domestically efficient Phoebe, Holgrave renounces his wanton ways, declaring himself a conservative eager to set out trees and make fences—even, he says, to build a house for another generation.

But Phoebe seems no match for Holgrave. True, her contact with Hepzibah and Clifford has matured her, but she resists the puzzles and perplexities that beset Holgrave and, one assumes, Hawthorne. Her realm is the Actual, her sphere the concrete, and she aspires toward nothing more than "a house and a moderate garden-spot of one's own." But if the reference to Voltaire is lost on Phoebe, it means something to her crafty creator. Cultivating one's garden of plebeian vegetables and aristocratic flowers may be, after all, the best one can do, "a truth," writes Hawthorne, "that has the bitter and the sweet in it."

Phoebe's innocence and Holgrave's volte-face constitute for Hawthorne the "setting sunshine" he said he wished to pour over his book's close, a jerry-built conclusion that perplexes many readers who find its quick, happy denouement a bit disconcerting. With Judge Pyncheon dead, Clifford exonerated of past and present crime, and Phoebe and Holgrave betrothed, the characters, including Hepzibah and the vagabond Uncle Venner, suddenly find themselves beneficiaries of the Judge's wealth, which happens to include an elegant country estate. To this new home they speedily repair, no longer chary of ancestral houses and ill-gotten gain, in a handsome dark green barouche.

In arranging the hasty departure of his characters, with the significant exception of Uncle Venner, who presumably will follow later, Hawthorne suggests that Hepzibah and Clifford and Phoebe and Holgrave, like Huck Finn, light out to a territory of the romancer's conjuring, a pastoral world of happily ever after, free from the contingencies of time and the vicissitudes of fortune, a place without death and history and old age or economic turbulence. It's the utopian dream Holgrave relinquished, a province of marvelous make-believe and romance that Hawthorne, ironies notwithstanding, still holds dear.

Small wonder that, at book's end, the wise Uncle Venner thinks he hears a strain of music and fancies that the ghostly Alice Pyncheon, "after witnessing these deeds, this bygone woe and this present happiness," has taken up her harpsichord again. Looking down at the scene below, her ancient eyes glittering, she begins to play plaintive tunes that, like the romancer's, sing of what is past, and passing, and to come.

—Brenda Wineapple

SELECTED BIBLIOGRAPHY

Works by Nathaniel Hawthorne

Fanshawe: A Tale, 1828 Novel
Twice-Told Tales, 1837; enlarged 1842 Stories
Grandfather's Chair, 1841 History
Mosses from an Old Manse, 1846 Stories
The Scarlet Letter, 1850 Novel
The House of the Seven Gables, 1851 Novel
The Snow Image, 1851 Stories
A Wonder-Book for Boys and Girls, 1852 Stories
The Blithedale Romance, 1852 Novel
Life of Franklin Pierce, 1852 Biography
Tanglewood Tales, 1853 Stories
The Marble Faun, 1860 Novel
Our Old House, 1863 Stories and Sketches
The English Notebooks, 1941 Journals
The American Notebooks, 1972 Journals
The American Claimant Manuscripts, 1977 Unfinished
    Romances
The Elixir of Life Manuscripts, 1977 Unfinished
    Romances
Hawthorne's Lost Notebook: 1835–1841, 1978 Journal
The French and Italian Notebooks, 1979 Journals

Biography and Criticism

Baym, Nina. *The Shape of Hawthorne's Career*. Ithaca, NY: Cornell University Press, 1970.

Bell, Millicent. *Hawthorne and the Real: Bicentennial Essays*. Columbus: Ohio State University Press, 2005.

Berlant, Lauren. *The Anatomy of National Fantasy: Hawthorne, Utopia, and Everyday Life*. Chicago: University of Chicago Press, 1991.

Bloom, Harold. *Nathaniel Hawthorne*. New York: Facts on File, 2001.

Brodhead, Richard H. *Hawthorne, Melville, and the Novel*. Chicago: University of Chicago Press, 1982.

———. *The School of Hawthorne*. New York: Oxford University Press, 1986.

Brown, Gillian. *Domestic Individualism: Imagining Self in Nineteenth Century-America*. Berkeley: University of California Press, 1990.

Budick, Emily Miller. *Engendering Romance: Women Writers and the Hawthorne Tradition 1850–1900*. New Haven, CT: Yale University Press, 1994.

Charvat, William. *The Profession of Authorship in America, 1800–1870*. Ed. Matthew J. Bruccoli. New York: Columbia University Press, 1992.

Cheever, Susan. *American Bloomsbury: Louisa May Alcott, Ralph Waldo Emerson, Margaret Fuller, Nathaniel Hawthorne, and Henry David Thoreau: Their Lives, Their Loves, Their Work*. New York: Simon and Schuster, 2006.

Colacurcio, Michael J. *The Province of Piety*. Cambridge: Harvard University Press, 1984.

Crews, Frederick C. *The Sins of the Fathers: Hawthorne's Psychological Themes*. Berkeley: University of California Press, 1964.

Erilch, Gloria C. *Family Themes and Hawthorne's Fiction: The Tenacious Web*. New Brunswick, NJ: Rutgers University Press, 1984.

Hawthorne, Julian. *Nathaniel Hawthorne and His Wife*. 2 vols. Boston: Osgood, 1884.

Herbert, T. Walter. *Dearest Beloved: The Hawthornes and the Making of the Middle-Class Family*. Berkeley: University of California Press, 1993.

Hunter, Gordon. *Secrets and Sympathy: Forms of Disclosure in Hawthorne's Novels*. Athens: University of Georgia Press, 1988.

James, Henry. *Hawthorne*. New York: Harper and Brothers, 1879; reprint, Ithaca, NY: Cornell University Press, 1998.

Lawrence, D.H. *Studies in Classic American Literature*. New York: Thomas Seltzer, 1923.

Leverenz, David. *Manhood and the American Renaissance*. Ithaca, NY: Cornell, 1989.

Levine, Harry. *The Power of Blackness: Hawthorne, Poe, Melville*. New York: Knopf, 1958.

Matthiessen, F.O. *American Renaissance*. New York and London: Oxford University Press, 1941.

Mellow, James R. *Nathaniel Hawthorne in His Times*. Baltimore: John Hopkins University Press, 1998.

Millington, Richard H. *Practicing Romance: Narrative Form and Cultural Engagement in Hawthorne's Fiction*. Princeton, NJ: Princeton University Press, 1992.

Moore, Margaret B. *The Salem World of Nathaniel Hawthorne*. Columbia: University of Missouri Press, 2001.

Pearce, Roy Harvey, ed. *Hawthorne Centenary Essays*. Columbus: Ohio State University Press, 1964.

Pfister, Joel. *The Production of Personal Life: Class, Gender and the Psychological in Hawthorne's Fiction*. Stanford, CA: Stanford University Press, 1991.

Reynolds, David. *Beneath the American Renaissance: The Subversive Imagination in the Age of Emerson and Melville*. New York: Alfred A. Knopf, 1988.

Reynolds, Larry J. *A Historical Guide to Nathaniel Hawthorne*. New York: Oxford University Press, 2001.

Schreiner, Samuel A. *The Concord Quartet: Alcott, Emerson, Hawthorne, Thoreau and the Friendship that Freed the American Mind*. New York: Wiley, 2006.

Tompkins, Jane. *Sensational Designs: The Cultural Work of American Fiction, 1790–1860*. New York: Oxford University Press, 1985.

Turner, Arlin. *Nathaniel Hawthorne: A Biography*. New York: Oxford University Press, 1980.

Waggoner, Hyatt H. *Hawthorne: A Critical Study*. Rev. ed. Cambridge, MA: Belknap Press of Harvard University Press, 1963.

Woodson, Thomas L. Neal Smith and Norman Holmes Pearson, eds. *The Letters of Nathaniel Hawthorne*, 1843–1853, Vol. 16. Columbus: Ohio State University Press, 1985.

Wineapple, Brenda. *Hawthorne: A Life*. New York: Knopf, 2003.